THE LAST
PLUMB LINE

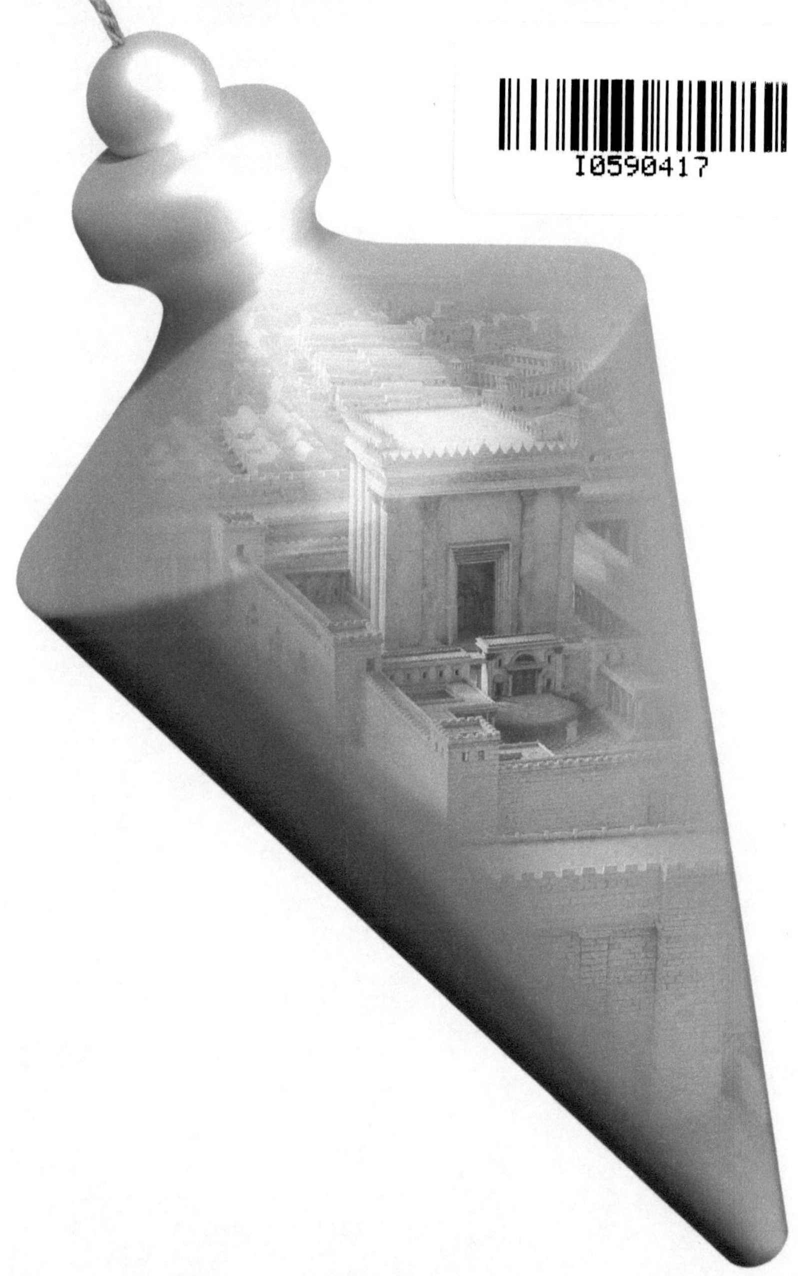

I0590417

THE LAST
PLUMB LINE

JULIE BRIDGES

Revelation 22:7
And behold, I am coming soon.
Blessed is the one who keeps the words of the prophecy of this book.

To my mother, Peggy—

It was you who first lit the flame of faith in my heart, a flame that still burns today. You planted the seed and nurtured it with your prayers, insight, and deep love for Scripture. Before I even knew what prophecy was, you were already teaching me to listen for His voice and look for His return. Your example taught me how to build a life rooted in Christ. You were the first to spark my interest in the Word and helped me grow a deep hunger for truth. We've studied prophecy together, and your wisdom has shaped me in ways I can never fully express. This book is just as much yours as it is mine. You're not just my mom—you're one of my closest, dearest friends. I treasure the bond we share, and I thank God every day for the love, strength, and encouragement you've poured into my life. I love you more than words can say.

And to those who are seeking truth in a world filled with uncertainty,

May this book serve as a guide—a reminder that God's Word stands firm, and His promises are unshakable. May it be a light on your path, pointing you to the One who holds all things in His hands.

ACKNOWLEDGMENTS

First and foremost, I want to thank my Lord and Savior, Jesus Christ. Without His guidance, mercy, and grace, this book would not exist. Every page was written through prayer and with the hope that it brings Him glory.

To my incredible husband, Steven—thank you for your unwavering support, love, and patience. This past year, you carried more than your share, taking on extra responsibilities at home while I disappeared into my writing world. You've always been my steady anchor, and I'll forever see you as one of God's greatest gifts to me.

To my boys, Trevin, Dylan, and Andrew—thank you for cheering me on and understanding when Mom needed a little extra quiet. I thank God daily for the gift of being your mom, and I pray you always walk closely with Him and trust His purpose for your life.

To my dear friends and family—Mom, thank you for your patience, your constant encouragement, and for always being open to my wild ideas. Whether it was late-night brainstorming or sharing your insights, I couldn't have done this without you. Dad, Jenni, and Jake, your support, love, and encouragement meant more to me than words can express. Camille, your inspiration, friendship, and belief in me have been a foundation I could always rely on throughout this journey, and I'm so thankful God brought us together. To all my friends and family, thank you for standing by me, for lifting me up with your love and laughter, and for being the encouragement I needed to keep moving forward. I will forever cherish each of you.

A special thank you to the late Hal Lindsey. Though we never met, your passion for biblical prophecy shaped my own. Your work inspired me deeply, and I will always consider you a mentor through the pages of your books.

And finally, thank you to God Manifest Publishing—Jonnathan and Olivia Truong—for helping bring this book to life. Your guidance, care, and willingness to answer my endless questions made this entire process a joy.

God
MANIFEST | PUBLISHING
www.GodManifestPublishing.com

This book and all other God Manifest Publishing books are available on Amazon.com.

Cover designed by Jonnathan Zin Truong
Interior designed by Jonnathan Zin Truong

For more information on foreign distributors,
email: *publishers@godmanifestpublishing.com*

Paperback ISBN: 979-8-9920028-9-8
Hardback ISBN: 979-8-9991501-0-3
eBook: ISBN: 979-8-9991501-1-0

TABLE OF CONTENTS

PRELUDE

Present time

Jayne slowly came to, her body resisting the command to move, every muscle protesting as though the weight of the world had pressed her into that cold wooden floor. Exhaustion clung to her like a relentless ache buried deep in her bones that no rest could cure. The air in the dim church was stale, thick with dust and silence, broken only by the faint sounds of sleeping breaths around her.

Trembling, she wiped at her face, but the gesture only smeared dirt across her skin, a reminder of how long it had been since she'd felt clean—weeks, maybe months. She wasn't sure anymore. Summoning her strength, she pushed herself up, her hands shaking under the effort, every movement a battle against the weariness that threatened to consume her.

Moonlight streamed through the fractured windows, pale beams illuminating the crumbling room. Landon and Andrew lay near the door, their positions awkward, their bodies contorted on the unforgiving floor. Landon's broad shoulders and the set of his jaw stood out in contrast to the boy she had raised. He was the protector now, taking on the mantle of a man who now had to keep their family together, safe. Andrew was sleeping nearby, his posture stiff and vigilant. She saw the lines of manhood in him now, the soft, carefree youth long gone. Seven years without his family. Three years without a single word from them.

But it was her daughter—her grown-up daughter—who pulled Jayne's gaze. Sophie was sleeping on a nearby pew, curled into the shadows, her face slack with fatigue, her breath slow and steady. She should be finished with college by now, maybe even planning a wedding or holding her own child in her arms. But instead, here she was—caught in a world that had torn away everything. Jayne's chest ached as she looked at her. There was a time she would've brushed the hair from her daughter's face, whispered promises about the future. Now, all she could do was watch and wonder how much more this life would take from her. The girl she'd raised was gone—not lost, not broken—but changed in ways Jayne could barely comprehend. The change had quietly woven itself into Sophie, a transformation Jayne had only now fully seen. It wasn't a single moment, but a slow shift, shaped by survival and struggle. Before her was no longer the girl with the innocence she once had, but a woman—strong, hardened by the world. In that quiet moment, Jayne recognized the adult Sophie had become, with all the strength and resilience that came with it

Near the altar, Jennie slept with her small daughter, holding the child against her chest as though she could shield her from the broken world around them. Her tiny breaths were peaceful, oblivious to the heaviness in the room. Above them, the wooden cross loomed on the wall, stark and splintered against the cracked plaster. Jayne's chest tightened at the sight. What kind of world would that baby grow up in now? What would become of her in this shattered, destroyed place? How could God let this happen to them? It felt cruel. The pain of it was too much to contain, and her body trembled with heartache and rage as she thought of her own husband who was now gone.

It was too much. The baby shouldn't grow up like this. None of them should.

Her throat constricted, anger and grief threatening to choke her. The questions she'd kept buried clawed their way to the surface. *Why?* she wanted to scream. *Where are you now, God?* The silence from heaven had stretched on too long, and the pain of it was unbearable.

She forced herself to her feet, her legs unsteady beneath her. The effort left her lightheaded, and she leaned against the wall for support. She needed space. The walls of the church felt like they were closing in, suffocating her. Her breath came in shallow gasps as she stumbled toward the back of the building.

The bathroom door creaked as she pushed it open. Inside, the air was damp, the faint stench of mildew clinging to the peeling walls. A cracked mirror hung above the sink, and for a moment, she avoided her reflection. She wasn't ready to face the stranger she'd become.

But the pull was too strong. Slowly, she lifted her gaze.

She hardly recognized the woman staring back. Her face was hollow and pale, with dark circles etched beneath her eyes and skin that was dry, cracked, and scorched by the relentless sun. Her lips were chapped and raw, and her hair hung in limp, tangled strands that framed her gaunt features like a shadow. When her trembling fingers brushed against her blistered skin, a sharp sting made her flinch, a souvenir of how deeply the world had worn her down.

Jayne let out a ragged breath, turning away from the mirror. Her fingers fumbled for the towel in her bag, and she pressed it against her face, scrubbing harder than she should have. The dirt wouldn't come off. It clung to her as if it had become part of her.

She closed her eyes, sinking onto the edge of the sink. Her tongue throbbed, swollen and raw from the thorns she'd pulled from her mouth. The bitter flesh of the cactus they'd found yesterday had barely been enough to hold off hunger, and the moisture it contained had done little to ease her thirst. It was a cruel mockery of survival—just enough to keep going but never enough to truly feel alive.

She wasn't sure why she was still trying, why she was attempting to make herself look anything other than what she had become—broken, beaten down by a world that had no mercy left. She reached for her bag, hands shaking, lifting it as a thud sounded from the ground. Her eyes flicked down, and there it was—the Bible. Ruth's Bible. It lay open-faced on the ground, its pages worn, its cover cracked and faded from years of use. She stared at it for a moment, the sight of it stirring a swell of frustration deep inside her. It felt like a cruel reminder of everything she had lost.

Her hands tightened into fists. She didn't want to keep going.

Her breath came in ragged gasps, and the room seemed to close in around her as she fell to her knees, fists clenched so tightly that her nails dug into her palms.

She couldn't breathe. The burden of it all was crushing her chest, suffocating her, drowning her in a sea of hopelessness.

"Where are you, God?" The words came out barely above a whisper.

Tears swelled in her eyes as her voice rose, shaking with fury. "Where are you? Why have you left us here? Why don't you take me?" she choked. "Why don't you just end this? I can't—I can't do this anymore!"

The words burned in her chest, as though she had been carrying them for lifetimes.

Her face yielded in desperation, tears blurring her vision. "I can't do this anymore!" she shouted, her voice cracking. "I've tried—I've fought with everything I have, and it's never enough. I can't keep going. I can't keep pretending. I just … I just want to see you. I want to be done with all of this—done with the pain, done with the emptiness. Just … take me home, Lord." Her body wracked with sobs, her words lingering in the air long after she had fallen silent.

She needed more—needed Him. "Where are you?" she cried, the words torn from her like a scream from the deepest part of her soul. "I need you *now*!" Her voice cracked and broke, raw with every unanswered prayer, every moment of silence that stretched longer than she could stand. She shook, her body trembling with a rage and desperation she could no longer contain.

The silence that followed felt like a final blow.

Her stomach turned. She didn't want to touch the fallen object. She didn't want to be reminded of the faith she had once clung to. It had failed her—had failed all of them. The promise of salvation felt distant, a lie whispered into the wind.

Still, her fingers found the Bible, and with a sharp breath, she threw it against the wall. The force of the impact sent it sliding to the floor, the pages fanning out like a prayer she no longer wanted to hear.

She collapsed in the dust on that cold bathroom floor, her breath coming in short, jagged gasps. Tears mixed with the dirt on her cheeks as she cried, the sobs wracking her body, making her feel weaker than she ever thought possible.

And then, as if the world was offering her a final cruelty, her eyes caught something—a note—poking out from the edge of the broken Bible's casing, almost taunting her with its presence.

For a moment, she stopped crying, the tears still running down her face, but her curiosity won out. She reached for the note, the paper crinkling beneath her fingertips. She unfolded it carefully, unsure of what she would find, and began to read.

My Dearest Jayne ...

CHAPTER ONE

A FRAGILE CALM

7 years earlier
Day 1, USA

In the distance, the soft whistle of a morning train echoed, reaching across a mile of river bottomland to find Jayne on her back deck—a gentle reminder of life beyond her quiet haven. The town hugged the banks of the muddy Brazos River, and nearby birds chirped, creating a melodic backdrop to her peaceful surroundings. As she gazed down the sloping lawn, beyond live oaks adorned with cascading Spanish moss, she saw the sun glinting on the river, winding its way toward the coastal Gulf waters.

The deep-rooted town of Thompsons nestled itself on the back porch of the sprawling metroplex of Houston, Texas, embodying a tranquil charm that Jayne cherished. Her neighborhood, a small-acreage community, was a true sanctuary. Colorful flower beds adorned modest homes along the streets, while deer moved gracefully, their silhouettes appearing against the dawn. Named for its roots in sugar production, the nearby city of Sugar Land brought back memories of childhood visits to the sugar plant, where her eyes widened with wonder as she learned about the sweet process of turning cane into sugar.

Seated on her back porch, Jayne cradled a steaming cup of coffee, its aroma enveloping her senses. As she gently swayed on an old wooden swing, the creaks synchronized with her thoughts. The morning sun rose, casting golden rays over the sprawling pecan orchard in the distance, with each tree creating long shadows on the dew-kissed grass. The familiar scents of earth and foliage mingled with her coffee, reflecting the richness of her town and offering a moment of solace. It was fleeting, though, for as she savored the stillness, the heaviness of the long day ahead began to settle in.

With a sigh, she glanced at the clock on her phone, feeling the pull of reality draw her away from the calm of the morning. The serenity she'd briefly enjoyed was slipping through her fingers, replaced by the demands of the office and the trial that was steadily approaching.

Jayne's eyes skimmed the case files in front of her, her mind absorbing every detail with the kind of intensity that only years of preparation could bring. As a prosecutor for the Harris County District Attorney's Office, she had worked tirelessly for this moment. This was the kind of case that could establish her legacy, determining whether she was worthy of the chief prosecutor role she'd been eyeing for years.

Her office mirrored her approach to work: clean, methodical, and efficient; each piece of paper stacked neatly; each file in its place. The walls, devoid of personal clutter, reflected her focus—there was only the work, and right now, the trial before her was everything. There was no room for distractions. No second chances. This was the trial that would make or break her, and she would do whatever it took to win.

Her suit, a perfectly tailored navy number, exuded confidence without being flashy. Her straight blonde hair, styled to fall just past her shoulders, framed her face in a sleek, polished look that was both professional and stylish. Her blue eyes were sharp but warm, reflecting both a keen intellect and a kindness that could put others at ease.

Jayne had learned long ago how to balance her life: work and family, the job that demanded her time and the people who expected her to show up. She'd always prided herself on being able to juggle both without dropping the ball. At work, she was a bulldog—relentless, sharp, with a deep conviction to always do what was right. In her personal life, she was the one others relied on, the glue that kept things together. And when the time came, she could shift effortlessly from one role to the next.

She glanced at the clock. 5:15 p.m. Her mind was still miles ahead, ticking through legal strategies and witness testimonies, but part of her was already thinking about Lawson, about dinner at home, about the quiet evening that awaited.

Lawson was her anchor. He had always been there, steady and unwavering, providing a sense of security that she deeply cherished. His warmth and caring drew people in, and his intelligence and wit never failed to impress her. He had a knack for current events, easily weaving them into their conversations, making their discussions both engaging and enlightening. Over the past twenty-eight years, they had built a life filled with love and laughter, and Jayne admired how he always made her feel safe, his presence a constant source of protection for their family.

As she wrapped up her day and made her way home, Jayne felt the familiar mix of relief and exhaustion. Heavy traffic conspired against her eagerness, keeping her inching along at a snail's pace. Just as she began to lose herself in thought, her phone rang. Sophie's name lit up the screen, and Jayne felt herself smile.

❋ ❋ ❋

"Mom! You won't believe it—I got an A on my textiles project!" Sophie said, her voice full of excitement. Jayne felt a smile spread across her face, the news lifting her mood instantly.

"I'm so proud of you, Sophie!" Jayne replied.. "What was the project?"

"I had to design an outfit for a mock runway show. We had to pick a theme, so I chose a masquerade dress. Since the Zeta social was this weekend and it was a masquerade ball, I thought it would be perfect," Sophie explained, her voice full of energy. There was a new confidence in her tone that Jayne recognized immediately.

"That's awesome, Sophie! I forgot the social was this past weekend. How was it?"

"It was amazing! The masquerade theme was so much fun—everyone went all out with glittery masks and fancy dresses. It felt like a scene from a movie!"

"Sounds like a blast! Did Matt come with you?" Jayne asked.

"Yeah, he did. He looked so good in his suit," Sophie said. "We even matched our outfits!"

A soft laugh escaped before she answered. "Did he have fun?"

"Yeah, I think so," Sophie said. Her voice wavered at the end—just enough to make Jayne sit up a little straighter.

Jayne shifted the phone. "What happened?"

Sophie hesitated for a moment before letting out a sigh. "Well, Matt and I got into a fight after the party."

"Oh no, why?" Jayne asked, her concern growing.

"He got mad at me for drinking," Sophie said quietly. "Ever since he joined that Young Life group, he's been different."

Jayne picked up on the change in Sophie's voice. "Different how?"

Sophie took a deep breath. "He keeps asking me to go with him to their meetings, and I tried it once. It was so uncomfortable, Mom. They were singing worship songs I didn't know, and everyone was raising their hands like they were at a concert. I don't judge them … it just isn't my thing, you know?"

Jayne nodded, understanding the struggle her daughter was feeling. "How does that make you feel about Matt?"

"I think he's upset that I still want to go out and have fun. But that's what college is about, right?" Sophie said, her voice tinged with frustration. "I want to enjoy these years before they're gone. But he seems to think I should be doing something else just because he found this new faith."

Jayne paused. "It sounds like you both are in a tough spot. It's hard when your beliefs don't line up with the person you've been dating for a while. Have you talked to him about how you feel?"

Sophie's voice softened. "Not really. I'm afraid it'll just make things worse."

Gently, Jayne said, "Maybe it's worth talking it out. You both need to be honest about what you want from each other."

"Yeah, I know. I just don't want to lose him over this," Sophie said, her voice full of uncertainty.

"Relationships aren't easy, especially when you're still figuring things out. But it's important to set boundaries and, above all, be honest with each other."

Sophie was quiet for a moment, contemplating her mother's advice. "Thanks, Mom. I'll think about it."

As they wrapped up the conversation, Jayne felt a renewed sense of connection with her daughter. She knew this phase of life was filled with challenges, but hearing her daughter's words brought Jayne a mix of emotions. She was thrilled to hear Sophie was doing so well in school and enjoying the pleasures of her college years, yet beneath that facade, concern for Sophie lingered. She wanted her daughter to be happy, to find her way in a world that often felt overwhelming. She and Lawson hadn't raised their kids in the church, aside from obligatory Christmas and Easter services. They were agnostic, always holding a vague belief that there might be a god out there, but never fully committing to any faith. Yet Jayne felt a quiet sense of gratitude as she watched Sophie carve out her own path, exploring her beliefs and growing into the person she was meant to be.

As Jayne stepped into her quiet home, the burdens of a long day began to fade away. The house was quiet, filled only with the soft whispers of memories—echoes of laughter and the warmth of family gatherings that once packed every corner. She was eager to share the evening with Lawson, as it was these small victories, these moments of connection, that reminded her of the fragile calm they had cultivated in their lives—a calm that, for now, felt unshakeable.

Jayne entered the dining room, smiling at Lawson, who looked up from his plate with a soft expression. "You're just in time," he said, gesturing to the steaming dish. "I saved you the best pieces."

She laughed lightly. "You know just how to spoil me." Jayne took a seat, inhaling deeply. The smell of roasted chicken mixed with herbs made her stomach growl.

As they settled into the familiar rhythm of their meal, the chatter from the television faded into the background. "How was your day?" Lawson asked, with genuine interest.

"It was hectic, as usual, but I'm here now. What about you?"

"It was good. Caught up on some projects, and I even managed to sneak in a quick workout."

They shared stories from their day, the conversation flowing easily between them. For a moment, the world outside seemed far away, the chaos of daily life fading into the background. The aroma of Lawson's chicken filled the room, its golden skin perfectly crisped and glistening under the soft light.

Accompanying the roast were vibrant, roasted vegetables—carrots, Brussels sprouts, and potatoes—each drizzled with olive oil and sprinkled with a hint of sea salt. With every forkful, Jayne was reminded of the simple joys they cherished together.

"Let's make a habit of this," Jayne suggested, lifting her glass of wine in a toast. "Quiet dinners, just us."

"Absolutely," Lawson agreed, clinking his glass against hers. "We need more moments like this."

As they continued to eat, the laughter from the television mingled with their own and Jayne felt grateful for this slice of normalcy.

Just then, a breaking news alert flashed across the screen. The anchor's serious tone caught Jayne's attention.

"We have an urgent update from Maxx News: Multiple nations, including Russia, Iran, and several other Arab countries, have launched coordinated air strikes into Israel, overwhelming the Iron Dome, the Arrow System, and David's Sling. Reports are flooding in from our Israeli news correspondents, detailing widespread devastation in key cities, including Jerusalem, Tel Aviv, and Haifa. Tensions are escalating rapidly, and officials are urging citizens to stay tuned for further developments.

"Local authorities in Israel are now advising residents to seek shelter immediately, as air raid sirens wail across the country. Emergency services are on high alert, and the situation is evolving by the minute. Families are being urged to stay indoors and follow official guidance as the threat level continues to rise. This is a critical moment," the anchor concluded, her voice steady but filled with urgency. "We will keep you updated as more information becomes available."

A chill ran through Jayne, raising the hairs on her arms, though she couldn't quite say why. She exchanged worried glances with Lawson, those words shifting everything in that moment, overshadowing their peaceful dinner. Israel had been in the headlines for weeks—more like years—but hearing that their mighty Iron Dome had been breached felt different, somehow more ominous. Why was this silly war intensifying? What was it even about?

As they settled back into their meal, Jayne felt a flicker of unease. She chalked it up to nerves about her upcoming trial—her mind running through everything she needed to prepare. Pushing the thought aside, she reminded herself that rest was what she needed most now. She finished her meal, helped Lawson clean the kitchen, and retreated to her room. Changing into soft pajamas, she climbed into bed, hoping sleep would still her restless thoughts.

✳ ✳ ✳

Jayne stood in front of the jury, every muscle taut with purpose. Her eyes swept over the faces of the twelve strangers who held the power to determine the fate of a life. She had delivered her case with precision, but now, as she prepared to make her final argument, she knew it was not just the evidence she needed to present—the stakes were far higher than that.

The courtroom felt charged, the oppressive silence thickening with each passing second. A single beam of light sliced through the tall windows, catching the wood of the jury box and reflecting off the polished surface of the table in front of her. The courtroom was still, all eyes fixed on her. For a moment, nothing moved—not the flutter of papers, not a shift in a seat—only the power of their gaze pressing in, sharpening her focus as her thoughts gathered.

She stepped forward in confidence.

"Ladies and gentlemen of the jury," she began, her voice steady, slicing through the tension, "You have seen the truth laid out before you. The evidence is undeniable. The fingerprints on the weapon. The video that captured the brutal, final moments of a young girl's life. And the witnesses, who placed him squarely at the scene." She paused, allowing her words to sink in. "This is not a matter of circumstantial evidence or a series of coincidences. This is the truth, plain and simple, woven together with a clarity that cannot be ignored."

Her eyes flickered briefly to the defendant. The man who had taken the innocent life of a child. His face remained unmoved, the same mask of indifference he had worn throughout the trial. A chill slithered down her spine, but she pushed it away.

"This is not just a case about one life lost," she continued, her voice gaining strength. "This is about all of us. About what happens when evil is allowed to slip through the cracks, when those who should be held accountable walk free, unchecked. You must ask yourselves: What happens to the rest of us if we allow him to go free? What message does that send? You have the power to restore the balance of justice that has been disrupted. I ask you to remember the young soul that was stolen, the future taken from her, from her family. Justice is not just about a conviction—it's about sending a message. A message that in the face of this unspeakable evil, we will not look away. We will not let it go unpunished."

She felt the full significance of the moment settle in, each word heavy with the burden of responsibility. She scanned the faces of the jury, their eyes locked on her, unreadable. She could almost hear their thoughts—or perhaps it was just her own anxiety gnawing at the edges of her resolve. She exhaled, taking a steadying breath. Her words had made their mark. Now, she would wait, meeting each gaze. She let the silence linger in the room, taut and poised.

"Guilty," she said softly but with an unwavering certainty, letting the word echo through the courtroom.

The jurors stared back, motionless. Jayne waited for the judge to dismiss them, expecting them to rise, file out, and begin their deliberations. But they didn't move. They remained seated, their expressions unreadable, as if they were merely actors in a play, waiting for the next line to be delivered. The silence stretched uncomfortably, and a knot of unease twisted in her stomach. Why weren't they leaving?

She glanced at the judge, expecting direction, but he remained still, almost mechanical, his gavel resting lightly in his hand. Her eyes darted back to the jury box, her mind racing. Something wasn't right. The foreman, stiff and robotic, slowly rose to his feet, his movements eerily deliberate, as if controlled by invisible strings.

And then came his voice, flat and uninterested. "Not guilty."

The world shattered.

Jayne's breath caught in her throat, the words hitting her like a physical blow. Not guilty. The phrase hung in the air, an impossible contradiction to everything she had just laid out. Confusion swept over her—how could they have reached a decision? They hadn't even deliberated yet. The verdict came too fast, too clean, as if the decision had already been made before they'd even left the room. Her mind raced to make sense of it, but the more she tried, the less sense it made. Could there have been some mistake? The evidence had been so clear.

The room seemed to tilt. Her hands—once steady—began to tremble. Her legs felt unsteady beneath her, as if the ground had shifted without her noticing. The sweat on her palms slicked the edge of the table, and she gripped it to steady herself. She wanted to speak, to demand clarity, but the weight of the moment made her words pointless. The room was already shifting, as if the reality of what had just transpired was being rewoven around her.

The judge's voice was distant, already addressing the next case as though nothing had happened. The gavel fell, signaling the end, but Jayne remained rooted in place. Her gaze swept over the jury, desperate for some sign, some flicker of humanity. But they avoided her eyes, busying themselves with their papers and bags, indifferent to the enormity of their decision.

And then, she felt it.

The air around her grew cold, her breath coming in sharp, shallow gasps. She turned, instinctively, and met the eyes of the defendant—his cold, lifeless stare locking onto hers. But it wasn't just a look. It was something more, something deeper, darker. A predatory gleam.

As their eyes locked, a bone-deep chill surged through her, paralyzing her momentarily. In that instant, his features contorted grotesquely, his face morphing into a demonic visage that seemed to pulse with malice. Jayne's heart raced, every instinct screaming to look away, but she was rooted to the spot. Just as quickly as it had appeared, the horror vanished; he was just a man again, but the fleeting glimpse of his true nature lingered in her mind like a dark stain.

She felt a rush of fear; this was more than just a man acquitted of a crime—this was a harbinger of the evil that lurked just beneath the surface of society. Before he turned to leave, he leaned closer, his voice a chilling whisper: "Time's up, Jayne!"

CHAPTER TWO

THE UNRAVELING

Day 2, USA

Jayne jolted awake, her heart racing and cold sweat drenching her skin. The remnants of the dream clung to her like a persistent shadow, every detail sharp and unsettling. She could still feel the icy grip of fear around her, a chilling reminder that hinted at something far worse than a vision. Her breath came in shallow bursts, her skin clammy and cool against the sheets. She could still see it—the twisted face, the sharpness of the moment, the feeling that something terrible was about to unfold. It wasn't just a nightmare. It felt real. Too real.

She sat up, trying to shake off the lingering unease, but the dream was stubborn. She glanced around, seeking comfort in the familiar surroundings. But as the words "Time is up, Jayne" echoed in her mind, an unsettling question loomed: What could that possibly mean?

Jayne sat dazed, the alarm blaring insistently and pulling her further back to reality as sunlight streamed through the curtains. She glanced at the clock—7:00 a.m. *She'd overslept.* It was going to be one of those frantic mornings where everything felt rushed, and she was already behind. Pushing the dream aside, she quickly scrambled out of bed, throwing on clothes as the clock ticked louder in her ears. She didn't have time to linger.

Downstairs, the smell of coffee drifted into the hallway, and Jayne spotted Lawson at the counter, his back to her. "Jayne, you're going to be late," he called, his voice carrying a familiar note of concern.

"In a minute," she replied, trying to rush without panicking. She snatched her keys from the table and hurried through the living room. As she passed Lawson, she paused, offering him a quick, apologetic smile. "I'm sorry I didn't eat with you. I'll make it up to you tonight, I promise."

He turned, a small smile tugging at his lips, but the worry didn't leave his eyes. "Just be safe. I'll hold you to that. Love you."

"Love you, too," she called over her shoulder as she headed out the door. But the words didn't feel like they usually did, light and reassuring. Today, they sounded almost hollow.

The air outside was warm with the promise of summer, the sky a cerulean blue, yet she had no time to appreciate it. Her mind buzzed with the day ahead—a crucial meeting with her division chief, lunch with Peggy, and drafting a legal motion for the upcoming trial still lay ahead.

The drive to work was usually uneventful—predictable, routine, safe. But today, as she merged onto the freeway, something felt off. It wasn't just the usual morning rush. There was an unsettling tension in the air. Cars weaved erratically, braking without warning, drivers' faces showing the same confusion she felt. Something was amiss.

She tightened her grip on the wheel, trying to shake off the growing sense that something wasn't right. A few more miles and she was sure she'd make it—just had to get through this traffic jam. But then it happened.

In a shocking moment, a car hurtled past her, its driver's seat vacant. Panic gripped her chest like a vise. How could a vehicle be moving without someone behind the wheel? Was she dreaming? Jayne gasped, adrenaline flooding her system. It instantly felt surreal, as if she had stumbled into a twisted nightmare.

One by one, other cars began to glide off the road, some eerily empty, moving as if guided by invisible hands, while others contained bewildered drivers who were just as confused as she was.

The commotion sent her heart racing even faster. A sudden panic emerged, and her thoughts began to quicken. What was happening?

Was there some emergency up ahead? The traffic was so congested, far worse than usual. Had she somehow missed an emergency alert or a news flash? Her mind raced with questions as the chaos around her grew. Vehicles collided, metal crunching and glass shattering. Suddenly, a car swerved across her lane—Jayne slammed on the brakes, her car jerking to a stop in the middle of the road. The cacophony of horns blaring and people shouting filled the air, blending into a muddled symphony of fear. A few drivers stumbled from their cars, dazed and confused, their faces pale with shock. Jayne honked her horn, urging them to clear the road, but it felt futile.

Just as her anxiety reached a fever pitch, Jayne's eyes widened in horror as she caught sight of an airplane soaring far too low, veering downward toward the city—its descent erratic and terrifying. Her breath hitched in her throat, a primal instinct screaming that something was terribly, irrevocably wrong. The aircraft's descent was steep, almost predatory, and terror clawed at her insides as she watched it plummet. Time seemed to stretch as the plane barreled directly over the freeway, engines roaring with a deafening intensity that drowned out the honking horns and panicked shouts below. In a heart-stopping moment, it crashed into the parking lot of a nearby Costco, the impact reverberating like a thunderclap through the air.

The moment it struck, a cataclysmic explosion erupted, sending debris flying in all directions. The ground shook beneath her, and the sound of breaking glass and twisting metal filled the air. Flames shot upward, illuminating the sky with a horrifying glow, while thick, black smoke billowed out, twisting and curling into the atmosphere like a sinister serpent.

From where she sat, she had a clear line of sight to the shopping center just ahead. The scene transformed into a hellish tableau: the parking lot engulfed in flames, cars nearby caught in the inferno, their paint blistering and melting away. The vibrant colors of the storefront were swallowed by the monstrous fire, which crackled and roared, sounding alive as it consumed everything in its path.

Panic surged through Jayne as she gripped the steering wheel, her knuckles turning white. Around her, more cars screeched to a halt, some drivers leaping from their vehicles, eyes wide with disbelief and terror. People stumbled, confusion etched on their faces as they tried to comprehend the catastrophic event unfolding before them. Her heart pounded in her chest as she battled the instinct to flee, desperate to break free from the turmoil that loomed like a storm ready to swallow her whole.

Everything felt alien, each detail heightened, as if the edges of her world were fracturing. The sun's glare felt accusatory, and the sounds of screeching tires and blaring horns created an unsettling backdrop. Her eyes flickered to her rearview mirror, despairingly searching for any hint of normalcy, but the road behind her offered only the same unsettling scene. In that moment, she caught sight of a car barreling toward her from behind, racing dangerously fast, its driver seemingly unaware of the impending danger.

Jayne swerved to avoid the collision, narrowly missing a vehicle that had come to a sudden stop in the middle of the highway. She struggled to stay focused. The world outside felt unreal. The highway stretched ahead but had transformed into a battleground of crumbled vehicles and disorder, prompting her to make her way onto the adjacent feeder road.

As she approached an intersection, the traffic lights flickered erratically. Horror washed over her as another car rolled past, yet the driver was nowhere in sight. In that moment, her heart raced even faster, a primal instinct urging her to escape, to get home to Lawson.

Turning onto a side street, Jayne hoped to navigate around the turmoil, but the disarray followed her relentlessly. Empty cars lined the streets, their doors flung wide open as if their occupants had vanished mid-step, leaving behind the remnants of their lives—coffee cups in cup holders, half-eaten breakfasts on the passenger seats, and articles of clothing strewn across the cushions where their bodies once sat. As she drove, she caught sight of a lawnmower idling on a front lawn, its engine buzzing monotonously. No one was in sight—only a crumpled pair of dirty jeans and a T-shirt lay in the grass, as if someone had vanished mid-chore. Her gaze shifted to a work crew gathered near a house, their expressions a mix of confusion and fear. They stared up at a tall ladder that reached toward the roof, but there was no one at the top—just a set of clothes hanging lifelessly from the rungs, fluttering slightly in the breeze. Below, the workers looked up, eyes wide and mouths moving, but their voices were lost in eerie silence.

More idle cars cluttered the streets, some abandoned, others crumpled into homes or smashed against each other. A minivan sat crookedly against a mailbox, its front end crumpled like an empty soda can, while a pickup truck had collided with the porch of a nearby house, splintered wood framing the scene like a surreal painting.

With each turn, the reality of the moment became clearer, as if the world she had known was unraveling, thread by thread. She had to get home, to Lawson.

✳ ✳ ✳

Jayne's tires screeched as she whipped the car into the driveway, her heart pounding in her chest. The world outside had become a nightmare she couldn't even begin to understand. She didn't pause to catch her breath—she was already halfway to the front door. Her mind was racing, and her body was working faster than her thoughts could keep up.

She fumbled for her keys, but before she could even unlock the door, it swung open. Lawson stood there, his briefcase in hand. The sight of him, safe and unaware, nearly broke her.

"You're home," he said, his voice steady but laced with an undercurrent of worry and confusion.

Jayne took a shaky breath, trying to calm her racing heart. "Lawson … the cars. There were cars driving by themselves, empty."

Lawson blinked in confusion, his eyebrows knitting together as he set his briefcase down on the ground. "Wait, what are you talking about?"

He took a step back, his voice tentative. "What's going on?"

Jayne was breathing too fast, her words tumbling over each other. "I don't know! It's like the world just stopped. Cars driving themselves, no one behind the wheel. I saw a plane crash, Lawson—right in front of me! Like it just … dropped out of the sky. The freeway was a war zone. People were just vanishing. No warning, nothing!"

Lawson's eyes widened, a flicker of concern crossing his face, but he was still trying to process what she was saying. "Hold on. Are you sure you're OK? You, you're talking about … a plane crash? People disappearing?" He stepped forward, his voice strong but filled with growing concern. "Jayne, calm down. You need to slow down."

Gently, he placed a hand on her shoulder, guiding her inside as she stumbled a little on her way through the door. Her breath was still ragged, and her hands shook as she clutched her purse. He led her to the couch, his grip firm but comforting. "Sit down, OK? Take a deep breath."

Jayne sank into the cushions, the frantic energy inside her not quite matching the calmness Lawson was trying to bring. Her eyes darted nervously toward the window, as if expecting the world outside to break apart at any moment.

"They just vanished," Jayne said, her voice unsteady as the words spilled out. "I didn't even make it five miles before it all started. The neighborhood was fine when I left, but once I hit the freeway … everything changed. Cars, driving themselves—empty, just veering off the road, crashing into each other. Wrecks everywhere. I watched a plane go down, Lawson—right in front of me. It just kept getting lower and lower, then crashed straight into Costco, exploded on impact. I tried to get off the freeway and head home, but it's the same thing everywhere. Cars wrecked, people gone. I saw a work crew—it was clear one of them had just vanished. And I swear, I saw a lawnmower running in someone's yard. No one around, but his clothes were just lying on the ground without a body. What the hell is happening?"

Lawson remained silent, his face tight with concern. He didn't speak. He simply listened, likely trying to make sense of what his wife was struggling to explain.

"I'm not imagining this!" she snapped, taking a deep breath, trying to steady herself. "It's real, Lawson. Something is happening out there. I don't know what it is, but it's spreading. I was on the road, and it was like … like I was the only one left who wasn't …" She stopped, realizing how crazy it all sounded. "I know it sounds insane, but you have to believe me."

"Okay, OK," Lawson said, raising a hand in a calming gesture. "Just breathe. Let me make sense of this. What do you mean, people disappearing?"

Jayne ran a hand through her hair, frustrated. "I don't know. It's like … I don't even know how to explain it. Cars without drivers, planes falling from the sky. And people, Lawson—people just gone. I thought I was losing my mind."

Lawson moved quickly to the TV and hit the power button. The screen flickered to life, showing a live broadcast. The reporter, standing against the backdrop of a wrecked plane with thick smoke rising in the distance, spoke urgently, his voice strained against the noise of the unfolding crisis.

"…authorities are grappling with a staggering, unprecedented event. People—entire families—have vanished without a trace. Cars continue to move, planes remain in the sky, but the occupants? Gone. The cause remains a mystery, and no one can explain how or why it's happening. What we are witnessing is not an isolated incident but a global phenomenon. It's happening everywhere. From small towns to major cities, there are reports pouring in from all corners of the world. We are witnessing what experts are calling The Day of Disappearance."

Jayne's chest tightened as the news anchor confirmed the one thing she had feared: It wasn't just her, and it wasn't just here. The world was unraveling.

"What in the …" she whispered, her breath catching.

Lawson turned to face her, his face pale, his eyes wide with a mixture of disbelief and concern. "It's not just us, Jayne. It's everywhere. This isn't some localized freak accident. This is global. It's—my gosh, it's like the world is … disappearing."

Jayne's hands shook as she pulled out her phone, dialing Sophie's number first, the screen showing it ringing but not connecting. She tried again, but it went to voicemail after only a couple of rings. "Sophie, it's Mom," she said, striving for calm. "Please call me back as soon as you can. I need to know you're OK. We're in the middle of something … strange. Call me, please." She hung up and immediately dialed Landon, leaving a similar message.

Jayne's stomach twisted. She tried Sophie's number again, but again, nothing. The phone rang, then went to voicemail.

"Come on, come on …" she muttered under her breath.

Lawson looked at her, his face softening. He reached for her, gently pulling her into an embrace. "I'm sure the kids are fine. They're probably just—"

Jayne pulled back slightly, her eyes wide with panic. "I can't just sit here and wait, Lawson. I need to know they're OK."

She quickly texted them both: *I can't reach you. I need to know you're safe! Please call me! It's urgent!* She stared at the screen, willing them to respond, but all she saw was the dreaded Delivered with no reply.

"Come on, kids," she muttered under her breath, trying Sophie's number once more. "Answer your phones!"

"No answer," she said quietly, a layer of fear creeping into her voice. Her hand fell to her lap, her phone now feeling like a foreign object. "What if something's happened to them? What if they—"

Lawson stepped closer, kneeling down beside her. "Jayne, I'm sure it's nothing. Maybe they're still in class? Or it could just be the phone lines—"

"I can't wait for this to blow over," she said, cutting him off. Her mind raced. "I've got to go. I need to see them, Lawson. I need to make sure our children are safe."

She stood up abruptly, already thinking of the quickest route to the highway.

Just then, a knock at the door interrupted them both. Jayne froze. Lawson glanced toward the door. "Who's that?"

✳ ✳ ✳

Jayne found Camille and David standing at the door, their faces drawn with concern. They lived just a few houses down on the cul-de-sac—good people, the ones who always showed up when it mattered most. "Hey," Camille said softly, almost hesitantly, her eyes scanning Jayne's face. "We just wanted to check on you two. Make sure you're OK."

Jayne leaned over and wrapped her arms around her friend, pulling her into a tight hug. "We're OK. We're just—" She pulled back, shaking her head as the weight of the morning's events settled in. "I don't know, Camille. I witnessed all of it on the way to work … it was all so surreal."

David shifted his weight, his expression tight. "I was out back when it happened, just gone. Poof. A guy walking his dog disappeared right in front of me."

Camille stared in disbelief. "What … what in the world is happening?"

Jayne stepped back and looked at Lawson, his expression darkening with every word. "I don't know. It was like the world just … stopped. It was like nothing I've ever seen."

Jayne opened the door wider. "Come in."

As they stepped inside, Jayne's gaze lingered on them. She'd always loved David and Camille. She had always admired how they'd found each other again—once childhood friends, they'd reconnected at a high school reunion and turned an old crush into a second chance at love. Now married fifteen years, they moved through life with quiet strength and deep affection. Camille had two daughters from her previous marriage, and David, who'd never married before her, had stepped into their lives without hesitation—never trying to replace anyone, just loving them as his own. Though Camille was nearly twenty years her senior, she'd become one of Jayne's dearest friends—wise, steady, and full of warmth. "Jayne, have you heard from the kids?" Camille asked, her voice low with anxiety.

"No, not yet," Jayne replied quickly, her stomach turning. "I've been trying, but they aren't answering. Have you heard from your daughters?"

Camille nodded, relief in her voice. "Yes, they're fine. Nicole's husband is on a business trip, but she's talked to him and he's OK for now. Just wondering how he'll make it home at this point." She paused for a moment, a shadow of worry flickering in her eyes.

Just then, Jayne's phone buzzed in her pocket. She pulled it out, her hands trembling slightly as she saw the name on the screen. Stepping away from her neighbors, she walked into the kitchen to take the call.

"Landon!" she exclaimed, answering quickly, relief flooding over her. "Landon? Oh, thank God, are you OK?"

"Mom, what in the world is going on? It's crazy here!" Landon's voice trembled, thick with panic. In the background, horns blared and distant shouts echoed through the chaos. "I'm in the car with Andrew. We were in class when it happened. One minute everything was normal, and then, suddenly … people just vanished. The kid sitting next to me was there one second, and the next—he was just gone. Mom! He disappeared. His clothes were still there … even his watch."

Jayne's heart sank at his words, the picture of what Landon had just described forming in her mind. "Where are you?" she whispered, struggling to process the enormity of what he was saying. "Are you safe?"

"Yes, I'm fine," He said, his voice trembling.

"Have you had any contact with Sophie?" she asked, anxiety gripping her.

"Yes, she's fine. We're on our way to Matt's now to pick her up. She's freaking out because she can't find him," Landon replied, his voice filled with a mixture of annoyance and fear. "What the heck is happening? Where did everyone go, Mom? People don't just disappear!"

"Oh, thank God she's OK. Do not let her out of your sight once you get to Matt's!" Jayne said with urgency. "I don't know, Landon. I just don't know," she said. "Honestly, it might be better for you to come home now. Things could escalate, and I don't want you in a big city with everything going on. If you can leave, you should," she urged, her voice steady despite her own fear. "I know it feels overwhelming right now, but it seems like it's only going to get worse. Are you sure you don't need me to come get you?"

"No, Mom, we'll be safe," Landon replied, in what was probably meant to be a reassuring tone.

"All right, but listen to me. Stay off the main roads and take the back ones. It might be safer that way," she said. "And please, keep in touch throughout the drive. I want to know you're OK."

"I will, I promise," he said.

"All right," Jayne said, her thoughts returning to concern for Sophie. "Please call me as soon as you pick up Sophie! She's refusing to answer right now, so I need to know she's with you. Just be careful, Landon. Keep your phone charged and call me if you have any trouble."

Landon's voice came through the phone, tinged with worry. "OK, I promise. Mom, Andrew doesn't want to go home right now. His parents are still out of town."

Jayne gasped as she remembered her last conversation with Andrew's mother, Lilah, who had excitedly mentioned their trip to Israel to visit family. "I just saw the news about that attack last night. Has Andrew been able to talk to his parents at all?"

Landon was quiet for a moment. "No … nothing."

Jayne was alarmed at the thought of Andrew's parents being so far away during such an unpredictable time. She took a deep breath, trying to steady herself. "Of course he can stay with us! I'm sure he's terrified. I want him here until we can figure this all out."

"OK, we'll pick up Sophie and be home soon."

Jayne's voice softened. "Keep an eye on the roads and let me know if anything changes. It's important that y'all stick together and take those back roads."

"Definitely," Landon assured her. "We'll keep our phones on, and I'll text you before we head out."

As they wrapped up the conversation, Jayne felt a mix of relief and insecurity take root. She knew they had a plan, but the uncertainty of the situation loomed large.

Jayne thought of her children, both attending the University of Texas in Austin, only a few short hours away. Landon, a business major in his senior year, had dedicated himself to his studies, dreaming of a bright future. With graduation just weeks away and a job offer already secured, she couldn't help but worry about what this upheaval could mean for him.

At the same time, Jayne felt grateful that Sophie was a freshman on the same campus. Having her older brother nearby brought a sense of comfort. Landon, tall like his father with dark hair and deep brown eyes, was studious and reserved, preferring the company of a close-knit group. Sophie, in contrast, was short with blonde hair, full of energy and charm. She thrived in the social side of college, joining a sorority and embracing the fun experiences, all while excelling in her fashion major.

Landon and Andrew had been friends since kindergarten, their bond forged over years of shared experiences. Andrew was the kind of friend every kid dreamed of—loyal, supportive, always there to lift Landon up. Jayne knew how much Landon admired him, not just for his character but for his dedication to his own ambitions. She remembered the excitement on Landon's face as he prepared for Andrew's bar mitzvah. She could still see him in his dress shirt and tie, beaming with pride like it was his own celebration.

What would this mean for the boys' futures? Would they still graduate together, chase their dreams side by side? The thought that they might not saddened her. She had hoped for so much for them all—careers, relationships, the freedom to explore the world. But now, everything felt like a fragile house of cards on the verge of collapse.

Jayne walked into the living room, her hand still clutching the phone. She let out a shaky breath as she found Camille and David sitting with Lawson, all of them looking up at her expectantly.

"The kids are OK," she said, her voice sounding steadier than she felt. She gave Lawson a quick, relieved smile. "Landon and Andrew are in the car. They're on their way to pick up Sophie. They're safe for now."

David and Camille exchanged a glance, a mix of relief and lingering concern on their faces.

"That's good news, Jayne," Camille said. "I'm so glad they're all right."

Lawson's face softened. "Thank God," he murmured, rubbing his hands over his face. The tension that had been knotting his shoulders seemed to ease just a little.

Jayne's mind, however, was still swirling. "I'm still worried about the roads," she said, her voice tight. "Landon said they were on their way home, but the highways—there's no telling what they might run into out there."

"I know," Lawson said, his tone firm. "But they're smart, and they'll keep in touch. I'm just glad they're OK."

Jayne let out a long, slow breath, willing his words to be true. "I know. I just wish we knew what in the world was going on."

Just then, there was a sharp knock at the door. Lawson stood up immediately, his eyes narrowed, uncertainty flickering across his face. He opened it to reveal Sarah and Trevin, their next-door neighbors. Sarah was visibly upset, her eyes red and puffy, and her breath came in short, frantic bursts. Trevin stood beside her, looking concerned but trying to remain calm.

Without saying a word, Lawson stepped aside and motioned for them to come in. As soon as they crossed the threshold, Sarah's composure cracked, and she began to cry, her shoulders shaking.

Camille and Jayne rushed to her side, both women instinctively reaching out to comfort her.

"Sarah, what's wrong?" Jayne asked, her voice soft but filled with worry. "Are you OK?"

Sarah sat on the couch, her hands trembling as she clung to her children's clothes, the fabric bunched tightly in her fists. Tears were streaming down her face, but her eyes were hollow, lost in a place beyond the room. Beside her, Trevin sat motionless, his silence speaking volumes about the ordeal they had just endured.

"I don't know how to explain it," Sarah whispered, her voice ragged. Her eyes brimmed with new tears, but she fought to keep them in check, wiping her face. "I had to go to the school to find them. I thought for sure they'd be there. I couldn't just wait … I had to know."

Jayne watched Sarah's words falter, grief tightening her throat. Sarah clutched the clothes in her lap— not for comfort, but as if holding onto something solid might keep her from unraveling completely. "We drove to the kids' school, but it wasn't what I expected. The streets were eerily silent. Cars sat abandoned, some wrecked, others just left on the side of the road. People were around, but it was like they weren't really there. They were … standing still, staring at nothing, as if they'd forgotten how to keep going."

Sarah paused, her chest rising and falling in uneven breaths, her hands trembling beneath her own grip.

"When we got to the school, I thought it would be better. But it wasn't. The gates were open, like they'd been waiting. Parents were everywhere, frantic, demanding answers, but nobody had any. Inside, the building was wrong. It wasn't just quiet—it was empty. Kids' drawings still hung on the walls, but backpacks were tossed aside. Lunchboxes left behind, but not a single child in sight. I couldn't make sense of it. Like the kids had never been there at all. And then I saw the playground." Her voice caught, a sob threatening to break through.

She exhaled shakily, her hands curling around the fabric in her lap, her grip tightening almost instinctively.

"I found Cassi's dress … her birthday dress." Jayne's heart sank as Sarah held up a pale pink dress adorned with delicate smocking. The intricate white stitching around the collar formed tiny, swirling patterns—details that had made Cassi beam with pride when she first wore it.

This was the dress Sarah had bought for Cassi just weeks ago, a special treat for her daughter's seventh birthday. Jayne had seen Cassi twirling in it, giggling as the fabric swirled around her. With her curly brown hair framing her face and bright green eyes sparkling with mischief, Cassi had a smile that could light up any room. Seeing the dress in Sarah's trembling hands sent a wave of grief crashing over them both, a reminder of the vibrant little girl who should have been wearing it.

"She was so proud of it, so happy. And now, it was just lying there, as if she never wore it. Just a piece of cloth that held nothing. I wanted to scream, to wake up from this nightmare, but I knew. Deep down, I knew something terrible had happened."

Her voice faltered, her words running together.

"This is Dylan's," Sarah choked out, clutching a pair of jeans and a red Nike shirt with a baseball graphic that read Never Give Up. She held the clothes as if they were lifelines to wherever he might be. Her trembling hands brushed against the fabric.. "I remember this morning; he was laughing as he put on his favorite sneakers. He pointed out the little hole in the right shoe he got while playing outside. 'Just battle scars, Mom!' he said." Sarah's voice cracked. "Now, that scuffed shoe... it's all I have left.."

Jayne's heart broke seeing her friend in despair. It was one thing to fear for children; it was another to hold the tangible remnants of their presence. Kneeling beside Sarah, Jayne felt her own tears threaten to spill over. "We'll find them," she promised, her voice trembling. "They're out there somewhere."

"I couldn't stop looking," Sarah continued. "I thought if I searched just a little longer … maybe, just maybe, I'd find something. A sign. A clue that they weren't really gone. I kept searching, hoping that if I looked hard enough, I'd see them hiding somewhere. But all I found were clothes. Hundreds of items. Stacked on top of the lawn, scattered across the playground like forgotten reminders. And still, nothing. They weren't there."

Her breathing grew shallow, and she pressed her hands to her face. Her voice, barely audible, trembled with disbelief.

"All the kids were gone?" Jayne asked softly, her face pale, eyes wide with confusion. "Why were all the kids gone?"

Sarah closed her eyes, her lips shaking as she spoke, the words strangled and raw. "The teacher said … all the elementary kids were gone. Some of the staff, too. They're saying some are missing at the middle and high school. There are reports. Kids … and staff just vanished. No one knows where they went. They're just … gone."

Jayne instinctively gasped, holding the palm of her hand over her mouth, her eyes darting down to the clothes Sarah clutched. "But the clothes … Why were all the clothes left behind? How could they disappear but leave their clothes?"

Trevin spoke then, his voice deep and firm, as if trying to ground them both in the reality they were still struggling to accept. "They'd gone outside for a routine safety drill—something they do every month.

And then … everything happened. They were out on the playground, and in an instant, they were gone. But their clothes—those stayed. Lying there, like they'd just stepped out of them."

The room was oppressive with the silence that followed Trevin's words, a tangible tension settling over them. Jayne sat frozen. She could only stare at her friend, struggling to process the images Sarah and Trevin had just described, each one more impossible than the last.

"Everyone just stood there," Trevin added quietly. "No one knew what to do. We kept hoping we'd see them. Some sign. But there was nothing. Just clothes. And nothing else."

"They made us leave," Sarah said, her voice quivering again. "Said it was a crime scene. Told us we had to go. But I couldn't. I couldn't leave without them. I kept thinking—what if they're scared? What if they need me? I kept looking back, thinking that if I could just see them one more time, it might all go back to normal." She paused; her hands clutched in her lap. "But they were gone. I couldn't stop it."

She exhaled sharply, tears streaming down her cheeks as she wiped at them again, her soft cries now turning into uncontrollable sobs. "I didn't want to leave. I didn't want to believe they were gone. But when we had to … I looked around at the other parents. Some of them were still standing there, lost, like me. And then I realized, it wasn't just my kids. It was all of them. All of ours. And that—that's when it hit me. This isn't just about us. It's bigger. It's too much."

She let out a shaky breath. "I couldn't protect them. I couldn't save them. And now … I don't know where they are. I don't know what happened. I don't know what to believe anymore."

Jayne felt her heart break, the devastation in Sarah's voice tearing at her. "But—how? Why?"

"There's no answer," Trevin replied softly, comforting his wife as he gently wrapped his arms around her. "No reason for any of it. They were there, and then … they weren't. Just gone."

A silence fell over them. No one knew what to say or how to comfort someone who had lost everything.

A few moments stretched between them, and Jayne felt every second like a push against the stillness. Her mind raced through the chaos of the morning, trying to grasp hold of what needed to happen next. Everything felt uncertain, unpredictable—each moment slipping away as quickly as the last.

Camille's voice broke the quiet, calm but urgent. "Let me walk you home, Sarah," she said, her eyes filled with concern. "David and I will stay with you for a while. Trevin, Lawson—why don't you two go get some supplies? Things are about to get chaotic. The stores will run out fast. Jayne, why don't you check on the rest of the neighbors and let's meet tonight at Sarah's around six? Does that work?"

Trevin nodded, his eyes reflecting the exhaustion and worry that seemed to press down on him. He looked at Sarah, his expression quiet but determined. "I'll be back soon. We'll figure out what to do next. Stay with Camille, OK? We'll meet back here later tonight."

Sarah's eyes met his, and she nodded slowly.

Camille gave Sarah a reassuring smile, though her own worry was evident. She turned to Trevin and Lawson, her voice steady but soft. "You two go get what you need. I'll take care of things here."

Trevin gave a brief, tight nod, then glanced at Lawson before heading for the door. "We'll be quick."

As the men gathered their things to leave, Sarah stood, her legs shaky, still holding the clothes. She glanced up at Camille. Camille stepped closer and put an arm around her friend, guiding her toward the door. "Let's go. We'll get you back to your place."

Sarah hesitated, looking one last time at the room. "I don't know how to do this," she whispered, almost to herself.

"You don't have to do it alone," Camille said gently. "We'll take it one step at a time."

Jayne looked at Trevin and Lawson, knowing they had to keep moving. Outside, the world was changing, and they needed to prepare for whatever was coming.

"Let's go," Trevin said quietly, his voice resolute. "We'll meet back at our house later tonight."

Jayne nodded and stood up, her eyes sharp with purpose. "I'll check on a few neighbors, spread the word about the meeting. We need to keep everyone in the loop."

As Camille led Sarah toward the door, she offered a silent but reassuring glance at Trevin.

Jayne watched them leave, then turned to head out herself. As she stepped toward the door, her phone suddenly buzzed in her pocket. She pulled it out quickly, letting out a deep sigh of relief when she saw the message. It was from Landon.

"Have Sophie. On our way. Love you."

Her fingers hovered over the screen for a moment, the message sending a sudden rush of emotion through her. It was a small bit of comfort, a reminder that her family was still holding together, even in the midst of everything falling apart. She glanced at the door, then back at the screen. *Love you.* The words, so simple, carried a weight that felt more important now than ever. It was a promise. A lifeline.

Jayne clung to that fragile reassurance, even as a deeper unease settled in the pit of her stomach. How long could safety last in a world that was spiraling out of control? She pressed her phone against her chest, silently whispering a thank you, grateful for this fleeting moment of peace. But she couldn't shake the feeling that the storm was far from over.

CHAPTER THREE

THE GATHERING STORM

Jayne hurried down the street, her steps quick and determined. The once-familiar neighborhood felt strangely foreign, each house standing as a silent witness, its door a potential gateway to answers or shared grief. She reached the first house and knocked softly. Only silence greeted her. Swallowing her growing unease, she moved on, the emptiness of each unanswered door deepening her sense of isolation—and feeding her fear of the unknown. She didn't know which of her neighbors were still here and who had vanished, leaving her to wonder if the world she once knew would ever feel the same again.

At the next house, a neighbor opened the door, her expression a blend of fear and confusion. They spoke for a few moments, and as Jayne continued her rounds, she gathered snippets of stories that mirrored her own friend's turmoil. Parents searching, children missing, spouses unreachable. "I haven't heard from my wife since this morning," one man said, his voice breaking. "I tried calling, but it just goes to voicemail."

Another neighbor, a woman with tear-streaked cheeks, shared how her son had also vanished during a routine drill at school. "He was right there one moment, and then … nothing," she said, looking down, as if the ground might provide answers.

Yet not every interaction was welcoming. Some neighbors, faces set in stone, simply shut the door in her face without a word. It was disheartening, especially since she recognized these individuals—people who had always maintained a distance, rarely offering help or kindness. Their coldness contrasted sharply with those closer to her, who had always been willing to lend a hand.

Jayne recalled instances where these distant neighbors had brushed off her greetings or ignored her pleas for support. They seemed more concerned with their own lives than the shared struggles around them. The sight of garage doors closing shut immediately after a car pulled in had become all too familiar, a symbol of retreat into isolation.

As Jayne reached the final house on her route, a new wave of concern settled over her. This was the home of her other next-door neighbors, a couple she had grown close to over the years. They were older, kindhearted, and like family to her. She had saved their house for last, dreading the thought that they, too, might be missing. The familiar flower beds, once a comforting sight, now seemed out of place, their bright colors standing in contrast to the dread knotting in her stomach. She stopped at the door and took a deep breath as she prepared herself for what she might find. With a quiet sigh, she rang the doorbell. The silence that followed was broken only by the anxious barking of Finnley and Charlie echoing through the stillness.

"Oh, please let them be here," she murmured, the knot in her stomach twisting tighter. Anxiety gripped her as she stood frozen, the barking growing louder and more frantic.

Determined, Jayne turned on her heel, her resolve solidifying. Ruth had entrusted her with a spare key for emergencies, and this felt like one of those moments. She hurried back home, thoughts racing as she retraced her steps.

Once inside, she moved quickly to the drawer where she kept important items. After rifling through a jumble of papers, her fingers finally closed around the familiar smooth metal of the key, attached to a vibrant purple lanyard—a color Ruth had chosen for its visibility. She recalled the warmth in Ruth's smile when she had first given it to her, a tangible sign of their friendship, a bond rooted in trust.

Key in hand, Jayne rushed back to Ruth and Isaac's house. As she approached the door again, she glanced at the lanyard, its plum hue standing out sharply against the dark wood. Taking a deep breath, she steeled herself for whatever awaited her inside. If the dogs were in distress, she needed to act quickly. With a firm grip, she inserted the key into the lock and turned it.

Inside, the cozy home was too quiet. "Ruth? Isaac?" she called, but the silence that met her was unsettling. The dogs' barking echoed from another room, frantic and desperate, urging her to investigate further.

She made her way down the dimly lit hallway. "Ruth? Isaac?" she called again, her voice cracking slightly as it bounced back at her from down the hall.

Pausing at the bedroom door, she took a deep breath and pushed it open. The sight of the bed before her sent a chill down her spine: two pairs of neatly laid pajamas peeked out the top of the sheet, as if Ruth and Isaac had just been sleeping there, leaving their clothes behind. It struck her as if they had vanished instantly.

Everything felt wrong—too quiet, too unsettling. Jayne's mind raced as she took in the scene. The bed was a reminder of their presence, yet the absence of Ruth and Isaac felt cold.

"RUTH! ISAAC!" she called out, but only the emptiness of the house responded. "They're gone," she whispered, her voice breaking. The thought that they had vanished—without a trace, without any explanation—was almost too much to bear. Her mind raced, trying to make sense of it, but the fear gripped her, refusing to let go.

Shaking her head to push back the rising panic, Jayne turned and headed for the living room, where the dogs' barking grew louder. Kneeling beside them, she forced herself to take a steadying breath. "You guys OK?" she murmured, her hand brushing gently over their fur, trying to calm them—and herself.

"Are y'all thirsty?" she said, her mind racing with questions as she moved toward the kitchen.

As she filled the dogs' water bowl, something on the kitchen table caught her eye. Intrigued, she walked over, drawn to the clutter of books and papers scattered across the surface. Each item seemed out of place, as though they held secrets, their presence almost deliberate—they were fragments of a mystery, a puzzle waiting to be pieced together.

As she approached the table, her eyes drifted over the disorganized stack of books. *The Final Hour: The Last Days on Earth* and *God's Wrath Revealed* sent a shiver through her. The titles and the crisis unfolding around her felt connected, as if the books themselves were whispering a grim prediction of their reality—one she wasn't sure she was ready to face.

Curiosity piqued, Jayne pushed the books aside, her gaze drawn to a sheet labeled "The Last Plumb Line," which contained a detailed outline. Flawless writing filled the margins, referencing the timeline of events, alongside disturbing images that left her more confused. As she flipped through the pages, she uncovered maps, charts, and haunting illustrations—one showed a world engulfed in flames, while another depicted a serene vision of heaven.

"Ruth, what in the world are you working on?" she murmured, pondering the implications of what she was uncovering. What had she stumbled upon? Each page felt like a step deeper into a confusing maze, and she couldn't shake the feeling that something significant was at play. Her instincts urged her to put it all down, to walk away, but she felt inexplicably tethered to that table, drawn to the gravity of the knowledge it held.

The weight of her discoveries settled over her, a suffocating presence. *Could this all be connected?* The thought lingered as she glanced at the stack of books and papers. Ruth's notes pointed to something dark—an outline of a tribulation marked by years of suffering, where many would face unimaginable judgments. A reference to the sudden disappearance of believers drew her in, as if the vague teachings of her past were suddenly merging with the terrifying reality before her.

Her gaze lingered on the scattered papers, and a nagging thought crept in. She wasn't sure if it was right to take them. She wasn't sure what they meant or if they were truly relevant, but they felt important, and she was afraid of missing something that could explain what was happening. It felt like prying into Ruth's private life—like crossing a line she shouldn't. But if Ruth was gone, perhaps understanding what she'd been researching was the only way forward.

With the dogs seemingly content, Jayne reluctantly stepped away from the table. She gave the papers one last glance, something about them made her pause. But she needed to get home. Still, as she turned to leave, a quiet thought followed: what if the answers she needed were sitting right there?

Outside, Lawson and Trevin approached the grocery store, the scene oddly familiar and jarringly chaotic. A long line snaked outside, with anxious shoppers jostling for space, faces a mix of determination and panic. The atmosphere buzzed with energy; it was clear everyone shared the same instinct—to stock up before it was too late.

"Looks like we're not the only ones with this idea," Lawson said, scanning the crowd. The sight of frantic shoppers only heightened his feeling of urgency.

As they pushed through the entrance, they were met with a discordance of raised voices and the rustle of hurried movement. Inside, the aisles were packed, and half the shelves stood eerily bare, remnants of what had once been a well-stocked store. People were throwing food into their carts as if it were a race, a desperate attempt to grab whatever they could before it vanished entirely.

Lawson and Trevin navigated through the crowd, witnessing a woman struggling to reach a box of cereal just out of her grasp. Before they could offer assistance, another shopper barged past her, snatching it up with little regard. Voices escalated nearby as two men began to argue over a case of bottled water, shoving and shouting as the situation spiraled into a brief but intense scuffle. This wasn't just grocery shopping; it was survival. The aisles were cluttered with frenzied shoppers, their faces etched with worry as they urgently grabbed items off the shelves. Lawson pushed his cart through the aisles, its wheels constantly squeaking.

They quickly filled their cart with essentials—canned goods, boxes of pasta, jars of sauce, and bags of rice—all nonperishables that might sustain them in the days ahead. They bypassed the fresh produce section, where fruits and vegetables lay neglected, as they knew they wouldn't last. Instead, they zeroed in on items with long shelf lives, each selection feeling like a small act of defiance against the world outside.

As they navigated the store, they avoided the congestion whenever possible, sidestepping families bickering over the last loaf of bread and individuals scanning the shelves with wild eyes. The atmosphere felt charged with desperation, and as they turned into the next aisle, Lawson and Trevin caught sight of a burly man who was wrestling with a young father trying to pry a pack of diapers from his hands. Lawson stared in disbelief as he realized the depth of fear that had taken hold of the community.

He turned to Trevin, his voice low and firm. "We need to grab what we can, fast. Things are about to get worse." He glanced down the aisle, scanning the shelves. "We'll need water, canned food, flashlight, and some cleaning supplies—just the basics." Trevin nodded, his expression tense. "We should grab batteries, extra medicine... whatever we can find." Lawson's eyes narrowed as he scanned the aisles. "And I need to hit the pharmacy for more doxazosin...just in case." Once their carts were stocked, they made their way to the pharmacy section. Shelves were ransacked and the air was thick with the sounds of panicked voices. People were grabbing whatever they could reach, and the pharmacist looked visibly stressed, trying to keep up with the demands of agitated customers.

Lawson stepped up to the counter, in disbelief at the sight unfolding in front of him. Behind the pharmacist, people were acting erratically, shoving and scrambling to get behind the counter to snatch the medications they desperately wanted. "Excuse me," he began, trying to maintain a calm tone amid the disorder. "I need to pick up some extra medication for my high blood pressure—doxazosin. Is there a way I can …"

Before he could finish, the frightened pharmacist reached under the counter and handed him a bottle with a disheveled smile.

"Here you go, just take it. Make sure to follow the instructions," he said, his tone professional but strained.

Relieved, Lawson took the bottle, grateful for the pharmacist's help. He glanced back at Trevin, who was still scanning the shelves, and he knew it was time to leave. They had what they needed and were ready to face whatever came next.

The lines at the checkout stretched endlessly, a sea of people doing their best to pay for the supplies they needed. But among them, others, driven by fear and panic, began to lash out. In their frenzy, they vandalized the store, grabbing whatever they could, disregarding the line and the rules without a second thought.

Trevin and Lawson exchanged worried glances as they navigated through the throngs of people. While some clutched their carts, eyes darting nervously, others were caught up in the fury, their actions driven by an instinct to survive at any cost. The difference was glaring—those willing to pay amid the turmoil and those abandoning all sense of order.

As they finally reached the checkout, the tension only intensified. The cashier's hands trembled slightly as she scanned their items and cast anxious glances toward the unfolding pandemonium just outside. Lawson's nerves were on edge, knowing they needed to leave quickly before the situation escalated further. He could feel the urgency of the moment, each second feeling more critical than the last.

Amid the commotion, he could hear mumbling coming from behind the counter. Phrases like *missing* and *the end times* slipped from her lips, each word steeped in disbelief and fear. Lawson leaned in, straining to catch her words.

"What are you saying?" he asked in confusion.

"It's the end times," she replied, her voice barely audible. "I heard it from friends. They said God is going to come back, and people will go missing."

Lawson's mind raced as he processed her words. "What do you mean, the end times?" he pressed, struggling to grasp the significance of her claims.

The cashier met his gaze, her eyes wide with fear. "People have been talking about it for a while now. They say this is just the beginning."

❋ ❋ ❋

As Lawson and Trevin stepped out of the store, the gravity of the cashier's words lingered. The parking lot was a scene of hurried movements and frightened faces, but all Trevin could think about was the conversation he'd just had.

"Did you hear what she said about the end times?" Trevin asked, shaking his head in disbelief. "It's like something out of a movie."

"Yeah, I did," Lawson replied. "But what does that even mean?"

They walked briskly toward the car, the chatter of panicked shoppers fading into the background.

"I never thought I'd hear anyone talk about that stuff seriously," Lawson continued once they were in the car. He gripped the steering wheel tightly as they pulled out of the lot. "It's always been something you hear in church or read in books. But now ..." His voice trailed off, a mix of disbelief and frustration surfacing.

"What the hell is going on?" he cursed, shaking his head, anger rising. "These people have lost their minds." He thought of the guy who had rushed to cut in front of them at the checkout, his impatience radiating like heat. "I thought I was going to get into a fight with that guy in line," Lawson admitted, his frustration bubbling over.

"Now it feels real," Trevin continued, looking out the window at the hurried lives around them. "What if it is the beginning of the end?"

"End of what?" asked Lawson.

"What if this is the end of life on earth as we know it? Missing people, vanishing into thin air, every belonging they have is left behind, but it's like their bodies just evaporated." Trevin paused. "People are going nuts out here, and it's only been a few hours. How bad is it really going to get, and what does this mean for humanity?"

Lawson's voice grew firm, determination filling him. "I will protect my family at all costs. No one gets to them."

CHAPTER FOUR

THE OUTLINE

At precisely six o'clock, neighbors began arriving at Trevin and Sarah's home, their faces marked with worry and uncertainty. Jayne stood by the door, greeting each familiar face. The living room, once a space of warmth and joy, now carried an unspoken seriousness.

David and Camille stepped inside, their expressions tense. David, with the unmistakable bearing of a seasoned Navy veteran, stood tall and composed. Jayne observed the sharpness in his attentive eyes, a reflection of his storied past. He scanned the room with a steady gaze, ever watchful for signs of distress. Having served on the neighborhood HOA board for years, he had built strong relationships with many of the residents and often extended a helping hand to those in need, a role he seemed to embrace with a sense of duty and pride.

Camille stepped toward Jayne and pulled her into a warm, steadying hug. "Thank you for staying with Sarah earlier," Jayne said, as she pulled back slightly to meet Camille's gaze. "It meant so much to her." Camille gave her a soft smile, her eyes full of understanding. "Of course." Her presence radiated tenderness and compassion, soothing the turmoil around them. Jayne couldn't help but admire the gentle smile on Camille's soft features, knowing it was her remarkable gift of listening, providing solace and understanding during uncertain times, that made her so special. Jayne felt thankful for the comfort Camille had offered, not only to Sarah but to the entire community. As Jayne watched them settle onto the well-worn sofa, she noticed its familiar creak, a haunting reminder of countless gatherings now overshadowed by the current crisis.

Next to arrive were Maria and John. Maria, with her short frame and long, wavy black hair, walked in with a quiet grace, her olive complexion giving her an air of warmth. Jayne greeted them both with a hug.

"Where's Lawson?" John asked, his voice calm as always.

Jayne pointed toward the kitchen. "He's in there, talking to a few of the others."

John gave a slight nod, then followed Maria into the room. Jayne watched as he quietly took in the space, his steady presence grounding the atmosphere. His calm demeanor was a perfect balance to Maria's usual exuberance, which was notably subdued. John's meticulous nature showed in everything he did, from his work at the auto body shop to the way he maintained his home garage, where every tool had a specific place.

Maria set down a tray she had brought from home, the familiar, sweet aroma of baklava filling the room. The flaky Greek pastry was something she was known for, and Jayne couldn't help but smile as the smell filled the space, bringing with it a sense of comfort and tradition. Maria's Greek heritage was something she always took pride in, and she shared it through food, hospitality, and the stories of her family.

Jayne peeked into the kitchen, where Jeremy stood at the counter, picking at a plate of food he'd brought with him. Tall and broad-shouldered, he moved with the relaxed ease of someone who didn't need to prove himself. His dark, close-cropped hair framed a face marked by quiet intensity, and his steady, thoughtful eyes missed little. Jayne knew he'd grown up in the Bronx, raised by his grandmother, and she'd always admired the quiet resilience in him—like he'd weathered storms long before any of this began.

Nearby, Tiffany leaned against the counter, her purple-streaked hair and nose ring reflecting her bold personality. Without hesitation, she'd helped herself to the liquor cabinet, rummaging through its contents with ease before pouring herself a drink. The sound of the bottle cap twisting off and the liquid splashing into the glass drew a few glances, but Tiffany was unfazed. She added ice with a casual clink, then leaned back against the counter, taking a slow sip.

Jayne noticed the shift in the room as Tiffany's eyes moved over the neighbors. A few stiffened under her gaze, while others exchanged uneasy glances. She had a reputation for stirring up complaints, calling the HOA over minor issues, and manipulating situations to fit her needs. People were polite, but the discomfort was clear.

As more neighbors trickled in, the atmosphere shifted from uncertainty to collective concern. The low hum of the news played in the background, its unsettling reports drawing some people to the television like moths to a flame. The mayhem on screen mirrored their own fears: stories of people vanishing into thin air, planes crashing with empty cockpits, and boats lost at sea, their crews unaccounted for. Refineries burned, and entire neighborhoods were engulfed in flames, with scant fire crews struggling to respond. The roads were choked with abandoned cars, a testament to the panic that had seized their town and countless others across the globe. Everywhere, people frantically searched for their loved ones, to no avail.

Sarah sat among the crowd, her eyes hollow, shoulders slumped beneath the burden of her despair. Jayne saw that she clutched Cassi's teddy bear, cradling it like a lifeline. Absently, she traced her fingers over a water stain on the coffee table beside her. The pain etched on her face revealed just how tenuously she was holding it together. Jayne could see the struggle in her friend's eyes, the desperate hope battling against the crushing reality.

Lawson and Jayne moved through the crowd, offering water and snacks in an effort to foster a sense of normalcy. They knew everyone had gathered for the same reason: to seek answers, find comfort, and support one another in the face of this terrifying uncertainty. The muffled sounds of distant sirens outside served as a reminder of the danger they faced.

"Thank you all for coming," Trevin began, his voice steady as he scanned the room filled with worried faces. "Why don't we start tonight by sharing what we've heard or know about what's going on?"

Tiffany spoke up, her colorful tattoos peeking from beneath the sleeves of her shirt. "I've been seeing so many posts lately—videos, stories, people talking about these strange lights in the sky. They say people are being taken by aliens. It's all over the internet." Tiffany crossed her arms and looked around the room, her voice matter of fact. "Listen, I've been seeing these videos everywhere. People talking about these orbs and drones in the sky, it's like they're all over the place now. You can't scroll through your feed without seeing one. And I read this article that said the disappearances—the kids, the families—it's all connected to alien abductions. I know it sounds wild, but the evidence is right there. They're being taken. I'm telling you, it's happening."

Tiffany's voice gained strength as she continued, her eyes flicking around the group. "Don't y'all remember all the drones and orbs we've been seeing lately? It's not new, it's been going on for decades, but y'all definitely remember how they really started showing up in 2024. I mean, it was all over the news. And just last month, I saw a video from the US House Committee on Oversight and Accountability, they presented it to Congress—talking about the unidentified anomalous phenomena. They're exposing the truth now, people! It's not a coincidence anymore. These are aliens. They've been here all along, and now they're starting to make themselves known. It's right there in front of us, plain as day."

David shook his head, a look of disbelief crossing his face. "I saw that congressional hearing too, but I don't buy the whole alien story. I think they're using the idea of aliens to cover up something they've been doing." His tone was firm, and Jayne could hear his skepticism. "It's too convenient, you know? They want us to focus on that while they keep the real truth under wraps. I heard it's related to some kind of government experiment gone wrong."

Trevin raised an eyebrow, clearly intrigued. "What kind of experiment?"

David shook his head slightly as he continued. "My cousin works in research and mentioned something about a project that got out of hand. He didn't give me many details, but he said they were working on advanced technology, something to do with human enhancement or behavioral control. He implied they were testing it on people without their consent. Then suddenly, poof! People just started disappearing." He leaned back, rubbing his temples as though trying to make sense of it all. "It sounds crazy, but when you start connecting the dots … it all starts to add up. Maybe this is just them covering it up—making it look like aliens, when it's really them messing with stuff they shouldn't have."

The room grew quiet as everyone seemed to process David's implications. Even Tiffany seemed to hesitate, her certainty wavering for a moment.

Jayne felt the tension rise as Maria admitted, "I used to roll my eyes at conspiracy theories, but with everything happening, I feel like we can't dismiss anything anymore. What if those people really are being taken?"

A murmur of agreement rippled through the group. Maria's words seemed to unlock a door to their collective anxiety, revealing a shared fear of the unknown.

"It feels like we're living in a horror movie, but this is real life. And that's what scares me the most," Maria added, her eyes wide. "I mean, people don't just disappear!"

A murmur of disbelief swept through the group, but Jayne sensed curiosity beneath it. Camille's eyes widened as she added, "It's always been the stuff of conspiracy theories, but now? It feels like anything could be true."

As the conversation deepened into theories and fears, Jayne felt the stress level in the room climb. The collective apprehension and uncertainty were evident, forming an invisible bond that felt like it connected their hearts and minds in this moment of crisis. She realized that, whatever the truth was, they were in this together, facing an unknown that loomed larger with every passing minute.

Jeremy, who had been observing quietly from the back, slowly stood. "I came across a theory about the end times," he said, his voice calm. "People are suggesting this could be a sign, that it was all predicted in ancient texts. There are historical precedents for this kind of upheaval—plagues, wars, natural disasters—all linked to similar predictions. I know it sounds far-fetched, but I can't shake the feeling that it's connected. This doesn't feel random; it feels orchestrated, like a force beyond our control."

The room fell silent, his words sparking curious looks.

"What kind of texts?" Trevin asked.

Jeremy surveyed the group before he continued. "The Bible, for starters. There are passages that discuss a great tribulation, a time when many would vanish without explanation. Some believe this could be the beginning of that prophecy coming to life. I don't know much about it, but I remember my grandmother telling me stories when I was a kid—tales filled with warnings and signs of the end times. She spoke with such conviction, her voice trembling as she described things that seemed so far-fetched back then. But now … those stories might hold some truth."

Lawson spoke up. "I've heard similar things. There are groups online discussing it, sharing interpretations. Some believe these disappearances are a warning, a call to prepare for what's to come. It sounds odd, but what if there's truth in it?"

Murmurs rippled through the room as everyone grappled with the implications of Jeremy's assertions.

"But what can we do?" Tiffany asked, frustration creeping into her tone. She helped herself to another drink, sloshing a few drops onto the counter without noticing or caring. "If this is really happening, what's the point of trying to make sense of it? Shouldn't we focus on survival?"

"That's the dilemma, isn't it?" Jeremy replied, lowering his voice. "Do we prepare for the worst while hoping for the best? We can't ignore the signs, but we also can't let fear dictate our actions. We need to help each other, no matter what this is—whether it's a government experiment, a prophecy, or something entirely different."

The group was silent. Jayne felt like they were navigating a labyrinth of confusion, each yearning to grasp the truth behind the day's bewildering events. In the background, the television flickered with images of conflict in Israel, news anchors discussing swelling tensions and urgent developments.

Lawson broke the silence, glancing at the screen. "Has anyone been watching the news on Israel?" His question sparked a wave of anxious murmurs.

"I caught part of it earlier," Maria replied. "They're saying it could escalate into an all-out war. Russia and Iran are both mobilizing troops, and the neighboring countries are gearing up for an invasion. It looks really bad for Israel."

"Yeah, it does," David added, frowning. "They're talking about a coordinated attack. The Iron Dome has been breached—missiles are getting through. It feels like Israel could get completely wiped off the map if this continues."

Jeremy nodded. "There's reports of airstrikes already happening. The situation is incredibly volatile, and it's hard to see how they'll recover from this. I feel horrible for the people stuck there that can't get out."

Jayne listened intently, her mind flickering back to her earlier conversation with Landon. He had mentioned that Andrew's parents were still in Israel, visiting family. She wondered if they were safe. The thought gnawed at her, adding to her anxiety. The conversation shifted, and she realized that their community was grappling with more than just a worldwide phenomenon.

"Is this even relevant?" Camille asked. "Israel has been fighting off threats for years. What makes this time different?"

John spoke up. "I spoke to a friend today who thinks this war could be biblical. They're linking the people who've gone missing to prophecies, like what Jeremy described. It's almost as if they're saying this war in Israel is the beginning of something much bigger, some kind of religious event unfolding right before our eyes."

The discussions about the Bible and the war in Israel triggered a memory for Jayne, reminding her of the unsettling books she had seen at Ruth's house, their titles pointing to the end times. She recalled the outlines and notes that connected significant prophetic events to the present situation. The gravity of those writings now felt more profound, as though Ruth had sensed something ominous on the horizon.

Jayne cleared her throat, feeling the urgency to tell her friends. "I remember seeing some disturbing materials at Ruth's house. There were books about the end of time. She has papers that include an outline with a specific order of events to come, along with upsetting images and maps of Israel. There might be a connection to everything that's happening."

A low buzz of murmurs filled the room as her words seemed to settle among them. John, his eyes wide with intrigue, encouraged Jayne to go back and retrieve the materials, suggesting they might provide valuable information.

Jayne nodded, a surge of determination rising within her. "I'll go get 'em right now."

With a newfound sense of purpose, Jayne made her way back to Ruth's house, her mind racing with possibilities. She was met with the familiar sound of Finnley and Charlie barking excitedly. She quickly checked on the dogs, ensuring they had food and fresh water. She tested the dog door on the back kitchen door, relieved to find it still working, giving the dogs access to the backyard if they needed to go out. As she gathered the materials, important documents and books in hand, she made a mental note to return the next day to bring the dogs to her house and care for them now that Ruth was gone. With everything secured, Jayne set off to rejoin the group.

As her neighbors gathered around, they began to sift through the scattered materials. The first thing that caught the group's attention was a stack of books, each one more unsettling than the last. Their titles focused on surviving the end times and the prophecies that foretold them. Their pages seemed to have an uncanny relevance to the crisis at hand.

At the center of the pile rested an old, well-loved Bible, its pages yellowed and frayed from years of use. Highlighted verses bore witness to Ruth's attention, each mark a reminder of her inquiries into themes of faith and hope amid profound uncertainty.

Tucked carefully within the pages of the Bible was the meticulously folded outline titled "The Last Plumb Line." As Jayne examined it, she could see that it was an extensive study. The outline was a timeline, presenting a chronological sequence of significant events anticipated over a period of seven years, collectively referred to as the tribulation. Each point was thoughtfully annotated, indicating specific occurrences such as natural disasters, political upheaval, and the emergence of key figures, all carefully woven together with biblical references.

Ruth had linked these events to prophecies from historical biblical figures like Daniel, John, and Ezekiel. As Jayne traced her handwritten notes, it became clear that Ruth had attempted to decode ancient texts and relate them to the current turmoil. Her insights appeared framed with an obvious belief that these events might soon come to pass.

Scattered among the books and outline were papers with intricate maps of the Middle East and Europe. Prominently displayed on one map were three large red circles: One around Jerusalem was labeled as a future religious control center. Another circle encompassed an area in Iraq, boldly marked Babylon, identified as the economic hub crucial for trade and resources. The third circle surrounded Rome, with annotations indicating it as the political base—suggesting a possible headquarters for decision-making and governance.

Jayne could see the intrigue and concern in her friends' eyes as they leaned in closer, absorbing the information.

"These places are more than just dots on a map; they represent control—political, economic, and spiritual. If the world is shifting toward a new government structure, what does that mean for us?" she asked.

Ruth's notes told the interconnectedness of these locations and painted a troubling picture, illustrating a potential new world order that could reshape global alliances and influence. Jayne considered the implications, realizing these centers of power were not just theoretical; they could soon dictate the very course of human existence.

Lawson shook his head in disbelief. "This is unbelievable. There's so much here—look at all these maps and books. Ruth must have dedicated years to compiling all of this. What else is in here?"

Within the original map, another series of maps depicted potential conflict zones and significant locations mentioned in the highlighted Scriptures, including the prophesied site of Armageddon, prominently marked in the Megiddo Valley in Israel. Scribbled notes in the margins expressed Ruth's fears and insight, blending academic rigor with personal reflection. There were markings indicating where a spiritual two-hundred-million-man army would cross the Euphrates River, amplifying the sense of impending unrest.

The group felt the significance of Ruth's dedication, and as they absorbed the information, they knew they were stepping into a foreign world, both seen and unseen.

Maria glanced at Jayne, who stood beside her, thoroughly shaken.

"Do you really think this could be real? That we're actually facing something like this?" Maria's voice trembled, her eyes wide with disbelief.

"Maybe," Jayne replied, striving to keep her tone steady.

Jeremy leaned in, studying the map that outlined potential conflict zones. "It's all interconnected," he murmured, "whether it's prophecy or a string of unfortunate events."

His gaze shifted to another map highlighting the United States, pinpointing three nuclear missile sites: the 90th Missile Wing at F.E. Warren Air Force Base in Wyoming, the 341st Missile Wing at Malmstrom Air Force Base in Montana, and the 91st Missile Wing at Minot Air Force Base in North Dakota. Nearby, diagrams marked safety bunkers within the Cheyenne Mountain Complex, designed for shelter in times of crisis. Other markings indicated potential refuge locations, like the Bridgeland and Crestview caves in New Mexico, emphasizing their importance for survival.

Lawson finally broke the silence, confusion clear in his tone. "What does it really mean?"

Jayne began sifting through the stack of papers, searching for the outline Ruth had prepared, labeled "The Last Plumb Line." As her eyes moved across the page, a growing sense of unease settled over her.

"This outline seems to be a chronological timeline, almost like a play-by-play of what's to come, based on the biblical book of Revelation. With each event, Ruth added additional notes and Scriptures to provide context. In the introduction, Ruth refers to a seven-year timeframe as the tribulation, a span during which God's wrath would be unleashed on the world. She also mentioned that, at the start, people would suddenly vanish all over the world—a phenomenon Ruth describes as the *rapture*, when God's believers would be taken away in an instant, leaving only their belongings behind. This event would include people of all ages, particularly children, who had not yet reached an age of accountability to understand their faith."

Maria, who had been listening quietly, spoke up, her voice tinged with confusion. "Wait a minute. What do you mean, *believers?* Believers in what? I go to church every Sunday. I believe in God. If this is true, why wouldn't I be part of the rapture?" She looked around the room, waiting for an explanation.

Jayne sat back, feeling the bulk of Maria's question. She didn't have an immediate answer. "I don't know, Maria," Jayne admitted. She looked at her, wishing she could offer a clearer explanation, but all she could do was offer what she had. "Maybe we need to read more of this. Ruth's notes ... maybe they'll help us understand what we're missing."

She paused, reading more before continuing. "According to this outline, the tribulation is divided into two phases, each lasting three and a half years. Before this seven-year tribulation begins, Ruth indicates the rapture takes place. She also indicates it will begin with a massive conflict involving Israel—one that will include not only Iran and Russia but several neighboring countries attacking. This isn't just any war; it's described as the pivotal moment that sets everything in motion."

Jayne continued to sift through the pages, her eyes scanning the notes she had left behind. "Ruth's notes talk about this war with Israel. They say this war must happen just prior to the beginning of the seven-year tribulation," she explained. "She references a passage from the Bible—Ezekiel 39:9–13 —that says Israel will spend seven months burying the dead and seven years burning the weapons left behind after the battle. Since it takes seven years to burn the weapons, this war must occur before or at the start of the tribulation."

She paused, allowing the implications to sink in before flipping through the pages. "After this war, there's supposed to be a peace treaty. But it's a false sense of security. That's when a new world leader that the Bible refers to as the Antichrist steps onto the scene, presenting himself as a savior of sorts, offering solutions to the world."

David frowns. "And that's when things really get dark, right?"

"It appears that way," Jayne replied. "The notes detail a series of catastrophic events that follow, each more horrific than the last. They are called judgments and will begin with natural disasters, famines, and plagues."

Maria's eyes widened. "But it doesn't stop there?"

"No," Jayne continued, tracing a highlighted section with her finger. "It mentions God pouring out His wrath on the earth. There will be terrifying signs, like earthquakes and celestial phenomena, ending with a great battle called Armageddon. The suffering and deaths will be immense, and those who remain will face unimaginable trials."

Lawson leaned in, looking troubled. "And this is all part of the tribulation?" he asked, glancing at his wife. Jayne caught the flicker of worry in his eyes, the kind that spoke of deeper fears about what this could mean for their family.

Jayne nodded solemnly. "Yes. The outline shows that the tribulation will be a time of judgment for those left behind, where humanity confronts the consequences of its choices to not believe in Christ. Those who remain faithful will be tested, while many others will be led astray by the Antichrist."

She took a deep breath and cleared her throat, sensing the collective tension in the room. "This isn't just a story or theory; these notes imply it's a warning. If this truly unfolds as described, we need to be prepared—not just physically, but spiritually."

The group fell silent at the heaviness of Jayne's words. The reality of the future felt more daunting than ever as she faced the possibility that Ruth's notes might truly be correct.

"What does that mean for us?" Camille asked, her eyes wide with fear.

A murmur of apprehension rippled through the group. David nodded slowly, a thoughtful expression crossing his face. "This is all so surreal. I always thought of these stories as fairy tales, but now it feels like we're living through a prophetic nightmare. What does it mean for all those who are missing? I have family who disappeared too. Why would some people be taken and others left behind?"

Sarah's eyes glistened with unshed tears. "My kids should be home by now, and it feels like an eternity since I last saw them. The only message I got from the school was a generic email sent to all parents, expressing their concerns." She buried her face in her hands and cried.

Beside her, Trevin sat with a tense jaw. He reached out, gently placing a hand on her back, offering silent support as they both wrestled with their fears.

As the group voiced their opinions, Jayne turned her focus back to Ruth's notes, searching for answers. She flipped through the pages until she found the section on the rapture. As she read aloud, the concept unfolded: the faithful being taken up to meet God, leaving the rest to confront the tribulation. Her eyes caught a highlighted passage that read "The Rapture," and she leaned in to read from 1 Thessalonians 4:16–17: *"For the Lord himself will descend from heaven with a cry of command, with the voice of an archangel, and with the sound of the trumpet of God. And the dead in Christ will rise first. Then we who are alive, who are left, will be caught up together with them in the clouds to meet the Lord in the air, and so we will always be with the Lord."*

Next to "caught up", Ruth had written *Harpazo* in bold. Jayne frowned, trying to grasp its significance. "What does *Harpazo* mean?" she asked the group.

Maria looked up, her expression stark. "It's a Greek word meaning 'caught up or snatched up,'" she explained, her accent and obvious heritage adding warmth to her words. "Here, it implies a swift removal."

As Jayne continued reading Ruth's notes, she came across a section that distinguished between the *first coming of Christ, the rapture,* and *the second coming*—three pivotal events in the biblical timeline. Ruth had made it clear that these events were distinct from one another, each serving a different purpose in God's plan.

Jayne began to read aloud again, her voice steady as she absorbed Ruth's explanations. "The first coming of Christ occurred over two thousand years ago. Jesus came to earth as God in the flesh, born of a virgin, lived a sinless life, and died to take on the sins of humanity. This was the fulfillment of many Old Testament prophecies and the cornerstone of the Christian faith. He came to offer salvation through His sacrifice and to establish the foundation of God's kingdom, but not everyone accepted Him as the Savior." Jayne paused, reflecting on the weight of that truth.

She flipped the page, her fingers tracing Ruth's handwritten notes. "The rapture," Ruth had written, "is where Jesus will take His believers, the ones who did accept Him, out of the world to protect them from the coming tribulation. It is a time of deliverance for the faithful, keeping them from experiencing the horrors of the seven-year period when God's wrath will be poured out. However, the second coming of Christ is vastly different, and yet to come."

"The rapture," Ruth wrote, "is a private event between Jesus and His believers. It will happen suddenly, without warning, and the world will not witness it. Those who are taken will be snatched away in the blink of an eye, and this will lead to confusion, doubt, and false theories—some will claim it's aliens, others will find alternative explanations. But this is God's intervention to remove His faithful before the chaos of the tribulation begins."

Jayne continued reading. "The second coming," Ruth wrote, "will happen at the end of the tribulation. Christ will return to earth, this time with His believers, also referred to as His *saints*, and every eye will see Him. It will be a public event—unmistakable and undeniable. Christ will come to defeat His enemies and establish His kingdom on earth. The world will know, without a doubt, that Jesus is Lord. It's not going to be something subtle or hidden like the rapture. It'll be loud, undeniable, and visible to everyone."

Jayne looked up from the notes, her voice steady as she shared the verses with the group. "In 1 Thessalonians 3:13 it says, '*So that he may establish your hearts blameless in holiness before our God and Father, at the coming of our Lord Jesus with all his saints.*' This is when He comes with His believers to establish His kingdom."

"The rapture," Jayne continued reading, "will be a quiet event, while the second coming will be a dramatic and public display. No one will be able to deny who Jesus is when He returns in glory at the end of the tribulation. He will defeat all opposition, and every knee will bow before Him."

The words hung heavy in the room as Jayne finished reading, the implications sinking in. The distinction between the rapture and the second coming was clear: One was a quiet, swift event for the faithful, while the other would be a cataclysmic and irrefutable return for the entire world to witness. It was also clear that Ruth had been diligently studying Scripture, understanding both events in depth, and somehow preparing others for what was to come.

Around her, some sat silently while others began to cry, their tears a blend of despair and realization. They faced the possibility that their loved ones might be among the missing, swept up in this promise. Jayne saw there was a bittersweet awareness that perhaps those they loved were the safe ones, yet also the fear of what they would soon face.

The group murmured among themselves, grappling with the implications of what Jayne had just laid out.

"If this is what they call the rapture," Camille asked, anxiety creeping into her voice, "what does that mean for us?"

Jayne took a deep breath, her resolve strengthening. "So, we know the tribulation will last seven years," she repeated, her voice trembling slightly. "Ruth's outline is like a playbook for what's to come. It begins with this war involving Israel, Iran, Russia, and other neighboring nations. After that, there will be a peace treaty, and then the Antichrist will emerge. These next seven years will be unlike anything we've ever seen. Her notes expand on how this war is seen as a precursor to the tribulation, but it clearly states that the seven-year countdown hasn't begun." Jayne's voice was steady. "It illustrates a struggle between good and evil, a conflict that transcends the physical."

Camille interjected. "What comes next? What happens to Israel during this war?"

Jayne rifled through the notes, searching for the relevant passage. "Ruth's writings detail that this conflict will be catastrophic. It describes how Gog, the chief prince of Magog—a leader from what we recognize as Russia—will gather a coalition of nations to launch a devastating attack on Israel." She glanced at the group, her expression serious. "Judges 2:3 states that Israel will become a thorn in the side of these nations, leading to a coalition against them."

Her voice rose. "The writings specify particular countries involved in this conflict. It lists their ancient biblical names in reference to where they are today. Magog is the region known as Russia, Persia is identified as modern-day Iran, Cush corresponds to Sudan and Ethiopia, Put is Libya, and various neighboring Muslim countries will also join forces against Israel."

Her words lingered as the group exchanged worried glances. Jayne could tell they were realizing these weren't just distant threats; they were real nations already embroiled in geopolitical tensions with Israel. The implications of Ruth's notes were profound, casting a long shadow over the group's understanding of the unfolding events.

The room fell silent as Ruth's revelations settled in. "This war will not only be significant but could have devastating consequences for Israel and the world," Jayne added. "The notes paint a grim picture, filled with strife and conflict that will engulf the region and test everyone's resolve."

Jayne grew somber as she turned the pages of Ruth's notes. "The Gog and Magog war doesn't just end with conflict. According to these prophecies, it concludes with a dramatic intervention." She glanced around at the attentive faces in the room. "As the nations prepare to attack Israel, there's said to be a divine response—a miraculous defense that turns the tide.

"According to these notes, one sign of this intervention will be a great earthquake." She recited the Scripture Ruth had meticulously noted: "In Ezekiel 38:18–20, it reads, *'But on that day, the day that Gog shall come against the land of Israel … On that day there shall be a great earthquake in the land of Israel. The fish of the sea and the birds of the heavens and the beasts of the field and all creeping things that creep on the ground, and all the people who are on the face of the earth, shall quake at my presence."*

Her words filled the room with silence, and the vivid imagery of destruction danced in her head. "Ezekiel was warning of a monumental shift," Jayne continued, looking around at her neighbors. "This isn't just about a war; it's about the very foundations of the world being shaken."

She took a moment before continuing. "In Ezekiel 38:21, it states, *'Every man's sword will be against his brother.'* Then in verse 22, it adds, *'With pestilence and bloodshed I will enter into judgment with him, and I will rain upon him and his hordes and the many peoples who are with him torrential rains and hailstones, fire and sulfur.'* Finally, in verse 23, *'So I will show my greatness and my holiness and make myself known in the eyes of many nations. Then they will know that I am the LORD."*

She glanced around at the group, gauging their reactions. "It sounds like after the earthquake, there will be immense confusion, and the enemies may start fighting among themselves."

David nodded, a serious expression crossing his face. "That sounds like friendly fire."

"Exactly," Jayne confirmed, her eyes widening with shared understanding. "The chaos that follows could lead to infighting among the nations that come against Israel. And as the notes indicate, Russia will face destruction; God will unleash hailstones and fire upon them, leading to their downfall. It will be apparent to these nations that God was the orchestrator of Israel's defeat."

A murmur rippled through the group as they seemed to process the implications. The concept of divine intervention, both catastrophic and transformative, began to take shape in Jayne's mind, and she felt their collective urgency deepen.

Trevin, looking skeptical, finally spoke. "So, is this really what's going on? Can we actually believe this? I mean, I don't think a country like Russia is going to go down that easily. They're a global superpower. It seems too far-fetched."

Jayne considered his words carefully. "I get where you're coming from. It sounds impossible, but the notes detail a series of events that align with what's happening in the world today. If these prophecies hold any truth, we have to take them seriously."

Maria chimed in, "But what if it's just a coincidence? We're all scared right now, looking for answers. Does that make it true?"

The voices in the room faded, each person seeming to wrestle with doubt and fear. Jayne nodded, acknowledging their concerns. "I get it. This is all overwhelming. But think about the patterns in history—so many people have dismissed prophecies until they unfolded right before their eyes. We can't ignore what we've found, especially when it feels so connected to current events."

Jayne's gaze fell upon Ruth's notes once more, drawn to a striking sketch that demanded attention. A massive hourglass dominated the page, its contours bold and commanding. In emphatic lettering that seemed to leap off the paper, it read: **"THE TIME CLOCK STARTS HERE! THE TRIBULATION BEGINS!"** An arrow pointed to the notation about the signing of a peace treaty with Israel and the enigmatic figure of the Antichrist.

Jayne's gaze lingered on the dark lettering, her thoughts swirling as she flipped through Ruth's meticulously detailed notes. A section caught her eye—its underlined heading read: The Rise of the Antichrist. She began to read aloud, her voice steady yet reverent.

"For the mystery of lawlessness is already at work. Only he who now restrains it will do so until he is out of the way. And then the lawless one will be revealed" (2 Thessalonians 2:7–8).

She paused, her fingers brushing over Ruth's handwritten annotations in the margins. "He who restrains," Jayne murmured, "is the Holy Spirit. Ruth's notes make that clear." She scanned the rest of the page, the weight of the truth pressing on her.

Ruth's notes elaborated: "The Holy Spirit, dwelling within every believer, holds back the forces of darkness. When the rapture occurs, believers—who are indwelt by the Spirit—are removed. The Holy Spirit's restraining presence is withdrawn. Only then can the Antichrist rise and begin his reign. With the Holy Spirit removed, the lawless one—the Antichrist—will then be revealed to the world. Following his rise, the signing of the peace treaty will mark the official start of the tribulation."

Lawson studied the notes with concentration. "If this is true, we need to keep an eye on the news for any signs of what we've just learned. If these events unfold as Ruth predicted, then we'll know these notes are valid. It could be our only way to prepare for what's coming."

David added, "Even if we're skeptical, we still need to prepare for what could happen next. Whether or not we believe the specifics, we should be ready for any scenario."

The group exchanged determined glances, and Jayne could tell they recognized that despite their uncertainties, the time for action was now.

Jayne continued, drawing from Ruth's notes. "This war is more than just a battle; it serves as a catalyst for the events leading to the final days." She paused and a hush fell over the room.

"It sets the stage for the return of Jesus Christ."

Everything she had thought was real in the world was suddenly shifting in her mind. She had never truly believed in a divine entity, only the concept of a creator. She had always dismissed the notions of a savior or a divine being like Jesus Christ, viewing the stories of the Bible as merely books written by men to help guide moral behavior. But now, with people vanishing and disturbing notes detailing what was happening, she couldn't shake the feeling that it might actually be true.

Questions swirled in her mind: What about heaven and hell? How could any of this be real? The foundations of her beliefs felt shaky, and she found herself grappling with the possibility that everything she had once dismissed could hold some truth. As unsettling as it was, she felt a growing urgency to confront these thoughts, realizing they had to find a way to navigate the uncertainties ahead, armed with the knowledge Ruth had left them. It was time to come together, not only to protect one another but to understand the profound changes their world was undergoing.

Jeremy broke the silence. "If this is real, then we have a responsibility to prepare ourselves and help others. We can't just wait for answers; we need to be proactive."

In that moment, Jayne recognized they had discovered something profoundly significant: the strength of their community and their capacity to endure uncertainty together. While they might not have all the answers, they had each other—and they held the critical information Ruth had left behind. This knowledge could serve as a guiding light through even the darkest times.

David spoke up, his expression somber, his experiences clear in the way he carried himself. "I think we need to secure the neighborhood. We can't afford to sit back and hope for the best. I have connections— some of our neighbors are Marines while others serve as police officers or in the National Guard. Tomorrow, I'll reach out to them to discuss setting up a security detail."

He paused, scanning the room to assess his neighbors' reactions. "We need to create a system to monitor who comes and goes. This is about protecting our families and ensuring everyone feels safe. I know these individuals have the skills and training necessary to help us establish around-the-clock security, not just at night."

David's gaze turned toward the door, as if he could sense the uncertainty lurking outside. "We can create a watch bill—like we did in the Navy—a rotating schedule where each of us takes turns keeping watch throughout the day and night. This isn't just about vigilance; it's about building trust within our community. If we're all looking out for one another, we can deter potential threats before bad things happen, and they eventually will."

Camille spoke up, her voice steady. "I think we should divide Ruth's notes and books. If we each take a section, we can review them individually and reconvene tomorrow, same place, same time. It'll be faster this way."

The group nodded in agreement. By pooling their efforts, they could better understand the full scope of the information Ruth had left behind and prepare for whatever lay ahead. With renewed purpose, they began gathering the materials.

As they said their goodbyes, Jayne and Lawson set off for home. Exhaustion clung to Jayne, her body weary from the emotional toll of the recent events, yet she couldn't shake the overwhelming surge of emotions that had enveloped her since discovering Ruth's notes. How remarkable it was that she had found them at such a crucial moment. How Ruth had entrusted her with the key that led her there. The years of meticulous research and preparation that Ruth had poured into those pages felt almost prophetic on their own. A sense of fear crept in as Jayne contemplated what lay ahead, the uncertainty looming large. Yet alongside that fear was a deep astonishment that she had stumbled upon this vital information just when it was most needed. With each step, she marveled at the wealth of insight contained within that outline, revealing a potential path for their future. This wasn't just a collection of thoughts; it felt like a lifeline. It seemed almost destined that she would uncover this treasure of knowledge at such a pivotal time.

As Jayne and Lawson walked home, they saw Landon's car pull into the driveway. Landon and Andrew got out, followed by Sophie, who was unloading their bags, noticeably exhausted. The sight of her children stirred a rush of reprieve in Jayne as she ran to greet them.

"Landon! Sophie! Andrew!" she called out in relief. The strain of the day began to lift slightly as she approached, eager to hear about their journey.

CHAPTER FIVE

AWAKENING THE WATCHERS

The day unfolded slowly, shadows of the previous day still lingering in Jayne's mind. She moved through her routine with an ever-present sense of nervousness, glancing at the clock more times than she could count. However, her kids were home, which offered a measure of relief. She brewed another pot of coffee, seeking the familiar aroma to distract from the swirling anxiety.

As she poured a cup, she noticed Andrew at the kitchen table, his phone in hand, scrolling through news updates. "Hey," she said gently. "Have you heard from your parents?"

He glanced up, his face marked with worry. "Yeah, I talked to them this morning. They're safe for now, but it's bad over there—like, really bad." He hesitated, his voice unsteady. "The situation in Israel is getting worse every hour. There's missiles coming in from all sides, and people are freaking out about it turning into a full-on invasion. My parents were at a wedding, but they had to leave when the sirens went off. They spent the night in a bomb shelter, but they're OK for now. My mom said everyone was just running around, trying to find somewhere safe. It's terrifying."

He let out a shaky breath and ran a hand through his hair. "And my brother, Sam—he's in Tel Aviv, reporting on the war for Maxx News. He's right in the middle of everything. He's literally working in a war zone. What if he gets caught in the crossfire? What if something happens and he can't get out? I just can't stop thinking about it."

His eyes darted around the room, seeming to seek reassurance. "My parents are really worried," he said with a sigh. "They keep trying to reach him, but cell service is spotty, and they haven't heard from him in hours. It's tough not knowing. I can't imagine what it's like for him—going through all of that—but I know he's resourceful." Andrew's voice steadied, giving off a sense of resilience.

Jayne's fear deepened as Andrew spoke. She had known Samuel was a correspondent but hadn't realized he had been sent to Israel during such a volatile time. Her worry intensified at the thought of him in the war's epicenter.

"I didn't know he was over there," she said, her voice barely above a whisper. "That must be terrifying for your family. I can't imagine the fear you're all experiencing. If there's anything we can do, just let me know."

He took a deep breath, his gaze distant. "My parents said the Iron Dome is struggling to keep up with the barrage of missiles, and people are rushing for bomb shelters, trying to find safety. But with the chaos in the streets, it's becoming really hard for families to protect themselves."

Jayne frowned. "I've heard of the Iron Dome. Isn't it supposed to be one of the most advanced defense systems in the world?"

"It is," Andrew replied. "But it's only built to stop short-range stuff, and there are way too many missiles coming in. The system can't handle it all. Whole neighborhoods could get destroyed, and people are freaking out—and honestly, I don't blame them."

In that moment, Jayne recalled Ruth's notes about the impending invasion. Her thoughts turned sharply to the chilling details—how the situation would worsen, leading to a series of disasters, including a massive earthquake that would shake the region to its core. *It's all connected*, she thought.

Jayne turned to Andrew, her voice steady as she tried to reassure him. "I know it's scary right now, but your parents are resourceful too. They'll do everything they can to stay safe." She placed a comforting hand on his shoulder. "Let's hold on to the hope that they'll find a way through this. They're strong, and you're strong too. Listen, Andrew, I think I should tell you …"

Without warning, the urgent alert of the emergency broadcast system cut through the room from the nearby TV, demanding immediate attention.

"Breaking news: Nationwide emergency declared. Citizens are urged to remain indoors. Reports of widespread civil unrest and law enforcement presence escalated in major cities," the alert blared.

As Lawson stepped into the room, his phone blared with urgent alerts as well. He quickly opened the news app, his expression shifting from unease to alarm as he absorbed the latest updates.

"This is serious," he said, tension creeping into his voice. "They're reporting that protests have turned violent in multiple areas, and the police are ramping up their response. It's like a powder keg about to ignite."

A chill coursed through Jayne. "My gosh, Lawson? Are we safe staying here?"

Lawson shook his head. "I don't know, but they're advising everyone to stay indoors unless it's absolutely necessary to go out. Cities are under lockdown. They're trying to contain the situation before it escalates."

The emergency broadcast system blared again, underscoring the urgency. Jayne exchanged anxious glances with Andrew, who looked increasingly distressed.

"What if the war spreads here?" Andrew asked, his voice wavering. "What if it gets worse?"

Lawson took a deep breath. "For now, we need to stay alert and wait for updates. Panic won't help."

Another notification chimed from the TV, linking to a live video feed from a local news station. The screen showed unsettling scenes from the city: crowds gathering, some waving signs, while others clashed with law enforcement amid the wail of sirens.

"Look at that," Jayne said, her voice trembling. "It looks like a war zone out there."

Lawson clenched his jaw, his gaze fixed on the unfolding scenes. "We need to keep the doors locked and remain vigilant. We really need to …"

Sophie burst into the kitchen, tears streaming down her cheeks, clearly distressed. "Mom, I can't get in touch with Matt!" she exclaimed, interrupting her dad mid-sentence. "I went to his apartment yesterday, but he wasn't there. I thought maybe he was just ignoring me because he's still mad about the other night, but with everyone going missing, I just need to hear his voice and know he's OK!"

Jayne looked up from her phone just as Sophie rushed into the kitchen. As the weight of her daughter's words sank in, Jayne glanced at Lawson. He was already watching Sophie, his expression heavy with what they now understood but couldn't yet explain. Their eyes met, and without a word, he gave her a look as if to ask, *Can you handle this?* Then he stepped out of the room. At the kitchen table, Andrew looked up from his phone, sensing the shift in the room. With a respectful nod to Jayne, he followed Lawson out, giving mother and daughter the space they needed.

"Sophie, when was the last time you talked to him?" Jayne asked gently, giving her full attention to their daughter.

Sophie wiped her eyes, frustration evident in her voice. "I don't even know! It was a couple of days ago, I think. I tried texting him yesterday, but he never replied. I just … I don't understand why he wouldn't answer."

Jayne paused for a moment, her thoughts recalling the discussion about the rapture from the night before and the unsettling number of missing people. She remembered her recent conversation with Sophie about Matt's newfound faith and his involvement in the Young Life group.

Jayne looked at Sophie, her concern deepening. "Sophie, sweetie, what has Matt told you about his faith?"

Sophie sighed, clearly irritated. "I don't know, Mom. It's not like he's calling me back right now! What does that have to do with anything?"

Undeterred, Jayne pressed on. "But what has he shared with you?"

With a reluctant huff, Sophie said, "Well, he joined a Christian group at school called Young Life. That's where all his friends are now, and he loves it. He's changed a lot over the past month—he doesn't want to hang out with my friends or party anymore. He talks a lot about God and all that stuff."

"I see. Can you tell me more about how it's affected him?"

Sophie crossed her arms, still feeling frustrated. "He's totally different now. He doesn't want to go out as much, especially where there are partiers and drinking. I get that his new faith is important to him, and it's changed him in a good way—he seems happier and more focused. But sometimes it feels like we are just drifting in two different directions."

"Has Matt specifically told you that he's a Christian or shared his views on being saved?"

Sophie nodded, her frustration shifting slightly. "Yeah, he has. He started reading his Bible after his roommate invited him to a Young Life meeting. He really liked it and just kept going. Before I knew it, he was getting baptized, talking about being born again and what that meant."

"He explained that being born again means having a spiritual renewal, like starting fresh. It's about turning away from his old life and committing to living a new one centered around his faith. The baptism was just a symbol of that transformation, like washing away the sins of his past life and being reborn into this new one."

Sophie paused. "He said it's not about the water itself saving him; it's more about what it represents. It's a way to publicly declare his faith and show that he's committed to following God now. I think that's what he finds so meaningful about it, but it just feels so different from the Matt I used to know."

Jayne shifted her focus, wanting to go deeper in their conversation. "Sophie, what do you know about all the people who are missing?"

Sophie sighed, frustration creeping into her voice. "All my friends are showing me these videos about aliens, saying the government is trying to cover it up. They think it's some kind of mass abduction or something. It's just so wild, Mom. I don't even know what to think."

Jayne felt a heaviness in her chest as she recognized it was time to share the truth with Sophie. Taking a deep breath, she steadied herself for what she was about to say.

"Sophie, there's something we need to talk about. It's important, and I need you to listen closely."

She searched her daughter's eyes for understanding, knowing that this truth might help Sophie accept the new reality—that Matt might not be coming back—and grasp everything that had happened and what was yet to come.

❈ ❈ ❈

The day passed in a blur for Jayne, her mind spinning with worry and uncertainty. She moved through the house on autopilot, searching for tasks to distract herself and keep her mind occupied until the meeting with neighbors later that evening. She prepared meals to freeze, reminding herself that having ready-to-eat food would be essential if things escalated. With roads growing more dangerous and more uncertainty about stores staying stocked, she wanted to make sure her family had enough sustenance without needing to go out.

As she chopped vegetables and sautéed meats, each meal felt like a small act of defiance against the unknown, a way to reclaim control over a situation that felt increasingly out of her hands. Between cooking sessions, she cleaned and washed sheets, her hands moving instinctively.

It felt as though she was preparing for something monumental, though she couldn't articulate what. Each beep of the washing machine served as a reminder of their impending situation.

Meanwhile, Lawson was on the phone with his boss, who had called to discuss the current state of affairs. With several employees missing and the city under lockdown, his boss had advised him to work from home for the time being. As a consultant for oil and gas companies, Lawson's projects were grinding to a halt. Hearing the confusion in his voice only added to Jayne's worry. The prospect that there might not be work for the foreseeable future loomed large, weighing heavily on her mind.

Glancing at the news intermittently, Jayne felt her unease deepen with each alarming headline. She wished she could silence her fears, but they lingered like shadows. The world outside seemed increasingly hostile, and she couldn't shake the feeling that something catastrophic lay just beyond the horizon.

Realizing it was almost time for the meeting with the neighbors, Jayne decided it was time to go get Ruth and Isaac's dogs and bring them back to her house. It was becoming clear they were among the missing—and might not be coming back. The thought still felt too heavy to say aloud, but the silence of their absence spoke volumes. Jayne figured the least she could do was make sure the dogs were safe and cared for.

Maybe having them around would cheer Sophie up too. She'd always loved those dogs, and with everything unraveling so quickly, a little familiar comfort might go a long way.

The moment she stepped inside, Finnley and Charlie rushed to greet her, tails wagging and paws clicking across the hardwood floor. Their joyful welcome tugged at her heart. She knelt briefly to rub their heads, whispering a soft, "Hey, guys," as if they too were trying to make sense of the quiet house.

She moved through the rooms, collecting their beds, food, water bowls, and leashes. As she gathered the last of the supplies, Jayne paused and looked around. The familiar scent of the home wrapped around her, and she took a deep breath, letting the quiet comfort of the space ease her tense mind and soothe her restless thoughts.

The walls were adorned with pictures that captured the essence of a life well-lived: Ruth and Isaac's wedding, their sons laughing together, family trips to the beach, and tender moments of their grandchildren being baptized. Each photograph felt like a window into love and joy, memories frozen in time, reminding her of the beauty that still existed in the world.

Her gaze fell upon framed Scriptures that hung like sacred mantras, whispering truths passed down through generations. A sign caught her eye that said "A family that prays together stays together." Those words resonated deeply, echoing in her mind with a significance she had never fully appreciated before. Amid the instability she now faced, they felt like a lifeline, a reminder that faith and connection could anchor them when everything else felt adrift. The crosses adorning the walls served as quiet sentinels of Ruth's unwavering beliefs, each one a testament to a life centered on devotion.

As Jayne took in her surroundings, memories of Ruth inviting her to church flooded back. Each time, she had offered polite excuses, leaving a series of missed opportunities that now weighed heavily on her heart. Regret settled in as she considered the community and faith that had so clearly defined Ruth's life, realizing she had turned away from something significant.

Surrounded by symbols of faith, she began to ponder the truths behind the Scriptures that covered the walls. Thoughts of God and His Son, Jesus, flickered in her mind—figures she had heard of throughout her life but had never truly sought to understand. Life had always felt too busy, too overwhelming to pause and explore the deeper meanings behind those teachings.

Yet now, in this moment of uncertainty and fear, she recognized that ignoring those invitations had been a mistake. A yearning stirred within her, urging her to seek out truths that could provide comfort and guidance. The notion that she might find strength in faith, and in a community united by shared beliefs, felt like a revelation. Perhaps, amid this crisis, she was being called to open her heart to something greater, something that could illuminate the path ahead and offer solace in turbulent times.

Snapping out of her thoughts, Jayne clipped the leashes onto Finnley and Charlie and walked to the front door. She took one last look around—the photos, the empty spaces where Ruth's presence lingered, the stillness of the room that felt untouched by time. It felt like walking out of someone's life, knowing they might never return. She opened the door and led the dogs outside, the silence stretching behind her like a farewell. The dogs trotted beside her as she stepped into the dusky quiet, heading home with more than just the weight of leashes in her hand.

As Jayne and Lawson made their way to Trevin and Sarah's house for the meeting, Landon, Sophie, and Andrew joined them. Jayne clutched a stack of Ruth's books tightly, including the detailed outline she had read earlier in the day. The evening air was thick with anticipation and unease, and she felt a surge of determination to share her discoveries. She knew the information could prove crucial for their conversations ahead, and she was ready to contribute to the group's understanding of the situation.

On their way, they spotted Tiffany striding toward them, a distracted look on her face. As she fell in step alongside them, her demeanor instantly shifted the mood.

"Hey, Tiffany," Jayne greeted, trying to infuse warmth into her voice. "How are you holding up?"

Tiffany rolled her eyes. "What do you want me to say? Everything's a disaster. My job's on the line, and it feels like the world's falling apart. Honestly, it's exhausting, and it's not like anyone around here cares."

Jayne exchanged a glance with Lawson, feeling the clout of Tiffany's negativity.

"It's tough for all of us," Lawson said cautiously. "But we're here to support each other."

"Sure," Tiffany said with a scoff.

As they continued toward Trevin and Sarah's, Jayne couldn't shake the feeling that Tiffany's attitude would weigh heavily on the group. She pushed those thoughts aside, reminding herself that they were all navigating uncharted waters together. The important thing was to focus on the meeting and the sense of community they desperately needed.

When they arrived at Trevin and Sarah's home, the atmosphere was eerily quiet. The dim light from inside spilled onto the porch, casting shadows on their faces. Sarah was inside, attempting to mingle but visibly fatigued; dark circles under her eyes revealed her sleepless night. Jayne felt a pang of empathy as she watched her; it was clear the burden of her missing children bore down heavily.

Inside, a few neighbors were already gathered, flipping through the notes they had brought from Ruth's materials. Whispers of discussion filled the room as they shared their findings, piecing together insights and theories. The urgency of the situation loomed large, everyone eager to make sense of their circumstances. Jayne took a deep breath, clutching her collection of Ruth's documents, ready to contribute to the conversation.

As the group settled in, Trevin took a deep breath and initiated the meeting. "Thanks for coming, everyone. How are you all holding up? Are there any immediate needs we should address?"

A few neighbors shared brief updates, expressing concerns but managing well given the circumstances. Camille and David mentioned they were keeping an eye on their supplies, while Jeremy offered to help anyone needing assistance around their homes.

However, the atmosphere shifted when Tiffany chimed in. "Honestly, I don't know how anyone can be OK right now," she complained, crossing her arms. "With everything happening, I'm just so tired of it all. I can't even think straight!" Her self-centered tone grated on Jayne's nerves, and she glanced around to gauge others' reactions.

David stepped forward, seeming to want to shift the focus. "I want to introduce some new faces to the group," he said, his voice steady. "These are neighbors I invited to join us tonight."

He gestured to a tall man with a strong build. "This is Michael, a fireman. He's here to offer insights on emergency preparedness."

Next, he pointed to a man exuding authority. "This is Decker, who works for the Fort Bend County Sheriff's Office. He'll provide updates on the local situation."

David continued, indicating a deputy standing beside Decker. "And this is Officer Jake Thayer, another deputy. He's been on the front lines and can share what he's observed."

Finally, he introduced a group of men who appeared ready for anything. "These are some ex-military guys: Leo, Travis, and Zeke, who goes by 'Red'—for obvious reasons." Laughter followed as everyone glanced at Zeke's bright red hair, the lighthearted moment easing the stress in the room.

Lastly, David gestured to a woman in scrubs. "And this is Dr. Katherine Vance. She's volunteered to help establish medical needs for the neighborhood."

The newcomers exchanged nods with the group, and Jayne felt a renewed sense of hope. With their combined expertise, they might navigate the future more effectively.

David stood up, taking a deep breath before addressing the group. "I want to share what we've been working on. We've formed a security team with Leo, Travis, Red, Officer Decker, and Jake as leads, along with other volunteers. Starting tomorrow, we'll begin implementing our plan to help keep our neighborhood safe."

He paused. "We'll be taking shifts around the clock. We're setting up entry control points at both entrances to the community. Only residents will be allowed to enter or leave, and any visitors must be preapproved and added to a list."

Tiffany huffed, her expression tight. "So, you're just going to stop our deliveries? What if I need groceries or something urgent? Who made you God?" Her frustration rippled through the room, eliciting a mix of sighs and eye rolls from the others.

"Tiffany, we're trying to protect everyone," Jeremy said from nearby. "This isn't about making life harder; it's about safety."

David nodded, focusing the group's attention back on the plan.

Tiffany leaned forward, her voice rising. "I get that, but this is unrealistic! Are we really going to halt all deliveries? What if someone's elderly or sick and can't get out? This feels excessive." Her anxiety amplified the tension in the room.

Jeremy tried to reason with her. "Look at what's happening outside. We have to take precautions for everyone's well-being."

"Yes, I know what's happening," she replied sharply, scrolling through her phone as if dismissing the situation entirely.

David kept his composure. "If you have a specific delivery, just put it on the list. We'll figure it out," he said, his tone steady but firm. Jayne exchanged looks with the other neighbors that reflected their frustration with Tiffany's insistence on her own needs over their collective safety.

David continued, his voice steady. "We'll also be conducting vehicle inspections on outsiders, even when contractors are allowed back in. Each section of our neighborhood will be designated A, B, C, or D, with roaming patrols to cover all areas. With 232 homes in our community, only 79 of which are currently vacant, we need to remain vigilant. The remaining 153 homes may have family members inside, even if some are missing."

To clarify his points, David distributed a map clearly labeling the different zones, allowing everyone to visualize their plan and the importance of their collective effort.

He gestured toward the tree line bordering their area. "We're surrounded by woods, which can be both a blessing and a risk. We'll need to patrol around the clock, reporting to our watch commander using military-style communications. The gated aspect of our community will help, but we need to combine our resources."

After David concluded his presentation, a few others shared news and discussed plans for the coming weeks to support the neighborhood, exchanging ideas about resources and strategies.

As the conversation began to wind down, Camille spoke up, her eyes bright with interest. "I wanted to mention the notes I brought home from Ruth. I found them incredibly insightful," she said, drawing everyone's attention. "There's so much wisdom in them about what we're facing and how to navigate it. She really had a sense of what was coming."

Several heads nodded in agreement, intrigued by the prospect of delving into Ruth's writings.

Camille began to share her findings, her voice steady and serious. "I came across some passages discussing the tribulation that's expected to arrive," she said. "Ruth highlighted key Scriptures from the opening chapters of the book of Revelation."

She paused, scanning the notes before continuing. "I think it's important to start at the beginning. Ruth's notes first highlight the Scripture from John 1:1–4, 14. Ruth makes it clear that this verse is foundational. *In the beginning was the Word, and the Word was with God, and the Word was God. He was in the beginning with God. All things were made through him, and without him was not anything made that was made. In him was life, and the life was the light of men … And the Word became flesh and dwelt among us, and we have seen his glory, glory as of the only Son from the Father, full of grace and truth.'*

"Before diving deeper into Revelation, Ruth indicates that it's important to understand this truth—that Jesus, the Word, has always existed, and He is central to everything that follows. She believed that grasping this would help us see the significance of everything that's coming because it's rooted in who Christ is. With that in mind, we can approach the rest of the Scripture with greater clarity and understanding."

There was a brief pause before Lawson spoke up, furrowing his brow. "Wait, I don't quite get it. So, Jesus is the Word—what does that mean exactly? Is He God, or is He the Son?"

Camille smiled gently. "He's both. Jesus is called the Son because He came from the Father and took on human form. But He's also fully God because, as we saw in John, He existed with God from the very beginning. That's the mystery of the Trinity: One God in three persons—Father, Son, and Holy Spirit. Jesus is God's Son, sent into the world, but He's also fully God, showing us God's presence here."

Jayne still looked a bit confused. "I'm still not sure I understand."

Camille paused for a moment to gather her thoughts. "The Trinity means that God exists as three persons in one: God the Father, God the Son, and God the Holy Spirit. God the Father is the Creator, the one who made everything. Jesus, the Son, is God in the flesh. He's fully God, but distinct from the Father because He was with God in the beginning. That's why we say He's both God and the Son of God. And the Holy Spirit is God in spirit, living in believers, guiding and empowering them."

She smiled and continued, "Think of it like an egg. It has three parts: the shell, the white, and the yolk. They're different, but together they make the egg. The same is true with the Trinity. The Father, the Son, and the Holy Spirit are distinct, but together they are one God."

Jayne nodded slowly, her face lighting up with understanding. "Oh, I get it now. Thanks, Camille."

Camille smiled as she picked up the notes to continue. "Ruth believed that understanding these Scriptures would help us navigate the uncertainty we're facing. They serve both as warnings and guides, providing clarity for the next seven years, helping us to stay faithful in the midst of trials and offering a clear picture of what is to come."

The room fell silent as everyone listened closely.

Her passion intensified as she elaborated. "The theme of Revelation is fundamentally about revealing who Jesus truly is. This book comes directly from God." She gestured for the group to gather closer, holding the notes up for all to see. "Look at this! The very first sentence states, *'The revelation of Jesus Christ, which God gave him to show his servants.'* His mission is to unveil these truths through His angel to His servant, John."

John couldn't help but interject with a light-hearted comment. "Well, I guess that means I'm in the Bible!"

Camille shot him a smiling glance. "Not quite, but you're in good company. Ruth also mentioned historical reformers like John Calvin and Martin Luther."

At this, Tiffany looked up in confusion. "Wait, you mean Martin Luther King is in the Bible?"

"No, no," Camille replied with a laugh, shaking her head. "I mean Martin Luther, the theologian who sparked the Reformation in the sixteenth century. He emphasized salvation by faith alone but overlooked many prophecies."

Lawson added, "That's likely because they were living in a different time. I doubt end-times prophecies would've made much sense to them back then."

Camille nodded thoughtfully. "Exactly. But now, given the events unfolding around us, these notes seem more pressing than ever. This shows that Israel is involved in many end-time prophecies, but they didn't even fulfill the prophecy of becoming a nation until 1948, and so much of what's described in the Bible on end times still hasn't happened."

She continued to sift through Ruth's notes, until her eyes landed on a specific reference. "Ruth wrote that God revealed to Daniel, an Old Testament prophet, that these words would remain hidden until the end times," she said, her voice thoughtful. "She also mentioned that sadly, many in the faith haven't explored these prophecies due to fears of misunderstanding, leaving much of this knowledge undiscovered." She paused, then added, "I guess there's a tendency to misinterpret theology, avoiding anything that might seem too dramatic or sensational. I think they fear it will be seen as exaggerated, like shock value, and not presented with the right context."

Trevin nodded. "It seems like they're afraid talking about it will only confuse people more than it helps. I've noticed that in churches today, too. When I was growing up, I never heard sermons about the end times—or even about Jesus, really. It was more like a motivational speech, designed to make you feel good. We hardly ever read from the Bible."

Jeremy shook his head slightly. "Same here. I went to church with my grandma growing up, but most of it felt like a ceremony, recited responses, songs I didn't know, and everything in a language I couldn't understand. I don't ever remember hearing a sermon that actually opened the Bible and explained it. It was beautiful in its own way, especially the stained-glass windows—but as a kid, I left each time not really knowing what any of it meant."

His comment drew a few knowing smiles. Camille smiled gently, then turned her focus back to the notes, as she read Revelation 1:3. "Listen to this," she said, her voice brightening. "It emphasizes the importance of what we're discussing: *Blessed is the one who reads aloud the words of this prophecy, and blessed are those who hear, and who keep what is written in it, for the time is near.*"

But her smile dimmed as a voice from the group interjected. "But why is this relevant to us now? If the rapture has already happened, doesn't that mean we're all doomed? What does it mean that 'the time is near'?"

Silence enveloped the room as everyone considered the question. If the rapture meant an end to any hope for salvation, what hope remained for those who were still here? Jayne looked around the group, uncertainty evident in everyone's expressions.

Camille took a deep breath, allowing the seriousness of her words to resonate. "These aren't just old texts; they're a call to action for us today. We're being urged to pay attention, to understand what's happening, and to share that understanding. This isn't solely about those who were taken; it's also for those of us who remain. There's still hope for redemption. Look here, we read this yesterday. At the end of this outline, it clearly shows that Christ returns! He comes back! Ruth labeled this as Christ's second coming. The messages in these Scriptures emphasize that while some may have been taken, there's still a chance for the rest of us. It's about recognizing the signs and returning to faith. We can still be saved if we hold firmly to the belief that Jesus is the only way to heaven."

Her gaze lingered on the Scripture. "This isn't only about the rapture," she said, her voice steadying with newfound understanding. "Revelation is, at its heart, a revelation of Jesus. It explains what follows when God comes for believers. He speaks not just to those who already believe, but to those who have yet to put their faith in Him. Do you see? God isn't just referring to that moment; He's talking about the ultimate return for all believers. There's still hope for everyone who remains, a future waiting to be fulfilled." Her realization resonated deeply with Jayne, a beacon of possibility, reminding her that even in darkness, light and redemption were within reach.

"I'm not saying it will be easy," Camille continued. "Just look at what's happening outside. But we're in this together, and together we can navigate the darkness, holding onto hope." The room fell silent as they absorbed her passion and the gravity of her message. Jayne glanced around, noting the engaged expressions of her neighbors, feeling a renewed sense of purpose in their gathering.

Camille again flipped through Ruth's notes, tracing the elegant cursive that filled the margins. "Look at this," she said, her voice bubbling with excitement. "Ruth clearly crafted this for someone specific to read. It feels so personal, doesn't it?"

"John was instructed by God to write about two things in this book: the events happening 'now,' which Ruth believed were pre-rapture, and the things that are to come—the tribulation period, the white throne judgment, the millennium, and ultimately, heaven."

The room buzzed with murmurs as everyone absorbed her words. "Ruth believed these writings could guide us through what lies ahead," Camille added, the conviction in her tone unwavering. "She saw the urgency in understanding what's coming, and I think it's crucial for us to take this seriously."

Camille glanced down at Ruth's notes and continued reading aloud, quoting Revelation 1:12–14. *"Then I turned to see the voice that was speaking to me, and on turning I saw seven golden lampstands, and in the midst of the lampstands one like a son of man, clothed with a long robe and with a golden sash around his chest. The hairs of his head were white, like white wool, like snow. His eyes were like a flame of fire."*

She paused. "I don't quite understand what the seven lampstands represent or the significance of this description of Jesus. What do they symbolize?"

Trevin chimed in, curiosity evident on his face. "What do the notes say about the lampstands?"

Camille smiled as she looked at the notes in the margins. "The seven golden lampstands symbolize the seven churches John was writing to. They represent each church's light and witness in the world.

"I have more notes," she added, "but they're from the end of Revelation. It might be better to go through it in order."

The group agreed and began to reorganize the notes, piecing them back together. As they worked, a sense of purpose filled the space. Once everything was sorted, they dove back into the text, eager to uncover more insights.

Tiffany looked puzzled. "So why is He so angry?"

"Angry?" Camille repeated, her expression shifting.

Tiffany nodded, disbelief in her voice. "Yeah, He comes back with white hair and fire in His eyes."

"Oh, I see what you mean," Camille responded. She took a moment. "Well, it seems the Jesus that we often see in illustrations or adorned on the walls is the one who came to earth first. He is gentle and loving, engaging with the poor and sinners. He came to show His love and reveal who He is as God in the flesh. He lived a sinless life but spent time with those who were broken. After His death, it became our responsibility to follow Him. Those who didn't were left behind during the rapture. Don't you see? We were left behind! We didn't understand before that He is the *only* way to heaven!"

As the weight of her words sank in, Camille continued. "But the Jesus who returns isn't the same as the one who came for His church. He's the Jesus who comes back with authority—majestic and powerful! His hair is white as snow and His eyes are like flames of fire. He comes to judge those who don't believe. He's coming to bring destruction!"

Her voice trembled, fear evident in her expression. "This is the Jesus who has authority, confronting the injustices of the world. The gentleness of His first arrival contrasts sharply with the judgment He will bring. He won't just be the savior; He will also be the judge. It's a frightening thought, but I finally understand." Tears streamed down her cheeks.

A profound silence settled over the room as Camille's words sank in. Jayne's breath caught as she tried to grasp the enormity of what had just been shared. The truth was clear, and she could feel it deep inside her. The room was still, each person processing the gravity of the revelation.

She looked around, noticing others wiping away tears. It was clear they all felt it, too. Jayne looked at Lawson, and for the first time, she saw a fear in his eyes, a fear that shook her to her core. It was the kind of fear that came when something terrifying finally became real.

Her eyes moved to her children, sitting quietly nearby, their faces pale with confusion. Her heart sank. How had she not shown them the truth before now? She had allowed so many moments to slip by without teaching them what truly mattered, without leading them toward salvation. The guilt hit her all at once. She had failed them.

Jayne's mind raced as the full impact of her past choices crashed over her. She had never truly known if there was a heaven or hell. She hadn't known if God was real, but she had convinced herself that, if it were true, their good actions would be enough. After all, they were good people. Surely that meant they would end up in heaven. She had never accepted Christ, never believed fully in the way she should have. She had dismissed the invitations from Ruth, distracted by life, and now she understood why it all felt empty. Being a good person wasn't enough. And now, the consequences of that denial, of that ignorance, were clearer than ever.

Not everyone in the room was convinced. A few exchanged skeptical glances, their faces showing doubt. Tiffany, arms crossed and tight-lipped, seemed unmoved. Others shifted in their seats. The divide between belief and skepticism lingered, creating tension amidst the shared sorrow.

Jayne wiped away her tears and took a deep breath. She knew the seriousness of the moment and felt the burden of what needed to be shared. Looking around at the group, she gathered her thoughts before speaking.

"Not to change the subject, but I need to discuss the situation in Israel," she began, her voice steady yet urgent. "Last night, we talked about what Ruth refers to as the Gog and Magog war, where Russia and its allies are escalating efforts to invade Israel. The situation is worsening, with reports of bombings claiming countless lives, particularly within the Jewish community."

As she detailed the situation, Jayne noticed Andrew's face clouding with confusion. She regretted not finishing their earlier conversation, wishing she could have explained her new findings before this meeting. "Ruth's notes explain that the intense hatred toward the Jews is tied to their covenant with God. This covenant is essential to understanding their role in biblical prophecy."

Jayne took a breath and then let her tone grow more fervent. "In Genesis 12:1–2, God calls Abraham, promising to make him a great nation. This promise, made over four thousand years ago, established Israel's special relationship with God. God reaffirmed this covenant with Abraham's descendants, especially Isaac and Jacob, making Israel His chosen people. In Exodus 19:5–6, He declares, *'You shall be my treasured possession … a kingdom of priests and a holy nation.'* This covenant carries both blessings and responsibilities, but it also invites opposition."

Jayne's gaze swept the room, sensing the weight of her words. "The hostility toward the Jews stems from this very covenant. As God's chosen people, they've faced persecution throughout history. Revelation 12:17 speaks of the dragon—representing the Antichrist—waging war against Israel, the woman. This spiritual struggle is rooted in the rejection of Jesus as the Messiah, as John 1:11 says, *'He came to his own, and his own people did not receive him.'*"

Her voice softened with compassion. "It's heartbreaking, but understanding this covenant reveals the larger picture of God's plan. Despite the suffering, there's hope. God has not abandoned Israel, and He remains faithful to His promises. Zechariah 2:8 reminds us that Israel is the apple of God's eye, and in Genesis 12:3, He promises, *'I will bless those who bless you, and him who dishonors you I will curse.'*"

Jayne's tone became serious. "This war will escalate. I can't say how long it will last—days, weeks, or even years—but it will intensify quickly. Like we discussed last night, Ruth's notes point to a coming earthquake that will shake the world's foundations, followed by hail and fire upon the nations fighting Israel. This won't be just a natural disaster but a sign of divine intervention. Afterward, many nations will fall into chaos, losing their leaders in the upheaval."

Jayne scanned the room, her heart heavy. "Then a new world leader will emerge—a figure Ruth believes will be of Roman and European descent, as described in the Bible. The world will be desperate for stability and will seek someone who can offer peace. This individual will be charismatic and eloquent, someone capable of swaying nations. The Bible refers to him as the Antichrist."

Murmurs rippled through the group, but Jayne pressed on, her conviction unwavering. "He'll unite nations, presenting himself as a leader who can bring people together. He'll sign a seven-year peace treaty with Israel, but this agreement will be deceptive. Israel will be unaware of its true nature, and according to Ruth's notes, this marks the beginning of the seven-year tribulation. The signing of this treaty starts the countdown."

"But why would anyone accept someone like him?" Trevin asked.

Camille and Jayne exchanged a knowing look, and Jayne spoke with urgency. "Look at the world around us. People are frightened—there are so many missing, and the unrest from wars, particularly in Israel, is overwhelming. When powerful nations like Russia and Iran weaken, a vacuum will form, and people will look for someone who can restore order and offer peace. The Antichrist may present himself as the solution to their fears, so that they overlook the true threat he represents."

"Do we have any idea who the Antichrist might be?" someone chimed in, eager for more information, their eyes scanning the faces around them for answers.

"We need to stay alert to the news, especially regarding Israel," Jayne said. "Pay attention to any developments concerning a peace agreement being signed. That moment will be pivotal. In the meantime, we must continue studying Ruth's notes to understand what's coming next."

Most of the neighbors nodded in agreement, their expressions weary but determined. As they began to wrap up, discussions shifted to logistics, how often to meet, where to gather, and what topics to cover in future conversations. They agreed to reconvene soon as a sense of camaraderie was forming, a collective resolve to stay informed and prepared.

As they got ready to leave, Camille turned to the group, her voice steady yet gentle. "I feel the need to say a prayer," she said. "If anyone would like to join me, you're welcome to."

A hush fell over the room, and Jayne and several others nodded in agreement. The atmosphere shifted, filled with a sense of hope and solidarity as they gathered in a circle, ready to lift their concerns and hopes to a higher power.

A few neighbors exchanged uncertain glances and chose to leave, Tiffany among them. She seemed to dismiss the gathering as a waste of time. But most of them remained, drawn together in a circle, hands clasped tightly. There was a sense of unity as they formed a bond, ready to share in this moment of prayer. Camille took a deep breath.

"Dear God, thank you for bringing us together in this moment. We are grateful for our neighbors and the community we've built, especially during these challenging times.

"As we gather here, we seek your guidance and strength. Please watch over us and keep us safe as we navigate the uncertainties in the world around us. We pray for those who are suffering and ask for peace in our hearts and in our community.

"We also come before you seeking forgiveness for not believing in your Son, Jesus Christ, when we had the chance. Thank you for still offering us the opportunity for salvation. As we read these notes from Ruth, grant us understanding and discernment. Guide us in interpreting her insights and your Word, applying them to our lives and what will come in the days ahead.

"Help us to support one another and to be a source of light and hope for each other. We are thankful for the blessings we have, even in difficult times. We trust in your wisdom and love. Amen."

As Camille concluded, a quiet "Amen" resonated through the room. A few wiped away tears, and Jayne felt her own eyes filling. The reality of their situation lingered in her thoughts, and she couldn't shake the fear about what lay ahead. Yet, in that moment of shared vulnerability, she found solace in the closeness of her neighbors, who felt like family, united in their collective concerns and hopes for the future.

CHAPTER SIX

TREMORS OF CHANGE

Day 2, Israel

The sun had set over Jerusalem, leaving the ancient stones of the Old City shrouded in shadow. Once, the air had been rich with the sweet scent of jasmine and the savory aroma of spices drifting from bustling markets. Now, Lilah was sure that it carried the acrid smell of bombs and the burning city.

Narrow cobblestone streets twisted through neighborhoods, their uneven surfaces a silent testament to centuries of history, but tonight, those familiar paths felt ominous. Just hours before, she and Ezra had strolled along HaNevi'im Street, their hearts light with anticipation for the upcoming wedding ceremony. Now, the gentle murmur of conversation was replaced by the distant wail of sirens and the sharp crack of explosions. The joyful laughter of children playing in the alleys had vanished, leaving an eerie, oppressive silence.

The vibrant colors of fresh produce had once spilled from the market stalls at Mahane Yehuda, where vendors called out prices, their voices weaving a lively tapestry of sound. The aroma of freshly baked challah had mingled with the earthy scent of olives and the sharp tang of pickled vegetables. The sun had glinted off the golden curves of the Dome of the Rock, its intricate mosaics shimmering against the clear blue sky—a sign of the city's rich spiritual history.

Yet now, those memories felt like an undercurrent of fear rippling through the air. The once-familiar streets—Ben Yehuda, where cafes thrummed with laughter, and Jaffa Road, alive with the clatter of trams—seemed increasingly distant. Lilah could almost hear the chatter of friends and family, savoring the sweetness of time spent together.

Not long ago, they had emerged from a joyous wedding, but now they found themselves huddled together in a bomb shelter, the world outside feeling alien and menacing. The dim light flickered as Ezra checked his phone for a signal, the screen casting a soft glow against the cold, concrete walls.

"Any word from Sam?" he asked.

"Nothing," Lilah replied. "I can't reach him or Andrew."

The shelter was filled with family—cousins, aunts, uncles—each grappling with the turmoil outside. The distant rumble of explosions served as a reminder of the war engulfing their homeland. It was hard to comprehend that just hours before, they had been celebrating love, and now they faced an escalating invasion with forces from Russia, Iran, and other neighboring countries.

Lilah tried to push aside the present, her thoughts drifting back to the past. Although they both grew up in Israel, their love story didn't begin until they met at NYU, each having chosen to study abroad. There, late-night study sessions evolved into deep conversations and shared dreams. Ezra had caught her eye before they ever spoke. He carried himself with a quiet confidence—tall, broad-shouldered, always focused. His deep-set brown eyes rarely strayed from his notes, and there was an intensity about him as if he had already figured out where he was headed. He was outgoing, the kind of person who easily drew others in with his energy and presence. Lilah, on the other hand, was more reserved. She was the shy one, content to listen and observe. After graduation, with job offers in hand, they moved to Thompsons, Texas—a quiet town just outside Houston. They later secured their dual citizenship, establishing a life that blended their Israeli roots with the promise of a new beginning in America.

During their time in the States, they had missed their families deeply and had eagerly anticipated this visit. They were staying at Lilah's sister

Miriam's house, a cozy home filled with warmth and love. Miriam had always been the more adventurous of the two sisters. Her laughter was infectious, the kind that made others smile without knowing why, and her dark eyes sparkled with a liveliness that drew people in. Striking waves of dark hair framed her face, mirroring the boldness of her spirit. They shared a bond that transcended distance; even when apart, they often found themselves on the phone late into the night, sharing dreams and fears.

This visit was especially meaningful since Miriam had recently announced her pregnancy, a surprise that filled her with joy. Her two older sons were nearly grown, but now, after years of thinking her family was complete, she was expecting a daughter. Even amid the current situation, Miriam's excitement was evident. She had confided to Lilah just days ago how much she had prayed for this child, the daughter she'd always wanted but thought would never come.

Miriam usually devoted herself to community service, spending countless hours volunteering at the hospital and coordinating events that fostered connection and unity. Her warm and outgoing nature perfectly balanced Lilah's quieter, more reflective demeanor. In these uncertain times, Lilah found comfort in her sister's steady presence and the sense of normalcy that family gatherings provided.

Lilah tried to hold on to that comfort as Jerusalem, once a symbol of spiritual strength, now felt trapped in a grim paradox—a place of sacred history overshadowed by the violence of war. Though Israel had endured its share of struggles, this time carried an unmistakable sense of finality. Lilah glanced at her family, their faces tense with unease as the overhead lights flickered, casting shadows across the shelter walls. She thought of Andrew, so far away in the United States, possibly unaware of the chaos unfolding just outside this hideout.

The underground bomb shelter was oppressively dim, its concrete cold and unyielding. Dust hung in the air, stirred loose with every distant explosion that reverberated through the ground like thunder. The vibrations rattled the shelves, dislodging small items and sending a few tumbling to the floor. The air was thick with a musty odor, mingling with the faint scent of bodies and perspiration. Supplies were neatly stacked in a corner—bottled water, canned goods, a battered first-aid kit—but their organization offered little assurance. The distant rumbles outside seemed to creep closer with every passing minute, shaking the walls and filling the room with tension.

Lilah flinched as another blast shook the shelter, dislodging a strip of paint from the ceiling. She looked over at Ezra, his focus fixed on his phone, endlessly scrolling through news updates. The look on his face said everything—regret, fear, and a weight she could feel deep in her chest. They'd both seen the warnings, watched the world shifting, but the need to be with family after so many years had made it feel worth the risk. But the trip to Israel had seemed like more than just a family visit—it was a chance to reconnect, not only with those they'd missed but with each other. Over time, what once sparked between them had slowly dimmed. As the kids grew up and moved out, quiet tension took the place of easy conversation. Something between them had unraveled slowly, almost imperceptibly. They hoped the time away—familiar ground, distant from old habits— might help them find what had been lost. Or at least remind them of why they began. She glanced back at Ezra, wondering if he was thinking the same thing—if he, too, was searching for a way back to what they once had. The world outside felt impossibly far away, yet the violence drew closer with every shudder of the shelter. Lilah tried to focus on the people around her—the familiar faces that were her anchor in the storm—but unease gnawed at her. What had been meant as a celebration of family and love had turned into a desperate effort to survive. And yet, despite the disturbance around them, the silent understanding they shared—their love, their unity—remained unshaken, the only fragile light in the growing darkness.

Suddenly, a sharp gasp broke through. All eyes turned to Miriam, who clutched her stomach, her face pale and stricken. Lilah rushed to her sister's side. "Miriam, what's wrong? Is it the baby?"

Miriam's breaths came shallow and uneven as she shook her head, her hands trembling. "I don't know," she whispered. "Something feels … different. Hollow. It's like … like she's not there anymore. I can't feel her."

Lilah's heart clenched as she crouched beside her sister, placing a gentle hand on Miriam's belly. "It's OK, Miriam. It's probably just the stress. You're seven months along, and all of this … it's overwhelming. But she's OK. I know she is." Lilah's voice wavered, though she tried to sound reassuring.

Miriam's husband, Yosef, knelt beside her, his dark curls slightly disheveled and his brow furrowed with worry. His words came quickly, almost in a rush, as he placed a steadying hand on her back. "Breathe, love," he murmured, his voice anxious but filled with care. "We'll get through this. The baby's fine, I'm sure of it."

Lilah nodded, echoing his words.

Miriam's eyes darted between their faces, her fearful expression still raw but tempered slightly by their presence.

Just then, Ezra phone vibrated against his knee, slicing through the thick stress of the shelter. "It's Samuel!" he exclaimed, swiping to answer. "Sam? Are you OK?"

"Dad! I'm fine," Samuel's voice crackled through. "I'm in Tel Aviv. There's a lot happening here, but I needed to check on you."

Lilah leaned in to hear. "We're OK, Sam, just scared. We're in a shelter with the others … There's explosions outside."

"Yeah, I know," Samuel replied, his tone turning grave. "They're escalating the conflict. I'm reporting live for Maxx News, and it's intense. Just finished covering the ground situation."

A bittersweet blend of pride and worry stirred within Lilah. Samuel had always been passionate about his work, but this was more than he had anticipated. "We're worried about you, too," Ezra answered. "You should find a safe place."

"I will, Dad. I promise. But how are you all holding up? Is Andrew with you?"

"Andrew's back in the US," Ezra said, guilt creeping into his tone. "We couldn't bring him. We thought we'd be safe here, just visiting family. We didn't expect this."

An oppressive silence hung between them. "I get it. You wanted to see family. But I wish you hadn't come either. It's a war zone out there."

Ezra nodded, even though Samuel couldn't see him. They had come to celebrate life, only to find themselves ensnared in a nightmare.

"Just stay safe, OK?" Samuel insisted, his voice urgent. "I'll keep you updated. Take care of yourself!"

Lilah's eyes glimmered with tears as Ezra ended the call. "He's OK for now," he said quietly, wrapping his arms around her in a steady, supportive embrace.

Samuel, their eldest son, stood tall and slender, carrying himself with a quiet assurance beyond his twenty-seven years. His dark hair framed sharp features, and deep-set eyes sparkled with intelligence. A graduate of the University of Texas, he had pursued dual majors in political science and journalism—a combination that mirrored his desire to understand the world and articulate its complexities.

Driven and insightful, Samuel always engaged fervently in discussions about politics and global affairs, earning respect among his peers for his well-informed opinions. Lilah and Ezra took immense pride in his accomplishments, knowing that his dedication would lead him to a future where he could make a meaningful impact.

As tension filled the shelter, Lilah found a quiet strength in her and Ezra's shared faith. The memory of **Yom Yerushalayim**, celebrated on the 28th of Iyar, gave their current struggles a deeper meaning. With the holiday approaching in the second week of May, they were reminded of its significance—not only as a time to reconnect with family and celebrate a wedding, but also to honor the unity and resilience of their people.

Yom Yerushalayim, which marks the reunification of Jerusalem and the return of Jewish sovereignty to the city in 1967, was a day of both joy and remembrance. Lilah remembered her grandmother's stories about the significance of this day—the reconnection to their holy city, the Temple Mount, and the resilience of their people. It was a day to honor their shared history and the renewed hope for their future.

Ezra looked at her, softly reminding her of their original plan to pray at the Western Wall for their family's protection. "We need that strength now more than ever," Lilah whispered, her mind lingering on their children.

As the holiday approached, they had hoped to find spiritual renewal among loved ones. But now, amidst the uncertainty and fear, their faith felt like the only anchor. Lilah silently vowed to hold onto their traditions and values, letting them guide them through the turmoil.

The soft hum of the shelter's lights was shattered by the blaring sirens, and Lilah felt Ezra tighten his grip on her hand. Explosions rumbled in the distance, shaking the ground beneath them. The harsh sounds of war seemed to reverberate through their bones, a constant reminder that the world outside had become a battlefield.

"I can't believe this is happening," she murmured, her voice barely rising above the noise. The fear twisted inside her, a knot she couldn't shake. "What if one hits us?"

Ezra shook his head, clearly trying to sound calm. "We're safe in here. The shelters are built to withstand this. We just have to wait it out."

But even as he spoke, the deafening blasts outside seemed to mock his reassurance, a constant reminder of the danger surrounding them. The sirens wailed again, a primal call to seek shelter, heightening the fear that gripped them all. Family members huddled together, their faces pale, exchanging worried glances and whispered prayers.

In the brief moments of silence between explosions, Lilah could hear the soft cries of her loved ones, a haunting echo of the escalating conflict just beyond their refuge.

The night had been restless, with sleep elusive for most. They spent the hours awake, softly murmuring prayers and reciting the Shema, their voices a quiet expression of faith. The bomb blasts and sirens had subsided, but the silence that followed felt heavy, and the anxiety still lingered, filling the space with unease. Lilah sat up slowly, her body stiff from the uncomfortable chair. The stillness was broken when her phone buzzed against the makeshift table, startling her.

She grabbed the phone, relief flooding through her as Andrew's name flashed on the screen, and she quickly swiped to answer. "Andrew!" she exclaimed. "Honey, is that you?"

"Mom! I'm so glad I got through!" Andrew's voice crackled with concern. "I've been trying to reach you for hours."

Lilah's heart soared at the sound of her son's voice, though it was quickly tempered by the heft of his words. "We're OK," she reassured him, glancing at the worried faces of family members. "We're in a shelter, but we're safe. What about you?"

"I'm at Landon's. We heard about the attacks on the news," Andrew said, urgency threading through his voice. "I was so worried when I couldn't get in touch. I thought … I thought something might have happened."

Lilah could hear the strain in his words, the underlying fear of a son separated from his family amid such dire circumstances. "We're fine, really. It was a long night, but we held on."

✳ ✳ ✳

"Good. I'm glad you're all together," Andrew said, though there was an unmistakable edge of apprehension in his voice. "What are you planning to do next?"

Lilah glanced at Ezra, who had just woken up and was now paying close attention. She hesitated, trying to find the right words. "It's hard to explain," she began. "The explosions were intense, and the sirens went off when we were at the wedding. Everyone was yelling to get underground. Missiles started coming in, so we had to move quickly. But we're OK!"

"Promise me you'll stay safe." Andrew's voice wavered slightly. "I can't lose you."

"We're fine," Lilah reassured him. "We'll stay strong. Just remember we love you, OK? Try not to worry."

"Mom, wait," Andrew cut in, desperation creeping into his voice. "Have you heard about the missing people? Thousands of people just vanished—gone. No one knows where they went."

Lilah was startled by his assertion. "What do you mean, *missing?*" she asked, a little confused. "Are you serious?"

"I'm serious," Andrew replied, his tone now sharp. "It's on the news—people just disappearing. I don't know how to explain it."

Could this be happening here too? she thought. She glanced at Ezra, her thoughts racing.

She kept the phone pressed to her ear, trying to steady her voice. "Andrew, where are you? Are you OK?"

"I'm safe, Mom," he said, his voice calmer now. "I decided to leave Austin and head back home with Landon. We're staying with Jayne and Lawson for now."

"Andrew—" Lilah began to respond, but just as she spoke, the connection dropped. She stared at the screen, her breath catching. "Andrew? Andrew!" she called, but only silence answered. "We need to get out of the shelter," she said quickly. "Maybe there's better signal outside to check our phones."

Stepping outside the shelter, Lilah and Ezra were met with a haunting scene. The air was thick with dust, remnants of the previous night's destruction strewn across the streets. Nearby buildings lay in ruins, their once-lively façades reduced to crumbling walls and shattered glass. The distant wail of sirens echoed.

A café that had once buzzed with life now stood hollow, its windows blown out, debris littering the ground. The acrid scent of smoke mingled with the bitter tang of burnt materials in the air. As they surveyed the scene, the contrast between familiar streets and the devastation struck Lilah like a blow.

Some structures remained upright, but they bore the scars of the night—cracked exteriors, exposed rebar, and scorched paint. A mural that had once brightened the wall of a community center now seemed a ghost of its former self, faded and marred by soot.

The street was unnervingly quiet, the usual bustle of Jerusalem replaced by a heavy silence. A few people stepped out of their homes, their expressions a mix of disbelief and fear as they surveyed the damage. Lilah couldn't help but wonder how long it would take for the city to recover or if the situation would only continue to worsen. Lilah's fingers instinctively reached for her phone, heart pounding as she tried to dial Andrew's number. The screen flashed an error message—no signal. She cursed under her breath and tried again. But before the call could even connect, her phone's screen flickered once and went black. No battery.

"Look over there." Ezra pointed toward a cluster of families, their faces marked by worry. As they moved cautiously through the debris, Lilah's heart ached for her city, for her family, and for the uncertainty looming like a dark cloud over them all.

As they approached the group across the street, the exhaustion was clear on the strangers' faces. A man with disheveled hair stepped forward, his expression serious. "You just came from the shelter?" he asked.

"Yes," Ezra replied. "We were hoping to find out more about what's happened."

The man nodded, glancing around as if to ensure no one else was listening. "The Iron Dome … it's been compromised. Missiles broke through last night. They're blaming Iran, but I've heard reports they're using Russian missiles."

Lilah exchanged a worried glance with Ezra. The Iron Dome had been Israel's safeguard against threats, and now its failure felt like a turning point.

Another woman from the group stepped forward, her eyes wide with fear. "Have you heard about the missing? It's true!" she said, her voice trembling. "Thousands are just gone—young children of all ages, along with some adults and the elderly. And it's not just here; it's happening around the world. It's horrifying."

Lilah's breath caught in her throat. "What do you mean, gone?"

"Vanished," the woman replied. "One moment they were here, and the next … gone. Families are searching everywhere, but none have been found."

The realization sent a chilling thought creeping into Lilah's mind. "Do you think it's a sign from God?" she whispered, the words slipping out before she could call them back.

Ezra nodded slowly. "It sure feels that way."

The group stood in heavy silence, processing what they had just learned.

Lilah glanced at Miriam, who stood nearby with her husband, her face pale and tense. Lilah stepped closer and rested a hand on her sister's arm. "Miriam, how are you feeling? Did you sleep at all?"

Miriam shook her head. "No. Something's wrong. I didn't feel the baby move all night. Not once."

Lilah's stomach tightened. She leaned in closer. "Let's get you home," she said. "You need to rest. We'll call the doctor as soon as we get there and figure this out. It's probably just the stress."

Miriam placed a hand on her stomach, her voice unsteady. "I don't know, Lilah. It doesn't feel right. It's like she's … gone."

Lilah pulled Miriam into a firm hug. "I don't want you worrying about this," she said. "We'll take care of you and the baby. Let's just focus on getting home."

Miriam nodded reluctantly, and they turned their attention back to the streets. The group began moving cautiously through the rubble as they made their way back to the house. As they approached the familiar building, they felt a deep sense of reassurance; the house had managed to withstand the destruction that had spread through the neighborhood.

The exterior stood as they remembered it—its warm stone façade a steadfast presence amid the dusty remnants of war. The front garden, once a beautiful tapestry of flowers, now lay scattered with debris from the blasts, yet the house itself stood resilient, a sanctuary in a world turned upside down.

✳   ✳   ✳

As evening settled in, the soft light from the setting sun filled the main living room of the house, offering a brief calm after the chaos of the night before. Lilah had just settled into a chair when her phone buzzed. She quickly picked it up, seeing Andrew's name on the screen.

"Mom! I'm so glad you picked up," Andrew said, relief in his voice. "I really need to talk to you. Landon's neighbors here are meeting every night now to come up with safety plans. It's been insane since all these people started disappearing, and they're trying to set up a network for everyone. But there's something else I need to tell you about what they've found."

Lilah leaned in, listening intently. "What's going on?"

"Jayne found some books and notes at a neighbor's house—one that's gone missing," Andrew explained. "The neighbors are talking about what's been happening around the world. They found all these books about the end times and notes that go with them. There's an outline with a timeline of events that's supposed to happen after everyone disappears. They're saying this war in Israel is part of it—the Gog and Magog war. It's all laid out there."

Lilah smirked, the name striking a chord but her skepticism clear. "Well, that's from the Bible, but we studied it in the *Tanakh* too, from the prophet Ezekiel. Gog and Magog… it's mentioned as a future war, but people interpret it differently. Some say it already happened, others think it's still coming."

"I know," Andrew replied, his voice steady yet urgent. "But everything I've been hearing in these meetings, it's starting to look like what's happening now. "And it gets worse. They say a massive earthquake is coming soon. It's supposed to hit Israel! They say after that, there'll be a peace deal, and then the Antichrist will appear."

Lilah, still shaken from the sleepless night, was trying to make sense of it all. "The Antichrist? Honey, we don't really believe in an Antichrist. This all sounds a little far-fetched."

"I wish it were," Andrew replied. "But people are taking it seriously. There's this feeling that something big is coming."

Lilah shook her head, still processing his words. She couldn't quite make sense of them. "Listen, Andrew, we're trying to find a flight to come home, but it's not looking good. The airport here is mostly destroyed, and I'm not sure about the surrounding cities. With the war going on, there might even be a no-fly restriction."

She paused, taking a breath. "Everything is so uncertain right now."

"Don't worry about me, Mom," Andrew said. "I'm safe at Landon's house. If you can come home, then do it. But don't stress over me."

"Stay safe, please," Lilah said with concern. "I'll keep calling as I hear more. I love you."

As she ended the call, she glanced down the hall only to see the closed bedroom door of her sister.

Miriam was resting in her bed after a long and emotional day. The doctor had come by earlier and confirmed what everyone had feared— Miriam had lost her baby. But the circumstances were baffling. There was no bleeding, no sign of miscarriage, no evidence of what had happened. Miriam's stomach, once full and rounded from her growing womb, now sagged as if the baby had been born. The skin hung loose, stretched from the pregnancy, but there was no baby. It was as if the child had simply vanished.

The doctor had tried to reassure her, but even he seemed unnerved. Miriam was the third mother he had visited that day with the same story—healthy pregnancies, but all the babies had been lost during the night. The bombings were the only common thread, but even that explanation didn't make sense. He had offered kind words, but nothing could comfort Miriam. She was devastated, the grief etched deep into her face, her hollow gaze fixed on the ceiling when Lilah last checked on her.

Lilah sat back in her chair, her mind heavy with everything that had happened. She glanced at her family sitting quietly in the next room, wondering if she should tell them what Andrew had said during their phone call. The urgency in his voice, the unsettling things he had told her about the disappearances, the neighbors' warnings—it all felt so surreal. But how could she bring it up now? Miriam had enough to bear, and the house was already steeped in a sorrow that no words could lift.

Still, she couldn't shake the feeling that the world was unraveling faster than they could keep up with. Her hand tightened on the armrest as she glanced toward the hallway, where Miriam lay in her room, her loss a heavy shadow that hung over them all.

The house jolted awake with a violent tremor that rattled everything in its path. The ground beneath Lilah's bed shifted as if the earth itself was breaking apart. She bolted upright, disoriented, and unable to catch her breath, trying to make sense of the commotion unfolding around her.

The rumbling grew louder, a low, guttural sound that seemed to come from deep within the earth. Light fixtures swayed above, casting erratic shadows on the walls. Glass shattered in the distance, and furniture groaned as it moved with a life of its own.

Lilah stumbled out of bed, the floor beneath her feeling unstable. She rushed to the living room, her feet unsteady. Ezra was already there, his face tense as he called out for her. "Lilah!" he shouted over the deafening noise.

The room was a blur of disarray. Chairs slid across the floor, and a bookshelf crashed down, books spilling in all directions. Miriam clutched her family, her eyes wide with fear.

"What's happening?" Lilah cried, clutching the walls as she tried to reach her husband.

"It's an earthquake!" Ezra shouted, his voice strained as he grabbed Lilah's hand and drew her into the threshold of the kitchen doorway.

Lilah's heart raced as the world around them continued to shake. The windows rattled violently, dust fell from the ceiling, and the walls creaked under the pressure. She shielded her face instinctively as debris swirled in the air.

They huddled together, hands gripping each other tightly, as the earth beneath them heaved and groaned. "Stay close!" Ezra urged, his voice barely audible over the noise.

Lilah squeezed her eyes shut, praying in silence, her body tense with fear as the tremors shook the ground beneath her. But even in the commotion, the feel of Ezra's hand in hers anchored her. Despite everything that had passed between them, his grip still offered protection—and in that moment, she knew their love remained, steady and enduring. Though fear gripped her, a flicker of hope sparked within her—that they would survive this.

The ground beneath them seemed to heave and split, as if the very earth was birthing a monster. Cracks and splinters of wood echoed through the house, the ceiling above them threatening to collapse. Dust filled the air, and the once-familiar home now felt fragile, like a dream unraveling. Each new shake sent a surge of adrenaline through her, forcing her to fight to keep her balance.

The violent upheaval seemed endless, though it only lasted a few minutes. When it finally stopped, a heavy silence fell, broken only by the faint creaks of the house adjusting to its new reality. Lilah opened her eyes. The living room had been torn apart—furniture overturned, books scattered, and dust hanging in the air.

She met Ezra's gaze, both of them acknowledging the devastation. The house was no longer safe.

"My gosh, if it's this bad in here, what do you think it's like outside?" Lilah whispered. Her stomach churned as she thought of Andrew's warnings. He had predicted this. She looked at Ezra, her resolve hardening. They had to find out what was happening beyond their walls—and what was coming next.

CHAPTER SEVEN

FROM HERITAGE TO HOPE: THE TRUTH REVEALED

Weeks had slipped by since the earthquake, and Lilah and Ezra—along with Lilah's sister Miriam and her family—sought refuge in a modest home belonging to some of Miriam's friends just outside the city. The tension of their recent past clung to them as they arrived, yet the rolling hills and olive groves that surrounded their temporary sanctuary offered a fragile sense of peace.

Asher and Adina had welcomed them with open arms, wrapping the family in warmth as they offered them their guest home. The airports in Israel, still bearing the scars of damage, offered limited flights, leaving Lilah and Ezra stranded with original tickets intended for a three-month-long stay. The uncertainty of when they would return pressed down on them, though knowing that Andrew was safe provided a touch of comfort.

It was hard for Lilah to watch the loss of Miriam's baby weigh heavily on her sister. Despite the peaceful surroundings, her grief lingered like a shadow, ever present and inescapable. She often retreated to the small bedroom she and her husband shared. Her once-cheerful demeanor had dimmed; her laughter, once so full of life, was now replaced with quiet moments of staring into the distance, her hand unconsciously brushing over her now-empty womb.

Lilah enjoyed how the home itself, though humble, brimmed with history and memory. Thick stone walls stood as a testament to resilience, and sunlight streamed through arched windows, spilling golden light onto the earthen floor and illuminating simple wooden furniture. A low, worn table surrounded by mismatched chairs served as the heart of the home, where family gathered to share meals and stories, laughter mingling with the scent of home-cooked food. The living area featured a well-loved sofa draped with a handmade blanket, inviting anyone seeking solace to sink into its embrace.

The modest bedrooms exuded warmth and invitation, offering just enough space for Lilah and Ezra alongside Miriam's family: her husband and two teenage sons, one seventeen and the other nearly nineteen. Each room was adorned with colorful quilts, hand-stitched with care, draped over sturdy wooden beds. Framed photographs lined the walls, capturing moments of family celebrations and milestones that seemed to echo with laughter. In one corner, a small bookshelf held a mix of sacred texts and children's stories, a sign of their Jewish heritage, and in the other, a small handmade wooden cradle stood, a quiet symbol of the family Adina dreamed of building one day.

In the kitchen, the comforting aroma of stew simmered gently on the stove, filling the air with rich notes of tender chicken, carrots, potatoes, and celery, all seasoned with fresh dill and a hint of garlic. This traditional dish, a staple in many Jewish homes, promised warmth and nourishment. Fluffy matzo balls floated delicately in the broth, their light texture contrasting with the hearty stew, creating a delightful harmony of flavors. Roasted root vegetables, their caramelized edges releasing a sweet, earthy fragrance, accompanied the meal, along with a crisp cucumber salad dressed in olive oil and vinegar. Each dish not only filled their bellies but also evoked a profound sense of belonging, rich with the traditions that bound them together.

As they gathered at the table, Lilah ladled the stew into bowls, her movements calm but focused.

"Samuel called again earlier," she said, passing Ezra a bowl. "He's still reporting nonstop. Said Tel Aviv looks like a war zone."

Ezra's hand paused over the breadbasket. "Is he safe?"

"He says he's moving around a lot. Reporting when he can, sleeping when he can't. But yes, safe—for now."

Miriam leaned forward, her spoon halfway to her mouth. "What did he say about what happened after the quake?"

Lilah glanced around the table. "He said the whole region erupted. Our enemies started firing—but not at us. At each other."

"They turned on themselves?" Miriam's husband asked, blinking fast.

Lilah nodded. "He said it was chaos. Missiles misfiring, communication breaking down... they ended up hitting their own. It wasn't even retaliation from us. They imploded. Like God confused them."

Ezra met her eyes. "That's what it sounds like."

Miriam's spoon clinked against her bowl. "Did he say anything about Jerusalem?"

"Some damage. Quiet streets. But he said the Western Wall is still standing. So is the Dome of the Rock. Some of the churches, too."

Miriam closed her eyes briefly. "So much has fallen, yet those places remain. It means something."

"It does," Lilah said, her brow furrowing. "I thought it was strange when we saw on the news that Chief Rabbi Weissman and the Prime Minister both addressed the nation. They called for strength and unity, but something about it just didn't sit right."

Miriam looked from one face to another. "So... what happens now?"

Ezra sighed. "We prepare. We pray. And we wait."

In their temporary home, Lilah often found herself gazing at the distant outline of the city, caught in a bittersweet mix of nostalgia and concern.

One evening, as the sun dipped below the horizon, Ezra gathered everyone in the living room. "We need to discuss what's been happening," he said, his voice steady yet imbued with seriousness.

Lilah and the rest of the family settled in, the flickering candlelight casting moving shadows on the walls. She sensed the tension as they waited for him to continue.

"News from the city is grim. Many are still struggling to find shelter, and resources are dwindling. The reports about the missing have only grown more troubling." Ezra paused, searching their faces before adding, "People are beginning to connect these events with what Andrew mentioned—Gog and Magog."

A murmur of unease rippled through the group. Miriam, seated beside Lilah, spoke up. "Do you think this is truly a sign? That something larger is at play?"

Lilah took a deep breath, uncertainty swirling within her like leaves caught in a breeze. "It's hard not to think about it. Andrew seemed so convinced … We remember he said all of this might be leading to the rise of some global leader—he called him the Antichrist."

Ezra frowned in disbelief. "But that's a concept from another faith. We don't believe in the Antichrist," he said, shaking his head as if to dispel the notion.

Miriam chimed in, her tone hesitant. "It sounds extreme, Lilah. Our beliefs don't include these ideas of an Antichrist or prophecies of that kind." The others nodded, their expressions a mix of skepticism and confusion.

Frustration rose within Lilah. "I know it sounds far-fetched, but Andrew is certain something significant is unfolding. Those notes were correct about Israel's defeat and the earthquake. Maybe there is truth about what's coming next." The others didn't look convinced, leaving the group grappling with uncertainty as they considered the implications of Andrew's warnings.

✳ ✳ ✳

As the days stretched on, the turmoil in Israel deepened, its conflict making headlines around the world. Yet the ripple effects of this crisis extended far beyond its borders. In the United States and other powerful nations, the political landscape was in shambles following the sudden disappearance of key leaders. Panic settled over the populace, a thick fog of uncertainty, as citizens clamored for answers, desperate for someone to restore order amidst the upheaval.

In their temporary refuge, Lilah and her family absorbed the harsh realities through news updates and Samuel's reports, which painted a grim picture of loss and instability. Governments faltered in their attempts to maintain control, their authority shaken. She and Ezra listened intently as Samuel told them privately of families desperately searching for loved ones, nations teetering on the edge of collapse. The death toll climbed relentlessly, a somber tally that included countless civilians and soldiers alike. Images flashed across the screen: Once-bustling streets now lay in ruins, the remnants of homes and businesses reduced to rubble, while charred vehicles marked the landscape like ghostly reminders of a world gone awry.

The reality of these scenes bore down on Lilah, each image a visceral reminder of the fragility of life. She found herself lost in memories of Israel's tumultuous history—the enduring struggle for identity and peace that had persisted since the nation's rebirth in 1948. But this moment felt different, as if a tide of despair threatened to engulf them. A deep sorrow gripped her as she thought of the lives lost, families shattered, and a future that loomed ever darker. Yet, amid the devastation, she grappled with disbelief that Israel had managed to emerge victorious, its enemies vanquished. It felt almost miraculous, a testament to what she believed was divine intervention, yet the burden of loss was evident.

Murmurs began to circulate about a gathering of influential figures at the United Nations and within the European Union. There was talk of a new leader emerging—one who might step into the void left by those who had vanished. This figure was not just any leader; whispers suggested they could unite nations under a single banner, a prospect both new and unsettling. Lilah could sense the mix of hope and skepticism in Samuel's voice as he relayed the latest developments, reflecting the deep yearning for stability in a world that felt increasingly fragmented.

"Good evening, I'm Samuel Cohen reporting for Maxx News. As the world grapples with unprecedented upheaval, many are searching for a figure to unite them during these challenging times. Reports indicate that citizens around the globe are calling for a leader who can restore calm amid the unrest. But pressing questions remain: Who will emerge as this unifying figure? Can anyone truly fill the void left by those who have vanished?

"People are searching for someone to restore order," Samuel continued, his tone zealous with the influence of such a monumental shift. "This new leader could wield unprecedented power, potentially ruling over a coalition of nations, but the question remains: Can anyone truly unify such a diverse world?"

Lilah exchanged a glance with Ezra, both of them grappling with the implications. The idea of a single leader guiding the course of nations felt both alluring and dangerous, a promise of hope intertwined with the risk of authoritarianism.

Lilah listened, concerned. Outside, the world felt like a time bomb, ready to explode at any moment. "Do you think this new leader will make a difference?" she asked Ezra.

"I don't know," he replied. "People are desperate for hope, but history teaches us that in times of crisis, the wrong leaders can rise to power."

The pressure of not knowing loomed, and as Lilah and Ezra navigated their own fears, they couldn't help but ponder what this emerging leadership would mean for their family and the uncertain future ahead.

✳ ✳ ✳

In the weeks that followed, families were left to navigate the aftermath of events that had upended their lives. A bright spot for Lilah was that Samuel's reassignment to report on the evolving situation in Jerusalem allowed him to frequently make the trek back to visit his parents in the countryside. Each return brought fresh updates about the shifting tides, not just in Jerusalem but throughout the world.

Though the rural area offered a fleeting sense of calm, Lilah and Ezra felt a gnawing unease about their prolonged stay. With airports closing and many airlines grounded due to staffing shortages from the missing, their original flights were repeatedly pushed back. Each new attempt to book an earlier seat only met with more frustration, leaving them adrift without any clear timeline for departure.

As the family gathered in the small living room of their temporary home, Lilah noticed the quiet tension between them. They switched on the television, and Samuel's familiar face filled the screen, his expression grave.

"Good evening, I'm Samuel Cohen reporting from Jerusalem," he began in a steady yet urgent tone. "The political landscape is shifting rapidly. We're witnessing a ripple effect as nations respond to the current crisis. It's crucial to stay informed as these events unfold."

As he spoke, Lilah leaned closer, intently watching the screen. "The world has chosen a new leader to guide us through these turbulent times," Samuel said. "After a vote by the European Union, the deputy prime minister of Italy has been appointed as the new global leader. With the pope's endorsement, his influence has quickly spread, uniting nations under his leadership."

"This man, a respected statesman and skilled orator, has captured the attention of many. Charismatic and persuasive, he seems poised to restore hope in a world yearning for stability."

As Samuel spoke, Lilah glanced at Ezra, who had a mix of curiosity and concern etched on his face. "What do you think he's really like?" Ezra mused.

Samuel adjusted his posture, his expression earnest. "He possesses a unique charm, a fervor that draws people in. The world appears to have rallied behind him. He is said to have an extraordinary ability to unite disparate groups, exactly what people are desperately seeking right now."

A flicker of hope stirred within Lilah at the thought of such a leader, but skepticism lingered. "Can one person really make such a difference?"

"I think folks are clinging to that possibility," Ezra replied, running a hand through his hair. "In these uncertain times, they want to believe that someone can lead them to peace."

The family sat in thoughtful silence as Lilah contemplated this newfound leader. Just then, the screen illuminated with the image of a tall figure at a podium, exuding an imposing presence as he addressed an eager crowd.

With his dark, slicked-back hair and striking features, he exuded an unsettling confidence. He carried himself with an authority that captivated and disconcerted in equal measure. The olive tone of his skin hinted at his Italian roots, while the strong lines of his jaw and high cheekbones lent him an air of nobility.

Dressed in a tailored suit that accentuated his formidable stature, he commanded the attention of all watching. The intensity in his deep-set eyes seemed to pull Lilah in, combining charm with an unsettling undercurrent. As the camera zoomed in, his polished smile revealed a veneer that seemed to mask a more ruthless ambition. Supporters waved flags and cheered, their enthusiasm amplifying the energy surrounding him. With each passionate gesture, he embodied a leader promising unity and hope.

His eloquence was striking; he spoke with a silver tongue, weaving his words together in a way that ensnared Lilah and the rest of his audience. Each carefully crafted phrase struck a chord, stirring emotions and igniting fervor among his listeners. With every commanding word, he painted a vision of unity and strength, compelling people to believe in his message and follow him wholeheartedly.

Samuel paused, his voice laden as he declared, "He is our new supreme chancellor, our global sovereign, our new world emperor. His name is … Nero Kesar."

With that, he concluded, "This is Samuel Cohen reporting live from Jerusalem."

As the weeks rolled on, the world began to take note of the remarkable rise of Nero Kesar. Samuel noticed how his charisma and persuasiveness captivated leaders and citizens alike, drawing support from every corner of the globe. Under Kesar's influence, a sense of unity emerged, as nations worked for stability in a world rife with uncertainty.

In a bold and unprecedented move, Kesar convened with the prime minister of Israel, Chief Rabbi Weissman, and leaders from neighboring countries to discuss a peace agreement. The air was tense, shaped by past conflicts, yet there was a sense of cautious optimism for a potential new beginning. Samuel had been on site, reporting live as the historic signing ceremony unfolded. After lengthy negotiations, they finally reached a consensus, signing a landmark treaty designed to last for seven years. The leaders stood side by side, their expressions a blend of resolve and hope, while Kesar spoke with passion, weaving a narrative of reconciliation and shared prosperity that resonated deeply with audiences everywhere.

Back at the modest hotel, Samuel called his parents to relay the news. "This is monumental," he declared, excitement and confusion warring within him. "A peace agreement signed by Israel and its neighbors? It feels like we're on the brink of something transformative."

His parents listened closely. "Can it really last?" his dad mused in a doubtful tone. "Seven years is a long time, and history has shown us how fragile peace can be."

"True," Samuel said. "But this feels different. Kesar has a way of inspiring people. It's as if he's reigniting their faith in something greater. Still, I can't shake this uneasy feeling …"

Lilah spoke, her voice steady but tinged with uncertainty. "It all seems strangely coincidental," she said, her gaze focused on the screen. "I remember Andrew's predictions and the notes he shared with us. It's hard not to wonder if this is part of something larger." She paused for a moment before adding, "We'll have to wait and see how it unfolds. For now, though, I hope it brings some relief to those who are suffering."

After a moment of silence, Samuel replied, "I'll keep you updated, Mom," before ending the call.

As the days passed, the world began to rally around Kesar's vision for peace. Samuel couldn't help but notice the shift in public sentiment, the air of anticipation filling the hearts of those yearning for stability. Families waited, dreaming of a brighter future, while others watched closely, weighing the implications of this new order. Conversations about rebuilding, healing, and reconciliation flourished, sparking a glimmer of hope in communities weary from strife.

Yet beneath the surface, a quiet tension lingered; many wondered if this newfound peace was sustainable or merely a facade hiding deeper issues yet to be resolved. The question loomed large—could Kesar's charisma genuinely foster lasting change, or were they on the brink of yet another upheaval?

As weeks turned into months, Samuel found himself deeply immersed in his work. His role had evolved into something significant as the world turned its gaze toward Israel, where a transformative wave was washing over the landscape. Together, Kesar and Chief Rabbi Weissman forged a partnership that inspired nations to unite in the pursuit of peace, a rare glimmer of hope in turbulent times.

In a bold move, new global centers sprang up almost overnight. Rome emerged as the political nucleus, becoming Kesar's base of operations, while an economic hub took shape near the Euphrates River in Iraq. Remarkably spared from the recent turmoil, this port became a lifeline for international trade, facilitating the movement of goods that kept economies strong.

Jerusalem transformed into the spiritual heart of the world, giving Samuel plenty to report on. With Chief Rabbi Weissman's guidance, an extraordinary level of collaboration blossomed between Muslims and Jews. A new Jewish temple was rising just a stone's throw from the revered Dome of the Rock, symbolizing this newfound harmony. Its location was a powerful gesture aimed at fostering peace and mutual respect between the two faiths.

Samuel's parents decided to extend their stay in the country, feeling a cautious relief as a sense of stability returned to the city. He was glad they had grown close to the owners of the home they were staying in, Asher and Adina. He knew the comfort of these newfound relationships gave them a sense of belonging.

News about the new temple's construction also ignited excitement within his parents. With this new era dawning, Jews were granted permission to resume sacrifices once the temple was completed, a long-standing tradition that had been on hold for generations.

Amid these transformations, Samuel began to forge new friendships, aided by his fluency in the language. He became part of a close-knit circle of men—young and old—who gathered regularly to share their thoughts and experiences. Yet, beneath their camaraderie, a current of skepticism rippled through their conversations. Many expressed doubts about Kesar's true intentions, and an unspoken agreement emerged to keep those concerns private.

As discussions deepened, some members began to question long-held beliefs, wrestling with the unsettling idea that perhaps their Jewish faith had been misguided. They contemplated the notion that Jesus might indeed be the Messiah, prompting a shift away from the Torah and Ketuvim toward Christian Scriptures. Samuel and the other Jewish men delved into end-times prophecies, convinced that these teachings were increasingly relevant to their lives. Drawn to the stories of hope and redemption within the New Testament, they sought answers in Jesus's teachings. The conversations grew more impassioned as they grappled with their identities and the implications of their newfound beliefs.

Feeling compelled to share these revelations, Samuel decided to visit his family one evening. As he entered the house, the sounds and smells of laughter and food drifted from the kitchen, where the women were busy cooking. The enticing aroma of freshly baked challah wafted toward him, and his stomach growled in response. The golden crust of the bread beckoned, while perfectly fried latkes, crisp and golden, sat alongside a dollop of applesauce. A colorful platter of gefilte fish, garnished with horseradish, completed the spread. Samuel couldn't help but smile, eager to join them at the table.

As they enjoyed their meal, Samuel cleared his throat and picked up his Bible. "I need to discuss something important with you all," he began. He felt the gravity of his words as he prepared to broach a topic that could alter the very foundation of their beliefs.

"I've been learning a great deal about the Bible and the prophecies within these pages," he said, opening the Bible to a marked passage. "I know this may seem like I'm drifting away from our Jewish heritage, but I believe there's a truth here that we need to explore."

His parents exchanged concerned glances. "What is it, Samuel?" his father asked, leaning in.

Samuel took a deep breath, aware that he was about to open a door to ideas that could change everything they had ever known.

"Are you saying you're abandoning our faith?" his mother said.

"Not exactly," Samuel replied quickly. "I'm saying we need to look at what's happening in the world and how it aligns with these prophecies."

He began reading passages about the end times, emphasizing the signs that seemed to mirror their current reality.

"Look here," Samuel said, pointing to a verse. "It speaks of a time filled with unrest, but also of hope and restoration. God has a plan, and I believe we're witnessing it unfold." He described how the Scriptures foretold significant events, including the Gog and Magog war, detailing the incidents that had engulfed nations.

He noticed the unease on his family's faces but pressed on. "This war ended almost miraculously—by an earthquake sent from God. The enemies turned on one another in confusion, and instead of Israel facing destruction, it was saved."

Miriam's husband leaned forward, curiosity beginning to replace apprehension. "Do you really think this is all connected?"

"I do," Samuel replied, sensing their growing interest. "And it goes even further. After this war, a man will rise to power, ruling over the entire world. He will form an alliance with another individual to broker a seven-year peace treaty with Israel. The Bible speaks of this figure, known as the Antichrist, who will ascend to power and deceive many."

Samuel turned to the Old Testament, tracing his fingers over the pages as he prepared to share what he had uncovered. "Look here," he said, guiding them to the relevant verses. "The Bible tells us that the Antichrist will be the leader of the world. He is prophesied to come from Roman descent. As for the man he aligns with, he is described as his false prophet, and the Bible indicates that he will be Jewish. Consider the events we've seen recently—the war, the rise of a new leader, the peace deal—it all aligns with biblical prophecy. And ... I believe the Antichrist is Nero Kesar, and Chief Rabbi Weissman has assumed the role of his false prophet."

"I understand how you might feel that way, Samuel," his mom said, her brow furrowed. "But our beliefs have been passed down for generations. It's hard to just cast aside everything we've held dear."

"I get that, Mom," Samuel replied gently. "But what if there's more to the story? What if we're being called to open our eyes to something new?"

Samuel's father shook his head, his expression serious. "It's not easy to let go of what we've always believed, especially when it has been our foundation for so long."

"I understand," Samuel said, sensing their struggle. "But I genuinely believe these signs are significant. We need to consider that what's happening might be aligning with the prophecies."

His parents exchanged glances, a mixture of concern and curiosity evident.

"We can't ignore how closely these Scriptures mirrored the events of the past several months," his dad said.

Miriam's eyes widened. "So you believe our chief rabbi is this false prophet?"

"Yes, I do," Samuel replied urgently. "These prophecies are unfolding before us. It's all connected."

As Samuel began reading scripture, he felt their shared heritage mingling with the new truths he presented. He hoped to guide them through these turbulent times, holding fast to their faith while exploring what lay ahead.

As they absorbed this information, Samuel watched their minds work, wrestling with long-held beliefs while considering the implications of his words.

Leaning in, he added a new revelation. "The new temple is nearing completion. Plans have been in the works for years, led by Jewish architects. Gershon Salomon, formerly the head of the Temple Mount Faithful, has long been a vocal advocate for the rebuilding of the temple. The movement he led emphasized not just the construction of a building, but the fulfillment of the redemption of the people of the Bible in the land of the Bible. Salomon once said, 'I cannot imagine an Israeli State or Israeli life in this country without the Temple Mount at the center of it.'"

Miriam looked between Samuel and his mom. "So you're suggesting that all of this—the rise of Kesar, the peace agreement, the rebuilding of the Temple—is part of a larger plan?"

Samuel took a deep breath, sensing the weight of the moment. "Yes," he affirmed, and opened the Bible, his fingers gliding over the pages until he found the passage he wanted to share, Jeremiah 33:14–16.

"'Behold, the days are coming, declares the LORD, when I will fulfill the promise I made to the house of Israel and the house of Judah. In those days and at that time I will cause a righteous Branch to spring up for David, and he shall execute justice and righteousness in the land. In those days Judah will be saved, and Jerusalem will dwell securely. And this is the name by which it will be called: 'The LORD is our righteousness.'"

Sam pressed gently. "The Bible tells us that the 'righteous Branch of David' refers to Jesus, the Messiah, who came to bring spiritual salvation to the world. He is from the line of David, as prophesied, and through His life, death, and resurrection, He provided a path for redemption, establishing the spiritual kingdom of God in the hearts of believers. His sacrifice made it possible for humanity to be reconciled to God.

"However," Sam continued, "during Jesus's earthly ministry, Jerusalem did not dwell in safety. Instead, the city remained under Roman oppression, and just a few decades after His death and resurrection, it was destroyed by the Romans in AD 70. The Jewish people were scattered, exiled, and persecuted for centuries. This shows that the prophecy wasn't fully realized at that time.

"But there's more. At the appointed time, after this seven-year period, Jesus will return—not as the suffering servant but as the reigning King. He will establish His eternal kingdom on earth, fulfilling every promise made by God. This will be the time often referred to as the millennial kingdom, when Christ will rule with justice and righteousness, and Jerusalem will finally dwell in safety. It is then that Judah, representing the Jewish people, will experience both physical and spiritual salvation. The prophecy looks ahead to this glorious future when Jesus will reign over all nations and the world will be restored to perfect peace under His rule." Sam paused, looking at his family. "Do you see what this means?"

Silence filled the room as the weight of the Scripture hung in the air. Miriam exchanged a glance with her husband.

"Sam, these are all from the Bible," his mother said skeptically. "But the Tanakh doesn't include the New Testament. The Scripture we follow doesn't recognize Jesus as the Messiah."

"Mom, I think we've been wrong all this time." He leaned forward, eager to make his family see his point. "All right, the book of Ezekiel is part of the Old Testament. It's one of the prophetic books in the Torah, found in the Nevi'im section of the Tanakh. It speaks about the temples, right?"

She nodded. "Well, yes. I know about the temples."

He continued, "Right, Ezekiel speaks about a future temple—but it's Daniel who warns us that the sacrifices will be reinstated and then suddenly stopped."

Sam's mother frowned slightly. "Daniel is in the Tanakh, yes—but he's not considered one of the prophets to us."

Sam took a breath. "I know. But hear me out. Daniel was a prophet in Babylon, and while his book is placed in the Writings—not the Prophets—in the Tanakh, Christians consider him a major prophet. And when you look at his visions alongside Ezekiel's, they line up. The two are connected. Listen to what Daniel 9:27 says: *And he shall make a strong covenant with many for one week, and for half of the week he shall put an end to sacrifice and offering.*"

He looked at his mom intently. "That's the Antichrist. He'll make a peace agreement with Israel for seven years—'one week'—but halfway through, he'll break it. That's when the sacrifices stop. Ezekiel's temple,

Daniel's prophecy—they fit together. And I believe this is how it's all going to unfold.

"And there's more," he said. "Have you heard about the red heifers?"

His mom nodded, her eyes widening with interest. "Of course, but what does that have to do with anything today?" she replied.

His family looked at him quizzically, and he continued, "The red heifer plays a crucial role in purification, especially for those who've been in contact with the dead. The Torah lays it out in Numbers 19: it has to be completely red, without blemish, and never yoked. That's the only way the people and the temple can be purified. Historically, these sacrifices stopped when the Second Temple was destroyed, but according to tradition, the red heifer is needed to purify the priests and the temple before sacrifices can properly begin again. That's why it matters so much to those preparing for the Third Temple."

His mother frowned. "But, Samuel, finding a red heifer without blemish—one that's never been yoked—that's nearly impossible now."

Samuel took a breath, letting the significance of his words sink in. "The Temple Mount Faithful had been working for years to find the perfect red heifers for the sacrifices—and now, they're here. Ranchers in Texas have bred these animals to be flawless, and some of them have already made their way to Israel. They're ready to restore the sacrificial system that's been central to our faith. Mom, this temple they're building is a direct fulfillment of prophecy—it's the one we've been reading about, the one that's supposed to come at the end of the age. But here's the twist: The Antichrist will deceive Israel into thinking it's ours. He'll let us restart our sacred traditions, including the sacrifices. But don't be fooled—this peace is a facade. In the middle of this seven-year period, the Antichrist will take control of the temple for himself, demanding the world worship only him."

She glanced at his father, who shook his head in disbelief. "Why does the world hate us so much? I just don't understand why."

Sam was eager to share details on this topic. "Well, I can explain. Let's go back and consider the attack on Israel that took place on October 7, 2023. Many believe that moment is tied to this prophecy. It was as if Israel had lowered its defenses, just as the Bible warns in Ezekiel 38:11: *'You will say, "I will go up against the land of unwalled villages. I will fall upon the quiet people who dwell securely, all of them dwelling without walls, and having no bars or gates."'* Israel had lowered its walls, or perhaps its symbolic walls, not knowing they were about to be attacked. But October 7 is also historically significant; it aligns with the Hebrew calendar day when King Solomon dedicated the First Temple to God, reading from the scrolls before its eventual destruction."

He paused, gathering his thoughts before continuing. "The ongoing conflict between Jews and Muslims over the land of Israel has deep historical roots, but it ultimately stems from God's covenant. God promised this land to Abraham and his rightful descendants, establishing Israel as a homeland for the Jewish people.

"In the Bible, Abraham was once commanded by God to sacrifice his son Isaac, a moment that was meant to test his faith in God. As he prepared to carry out this heartbreaking act, God intervened, providing a ram caught in the thicket as a substitute. This pivotal event occurred on the mountain of Moriah, now regarded as sacred ground. Through Isaac, God intended to fulfill His promises, establishing a lineage that would lead to the nation of Israel."

His dad nodded. "Yes, we know that, Sam. Israel has always been God's chosen people. But why is there so much hatred toward us for it?"

Samuel paused, looking at his parents before continuing. "Well, think about it, Dad. We know the story of Abraham and his sons, right? God promised Abraham a son who would inherit the land, but Sarah was barren. She gave Hagar, her maid, to Abraham, and Ishmael was born through that union. But this wasn't the son God intended. Later, Sarah gave birth to Isaac, the rightful heir. Ishmael's descendants became the ancestors of another lineage. That line eventually led to Muhammad, who Islam considers a prophet and messianic figure. The Dome of the

Rock, which stands on the very site where Abraham was prepared to sacrifice Isaac, is also believed by Muslims to be where Muhammad ascended to heaven. This land, sacred to both Jews and Muslims, has been fought over for centuries."

He looked around at his family, witnessing their expressions shift from confusion to contemplation. "This division has festered for generations. The conflict between the descendants of Isaac and Ishmael is not just historical; it represents a deep spiritual struggle that continues to this day."

"Iran's animosity toward Israel runs deep," Samuel continued. "They back groups like Hezbollah, the Houthis, and Hamas. The attack on October 7 came from Gaza, fueled by Hamas, which is orchestrated by Iran. These entities are run by the Sar Paras, a biblical term for the Prince of Persia, which points to the leader of Iran. The leader of Iran, Sar Paras, is fueled by the Red Dragon, whom Scripture identifies as the Antichrist!

"This recent war involving Israel is a reflection of the Gog and Magog prophecy. Magog is often associated with regions to the north of Israel, linked to modern-day Russia. According to Scripture, its leader, Gog, will ally with nations such as Cush, corresponding to Sudan and Ethiopia today; Put, which we recognize as Libya; Meshech and Tubal, connected to Turkey; and Persia, meaning Iran. Each of these nations contributes to the tensions we've been witnessing."

Samuel leaned in, his expression serious. "And we cannot overlook the new temple being constructed. Prophecies indicate that it plays a crucial role in our future. The fact that it is nearing completion is astonishing!"

His mom frowned, concern etched on her face. "But how can this be? The Dome of the Rock sits directly where the new temple is meant to be built. Doesn't it need to be removed first to make the prophecy true?"

"No, Mom," Samuel replied firmly. "The Muslims got it wrong! The new temple will rise just twenty-one meters from the Dome of the Rock. This proximity holds great significance for us." He opened the

Bible again, reading aloud with clarity. "In Ezekiel 40:5, it describes the temple's measurements, affirming that the new structure is being built in accordance with Scripture. This temple represents not merely a physical space but the restoration of our faith and connection to God."

His parents exchanged bewildered glances. "It seems the Old and New Testament prophecies are not mere concepts; they are unfolding in our lives," his mom said.

Ezra leaned back. A mix of disbelief and understanding crossed his face. Finally, he murmured, "So, you're saying that Jesus truly is the Messiah?" His tone was both rhetorical and incredulous, as if he were grappling with a truth that had suddenly come to light. A heavy silence settled over the room.

Miriam and her husband's expressions shifted from skepticism to curiosity. Their two sons, Moshe and Aharon, intrigued by the unfolding dialogue, began to ask questions about Jesus, their voices a blend of innocence and earnestness.

"What does it mean for us if He is the Messiah?" Moshe inquired. "How does this change everything we thought we knew?"

Samuel responded with urgency as he saw his family on the cusp of a revelation that could redefine their beliefs and future.

"It's crucial for us to understand the significance of believing in Jesus now. We've rejected Him once; we cannot do it again." Sam turned his Bible to the New Testament. "In John 10:25, Jesus tells the Jews, '*I told you, and you do not believe.*' Then in verse 38, He adds, '*Even though you do not believe me, believe the works [I do], that you may know and understand that the Father is in me and I am in the Father.*' Just look at what He is doing!

"My friends and I have started reading the Bible," Sam continued, "and what we've uncovered is profound. Jesus came as the Son of God, living a sinless life and ultimately sacrificing Himself on the cross, fulfilling ancient prophecies."

He recounted the pivotal moments of the crucifixion. "He was executed by the Romans, yet even in that moment of despair, He kept His promise. He rose again three days later, conquering death and offering us a path to salvation. This isn't just a story from the past; it speaks to us today. These offerings and sacrifices that our people are planning to make at the new temple aren't needed. Jews are still practicing these ancient traditions, still waiting for their Messiah. But they're unnecessary." He paused. "There's no need for these sacrifices because … Jesus was the sacrifice."

Miriam and her husband listened intently, their expressions showing contemplation. Moshe and Aharon exchanged looks of wonder. Samuel could see their minds working, each revelation prompting deeper questions about faith and heritage.

Miriam's husband, clearly intrigued, asked, "If Jesus is indeed the Messiah and the Antichrist is set to rule now, where does Jesus fit into all this? How do we reconcile His absence with what you're saying?"

"The next seven years are what the Bible refers to as the tribulation," Samuel said. "It's a time of great upheaval and testing."

"Andrew has been sharing similar views from his friend Landon," his mother said. "He's been staying at Landon's house, and his parents have been gathering with their neighbors weekly to discuss these topics. I didn't really understand it until now."

Samuel nodded. "These seven years will challenge our faith in Christ. This period will reveal God's wrath against those who do not believe. The faithful—the ones who vanished—were taken up in what is known as the rapture. It marks the beginning of troubled times.

"The tribulation started with a seven-year peace deal involving Israel. The Antichrist will rise to power alongside his false prophet, initially winning the admiration of many. At first, people will embrace him, but midway through, the truth will emerge—he is not who he seems. By then, it may be too late for many."

Samuel paused, gathering his thoughts. "A series of events will unfold in chronological order, known as God's judgments. We're talking about wars, famine, and calamities sweeping across the earth—consequences of rejecting divine truth."

Moshe leaned in, curiosity etched on his face. "How does the Antichrist gain his power? What makes everyone follow him so blindly?"

"It's essential to understand that the Antichrist's power comes directly from Satan," Samuel replied. "There's a Scripture I learned about Jesus being tempted in the wilderness. In Matthew 4:8–10, it says, *Again, the devil took Him up on an exceedingly high mountain, and showed Him all the kingdoms of the world and their glory. And he said to Him, "All these things I will give You if You will fall down and worship me." Then Jesus said to him, "Away with you, Satan! For it is written, 'You shall worship the LORD your God, and Him only you shall serve.'"*

"Now, that same offer is being made to a man who will accept it: the Antichrist. He's willing to take the deal, gaining immense power and influence. This is how he will manipulate the world, presenting himself as the solution to all its problems while ultimately serving a darker agenda."

Samuel grew more serious as he continued. "Because we didn't believe when we had the opportunity, God is now placing His judgments on the world, responding to the sin and rebellion it carries. The tribulation is a time when the consequences of our choices are laid bare—a reckoning for those who have turned away. God desires for us to return, but many will refuse to see the truth, and that refusal will lead to unimaginable suffering."

Samuel paused, considering his next words with care.

"You see, when Adam and Eve sinned, by eating fruit from the forbidden tree as Satan tempted them, humanity severed its connection with God. That sin caused us to lose our rightful claim to the earth. The only one who could redeem us and reclaim that title would need to be perfect, sinless—willing to sacrifice himself for the sins of all. When Jesus was crucified at Golgotha, He didn't just forgive our wrongdoings; He broke the hold that Satan had on the earth. God couldn't simply take it back; He had to pay the price to reclaim it. Jesus allowed Himself to be killed because He had to be our ransom. He could have stopped it, but He chose not to." *

"He has already begun reclaiming that title by taking believers up in the rapture. The rest can still be ours—if we believe now! The price has been paid. It was Jesus! He was the perfect sacrifice, and many still don't believe it. Yes, we may face tribulation, and countless people will suffer and die, but we still have the chance to spend eternity with Him!"

Moshe's face reflected deep concern. "Why didn't God intervene sooner?" he asked, his voice quivering. "People have been wicked for so long. Why does He still care enough to save us?"

"God is patient, Moshe," Samuel said. "He desires everyone to come to repentance. As it says in 2 Peter 3:9, '*The Lord is … not wishing that any should perish, but that all should reach repentance.'* He gives us time, hoping we will turn to Him willingly. It's not that He doesn't see the evil—His love is so vast that He allows us the freedom to choose. Even now, in these dark times, His grace is still offered to those who are willing to accept it."

His father turned to Samuel. "So, what comes next?" he asked, his tone steady but laced with apprehension. "What should we be preparing for?"

"The next seven years are going to be unlike anything we've ever seen," Samuel said, then inhaled deeply. "Many will die, and the suffering will be unimaginable. The Bible tells us that when Jesus came the first time, He came as a gentle lamb. But the next time He comes, it will be as a powerful lion."

Samuel's determination grew as he continued. "The Bible provides a detailed account of what lies ahead, and we need to start gathering regularly to study it together. I've connected with a growing group of Jewish believers. We're reaching out to others across the country, and each day more join us. I feel a deep need to share this truth with anyone willing to listen."

                    *Hal Lindsey

"Can we join your meetings?" Moshe asked, his voice full of conviction.

"Absolutely," Samuel replied. "The more, the better."

As the evening wound down, they shared heartfelt goodbyes. Samuel paused at the door and turned back to his parents. "Here," he said, handing them his Bible. "I want you to have this. Please read the Scripture I've bookmarked and reflect on it. It's a powerful reminder of God's love and promise."

His parents nodded, their hands clasped together.

"We will," his mom said. "Thank you for sharing this with us, Samuel." She reached out and squeezed her son's hand.

As he stepped outside, Samuel felt a mix of hope and responsibility. He knew this was just the beginning, and he was determined to keep spreading the truth and guiding those around him in their faith.

Just as he was about to leave, he heard his mother's voice calling him back. Curiously, he turned to see her opening the Bible he had left behind. She found the passage and began to read aloud, her voice clear.

"*'For God so loved the world, that he gave his only Son, that whoever believes in him should not perish but have eternal life.'* John 3:16."

As they stood in silence, Samuel hoped the Scripture they had read was echoing in their minds as well, weaving through the threads of their thoughts, unraveling a mystery they had never before comprehended. He saw that a new path stretched out before them all, its contours becoming clearer, like the first light of dawn breaking over a dark horizon.

CHAPTER EIGHT

A SYMPHONY WITHIN THE STORM

1 ½ yrs since start of tribulation

As dawn broke over the neighborhood, Lawson stepped outside, the sky heavy with clouds and a brisk breeze stirring the air. The wind had picked up, rustling the leaves, and the gray sky seemed to promise the arrival of a storm. He made his way to his car, the gravel crunching beneath his feet, when a glint of white caught his eye. A folded piece of paper rested precariously on the windshield, fluttering in the breeze.

A sinking feeling settled over Lawson as he approached the car and plucked the paper from the windshield. He unfolded it slowly, his eyes scanning the hastily scribbled words: **Be careful. They're watching.**

An unease gripped his stomach, and he glanced around, half expecting to see a shadowy figure lurking in the corners. What did they know? Who had left this warning? Questions swirled in his mind as he crumpled the note, stuffing it into his pocket as if to bury it from sight.

Upon arriving at the office, Lawson was met by the relentless hum of fluorescent lights and the stifling atmosphere that had become all too familiar. The space felt altered—hostile, almost claustrophobic. He settled into his cubicle, attempting to focus on his tasks, but the note gnawed at him, refusing to be forgotten.

A sudden uproar near the break room pulled his attention. Marcus, a fellow coworker, stood with his arms crossed, his face flushed with anger. "What do you mean you're installing tracking software on our phones?" he shouted at their boss, a man whose demeanor was as frigid as his sharp suit.

"If you don't like it, you can quit," the boss retorted, barely lifting his eyes from the tablet in his hands.

Lawson felt the tension in the room. Marcus's outrage resonated deeply within him. The invasive nature of technology revealed that each device was serving as a surveillance tool rather than a means of connection. It felt as if their privacy had been breached, their thoughts and conversations monitored.

Though he tried to focus on his work, the walls seemed to close in around him. It was staggering to reflect on how drastically life had transformed in just a year and a half. The ascent of Nero Kesar had reshaped their reality, though only for those willing to acknowledge the shift. Supply chains lay in ruin, grocery shelves increasingly bare as food grew scarcer. Medicines, once readily available, had become elusive, thanks to the government's refusal to import from China, which was deemed unworthy because of its defiance against Kesar's authority.

Lawson pondered the chilling truth: Any dissent had become a perilous gamble, a potential invitation to persecution. Freedom of speech was eroding, replaced by a culture of silence that stifled debate. Religious practices that diverged from the state-sanctioned ideology faced severe restrictions, while many worshiped whatever suited their fancy— everything except God. The world beyond felt wicked and unpredictable, a vast sea of uncertainty where trust was a fleeting memory.

With a determined shake of his head, he attempted to refocus on his screen, but the weight of his thoughts lingered. How much longer could they withstand this growing pressure? How soon would the warning on that note materialize into something more tangible—more dangerous? The thought was unnerving, and he resolved to tread carefully, acutely aware that unseen eyes were ever watchful.

Later that evening, Jayne stood at the kitchen counter, methodically rummaging through drawers in search of batteries and flashlights. The

Weather Channel hummed in the background, its urgent updates on Hurricane Van filling Jayne with a sense of uncertainty. Positioned just more than 130 miles away from Jayne and her family, Port Lavaca was bracing for one of the most formidable storms on record—a Category 6 with winds predicted to exceed 200 miles per hour.

Though they wouldn't face a direct hit, the storm's vast size—more than 200 miles wide—meant that the gusty bands could reach nearly 300 miles, potentially affecting Jayne's quiet town. They had weathered numerous hurricanes in the past, but the recent year and a half had brought an increase in the severity and frequency of natural disasters.

"Lawson!" she called urgently. "Have you checked the pantry for more flashlight batteries?"

"On it!" he replied, his voice calm as he moved through the living room toward the kitchen pantry.

Finally, Jayne unearthed a flashlight and tested it, the bright beam slicing through the kitchen's dim light with reassuring clarity. This routine had become a familiar ritual—boarding windows, filling jugs with water, gathering supplies.

Lawson emerged from the pantry and handed Jayne the extra batteries he had found. "Here, just in case," he said, his tone steady. "I'm going to check the roof." He glanced out the window at the dark clouds gathering ominously overhead. "Good idea," Jayne replied, her mind already racing ahead. "And don't forget to check the oil in the generator while you're at it."

As he headed toward the door, Jayne paused for a moment, taking a deep breath. She felt a swell of gratitude for the home generator they had had installed a few years back. It was more than just a practical solution; it had become a lifeline during storms, providing much-needed power when the rest of the neighborhood was plunged into darkness. So many of their neighbors had been left in the dark during storms, their homes powerless and cold, while hers stood as a beacon.

It wasn't just about convenience; it was about community. In those moments of crisis, her home had become a gathering place, sharing warmth and solace. Jayne felt a rush of appreciation for the foresight that had led them to invest in that generator, and she silently hoped it would serve them well once again.

She set the flashlight on the counter and stepped outside, her determination clear as she joined Lawson in preparing for the storm. The atmosphere felt charged, and as she moved through the yard, she began gathering the pool furniture and potted plants, ensuring that anything that might become a projectile was safely stowed away. The wind picked up, swirling around her, each gust a sharp reminder of the tempest looming on the horizon. She glanced up at Lawson, struggling to steady himself on the slope of the roof. He was silhouetted against the deepening twilight.

"Everything OK up there?" she called, her voice cutting through the rising chorus of the wind.

"Yeah! Just making sure nothing's loose!" he shouted back, his words barely audible.

Jayne turned to watch as Landon and Andrew worked diligently securing the last of the wooden boards over the windows, their faces set with determination. She appreciated their commitment. "Make sure to screw those in tight!" she called out, her voice mingling with the growing wind.

"We got it, Mom!" Landon replied, continuing to tighten the screws. Andrew nodded, glancing over to offer her a reassuring smile.

She turned her attention back to the task at hand, grateful for the familiarity of this routine. Each action grounded her, a reminder that even in times of uncertainty, there was still a sense of control. Jayne thought about the recent string of disasters—the wildfires that ravaged the West, the hurricanes that battered the Gulf Coast, and the tornadoes that seemed to touch down with increasing ferocity. It was a world transformed, one where the weather felt like an unpredictable adversary.

Jayne stepped back into the kitchen, the rhythmic patter of raindrops against the window urging her to move quickly. The wind had picked up further, whistling around the corners of the house—a haunting prelude to the storm's imminent arrival.

With the house preparations nearly complete, Jayne busied herself in the kitchen, pulling a bubbling lasagna from the oven. Though her hands moved steadily, a quiet unease lingered at the edges of her mind, threatening to disrupt her focus. As she meticulously arranged the lasagna on the counter, she couldn't shake the images of destruction the storm could bring—trees bending under fierce winds and debris flying through the air. The reality of the impending hurricane loomed, even as she focused on the comfort of her home and the gathering of friends.

The guest rooms were nearly ready; beds made crisp and inviting, air mattresses inflated and tucked into the corners of the living room, all set for the neighbors who would soon arrive. She glanced at the clock—her friends were expected around six.

As she turned to head down the hall, Jayne recalled that Sophie had promised to help but had not been seen for hours. Her frustration grew as she pushed open the door. Seeing Sophie curled up in bed ignited a mix of worry and irritation.

Sophie had been having a hard time adjusting to this new reality. She missed her friends, the social life she had at college, and the fun that seemed to be slipping away with each passing day. It hurt Jayne to see her daughter in such a state, especially when Sophie sometimes took her frustrations out on the family. There had been times when Sophie had snapped at Jayne for asking her to help with dinner or rolled her eyes when Jayne tried to engage her in conversation.

"Everything just sucks! You just don't get it," she had said during one heated moment, the words cutting deep.

Jayne knew Sophie was struggling to come to terms with the fact that this was their new life, one that felt increasingly bleak. The idea that the world outside was too dangerous to navigate made Sophie feel like a prisoner at home. Lost opportunities and a future now overshadowed by uncertainty left her feeling depressed and angry. This anger often manifested in sharp words and hurtful comments, leaving Jayne feeling both helpless and heartbroken.

With all that had been happening—the chaos and dangers looming beyond their door—none of them saw the point in trying to return to college. Landon and Andrew had managed to complete their last few classes online, finishing just three weeks shy of graduation. But the culmination of their hard work felt hollow; instead of donning caps and gowns to celebrate their achievements, their diplomas arrived quietly in the mail. Landon had forgone his new job entirely, unable to find meaning in it now.

As for Sophie, she never returned to campus. Jayne and Lawson felt it was safer for her to stay home, a decision made out of love and fear, but one that Sophie struggled with daily. She was obviously wrestling with the loss of her independence, her dreams, and the life she thought she was building. The frustration seemed to gnaw at her, simmering under the surface until it bubbled over in fits of anger. Jayne could see the pain behind her words, but it didn't make them sting any less.

Jayne was glad that Sophie had accepted that her boyfriend Matt wasn't coming back. But Sophie still grappled with the concept of the rapture and all the discussions her parents had been having with friends. Jayne could see the conflict in her daughter. Sophie had been attending meetings with the neighbors, but she was clearly unsure about her faith. While the rest of the family had embraced salvation and found solace in reading the Bible and praying together, Sophie seemed lost. She went along with it but often questioned whether believing in Jesus would really help. Jayne understood that this was a difficult transition for her, but the stubbornness only added to Jayne's growing concern.

Jayne's front door swung open just as the first heavy drops of rain began to fall, bringing with them a gust of wind that rattled the windows.

Their neighbors John and Maria stepped inside, bags in hand, with a sense of urgency that matched the weather outside. Camille and David followed closely, their faces a mix of determination and concern. Finnley and Charlie bounded toward them, tails wagging, eager to greet the familiar faces.

"Looks like we made it just in time," John said, shaking off the rain.

"Just in time for a feast," Jayne replied, her smile genuine, though the storm loomed in her mind.

As they settled around the kitchen table, the rich aroma of the lasagna wafted through the air, mingling with the fresh scent of the Greek salad that Maria had prepared. Jayne had layered the lasagna with care, each sheet of pasta cradling a hearty mix of seasoned meat, tangy marinara, and gooey cheese. It was bubbling and golden, the cheese stretching as she served it, enticing everyone with its warmth.

Just then, the door opened again, and in walked Trevin and Sarah, a welcome sight amid the growing storm. Sarah carried a large dish of her homemade banana pudding, the sweet scent drifting through the kitchen. Yet Jayne noticed the shadows beneath Sarah's eyes and the way her clothes hung loosely on her frame—a stark reminder of the weight she had lost in her grief.

"Hey, everyone," Trevin said, offering a warm smile. "We brought dessert!"

"Sarah's banana pudding is the best," Jayne said, her tone light, but the heaviness of the moment lingered. "It's a family tradition, isn't it?"

"Yes," Sarah replied, her voice steady but tinged with the sadness that had become a part of her. "I thought we could all use a little sweetness tonight."

Jayne watched as Sarah placed the dish on the table, its rich stacks of pudding and banana looking delicious. She appreciated her friend's effort, knowing that Sarah was still struggling but was trying to bring some comfort to their evening.

"I hope you're hungry," Jayne said, dishing out generous portions. Beneath the table, Finnley and Charlie sat patiently at their feet, eyes fixed upward, hoping for a taste.

"Oh, it looks amazing!" Camille exclaimed, her eyes bright with anticipation.

"And this salad looks and smells incredible, Maria," Lawson added.

Maria beamed. "It's a family recipe," she said with a hint of pride in her voice. "Fresh herbs make all the difference—oregano, basil, and a touch of lemon juice for brightness."

As Jayne dug in, the flavors danced on her tongue, each bite of lasagna rich and savory, perfectly complemented by the crisp, tangy notes of the salad. The laughter and chatter around the table provided a comforting contrast to the increasing winds outside, which howled like a distant train.

Lawson, glancing at the window, commented, "We've been through storms before, but this one's different."

Maria nodded. "With everything that's been happening lately—wildfires, floods—it's hard not to worry. But I'm glad we're together."

"Absolutely," Jayne replied, a sense of gratitude washing over her.

Their conversation flowed easily, punctuated by the occasional clink of silverware and the sound of rain beginning to pound against the roof. Each shared story and hearty laugh wove a fabric of camaraderie, creating a refuge of warmth.

Hours had passed since the storm's fury had settled into a relentless assault, the wrath now an unyielding barrage against their home. The wind outside had transformed into a howling beast, thrashing against the house as if trying to claw its way in. Jayne sat alone at the kitchen table, the glow of the television casting long shadows across her face, her heart pounding in rhythm with the gusts.

The lasagna had long since disappeared, replaced by an oppressive silence punctuated only by the distant hum of the generator now in use and the roar of the storm that lay just beyond their walls. Lawson was perched on the edge of his chair, eyes fixed on the screen, while the boys huddled together, whispers exchanged in nervous anticipation. Camille and Maria sat across from them, worry etched on their faces as they followed the weather report.

"Port Lavaca is currently enduring the brunt of what is being described as the worst storm in American history," the anchor stated, his tone urgent. "The eyewall is moving inland, and the reports of damage are already coming in. This storm is so large that its impact will be felt far beyond the immediate area. Meteorologists are warning that the scale of devastation will be unprecedented.

"In the past year alone, we've seen a disturbing increase in the intensity and frequency of storms, with entire cities turned into ghost towns and communities left in ruins," he said with a grave expression. "Places like the Bahamas and parts of the Philippines have been almost completely wiped off the map, their landscapes forever changed by nature's wrath.

"Officials are urging anyone still in the area to take the necessary precautions. The destruction we're witnessing isn't just a local phenomenon; it's part of a broader pattern that raises serious concerns. This storm could leave Port Lavaca unrecognizable, and the reality is that no one will survive if they remain. They're advising anyone who refused to evacuate to use a Sharpie to write their names and next of kin on their arms or legs. Identification may be crucial, as the likelihood of survival is dwindling with every passing moment."

As the anchor's voice faded into the background, Jayne found herself slipping into a reverie, her thoughts drifting back over the tumultuous year and a half since the rapture and everything that had changed thereafter. The world felt like a different place, filled with uncertainty, yet in the depths of her heart, she remained hopeful.

Her mind wandered to the weekly gatherings with friends and family, cherished moments spent discussing the notes left by Ruth. They had formed a tight-knit community, united in their quest for understanding, diving into Scripture and unraveling the intricate outline she had provided. Each passage served as a reminder of their shared hope, illuminating the path ahead.

Ruth's outline was proving hauntingly accurate. It spoke of Israel's salvation, foretold by an earthquake that would leave their enemies in disarray. It detailed the fall of Russia and its neighboring countries, the rise of the Antichrist, and the harrowing peace treaty he would broker with Israel—starting a precarious seven years that loomed over the future.

They had examined the four horses of the apocalypse, each rider a symbol of what was to come. The first, a rider on a white horse, signaled the Antichrist's arrival. The second, a fierce red horse, embodied the wars that would engulf nations. The third, a black horse, warned of famine and disease, while the final rider, pale and ghostly, represented death— the grim reality now manifesting with plagues sweeping the globe.

Jayne leaned back in her chair, memories pressing down like a leaden blanket. The storm outside mirrored the tempest within her, a swirling vortex of fear and insecurity. Each crack of thunder seemed to echo the turmoil in her mind, amplifying her anxiety. She grappled with the realization that the world was unraveling, each dire prediction from Ruth's notes morphing into a grim reality.

As Jayne sat in the dim light of the kitchen, shadows danced along the walls, mirroring the perplexity within her heart. She thought of America, a once-vibrant constitutional republic now shrouded in a fog of uncertainty and despair. Decisions that had once rested in the hands of its citizens were now dictated by a shadowy council, led by Nero Kesar, the new emperor of a world that felt increasingly foreign. The man's charm was profound, his speeches dripped with promises of peace, yet each word only deepened her disillusionment. Where was the peace he spoke of?

Instead, the world was ablaze with conflict. Nations once stable had become battlegrounds, with China tightening its grip on Japan and Taiwan, their sovereignty slipping like sand through desperate fingers. Civil unrest smoldered just beneath the surface in every nation, a disquieting reminder that harmony was merely a façade. In America, Jayne sensed a mixture of hatred and fear simmering in the hearts of strangers.

Reflecting on the years prior to the rapture, Jayne now recognized a gradual shift in society, where invisible lines were drawn between races, morals, faiths, and creeds. Initially subtle, these divisions deepened over time, morphing into obvious hatred. She recalled the whispers of discontent that grew louder, fueled by rhetoric that seeped from the highest levels of leadership, igniting tensions and promoting divisiveness.

What began as mere disagreement evolved into a chasm that pitted communities against each other, as political lines hardened into battlegrounds of ideology. Pro-life versus pro-choice, liberal versus conservative, each side armed with weapons of judgment and disdain. It became clear to her that these divisions were manifestations of a deeper spiritual conflict, a reflection of the eternal struggle between good and evil. The devil, it seemed, had orchestrated this discord, using human leaders to sow seeds of division, while the essence of God's love was overshadowed by an ever-increasing darkness. The leaders, in their speeches, had offered only canned responses, perpetually referring to reimagining the future as if the past were nothing but a series of great sins to be buried and forgotten.

Kesar's strongholds had been established in Rome, Jerusalem, and Hallah, just outside of Baghdad, yet none of them thrived as promised. The political center in Rome had stripped citizens of their voices, replacing the facade of democracy with an oppressive regime that demanded blind allegiance. She could almost hear the echoes of long-lost debates, where people once passionately voiced their opinions. Now, leaders danced like marionettes, strings pulled taut by Kesar's will.

Economically, the city of Hallah had fallen into turmoil. With import and export channels in disarray, food shortages loomed large, making it even harder for families already stretched thin. She thought of the empty storefronts, once bustling with life, now mere relics of a forgotten era. Many businesses had closed their doors, their futures snuffed out by the sudden absence of workers taken in the rapture. Jayne mourned not just for the loss of jobs, but for the vibrancy of community that had been so integral to their lives.

Ironically, this city was the same location referenced in Ruth's notes, the ancient city of Babylon, now described as the new Mystery Babylon. The parallels were striking; just as the original Babylon had faced its own destruction, Hallah now stood on the brink of a similar fate. The lessons from the past felt eerily relevant, and she couldn't shake the feeling that they were living in a modern-day reflection of a much older story—one marked by instability and the fragility of civilization.

The religious base, which had once promised solace, had become a breeding ground for despair. With countless Christians gone, a darkness had crept into society, infecting hearts and minds. Idolatry had taken root, with people embracing sun gods and other deities in bewildering rituals. She shuddered at the thought of the recent event in Mexico, where thousands had gathered to celebrate a sun god, their fervor a jarring contrast to the emptiness she felt. The image of worshipers dancing under the blistering sun haunted her, a grotesque spectacle that seemed to mock the void left by the faithful's departure.

It wasn't just the worship of fake gods and idols—it was the unchecked rise of witchcraft that set her on edge. Tarot cards, horoscopes, numerology: People flocked to these practices, believing they came from a higher, godly place. But they were deceived. It all stemmed from Satan, his cunning wrapped in the guise of enlightenment, leading countless souls astray. She thought about how, in years past, children had innocently played with Ouija boards, thinking it was a game. Now, those same kinds of practices—seeking answers from the supernatural, attempting to communicate with spirits—were widespread, embraced by all ages. What they didn't realize was that whether seeking answers through cards, astrology, or a board game, each practice was a portal, an opening to the demonic. They were inviting darkness into their lives, often unknowingly, but with devastating consequences. The worship of the dead became commonplace, with people communing with spirits they believed to be loved ones, seeking comfort in their whispers. Yet she knew the truth: These rituals weren't innocent; they were a direct line to the darkness, another ploy to disregard the only true path to heaven.

The world had traded faith for falsehoods, rejecting salvation in favor of lies that promised power and control but delivered only enslavement to sin. She trembled at the thought, knowing how many had been led away from the truth, their eyes veiled by the great deceiver's handiwork.

Her unease deepened when she thought of her boss, who had recently taken to burning sage in the office, convinced it would ward off demons. It was becoming a common practice in the world around her—people believing that natural herbs, crystals, or rituals could protect them from dark forces. The idea that sage could somehow cleanse the space, ward off evil spirits, or purify the atmosphere was nothing more than a misbelief. In truth, burning sage did nothing to protect anyone because it wasn't the herb that held power.

Jayne was sure that Satan, who reveled in these misconceptions, was laughing behind it all. The notion that a simple, earthly thing like sage could repel the demonic was absurd. Demons were not driven away by herbs or incantations; they were only afraid of one thing: the name of Jesus Christ. His power alone could cast out evil, but the world had turned its back on that truth, seeking refuge in misguided remedies that did nothing but keep them in the clutches of deception. It was heartbreaking to watch, knowing how easily people were led astray, while the only real protection—the true power—was available to them, waiting, if only they would turn to Christ.

In that moment, Jayne's heart ached with sadness and a profound sense of disturbance. The world around her had transformed into a twisted reflection of what it once was, her fears pressed down further, heavy and relentless. Each breath felt like a struggle, as she grappled with the unsettling truth that the worst was yet to come.

Jayne's reflective silence was violently interrupted by a resounding crash that echoed through the house, yanking her back to reality.

The lights flickered once, twice, then succumbed to darkness, leaving them enveloped in an unsettling quiet—except for the sudden bark of the dogs, their sharp voices cutting through the stillness. She felt her heart quicken, instinctively looking to the window, though the boards obscured any view of the outside. The howling wind had intensified, its fury now matched by the deep rumble of thunder that rolled ominously in the distance.

"Is everyone OK?" Lawson's voice cut through the dimness.

Jayne nodded, though the gesture was lost in the shadows. Her mind raced with thoughts of what could have caused the crash on the generator outside. Had a tree fallen, or was it something else entirely?

"Let me grab some candles and flashlights," Jayne said, rising from her chair. She moved quickly through the darkened kitchen, her hands steady as she located the candles and matches. Lighting them, she felt a small sense of reassurance as their warm glow filled the room.

Lawson stood by the door, concern etched across his features. "I think something must have crashed on the generator," he said, his voice low. "It's too dangerous to go outside right now."

His words only amplified the tension that had settled over Jayne. Shadows danced in the flickering candlelight, reflecting the unease that coursed through the room. She could see the worry in the eyes of her neighbors, a shared anxiety that knitted them closer in the uncertain darkness. Outside, the storm raged on, an ever-present reminder of the chaos unfolding beyond their fragile walls.

The darkness wrapped around Jayne, suffocating and oppressive. With the lights out, the house felt adrift in a turbulent sea, the howling wind outside transforming into a menacing roar. It echoed through the walls, a simple reminder of nature's unbridled power. Jayne sat beside the dogs, her hands gently resting on their backs, offering quiet comfort as they trembled at her side.

Rain slammed against the windows, relentless and aggressive. The sound was unyielding, a grim backdrop to the rising fear Jayne could sense in the group. They could hear the wind howling, a voice that seemed to mock them, whispering threats through the crevices of the old house. Shadows flickered ominously, creating distorted shapes that danced across the walls.

Jayne's heart raced, thumping against her ribs in response to the hurricane just outside. The storm felt personal, as if it aimed to tear apart their sense of safety, piece by piece.

"Is it supposed to be this bad?" Maria's voice trembled, barely audible over the howling wind. The question hung between them, its gravity settling in the silence indoors.

Sophie shifted nervously. "What if the roof gives in?" she muttered, glancing toward the boarded windows, as if expecting them to splinter under the assault. The wind responded with a fierce gust, rattling the shutters like an ominous warning.

They huddled close, the warmth of their bodies a fragile comfort against the penetrating chill that seeped into the room. Each crash of thunder reminded them of their vulnerability, each blow of the wind a looming threat. Jayne felt a sinking realization: They were caught in a waking nightmare, and the darkness was just the beginning.

Time dragged on, each minute stretching into eternity. The storm made the world outside feel distant; their reality was reduced to flickering shadows and hushed whispers. When Jayne pulled out her phone and noticed cell service was down, she felt cut off from the outside world, left to contend with her fears in isolation.

As the hours dragged by, Jayne heard the sounds of the storm outside ebb and flow, soft whispers of wind swelling into a tumultuous roar, only to recede once more. It was the hurricane's bands, coming and going, their rhythmic motion creating a haunting symphony of nature. Jayne listened as the winds softened, then gradually built in intensity, each swell mirroring the rise and fall of an orchestra tuning for a performance.

As the winds outside oscillated, Jayne found herself drifting into a cherished memory, one that felt so long ago but was as vivid as the storm raging beyond her walls. She could almost see the stage bathed in warm light and the hushed anticipation of the audience, their eyes fixed on the performers ready to weave magic through music. It was a night she had held dear—the evening Lawson had surprised her with tickets to the Houston Symphony for their anniversary. The symphony, *L'Italiana in Algeri* overture, had begun with delicate strains of violins that filled the hall, creating an atmosphere electric with possibility.

The memory washed over her, a wave of warmth and nostalgia. She recalled how the music had wrapped around her like a soft embrace, beginning gently before rising to a grand crescendo that filled every corner of the theater. The instruments seemed to dance, each note building upon the last, much like the wind now rushing against her home. She remembered the way the audience swayed in unison, their hearts lifted by a shared experience that transcended the mundane. Even Lawson, who usually kept his emotions close, had allowed himself to be swept away in the magic of that night.

In the enveloping darkness, the rhythmic patterns of the storm mirrored the emotions she had felt in that concert hall, blurring the line between the pandemonium outside and the beauty of the music. The storm became a living entity, echoing the raw emotions that had once captivated her in the symphony. In that moment, the outside world faded, and she clung to the memory—a beacon of light amid the uncertainty that surrounded her.

The morning light seeped through the boarded-up windows, illuminating the dust motes drifting in the stillness as Jayne blinked. Lawson leaned over and gently shook her shoulder, further rousing her from an uneasy slumber on the couch.

"Jayne, sweetie, wake up," Lawson said quietly. "The storm has passed."

As she stirred, the haze of sleep began to clear. Landon, Sophie, and Andrew were sprawled on air mattresses nearby, finally asleep after a night of unrest. The storm had kept them awake for hours—its winds howling, windows rattling—until the bands finally loosened their grip just before dawn. Only then had sleep come, fragile and fleeting. Watching them now, Jayne felt a quiet relief that Andrew was staying with them. His steady presence brought a measure of calm, especially for Landon.

"What's it like outside?" Jayne asked, pushing a stray lock of hair behind her ear as her anxiety returned.

Lawson rubbed the back of his neck, his brow furrowed with concern. "I haven't looked yet."

Jayne nodded, feeling a flutter of unease in her stomach. The storm had been unlike anything she had ever known, a force of nature that left her both in awe and apprehensive. "Let's wake them up," she said, her voice thick with sleep.

Lawson approached Landon, gently shaking his shoulder. "Hey, rise and shine. We've got to see what the storm did."

Andrew stirred first, blinking as if emerging from a dream. "Is it over?" he asked sleepily.

"Yeah, it's over," Jayne confirmed, the relief in her voice tempered by the uncertainty of what awaited them outside.

Sophie sat up slowly, rubbing the remnants of sleep from her eyes. "What time is it?" she mumbled, glancing around the dimly lit room.

"Early morning," Lawson replied firmly. "We should get moving before it gets too hot."

The boys exchanged knowing glances, a blend of anxiety and apprehension shimmering between them. Sophie, obviously not intrigued, pulled the covers over her head and fell back to sleep.

Jayne rose from the couch, her limbs stiff from the uncomfortable position she had occupied through the night. She joined Lawson at the back door, where he stood with the handle poised, ready to reveal what lay beyond.

As Lawson opened the door, Jayne stepped into the morning light. The sight that greeted them was both familiar and unsettling. Their backyard, once a serene sanctuary, now bore the scars of the storm's fury.

Ancient oak trees, towering sentinels of the landscape for more than a century, lay uprooted, their massive roots clawing at the air like skeletal hands reaching for something lost. The ground was a tangle of branches and leaves, remnants of the storm that had swept through. A profound sense of loss washed over her as she surveyed the devastation.

Beyond the yard, the Brazos River had overflowed its banks, its muddy waters creeping ominously into their property. The current stretched halfway up the lawn, swirling and churning. Jayne felt a pang of vulnerability as she watched the river's relentless advance, encroaching upon the boundaries of their lives.

The swimming pool, usually a gleaming blue oasis, had transformed into a grotesque sight, choked with leaves, twigs, and debris. Jayne grimaced at the view, the realization sinking in that restoring order would be no small feat.

"Looks like we've got our work cut out for us," Lawson remarked, his voice confident despite the scene before them. Jayne nodded, feeling a mixture of gratitude for their safety and sorrow for the beauty that had been lost. Together, they stood on the back porch, absorbing the situation, knowing they would need to summon their strength to confront what lay ahead.

Just then, Trevin and Sarah emerged from the dim light of the living room, rubbing their eyes as the fresh morning air wrapped around them. As they stepped outside, Jayne saw their expressions shift from groggy confusion to wide-eyed astonishment.

"Wow," Trevin gawked. "This is bad!"

Camille and David followed closely behind, their faces a mixture of shock and concern. David's gaze swept over the yard. "There's a lot of damage here," he said, his voice steady. "We'll need to get to work as soon as we can."

"Definitely," Camille added, glancing at the toppled trees that had stood for generations, their roots exposed like forgotten memories. "It's hard to believe how quickly everything changed."

Nearby, Maria and John stood hand in hand, their fingers intertwined as they surveyed the wreckage. "I'm just grateful the house is still standing," Maria said, her voice tinged with disbelief. "We were lucky."

"Lucky, indeed," Jayne echoed, her heart swelling with relief even as sorrow for the lost trees tugged at her. "But there's so much to clean up."

The group gathered in somber silence. They were alive, they were safe, but the world they knew had been irrevocably altered. Together, they shared a moment of gratitude amidst the wreckage. Jayne knew their bond was strengthened by the trials they faced even as the echoes of the storm still whispered through the air.

By midday, most of the aftermath of the storm still covered the ground. From across the yard, Jayne paused to watch Lawson standing in the harsh sunlight, sweat trickling down his forehead as he held a chainsaw. The machine's roar broke the stillness that enveloped their neighborhood, underscoring the hard work ahead.

Landon and Andrew, clad in well-worn jeans and sturdy boots, were busy prying boards from the windows. Each creak of the wood felt like a release to Jayne, as they unveiled the battered landscape outside.

As Lawson set down the chainsaw next to pieces of a massive oak, he glanced at the generator, now useless beneath a thick limb that had crashed down during the storm. "Well, that was nice while it lasted," he muttered, a tinge of sarcastic frustration creeping into his voice.

"Tonight's meeting is still on at Trevin and Sarah's," Jayne announced, wiping her hands on her jeans as she approached Lawson, who was surveying the yard with exhaustion on his face. "It's a little earlier today, though, since the power's out. We don't want to sit in the dark all night."

Lawson hesitated, running a hand through his hair. "I don't know, Jayne. I'm wiped out. We've got a lot of work to do out here."

Jayne placed a reassuring hand on his shoulder. "I get it, but we need to talk about what's been happening in the neighborhood—break-ins, thefts. David has some important updates to share."

He let out a long breath. "Do you think anyone will even go?"

"I think they will. It's important for us to stay connected right now," she said. "Why don't you take a quick shower? I think it will help." She pinched her noise and smiled.

Lawson rolled his eyes in return. "You're right." With a reluctant nod, he turned toward the house.

The atmosphere hummed with a mix of exhaustion and unease as Jayne and Lawson gathered with the others in Trevin and Sarah's living room. The group sat close together, their faces dotted with beads of perspiration, a token of the power outage that had left them without electricity.

"Most homes weathered the storm surprisingly well," Trevin began, fatigue evident in his voice. "But there's definitely some damage. A lot of roofs need repairs, and I noticed several trees down on my street."

Sarah nodded, her expression weary but focused. "We've got some minor flooding in the garage. It's not too bad, but clearing it out will take some effort."

"We should come up with a plan for those who need assistance," Camille said, rubbing her temples. "David, didn't you mention you had some reports on the damage?"

David let out a resigned sigh. "Yeah, I put together a list of the worst-hit homes. Most of the damage is minor, but a few places might need structural checks. We'll have to figure it out ourselves; it's not like we can call for services right now.

"But we need to address the break-ins," he continued. "The thieves are becoming increasingly bold and desperate, using the woods behind our neighborhood to slip in and out undetected. They're driving their trucks right through the thicket, targeting homes at the back. It's a worrying trend, especially with supply chains still disrupted and so many stores already closed."

Murmurs rippled through the group.

David pressed on. "Our security detail has increased their vigilance. They're conducting additional watches and have blocked off access points to the woods. We've also added early detection devices that will need monitoring.

"I don't expect the power to be restored anytime soon," he said. "The government isn't offering any assistance programs anymore, and with FEMA gone, it feels like we're on our own. Even the insurance companies are turning their backs, denying claims and leaving many without support."

Jayne took stock of the group's reactions. They were obviously concerned, but there seemed to be a shared resolve. "What can we do?" she asked.

"We'll have to rely on each other," David said. "Stocking up on essentials, sharing what we can—it's all we can do."

Clearing his throat, he shifted his tone. "I've been listening to my ham radio, tuning into some special frequencies where groups are quietly sharing information. There's a lot going on behind the scenes that we need to be aware of. The government's surveillance has ramped up in ways we didn't expect. They're not just tracking our phones anymore—they're monitoring our movements in real time."

"Isn't that tracking to help keep the peace?" Sarah asked.

"They want us to believe there's peace, but it's all a lie." David ran a hand through his hair, a grim look crossing his face. "It's like the world is spiraling, and people are too caught up in their own lives to notice. It feels like we're all on the *Titanic* and just hit the iceberg—some are starting to realize what's happening and scrambling to save themselves, while the majority are still acting like they're on a booze cruise in Cancun, completely unaware of the danger ahead."

His voice dropped. "What's even more concerning is that they've expanded their reach. Drones, advanced surveillance systems, they're everywhere now. I've heard reports of these devices being used in neighborhoods just like ours. It's a chilling reality, and we can't ignore it any longer.

"We need to stay vigilant—not just against thieves and looters, but against this increasing scrutiny. I think it's crucial we keep our conversations private and be mindful of what we say and do, even here at home. I know there's a lot of wandering eyes. It's a lot to take in, but we have to protect ourselves." David glanced around, seeming to gauge their reactions as people looked at their neighbors and began to murmur.

Jayne spoke up through the hushed conversations. "I've felt uncomfortable at work for a while now. It's like there's an unsettling presence, as if I'm being watched. We've been short-staffed since so many people went missing, and no one has been hired to fill those gaps. I find myself doing double the work, and it just adds to the tension."

She hesitated, then continued. "They're starting to install cameras in the office and other devices that track our phones, but my boss won't explain why. I've been working from home as much as I can, trying to avoid being there. It just feels like we are being monitored and under constant inspection."

"The same thing is happening at my work," Lawson said, nodding. "They've installed surveillance cameras everywhere, and I can't shake the feeling that they're watching our every move. It's like we're living in a glass house."

"Reports coming in through my ham radio indicate that this surveillance extends far beyond our community," David said seriously. "This technology, though quietly integrated into our lives for decades, is now revealing its true nature. Every smartphone and device we've embraced is capable of monitoring our every move. It's a threat that we have ignored for far too long."

He paused as if weighing the impact of his words. "Calls and texts are being scrutinized, their contents archived on servers, waiting for the right moment to be used against us. Corporations have long utilized this tactic with work emails, but the new regime demands it for personal communication as well. This data isn't just for tracking; it can be weaponized to coerce compliance."

Jayne noticed a flicker of unease crossing Sophie's face. She glanced back at her phone, seeming to contemplate the implications of his words.

The room was silent as David continued calmly but with an unmistakable urgency. "They've begun categorizing individuals into risk profiles based on all this information. Those who exhibit dissent are flagged and monitored more closely. This type of AI advanced technology has been here for a while now—evolving rapidly, utilizing data to target individuals based on their beliefs, even conversations held years ago. Social media isn't just a platform for connection anymore; it's a tool for surveillance. They're analyzing our interactions, scrutinizing our posts, and assessing our affiliations. Every action online feeds their algorithms, creating an intricate web of behaviors and patterns, especially aimed at those who challenge authority. And with facial recognition technology, they can even gauge our emotional responses, constructing detailed psychological profiles."

"That sounds like a dystopian novel," Sophie said dismissively.

"This isn't some fictional idea—it's already happening," David replied. "Take China, for example. They've implemented a social credit system where a person's behavior—online and offline—directly impacts their social and economic freedoms. Everything from your financial transactions to your interactions with others is tracked and scored. If you're caught engaging in activities deemed untrustworthy, like criticizing the government or even associating with people labeled as undesirable, your score drops. A lower score can mean restrictions on travel, fewer job opportunities, or even being barred from renting an apartment.

"On the flip side, if you comply with state-approved behaviors—like staying in line, promoting government messaging, or simply keeping a low profile—your score goes up, granting you privileges. It's a surveillance state that controls every aspect of your life, and it's creeping into our own systems here. Free speech is under siege. Any notion that contradicts their agenda is swiftly silenced. Our online searches are manipulated, diverting us from the truth and pulling us deeper into a fabricated narrative crafted by those in power. They aim to shape our beliefs, steering us away from reality and toward a carefully constructed illusion."

Jayne was glad when Lawson interrupted, breaking the tension. "Yesterday morning, I found a note on my car. It warned me to be careful, to stay quiet. It felt ominous. What do they know?"

"You're not alone," David said. "We already know Jeremy was arrested a few days ago. The reasons are still unclear." A murmur of concern rippled through the group.

Jayne's gaze swept the room. She had her suspicions about who might have been the one to talk—those faces that had disappeared from their circle over time, the ones no longer joining their group. She couldn't shake the feeling that betrayal was closer than they realized.

"With everything that's happening, I can't help but think about Ruth's notes." she said. "The surveillance, the control—it seems like they're laying the groundwork for the mark of the beast that we know is coming."

She glanced around the room, searching for reactions. "I think this is the precursor of what's to come. All this tracking and monitoring is normalizing the idea of surrendering our privacy before they take it away entirely. The Constitution, which once protected us from government overreach, now feels like a relic of the past."

"It's not just happening here," Andrew said. "My parents have noted similar trends in Israel, and my brother Sam has been receiving reports from inside sources. This isn't isolated; it's a global trend. They're gearing up for the mark of the beast."

Camille raised an eyebrow. "What do you think it will look like?"

"I don't know, but it will be something they implant or tattoo in some way—something in people's right hands or foreheads, a means to track and control," David said grimly. "Without it, you won't be able to buy or sell anything, not even groceries. They'll have a way to monitor everyone."

"And the Bible warns that anyone who receives that mark is doomed," Jayne added in a soft voice. "In Revelation 14:9–10 it says, *'If anyone worships the beast and its image and receives a mark on his forehead or on his hand, he also will drink the wine of God's wrath.'* It's like choosing to align yourself with the devil, sealing your fate." Her words enveloped the room in a quick hush.

Trevin's voice cut through the murmurs, urgent and clear. "The outline suggests the mark will be mandated halfway through the tribulation, which would be in the next two years. We need to prepare ourselves, just in case it's introduced sooner."

Lawson nodded thoughtfully. "We've got to be ready to head for those caves Ruth mentioned. Our plans need to be solid, and our supplies in order."

David shifted in his seat, his expression serious. "I've been monitoring chatter on my radio. There's an underground group—like an underground railroad—trying to get people to safety, away from the authorities."

Hope came alive in Jayne as the idea of an underground network sparked possibility.

"Then, should we head to the caves now?" Trevin asked, urgency lacing his words.

"They aren't ready yet." David shook his head. "They're stocking supplies for an expected influx. If we move too early, we could deplete their resources. Let's stick to our plan and remain alert. I'm working on securing safe stops along the way."

The group fell silent, and Jayne absorbed David's words. The caves represented safety, yet patience was essential.

Camille broke the stillness. "We're almost halfway through the first half of the tribulation. The first seal—the rise of the Antichrist—is upon us. The second seal, symbolized by the red horse, brings war, and we're witnessing that unfold."

She took a moment, scanning the faces around her. "The third seal, represented by the black horse, signals famine and disease. We've all been seeing reports of widespread starvation affecting nations worldwide, along with outbreaks of diphtheria and measles spreading quickly. And the rise in mpox cases is equally concerning."

A soft murmur swept through the group, and Jayne recalled the recent lockdown sparked by the Marburg virus. The emergence of COVID-19 had merely foreshadowed the turmoil they now endured.

"Then there's the pale horse, representing death. Many will succumb to these diseases and famine," Camille added.

"What comes after the pale horse? I can't remember. What's the next seal?" Maria's voice broke the tense silence from the back of the room, steady but laced with worry.

Camille exchanged glances with the others. "The fifth seal reveals the martyrs—the souls of those slain for their faith."

"And what about the sixth seal?" Landon asked, his voice barely above a whisper.

Jayne opened her Bible, her fingers brushing over the pages until she found the passage about the sixth seal. "Revelation 6:12–13 states, '*When he opened the sixth seal, I looked, and behold, there was a great earthquake, and the sun became black as sackcloth, the full moon became like blood.*' " She shuddered as she considered the implications. "Ruth's notes indicate this is likely nuclear war. The imagery of cosmic disturbances—darkened suns, blood-red moons, and falling stars—suggests the world is on the brink of destruction."

She glanced around at the group. "What's important to remember is that while the first six seals are presented in chronological order, they can unfold throughout the entire tribulation. It isn't until the next set, the trumpet judgments, that we see events occurring in a strict sequence. These next judgments will be the fallout from the nuclear war that's coming soon."

No one spoke, her words hanging in the air like an impending storm. Jayne's eyes narrowed as she flipped to the next passage.

She took a deep breath. "And then we have the seventh seal," she said, her voice barely above a whisper. "Revelation 8:1 reads, '*When the Lamb opened the seventh seal, there was silence in heaven for about half an hour.*' It's as if God is taking a moment—a pause—giving people a chance to catch their breath momentarily … and repent."

She looked around the room, her gaze steady as she absorbed the weight of the moment. "The Bible suggests that this half hour of silence could symbolize about six months. It's not just a brief pause; it's a significant period of reflection before the next wave of judgments begins."

"We need to keep doing what we're doing," Lawson interrupted. "When the time comes, we need to be ready to leave." He looked around, meeting the eyes of each neighbor. "Things are likely to worsen, and we have to prioritize our safety. Let's promise to communicate if we notice anything unusual. Listen to David—be mindful of what you say and do on any devices, and watch who you confide in. Keep our discussions private and limit conversations with outsiders to what's necessary."

A collective weariness seemed to settle over them as they all agreed with Lawson's words, a combination of the recent discovery along with the fatigue from the day's labor. Evening was approaching, and the room grew dimmer as Jayne realized it was time to retreat into the comfort of their own homes.

"Let's reconvene tomorrow," she suggested, her voice a soothing balm amidst the growing unease. "We can tackle the rest of the debris and mess from the hurricane together."

With nods of agreement, they began to gather their things. Jayne hoped the promise of the next day offered a glimmer of hope, encouraging them to be resolute in facing the days ahead.

As Camille began to lead them in prayer, her voice rose softly, weaving through the dimly lit room. Jayne closed her eyes, allowing the familiar rhythm of the words to wash over her. In that moment of collective devotion, a profound sense of gratitude enveloped her. She reflected on the people gathered around her—friends who had become family, each one a beacon of support in these turbulent times.

Thoughts of her loved ones wrapped Jayne in a comforting warmth. Amidst the uncertainty, their bond felt like a lifeline, anchoring her through the storm. As Camille's voice resonated around her, Jayne silently offered her own gratitude and prayers, asking God to use her as a vessel for Sophie or to send someone into her daughter's life who could guide her toward Christ and salvation.

CHAPTER NINE

FAITH UNDER FIRE

3 ½ years since start of tribulation

Lilah knelt in her garden, the earthy scent of freshly turned soil mingling with the sweet perfume of blooming rosemary and lavender. March had wrapped the Israeli countryside in a gentle embrace, where the sun dipped low in the sky, casting a golden light over the landscape. A soft breeze whispered through the citrus trees, carrying the intoxicating fragrance of their blossoms, while the distant notes of birdsong floated through the air, weaving a tapestry of sound that echoed the beauty of the season.

Lilah paused, her eyes drawn to the delicate sight before her. The small fingers of a child, soft and unblemished, curled around a ripe tomato, their gentle pressure squeezing it slightly as Lilah marveled at the simple beauty of the moment. The child's innocent fascination with the world around her stirred a warmth in Lilah's heart, a pure, quiet reminder of life's continuity amidst the unrest surrounding them.

She remembered the day of the child's birth, two years ago. It had been one of those soft, slow evenings when the rain fell gently outside, its rhythm matching the rhythm of life within. The men had gone hunting, leaving the women to prepare the evening meal in the warmth of the kitchen. Miriam and Lilah had gone to the main house to check on Adina, carrying food for her.

As they stood before Adina's bedroom door, they could hear the soft sound of her moaning from within. A few moments passed and they gently pushed the door open. The dim evening light filtered across the room, casting a soft glow on Adina's small form. She lay in bed, writing with each wave of pain, her fist pressed tightly against her mouth in an attempt to stifle the sounds of her labor.

Together, Lilah and Miriam prepared the room, setting up everything they needed for the birth. The night stretched on, with only the sounds of Adina's struggle and the steady fall of rain to accompany them. They stayed close by her side through every moment, providing comfort and support as the hours passed.

When dawn finally broke, the first rays of light found their way through the window, and the room seemed to hold its breath. There, in the dim morning light, Lilah looked down at the sleeping infant nestled warmly in Adina's arms. The baby's long, dark lashes lay gently against her skin, and her soft brown hair framed her angelic face. Her cheeks were like roses, flushed with the sweetness of new life.

Exhausted, Adina had whispered, "We will call her Shay, our little gift from God."

Shay had grown into their bright light—sweet, tender, and ever curious, exploring the world around her. Everyone adored her, vying for her attention, but she always seemed to rush toward Sam, eagerly greeting him whenever he came over.

Just as Lilah's mind lingered on the sweet memory, her phone buzzed sharply, pulling her back to the present. She glanced down. With a sense of urgency, she gestured for Miriam to take Shay, and Miriam, without hesitation, scooped the little girl into her arms.

Lilah answered the call, her fingers trembling slightly as she brought the phone to her ear, never knowing what news each call from him might bring.

They exchanged greetings—Andrew assuring her he was OK, and she telling him how much she missed him.

After a moment, her tone shifted. "We shouldn't have stayed, Andrew. I'm so sorry we aren't there with you. Things are falling apart. They've grounded all Jews from flying, and now they're registering us for a census. With our dual citizenship, we're trapped here."

She had thought her stay would be short, and she was initially filled with excitement at the prospect of witnessing the temple's rebuilding. The idea of participating in sacrificial offerings, a long-lost heritage, had once thrilled her. But since Samuel shared the truth of Christ with them, everything had changed. The rituals that once held so much promise now felt irrelevant, like shadows fading against the light of her newfound faith.

Silence enveloped them. Lilah felt the yearning to see her son. "I thought this was temporary, but it's like we're being cornered. I never imagined it would come to this."

"Mom, tread lightly with your words. The airwaves can carry more than just sound," he warned, his voice a cautious but sharp whisper. "Keep your thoughts wrapped tight."

She nodded, though he couldn't see her. "I know. I'll be careful. But it's hard not to feel hopeless." She scanned the garden, ensuring their words were private. "I wish I could just leave, but it feels impossible now."

"Stay strong," Andrew urged. "Our family is there. Lean on them. I'm with you, even from afar."

As they spoke, a breeze rustled the leaves, a soft reminder of resilience amid the unrest. "I'll try," Lilah replied, her voice steadier. "But it feels like the walls are closing in."

"Take it one day at a time," he said before his voice turned serious. "Mom, I'm OK. We have a plan in place, but it's crucial that you understand I might not be able to contact you for a while."

Lilah's heart tightened at the thought. "I knew this was coming, but it doesn't make it any easier, Andrew. Please be careful."

"I will. Just remember, I can't share all the details right now," he said, cautiously yet reassuringly. "You know why."

She nodded, understanding their situation. "We have a plan too, with Miriam and Adina's family. Your dad and Sam are involved, and we're ready to move when the time comes."

"Good," Andrew replied. "Please be careful. I love you."

Lilah felt a mix of worry and pride for her son, knowing he was facing challenges she could only imagine. The distance between them felt unbearable, yet she drew strength from their shared determination.

With a heavy heart, Lilah ended the call and gazed at her garden, once a sanctuary but now tinged with despair. The vibrant spring blooms stood in contrast to her growing unease. She straightened her back, resolved to protect her family and face the uncertainty ahead.

With her knees sinking into the soft earth, Lilah immersed herself in the garden's embrace. She worked diligently, preparing for the days ahead. They had butchered chickens, and drying strips of meat, carefully seasoned, were laid out under the warm sun to dehydrate. She had set aside baskets filled with vegetables—tomatoes, peppers, and squash—and sliced them into thin pieces before laying them on trays to dry, the colors vivid against the dull wood. She recalled the time spent storing seeds for the future, tucking them into small, labeled envelopes. Each seed represented hope, a promise of sustenance in the challenging times they anticipated. She could almost hear the whispers of her ancestors, echoing through the generations, reminding her of the importance of preparation and resilience. This ritual was not merely a chore; it was a way of holding onto life.

Three years had slipped by in a blur, and the thought of missing so much with Andrew gnawed at her heart. Birthdays, milestones, the simple joy of shared meals—all of it felt distant now, overshadowed by what was to come. Each bite felt like a reminder of the moments she longed to share, a poignant blend of hope and sorrow.

Lilah paused, wiping her brow and gazing out at the horizon. She cherished the vital life around her, yet a profound sadness settled within.

✳ ✳ ✳

As Lilah approached the house, her basket brimming with fresh vegetables and fragrant herbs, she noticed Adina and her husband, along with Ezra, gathered in the living room, their eyes fixed on the flickering screen. The voice of her son echoed from the TV, announcing the recent arrival of Nero Kesar in Israel. A buzz filled the air, yet the excitement felt hollow; people discussed his visit with fervor, eager to welcome him to the temple, blind to the dark intentions lurking beneath the surface.

Ezra shook his head. "This is bad news," he muttered. "They don't even realize he's here to establish his reign in the temple."

Suddenly, the broadcast shifted to disturbing reports of escalating violence across the nation and the world. Lilah watched as images flickered on the screen—rebellious scenes of Christians being captured and brutally killed, their cries lost in the din of a world descending into madness. Flames engulfed churches, their steeples collapsing like fallen giants, while hordes of people surged through the streets, fueled by a frenzy that seemed to drown out any remnants of civility. The graphic footage displayed bodies strewn carelessly. Outside the temple walls, the violence intensified, but the Jews within seemed undeterred, continuing their worship, detached from the chaos just outside.

Sam spoke clearly as he reported on the unsettling alliance forming between the Pope and various religious leaders around the globe, all echoing the troubling sentiment that there were many paths to salvation. Lilah reflected on the fact that the Catholic Church, once a bastion of faith, had strayed far from its roots, now embracing a pluralism that contradicted its teachings. Idolatry resurfaced with alarming enthusiasm as people flocked to altars adorned with trinkets and images, worshipping anything that promised solace. In this age of spiritual anarchy, the world seemed to have returned to the days of Noah, where faith in the one true God had been supplanted by a lawless blend of beliefs. Anything went, it seemed to her, except for the message of Christ's love and hope for humanity.

Lilah turned away from the TV, the heaviness of the news weighing heavily upon her. She joined Miriam and Shay in the kitchen, where she could still hear Sam's reporting but the comforting aromas of garlic and onions sizzling in olive oil filled the air. Together, they began to prepare dinner, a spread steeped in their culinary traditions.

The rest of the family sat in silence as Sam continued his broadcast. "Nero Kesar has just arrived in Israel, a move that's only heightened the tension already gripping the world. With the growing unrest, his presence here seems to fuel the fire. Despite the chaos, however, the Israeli government has rolled out the welcome mat—"

Sam stopped mid-sentence. From the kitchen, Lilah curiously leaned around the corner to catch a glimpse of the TV. His face had gone pale, eyes fixed on the screen in disbelief.

He shifted his weight uncomfortably, his gaze flickering between the camera and whatever new information he was receiving in his earpiece. A moment passed. Then, his voice dropped, barely audible. "I … I'm just getting word … Oh my gosh … We've just learned that Nero Kesar has been shot."

Gasps erupted from the living room. Ezra's hand shot to his mouth, his eyes wide with disbelief.

Adina's lips trembled as she whispered, "Shot? But … how? Is he …?"

Sam seemed frozen for a moment, still listening to his earpiece, his face a mask of confusion. "We don't know all the details yet … we're still trying to get confirmation …" His voice trailed off as he looked back to the camera, trying to regain composure.

Miriam poked her head out of the kitchen. "What was that?" she asked, her brow furrowing in confusion.

She and Lilah came all the way into the room just as the TV flashed the stark, red headline: BREAKING NEWS: Nero Kesar Shot.

Sam cleared his throat, his voice dropping to a near-whisper. "We now have footage from just minutes ago when Nero Kesar was shot."

The screen suddenly cut to Ben Gurion Airport in Jerusalem. Nero Kesar, flanked by his heavily armed security detail, was just stepping off his plane. The cameras focused on him as he made his way down the stairs, his stride confident and deliberate, the noise of the crowd swelling in the background. His arrival had been anticipated for days, and now the moment had finally arrived—his presence alone seemed to stir the air with tension.

But then, without warning, the footage shifted abruptly. The camera, seemingly unaware of what was to come, suddenly jerked with a sharp motion.

A single shot rang out, loud and clear, cutting through the air with terrifying precision. Kesar's body jerked, the impact of the bullet undeniable, and in the blink of an eye, he crumpled to the ground. The camera, now trembling with the operator's shock, struggled to capture the chaos that followed—his security detail lunging forward, their arms flailing desperately as they tried to shield him.

Panic swept through the crowd like a tidal wave. People screamed, scattering in every direction, their faces masks of terror. The screen flashed with raw, unfiltered chaos—shouting, running, confusion— and the once festive scene devolved into an overwhelming blur of bodies and fear.

In the living room, Lilah heard the gasps of the family fill the air, though she sensed no movement as she continued to stare at the screen, struggling to comprehend what she had just witnessed.

The camera held steady again on Kesar's body sprawled across the pavement, lifeless and unmoving. His once confident stride had been interrupted in an instant, and now he lay in a pool of crimson, surrounded by his frantic security detail. They tried to cover him and shield him from the ever-watchful eyes of the camera. But in the midst of the frenzy, Lilah became aware of one horrifying truth. As the camera zoomed in, the mortal wound was clear—a deep, dark hole at the center of Kesar's forehead, blood still oozing from it.

The air felt heavy as paramedics rushed to the scene, their faces grim as they worked swiftly, but with an undeniable sense of futility. Lilah watched as Kesar's body was lifted with grim precision, the lifeless weight of it a haunting reminder of the violence that had just unfolded. The ambulance doors slammed shut with finality, cutting off any hope of seeing Kesar rise from the nightmare.

As the vehicle sped away, the camera shook once more, then the screen flickered back to Sam. His face was pale, his eyes wide with disbelief, and for a moment, the words seemed to catch in his throat. Then, forced to speak, he let the weight of the moment sink in.

"We've just witnessed the unthinkable," Sam said unsteadily. "Nero Kesar has been shot … and we are awaiting further confirmation. This is a developing story. Stay with us."

Lilah watched helplessly as Sam stood in front of the camera, the grandeur of the newly completed temple rising behind him. The hustle of the crowd continued around him, but his focus was entirely on the earpiece in his ear.

He shifted his weight uneasily, his eyes flicking to the camera, then back to the crowd. People nearby were whispering in hushed tones, some praying, others shaking their heads in disbelief. But it was clear no one knew how to react.

Ezra leaned forward, his voice breaking through the silence. "Is he dead? His words came fast, like he was trying to make sense of it before the silence swallowed them whole. Lilah lifted her hand without looking at him, signaling for quiet. Her eyes stayed on the screen, watching Sam. He was listening to something in his earpiece, and she knew he was about to speak again.

His fingers gripped the microphone tightly. "We're still waiting for more information," he said, his voice betraying a hint of strain. "The world is holding …" Sam closed his eyes for a moment. When he opened them again, he looked into the camera, his voice lower, more solemn. "It's official," he said, his tone heavy. "Nero Kesar has been confirmed dead."

He paused, letting the words linger in the air. The crowd around him seemed to freeze in place. Some dropped their heads, others exchanged shocked glances, but all of them seemed to understand: This was the beginning of something that no one could yet comprehend.

Lilah returned her attention to the living room, which was eerily quiet, the air thick with the weight of the news they had just heard. Miriam sat in her chair, her hands still clenched in her lap, staring at the screen. Adina, sitting next to her, was lost in thought, her eyes distant. The room seemed frozen, time moving slower with each passing second. Lilah noticed the brief hesitation in Ezra's gaze as he swept over the family, almost as if he were asking a question he already knew the answer to. "So, what happens now?" he asked.

Lilah didn't respond right away, her gaze drifting from Ezra to the others in the room. When her voice finally came, it was calm but carried a weight of understanding.

"That's not the last time we'll hear his name."

She turned her attention back to Ezra.

"Revelation doesn't end here."

As the minutes passed, a quiet tension settled over the room. Lilah was eagerly awaiting the arrival of Sam and his cousins in time for dinner. While Sam wrapped up his segment at the news station, Moshe and Aharon were secretly meeting with a group of believers, sharing their message with anyone willing to listen.

Lilah threw herself into her tasks, rolling grape leaves stuffed with seasoned rice, pine nuts, and dill, arranging them meticulously in a pot to steam. The rhythmic movements of her hands offered a soothing distraction, allowing her to focus on the comforting ritual of cooking. Each roll felt like a thread weaving together the fabric of family and hope, a small act of normalcy in an increasingly tumultuous world.

Lilah also prepared crispy roasted eggplant, brushing the slices with olive oil and sprinkling them with za'atar, filling the kitchen with an intoxicating aroma. The scent mingled with the earthy fragrance of the garden. As she diced cucumbers, tomatoes, and red onions for a colorful Israeli salad, the kitchen transformed into a haven of warmth and familiarity.

An hour later, the door swung open. Samuel entered with his cousins and his cameraman Damion, their presence breaking the silence. Shay whipped her head around at the sound of Sam's voice, her eyes lighting up as she bolted toward him, rushing into his arms.

"You're here!" Lilah replied, relief washing over her.

Damion had become a familiar presence at their gatherings over the past year. His easy nature and genuine personality had made him part of their family. She felt grateful for the bond he and Sam had formed, one forged in the fires of shared experiences and challenges. The tension that had settled over the house broke the moment they entered, everyone instantly rising from their seats, rushing toward them with anxious expressions.

"Sam!" Lilah said when he didn't speak. "What is going on?"

Miriam stepped forward, her eyes scanning his face for answers. "We saw it happen," she said, her voice laced with disbelief. "We saw the footage. Kesar was shot in the head. They said he was dead."

Sam didn't answer right away. His eyes flicked toward the television, now dark and silent. A strange look passed over his face before he met his mother's gaze. "You haven't heard the news?" he asked, his tone edged with something unreadable.

Without a word, he strode across the room, grabbed the remote, and turned the TV back on. The screen flickered to life—live footage, the timestamp clear in the corner of the screen.

And there he was.

Kesar.

Alive.

He stood at the front of the new temple, greeting the prime minister and the chief rabbi. Weissman was close at his side, watching him with a look that was equal parts reverent and sinister. He praised Kesar, bowing slightly, and then placed his hands on Kesar's forehead as if blessing him—like a healer bestowing divine favor. The crowd behind them murmured in awe, the atmosphere charged with a sense of twisted adoration.

The room went still.

He was walking, talking—addressing a gathered crowd with the same commanding presence as before. His expression was calm, almost serene, his movements smooth and deliberate. The only evidence of what had happened was a small bandage over his forehead, a stark contrast to the brutal reality they had all witnessed.

Lilah's breath hitched.

Miriam took a step closer, shaking her head in disbelief. " Could it be?" she whispered.

Samuel turned to them, his voice low, steady. "He's not dead."

Shay clung to Sam's leg.

"How?" Ezra's voice was hoarse. "We saw it. The bullet—"

"I don't know how." Sam's grip tightened around the remote. His eyes stayed on the screen, on the man who should be lying in a morgue. "But we know what this means."

Aharon's voice came out hollow. "Revelation."

Sam nodded. "The beast that was slain but lived." His voice was eerily quiet, as if speaking it aloud would make it even more real.

A slow, suffocating dread crept over Lilah.

"Who can make war against the beast?" she whispered.

No one spoke.

Because the answer had just played out in front of them.

Because the moment they had feared had just arrived.

As the meal settled into a more normal rhythm, Samuel was comforted by Shay perching on his lap, being the center of attention again. Her tiny hands reached for a piece of bread, but instead of taking a bite, she held it out toward him, her face serious as if offering him a gift.

"Thank you, Shay," Samuel said with a grin, taking the bread from her outstretched hand.

But as soon as he took it, Shay's expression changed, and she quickly grabbed the bread back. With a cheeky giggle, she shoved it into her own mouth. "Mine!" she declared proudly, her eyes twinkling mischievously.

The table erupted in laughter, and Samuel, pretending to be hurt, gasped.

Shay responded by offering him a piece of her bread once more, this time with a sly grin. She held it up to his mouth, waiting for him to take a bite.

"All right, all right, little bird." Samuel laughed, leaning forward to take a small bite from the bread. "You are a little bird, aren't you?" He giggled as he tickled her sides. "That's what I'll call you from now on—you're my little bird."

Her face lit up in a big smile, satisfied with her success, and she proudly patted his cheek with her free hand, leaving behind a smear of butter.

Sam's mom shook her head with a smile. "She's got you wrapped around her finger."

Samuel grinned, brushing crumbs off his face. "I'll never win, will I?" he said, his heart full of affection for the little girl who had just stolen his dinner.

As the laughter subsided, the conversation shifted to more serious matters.

"But in all seriousness," he said, "it's incredible how our group has grown. We now have over 144,000 Jewish men across the nation coming together to support one another in faith. But we have to be careful; we're communicating through encrypted messages and frequencies. It's the only way to keep our discussions safe."

His dad looked concerned for his son. "This is dangerous territory, Sam. You know that Christians are being targeted. I worry for your safety, for all of you."

Samuel watched Moshe and Aharon exchange determined glances.

"We know the risks," Moshe said, his voice steady. "But we believe God is with us, protecting us as we witness to others. We're committed to this path."

Aharon nodded, his face solemn. "We're not alone in this. There are experienced and trusted leaders within our movement, guiding us and providing wisdom as we navigate these uncertain times."

Sam's dad leaned in with curiosity. "Who are they?"

Sam looked at Moshe before responding, "Their names are Moses and Elijah."

Ezra's eyebrows raised in surprise. "Moses and Elijah? Like in the Bible?"

"Yes," Sam said earnestly. "Moses is a scholar deeply versed in our faith, someone who can navigate the Scriptures with exceptional clarity. He brings wisdom and perspective to our discussions. Elijah, on the other hand, has this fiery passion; he inspires people with his boldness and conviction. Together, they're leading our meetings in Jerusalem, and their influence is reaching far and wide."

His mother nodded slowly. "What kind of risks are they taking?"

"Significant ones," Aharon interjected. "They're not just organizing discussions; they're actively working to safeguard our community. They constantly have to stay a step ahead of the authorities, who are increasingly hostile toward any Christian presence. Their determination is infectious. They genuinely believe they can make a difference."

"Their leadership gives us hope," Sam added. "They've brought together a diverse group of believers, and that unity strengthens us when times get tough. It's more than just survival; it's about sharing our faith and hope."

His father looked around the table, his concern evident. "It's inspiring, but it's a heavy weight to carry."

"God is with us," Moshe reassured him, placing a hand on his uncle's shoulder. "We're part of something much bigger than ourselves, and that gives us strength."

They moved on to other topics, but the influence of their mission lingered with Samuel, reminding him that a shared understanding united them as they faced an uncertain future.

A few months had passed, and the atmosphere in Jerusalem was unsettling. Sam and Damion stood on a bustling street corner, their cameras rolling, capturing the stark reality unfolding around them. Since the day Nero Kesar reappeared—after what many believed was a fatal head wound—the city had changed. The footage had been clear.

He was dead. But now, alive and stronger than ever, people had begun to look to him as the long-awaited savior. They couldn't explain it, so they worshiped it.

By his side, always, was the chief rabbi. Weissman. He moved with Kesar like a shadow, performing acts the crowds called miracles— healings, signs, wonders. Things that defied explanation. People were amazed. Enthralled. Blind.

Sam wasn't.

He knew what they were really witnessing. The false prophet, empowered not by heaven, but by hell. And no one seemed to care.

Kesar's alliance with the religious elite had been solidified, and the masses embraced it, continuing with their daily lives as if nothing were amiss. Reports of violence against Christians had surged, with radical groups actively seeking them out, their brutality now a grim spectacle in public spaces. Yet the crowds turned a blind eye, pretending not to see what was unfolding right in front of them.

The city's vibrant spirit felt hollow, overshadowed by a collective denial that allowed the horrors to flourish.

"Sam, look," Damion whispered, his voice barely audible over the noise.

Sam turned, his heart sinking as they spotted a group of captured Christians being led toward the Western Wall, their hands bound and faces marked by despair. The sight was jarring, a reminder of the atrocities unfolding in their world.

The captors shouted commands, their voices laced with venom, as the prisoners were forced into a line. Sam's gut lurched. The captured Christians—men and women alike—stood together, their expressions a blend of terror and defiance. Among them, one woman caught his eye. She stood slightly apart from the others, her features striking in their simplicity. Her dark brown hair, pulled back into a tight knot, framed a pale face, slightly freckled from the sun. She couldn't have been older than twenty, though the exhaustion in her eyes made her appear older.

Her clothing—a faded blue tunic—hung loosely from her slender frame, the fabric worn and frayed at the edges. A small silver cross glimmered softly against her chest, a bold symbol of her faith, a testament to her unwavering belief. Her eyes, dark and full of sadness, met his, and for a brief moment, time seemed to freeze. Tears streamed down her face, yet there was an undeniable serenity in her expression. It was as if, in the face of impending death, she had found a profound sense of peace.

Sam's throat tightened, the sickening churn in his stomach making it hard to breathe. His body flushed with a wave of heat, a prickling sensation creeping over his skin, as if his very cells were rebelling against the helplessness gnawing at him. He wanted to stop it—wanted to rush in and save her—but as his eyes locked with hers, what he had mistaken for fear was something else entirely.

It wasn't fear. It was something deeper. Something unshakable. In that instant, Sam realized she wasn't afraid of dying. Her calm wasn't born of resignation; it was something far more profound. There was peace in her gaze, a peace that transcended the brutality around her. A peace that no violence or hatred could touch.

She wasn't afraid. She knew where she was going. And in the face of all this evil, in the certainty of her impending death, that peace was louder than any scream, stronger than any fear. She was going home.

The captors began to taunt them, their jeers echoing harshly against the stone walls, their voices dripping with malice. They paced in front of the prisoners, their boots scraping against the stone floor, and every now and then, one would lash out with a cruel kick or shove, relishing in the fear and helplessness they caused. The captors laughed darkly as they yanked at the prisoners' hair or forced them to their knees. One man, his face twisted in sadistic glee, approached the woman Sam had noticed, and with a mocking grin, he yanked on her chain, pulled her head back, and spit on her face. "You think your God will save you?" he sneered. The others chuckled, a sickening sound that filled the air.

Damion's hands trembled slightly as he focused the lens on the woman. His camera clicked, the sound of it a quiet contrast to the shouts of the captors. Through it all, the woman remained steadfast, her lips moving in silent prayer, undeterred by the torment around her. It was a powerful image—a woman holding onto her faith in the face of brutality—a moment Sam would carry with him forever.

"Damion, we have to do something," he said, his voice filled with desperation. He felt the moment pressing down on him. This wasn't just news anymore; it was a call to action.

Damion took a step back, his expression grim. "We can't step in, you know that!"

As they prepared to broadcast live, Sam's heart raced. He knew the risks all too well, but the urgency of the situation left him no choice. The world needed to see the atrocities unfolding in their city, but more importantly, they needed to hear the truth of the violence that had seeped into every corner of their lives. His eyes flicked back to the woman, her gaze unwavering, filled with quiet strength as she stood in the midst of the chaos.

She glanced up at him, their eyes locking for a brief moment. In that silent exchange, Sam felt a deep connection, as if she, too, understood the gravity of what they were about to do.

"May God be with you," he whispered silently, hoping she could somehow feel the strength of his intention. He knew they were risking everything, but this moment was bigger than them. It was a fight for truth, a stand against the darkness that threatened to engulf their world.

As the broadcast began, the camera panned across the scene, capturing not just the evil but also the resilience of those lined up before the Western Wall. Sam faced the lens, his voice steady and unwavering. "What you're witnessing isn't just a headline; it's a profound human tragedy. These are lives hanging in the balance, and their faith is standing firm against relentless oppression."

The importance of the moment bore down on him, and in that instant, a connection with the suffering surged within him—a shared humanity that could not be extinguished by the encroaching hatred. The world needed to see this, and he was resolute in his mission to ensure they would.

He turned back to the group, and the woman's gaze found his once more. In her eyes, he did not see fear, but an unspoken truth—a quiet acknowledgment of what was happening and the power of their shared moment. It was as if she were silently telling him to not give up, to continue the fight. The brief, intense exchange between them felt like a vow, a promise to bear witness, no matter the cost.

Just then, the stillness shattered. A series of gunshots rang out, sharp and jarring. Sam's breath caught and a jolt of shock rooted him in place as he focused on the woman with the silver cross. Time seemed to slow as she flinched, her eyes widening in disbelief. The bullet struck her with a sickening finality, and she fell to the ground, the cross swinging gently in the aftermath, catching glimmers of light.

Crimson spilled forth, a glaring contrast against the worn stones of the ancient wall, painting a grotesque portrait of violence. Gasps erupted from the onlookers, but many turned away, unable or unwilling to confront the horror that had just unfolded.

Sam remained transfixed, the camera capturing every agonizing detail—the way her body hit the ground, the blood pooling around her. The world blurred into the background, his focus narrowing to the raw reality before him—a chilling testament to the brutality that had claimed yet another life. In that moment, he knew the truth had to be told, no matter the cost.

CHAPTER TEN

BOUND BY THE MARK AND THE RISE OF 666

Lawson eased into his battered SUV, the engine sputtering to life with a reluctant growl. The city outside his window told a story of decay—streets once alive with families and chatter were now lined with hollowed-out homes, their windows staring blankly like forgotten memories.

Over three years of disorder and instability had left scars everywhere, not least on Jayne. Her once-bright laughter had given way to quiet determination, her sunken eyes reflecting the toll of endless uncertainty.

Pulling out of the driveway, Lawson navigated the fractured asphalt of his neighborhood. Familiar landmarks had become shadows of what they once were. Near the exit, a checkpoint came into view. Officers Decker and Thayer stood at their post, both alert, their postures tense.

As Lawson slowed, rolling down the window, Thayer—Jake, as Lawson had always known him—stepped forward. His uniform was rumpled but still carried an air of authority.

"Hey, Lawson!" Jake called, striding over. "Where are you headed?"

"Just going to pick up some supplies," Lawson replied, forcing a smile.

Decker leaned against the patrol car, arms crossed. "You know it's risky out there. You should have someone go with you."

"I appreciate the concern," Lawson said, his voice steady, "but I need a few things. Unfortunately, I just can't wait."

Jake exchanged a glance with Decker. "Be careful. We've had reports of looting in the area. If things get out of hand, you need to get back fast."

As Lawson turned to leave, Jake called out, "Hold on a minute. I can't let you go alone. Travis is here to relieve me, so I'll ride with you."

Lawson paused, knowing Jake was right. He knew the streets were perilous, but having a cop beside him brought a strange sense of security.

"All right," he replied, watching as Jake approached his car.

As Jake slid into the passenger seat, Lawson felt a momentary sense of ease.

"Where are we headed?" Jake asked, adjusting his radio as Lawson pulled away from the curb.

"There's a guy I've been in contact with," Lawson said, keeping his tone casual despite the transaction looming ahead. "He's got some military-style gas masks that I need. In exchange, I'm trading him a half ounce of gold I've kept in my safe."

Jake raised an eyebrow. "Gold? You sure you want to part with that? It's getting harder to come by these days."

"I know," Lawson said, gripping the steering wheel tightly. "But with everything going on, I need those masks. They're critical for what's ahead."

Jake glanced out the window, the signs of a crumbling town flashing past—abandoned shops, graffiti-covered walls, and empty cars scattered along the sidewalks. "What do you know about this guy?" he asked as they neared the outskirts.

"His name's Dante. We've traded before—just supplies, nothing shady," Lawson replied. "But he's been on edge lately. Says he's worried about all the desperate people showing up. Can't say I blame him. Everyone's after something."

"Let's hope he keeps it together," Jake said with a nod.

As they approached Dante's place, the silence in the car deepened. The streets felt heavy with abandonment, a grim reminder of how quickly things had unraveled.

Jake leaned back in his seat, his eyes scanning the grim landscape.

"You see that?" he said, nodding toward a nearby alley. A group of men huddled together, exchanging furtive glances as they completed a transaction that was all too obvious. "Criminal activity is rampant. It's like the law doesn't even exist anymore."

Lawson swallowed hard at the implications. "It's sad. Just a few years ago, this place was full of life. Families, kids playing in the park …"

"Yeah, well, those days are long gone," Jake replied, his tone grim. "Most of the cops have thrown in the towel. They're outnumbered, and the rest are just trying to survive like everyone else. The city's become a free-for-all. It's kill or be killed."

As they passed the Social Security building, Lawson and Jake exchanged uneasy glances. A cluster of local officials and others stood outside, their expressions tense, and construction crews were setting up makeshift barriers and tents, hinting at something significant about to unfold.

"What do you think is going on there?" Lawson asked.

"Not sure, but it doesn't look good," Jake replied, his voice low.

Lawson felt a knot tighten in his stomach. "With everything that's been happening lately, I can't shake the feeling it has something to do with the next phase. Ruth's notes mentioned the mark of the beast is on the horizon."

"Right," Jake said, glancing at the growing crowd.

As they pulled up to the warehouse, Lawson's eyes swept over the grimy exterior and rusted metal doors. The building stood cold and uninviting. Jake scanned the area. Without a word, they stepped out of the car, and Lawson felt an unspoken understanding passing between them.

Dante appeared at the entrance, his compact, muscular frame silhouetted against the fading light. His broad shoulders and thick arms, covered in faded tattoos that traced stories of another life, flexed as he glanced over his shoulder with a sharp, nervous energy. His close-cropped black hair and scruffy beard framed a face that bore the hard edges of survival—deep lines around his eyes and a nose that had clearly been broken before. His dark brown eyes darted around, alert and calculating, before settling on them.

"Get inside, quick," he urged, his voice low but commanding as he stepped aside to usher them into the dimly lit interior. The glow of a single bulb illuminated the room, making the ink on his arms shift and blur like restless spirits.

Once inside, Dante's demeanor shifted. He handed Lawson four MCU-2/P gas masks, his voice low as he detailed their use. "Make sure the seals are tight. When you put them on, it's crucial to adjust the straps until they fit snugly. You don't want any leaks. The filters need to be replaced after a certain time, so keep an eye on them. If you smell anything unusual, replace the filter immediately."

Lawson nodded, the masks heavy in his hands. "Thanks, Dante." He slid a half ounce of gold across the table between them, grounding him amid the tension.

Dante raised an eyebrow, curiosity flickering in his eyes. "What do you need these for, anyway?"

Lawson hesitated, searching for the right words. "Just … precautionary measures. You never know when you might need them." He hoped the vague answer would suffice.

Jake, meanwhile, examined the rest of the items laid out on the table, his eyes adjusting to the dim light. "What else you got?" he asked, his voice steady as he motioned to various items scattered around.

Dante's eyes brightened with interest. "You're looking at antibiotics, some extra 550 cord, and a few weapons. I've got an AR-15, .308 rifle, and 9mm pistol, and plenty of ammo: 5.56 rounds, .308 rounds, and .22LR. For the 9mm, I can throw in some extra rounds. I also have iodine tablets, canteens, and full gas canisters—fuel's been hard to come by lately. Oh, and I've got a survival guide for the wilderness and some sleeping bags."

Lawson felt a flicker of hope. "How much for all of that?"

Dante considered it for a moment, a wry smile tugging at the corners of his mouth.

"You're bleeding me dry here," he said, letting out a low curse under his breath. "Three guns, ammo, and everything else—it's gonna cost you at least a couple more ounces of gold."

Lawson considered his remaining supplies, weighing his options. With a resigned sigh, he took out the rest of what he had and handed it to Dante. Necessity outweighed his hesitation.

Dante examined the gold, nodding in approval. "You've got yourself a deal. Just remember, out there, every bit counts."

As he began packing the items into a sturdy bag, Lawson felt relieved to finally have the supplies they needed. Each item represented a step toward being prepared for what lay ahead.

Jake curiously scanned the room one last time. "You got any NAK kits?"

Dante shook his head, a hint of frustration in his expression. "No, my supplier didn't come through. They robbed the train carrying the supplies last week. I do have one GP medium left, but it's missing a couple of poles and it's the smaller version."

Lawson was puzzled since he wasn't familiar with military jargon. "What exactly is a GP medium?"

"A GP medium?" Dante said with a chuckle. "It's a modular general-purpose tent system. They're durable and can house a good number of people. Perfect for temporary shelters or operations. You'll want one, especially if things get worse out there. Consider it a freebie. You'll need it more than I will."

"Thanks, Dante. I appreciate that," Lawson said as he began gathering his goods.

"You two planning to head out soon?" Dante asked.

Instead of answering, Jake asked, "Hey, do you know what's going on at the Social Security office?"

Dante shrugged, a skeptical look crossing his face. "Not really sure yet, but I've been hearing that the town's setting up a new system for people to buy goods. Seems like the government wants to help citizens get what they need since buying things has become so tough. It's some kind of new assistance program."

Lawson shot Jake an uneasy glance, the unspoken truth hanging between them. They knew what that meant for the future—more control, more regulation—the mark of the beast was coming in fast, but Dante remained blissfully unaware, his focus on the immediate transaction.

As Lawson adjusted the straps of his heavy pack, a sudden cold pressure of a muzzle pressed against the back of his head, jolting him into awareness.

"Don't move," commanded a gravelly voice laced with menace. "Drop the bag."

The atmosphere shifted. Lawson froze, but out of the corner of his eye, he could see Jake pull his weapon in one swift motion.

"Drop it!" he commanded, his voice steady and authoritative, cutting through the tension like a knife.

The robber, eyes wild, swung the gun toward Dante, but before he could pull the trigger, a shot rang out, striking the robber in the shoulder. Lawson turned to see his assailant stumble back, gritting his teeth in pain, but he didn't fall. Jake rushed forward, closing the distance. With a quick kick, he sent the robber's gun sliding across the floor, out of reach. In one fluid motion, Jake handcuffed the man, pinning him to the ground. As he secured the cuffs, Jake's eyes flicked toward the back of the room—just for a second—and caught sight of the door they'd come through. It was ajar. Not wide, but enough to suggest it hadn't latched. The guy had slipped in.

Lawson was shaken, his hands trembling as he processed the scene.

Dante glanced at the injured robber, still writhing on the floor, and muttered under his breath, "Man… you weren't playin'."

Then, turning to Jake with a nod of genuine relief, "Thanks. For real."

Jake raised the radio to his mouth, instinct kicking in. "This is Delta 3—"

"Whoa, hold up." Dante's voice cut in sharp, low.

Jake glanced over.

Dante took a step closer. "This warehouse is off the books. You call it in, it's gone. I lose everything. Just…think for a second."

Jake hesitated, the radio still in his hand. Years of protocol clashed with the reality in front of him. He looked at the injured suspect, then at Lawson, still pale and shaken, then back to Dante.

Static crackled.

"Delta 3, repeat your location. Do you need EMS?"

Jake pressed the button, his voice steady. "Affirmative on EMS. Suspect down. Location—uh, alley off 5th and Grant. Will meet responders at cross street. Over."

He lowered the radio slowly, eyes meeting Dante's.

Dante gave a tight nod. "Appreciate it."

"Let's move," Jake urged, glancing back toward the shadows._

Lawson quickly grabbed the supplies he'd scavenged earlier, tossing them into the back of his SUV. He slammed the trunk shut and slid into the driver's seat, his eyes darting around, ready for whatever came next. Dante took off in one direction, his expression a mix of frustration and concern, while Jake loaded the handcuffed man into the back of Lawson's car. Jake slid into the passenger seat, eyes sharp, always scanning.

As they pulled away from the warehouse, Jake glanced out the window. "Keep your eyes peeled," he said, watching the darkened sidewalks. "We don't know if that guy had any friends out there."

Lawson nodded, knuckles tight on the steering wheel. The city wasn't what it used to be—quiet didn't mean safe anymore.

As they neared the corner of 5th and Grant, the distant wail of a siren began to rise. Flashing lights appeared at the far end of the block.

"There they are," Jake said. "Pull over by the curb."

Lawson eased the car to a stop. Jake was already opening his door before the vehicle fully halted. He swung the back door open, grabbed the injured man, and helped him out. Another patrol car pulled up behind them, and a cop stepped out.

Lawson sat still in the driver's seat, his hands gripping the wheel as he watched Jake approach the officer. He couldn't hear their conversation, but he could see the way Jake gestured toward the backseat. The officer nodded, taking the man from Jake's hands.

EMS rolled up moments later, lights flashing in rhythm with the sirens. Lawson kept his gaze focused on the scene ahead, waiting.

Finally, Jake turned, walking back toward the car. He leaned down into the window. "Go on home," he said, his voice calm but firm. "I'll stay and finish up the report. Another unit'll give me a lift later."

Lawson gave a short nod. "You sure?"

"Yeah." Jake replied.

Without another word, Lawson shifted the car into gear and drove off. The flashing lights receded in the rearview mirror, but the tension of the night still clung to him, lingering in the quiet.

✳ ✳ ✳

A few days later, as Jayne filled the water bowls for Finnley and Charlie, the two dogs eagerly watched her, their eyes bright with anticipation.

Just as she reached for the dog food, a sharp knock echoed through the house, drawing her attention. She glanced toward the front door, curiosity piquing.

Setting the food down, she wiped her hands on a towel and walked to the door. Peering through the window, she saw David standing there, his expression serious. She opened the door and greeted him with a cautious smile.

"Hey, David. What's going on?" she asked, noting the urgency in his demeanor.

"I need to talk to both of you," he replied, his tone unmistakably serious.

Jayne stepped aside to let him in, her mind racing with questions. She called for Lawson before settling in the living room. Finnley and Charlie moved to rest by her feet, sensing the shift in the atmosphere.

"I've been listening to the news on my radio," David began as soon as Lawson walked in. "There's a lot of chatter from the underground groups that are trying to help people get out."

Jayne leaned forward, intrigued. "What are they saying?"

David hesitated, then continued, "It sounds like they're gearing up to put things in place for what we know is coming. It's serious. They're talking about the measures the government is preparing, and it's only a matter of time before it reaches us. It feels like there's a lot of activity surrounding the government's plans. If we don't act soon, we could find ourselves trapped here."

Lawson looked at David, his expression tense. "What are you hearing?"

David took a deep breath before responding. "The government is planning to implement the new social program for buying and selling goods. With the dollar's decline and everything else happening, they're positioning this as a way to help those who are struggling. But really, it's a method of control disguised as support, which you and I know to be the mark of the beast."

"We should've seen this coming," Lawson said, shaking his head. "The petrodollar system was the only reason America had so much global power. Everyone had to use our money to buy oil, so we basically controlled the game. But once countries started pulling away—joining up with BRICS, trying to replace us—it was only a matter of time. You know, after these last couple of years studying Bible prophecy, I've always wondered why America isn't mentioned. Now I get it. We didn't fall from an outside attack—we did this to ourselves. Our own leaders. And nobody saw it coming."

"I just drove by the Social Security office yesterday," Lawson continued. "There were work crews inside, setting up for something big. They were rearranging furniture, bringing in supplies, and putting up barriers outside to manage the long lines of people they're expecting."

David leaned in, his expression grave. "Officials are sending notices to people's phones, instructing them to go to the Social Security offices on specific days, based on their last names—A, B, C, and so on. If you don't show up within the given time frame, you could face serious consequences. They might even come to your home to arrest you."

Lawson frowned. "So, this 'government assistance program' really is what we've been waiting for?"

"Absolutely," David said. "If you don't comply, you won't be able to buy or sell anything. No more paying bills, no more groceries, and they could even take your house. You won't be able to shop at any stores since you'll have to scan for everything now."

Jayne leaned forward, listening intently as David elaborated. "The mark itself is a QR code that's digitally scanned on a person's right hand for identification. For those who can't use their hands, it's required to be placed on their forehead. It's chilling how organized this is becoming."

"What does it look like?" Jayne asked, already knowing the answer would be unsettling.

"It's a unique code for each individual, storing all their personal information such as name, address, family, religious affiliation, even their medical history and blood type. It functions similarly to a barcode, containing not just your individual Social Security number but also the prefix of Nero Kesar's personal identification number: 666."

Lawson scowled. "And that number's significance is clear."

David nodded as he continued. "It's derived from the numeric value of his name. Once someone gets the code tattooed, the office takes your personal phone and uploads the QR code. This activates the scan, enabling officials to track you. If someone doesn't have a phone, they'll be issued one. It's now illegal to be without it; they need a way to monitor everyone."

"So, when someone wants to buy something, they won't be using cash or cards anymore? They just scan their hand?" Lawson asked.

"Exactly," David replied. "And many people think it's just a government handout, not realizing the full extent of what they're signing up for."

"No, let's not forget—they will know exactly what they're doing," Jayne interjected. "This isn't just ignorance. People are making a conscious choice to accept the Antichrist. They are choosing to pledge their allegiance to him. The Scripture is clear about this."

"Right," Lawson said. "Revelation warns us about these times—how individuals will willingly accept a mark that signifies their allegiance to a false power. Revelation 13:16–17 states, *Also it causes all, both small and great, both rich and poor, both free and slave, to be marked on the right hand or the forehead, so that no one can buy or sell unless he has the mark, that is, the name of the beast or the number of his name.*"

"I've been working on plans for us to leave," David said. "The underground group has set up safe houses for people heading to the caves in New Mexico, but they're strict about who can stay and how many can be accommodated at each location. It's getting dangerous on the roads; checkpoints are appearing along major highways."

He spread out a map on the table, tracing routes with his finger. "I've pinpointed some back roads to avoid the blockades. Unfortunately, we'll need to split up for safety. Trevin, Sarah, John, and Maria will take one route and stay at a designated safe house. Camille and I will take Jake and follow another path to a different location, while you, Jayne, Landon, Sophie, and Andrew will head to yet another spot. Each group will have a separate place to stay."

Jayne frowned, processing the details. "What about the others?"

David, with concern etched across his face, gave a deep sigh and went on. "We don't have any more places for them to go at this time. They're going to have to wait here until more homes open up."

"Where is my family going?" Lawson asked.

"The first stop is a small town a few hours away called Rockdale, Texas," David replied. "An older couple there has a farm and is willing to take you in for a few days."

A sense of urgency gripped Jayne. "We need to move quickly. The sixth seal is next, and we're expecting a nuclear attack. We don't know where it'll hit, but we need to find safety fast."

David's eyes narrowed. "I know. We have to stay ahead of this. I'll inform the rest of the group about the plan and stress the need to prepare to leave soon."

David's phone buzzed in his pocket, interrupting their conversation. He pulled it out and glanced at the screen, his eyes scanning the message quickly. After a moment, he tucked the phone back into his pocket, his face hardening. He looked up at Lawson and Jayne.

"We leave tomorrow."

CHAPTER ELEVEN

BEHIND CLOSED DOORS

The old building loomed against the night sky as Sam approached, its crumbling exterior a bleak reminder of the earthquake that had rattled Jerusalem years ago. Chunks of stone lay scattered on the ground, thick with the scent of damp earth and decay. Once a beautiful gathering place, it now stood mostly vacant, its shattered windows reflecting the moonlight in peculiar patterns.

Once inside, he watched the shadows that moved along the walls as a group of men gathered, their hushed voices echoing off the cracked plaster. The candles flickered, illuminating the faces of those who had come to seek solace and strength amid the strife surrounding them. They met here in secrecy, knowing that discovery could mean a death sentence.

Sam found a spot near the back near Moshe and Aharon and turned his attention to the front of the room, where Moses and Elijah stood with reverence, their presence commanding yet comforting. Moses, with his long beard and piercing gaze, exuded a sense of wisdom, while Elijah's passionate demeanor drew the men closer. Sam joined in as the men led the group in prayer, their voices rising in unison.

"Lord, grant us courage in these dark times," Moses intoned, his voice strong. "Guide us as we carry your message into a world that has turned away."

Elijah continued, "We stand firm in our faith, united as brothers. Lord, let our words be a light to the world."

As this smaller assembly of men—part of a larger, diverse group of more than 144,000 Jewish believers—bowed their heads in solemn agreement, Sam felt the significance of their mission. Their task was to spread their newfound Christian faith in a land where such beliefs could invite severe persecution. Each man had unwavering determination and understood the risks they faced for their convictions.

As the prayer deepened, Sam could feel a sense of purpose fill the room. They were more than just a group of men; they were a movement, determined to spread hope amidst the despair. But outside, danger was closer than they knew, as whispers of betrayal began to circulate among those they once trusted.

After the prayer, Moses began recounting the stories of believers who had been martyred for their faith, his voice steady but filled with raw emotion. Each word he spoke was met with quiet attention, the men listening carefully. He reflected on the Ten Commandments, lamenting how society had strayed far from those moral foundations. As he drew parallels between the ancient past and their current reality, Sam listened intently.

He found himself pondering the origins of Moses, this enigmatic leader, a man they had known little about before now. Yet here he stood, guiding them with a wisdom that felt ancient. An undeniable aura surrounded him, an echo of a time long past, as if he were an old soul returned to fulfill a sacred purpose. Elijah stood beside him, amplifying this sense of significance, embodying a legacy of faith that connected their hearts to a greater narrative. In their midst, Sam felt the threads of history intertwining with the present.

"The mark of the beast has arrived," Moses declared. He explained how they had long anticipated this moment, now come to fruition as people willingly lined up to receive the mark on their hands or foreheads. It was alarming to Sam that so many were choosing to follow this makeshift messiah, who was, in fact, the complete opposite of what they believed. Many Jews regarded him as the long-awaited savior, while Muslims, too, were drawn to his deceptive allure.

Elijah then took his turn, his voice somber as he described the implications of the mark. "This is just the beginning. The Antichrist will soon announce himself to the world, declaring that he is the messiah. And shockingly, some will not only follow him; they will worship him. He will establish his reign in the new temple for all to see."

A leaden silence settled over the group as they all contemplated the implications of Elijah's words.

"Brothers," Moses urged, his gaze sweeping over the men before him, "stay steadfast in your faith. Cling to the Word of God and resist the temptations of the world. Protect your families. When the time comes, you must lead them to safety in the mountains."

He paused. "The Judaean Mountains await you—there, you will find refuge. Prepare now. Gather food, store seeds. Do not drink from the streams; they will be tainted, as bitter as wormwood. Instead, trust in the aquifers beneath the mountains; they will sustain you through the trials to come."

His eyes burned with intensity as he continued. "Destruction will descend upon the earth. The stars will fall from the heavens, the cities will burn with unquenchable flames, and the waters of the seas will turn to blood. The ships will be shattered, and there will be no escape for those outside. Evil will rise from the bottomless pit, seeking to lead you astray and destroy you. But I tell you, do not leave the caves. Remain hidden, for there the Lord will provide all you need."

"Endure this time," Moses said in a fervent tone, "for after the final war in the Valley of Megiddo, Christ will return."

His voice softened, but the urgency remained. "Our time with you is limited. Soon, we must depart."

A murmur of concern rippled through the group, and Sam stepped forward, fueled by desperation. "Where will you go? We want to follow you."

Moses's expression relaxed, a hint of sorrow in his eyes. "There will come a day soon when you will witness our death. The world will not mourn, save for my brothers in Christ. But do not fear or be saddened, for we will be with our Lord. They will see us rise after three days, just as our Savior did. It is then you must heed my warning: Leave everything behind and flee to the mountains! Do not look back for anything; your safety depends on your obedience."

The words struck Sam with sudden clarity. As if a veil had lifted, he saw it all—everything they had done, everything they were. Scripture, once cryptic, now burned bright in his mind. These weren't just brave leaders or faithful men. They were the two witnesses. The ones prophesied to come. The ones who would stand in Jerusalem, defying the darkness with God's authority until the appointed time.

Moses's words lingered, a solemn vow that underscored the magnitude of their situation. Sam sensed the weight of his prophecy and the trials that lay ahead. With renewed resolve to ensure what lay ahead, he knew the group was united in a mission far greater than themselves.

The hotel room was brightly lit, sunlight streaming through the large windows and casting a warm glow across the space. Sam stood by the desk, checking the time as he gathered his belongings for work. Damion sat on the edge of the bed, curiosity etched on his face—he'd stopped by from his own room a few minutes earlier, and Sam could see that he was still not ready to let the questions go.

"Hey, where were you last night?" Damion asked, glancing up from his phone. "I came by your room to see if you wanted to grab dinner."

Sam paused for a moment, hesitating. "I was at a meeting with the group," he replied, keeping his tone casual.

Damion leaned forward. "The group? What were you discussing?"

Sam took a breath, feeling an unexplained reluctance to share. "Just important matters about what's coming," Sam began, his tone serious despite the cheerful ambiance outside. "The rise of the Antichrist is imminent. He will establish himself in the new temple."

"What do you mean? What else did they say?" Damion asked, his interest clear.

Sam paused as an internal struggle took place. For reasons he couldn't fully articulate, he chose to withhold some of Moses's warnings.

"Are your parents planning to stay where they are?" Damion asked. "I thought they mentioned something about leaving when we were there last."

"They're just preparing for whatever happens next," Sam replied, avoiding direct eye contact as he shuffled through his notes.

A quiet fell over them, the space between filled with unspoken thoughts. Sam wondered if his discretion was leaving his friend feeling sidelined, but he couldn't ignore the prompting to be cautious.

"Right," Damion said finally with a trace of disappointment. "Just preparing, then."

Sam nodded, but the bright atmosphere of the hotel room felt oddly out of place, overshadowed by the quiet heaviness of their unaddressed thoughts.

More than a week had passed since Sam's last meeting, and the world had grown increasingly fraught. News reports flooded in daily, detailing a grim toll of violence and death—a constant reminder of a world collapsed.

Though Sam and Damion maintained their professional rapport at the news station, an undercurrent of tension lingered between them.

Each day, Sam felt the burden of his dual existence more acutely. The fear of discovery gnawed at him like an insistent specter, haunting his thoughts and invading the quiet moments. He couldn't shake the worry that someone might uncover the truth about his secret group, putting his family's safety at risk in a society that seemed increasingly hostile to their beliefs.

As dusk fell, Sam returned after another evening of hushed discussions among his peers. The walls of the hotel felt oppressive, amplifying his paranoia of being observed or pursued. Though he was accustomed to the urgency of these secret meetings, a feeling of unease stayed with him, persistent and nagging.

He approached Damion's door, knocking lightly, the sound echoing softly in the stillness. "Hey, you in there?" he called out, hoping for some semblance of normalcy.

Silence met his inquiry, stretching into an uncomfortable pause. Sam knocked again, a bit harder this time. The absence of a response sent a flicker of disappointment coursing through him. He had hoped they could share a meal as friends.

With a sigh, he turned away, glancing down the dimly lit hallway. He wrestled with the guilt of keeping Damion in the dark about the meetings. He rationalized it as a protective measure—safeguarding his friend from the potential fallout of their secretive mission.

Sam was acutely aware that Damion was not of Jewish descent and would never be accepted into the group, which was comprised solely of single Jewish men. As he made his way back to his room, the oppressive silence of the hotel surrounded him, amplifying his anxieties and leaving him to wonder how much longer they could navigate this treacherous landscape without drawing attention to themselves.

✳ ✳ ✳

"Good morning, I'm Samuel Cohen, reporting live from the steps of the new temple in the heart of Jerusalem," Sam announced, his voice steady as he faced the camera. The atmosphere buzzed with anticipation as a crowd gathered, eager to hear an important address from Nero Kesar, a leader who had captured the public's imagination with his promises of hope and renewal.

As Sam adjusted his microphone, he felt the weight of the moment. People around him exchanged excited murmurs, their eyes fixed on the podium where Kesar was about to speak. He glanced at Damion, who was adjusting the camera, aware that this event could shift the narrative in the region.

Finally, Kesar emerged, a tall figure clad in a dark suit, exuding charisma, followed by his officials, who stood a few paces behind him. The crowd erupted into applause, a wave of enthusiasm washing over the steps. He raised his hands to calm them, his voice smooth and alluring.

"Today marks a new chapter for our beloved Jerusalem!" he proclaimed, his tone infused with passion. "Together, we will build a future of unity and strength, where every citizen has a place. We must forget our differences and unite, together as one. The challenges we face are great, but together, we will overcome them."

The crowd roared in approval, hanging on his every word. Sam felt a mix of contempt and resignation; he secretly despised Kesar, fully aware of his manipulative nature. Yet he maintained a façade of indifference, knowing that any hint of dissent could expose him to danger.

Kesar's voice resonated with enthusiasm. "Together, we will forge a future that is bright and prosperous for all our citizens. As it is written in the Scriptures, *'Where there is no vision, the people perish.'* We are here to build a world with unity, strength, and hope!" His words stirred the crowd, a mix of admiration and eagerness rippling through the audience.

He paused, a subtle smile playing at the corners of his mouth as his voice took on a commanding tone. "I call on all of you to come together as one people, to cast aside the divisions that have long separated us. Let there be no conflict among you—only unity, only harmony. Together, we will create a perfect union of mind and purpose, a unity greater than anything the world has ever known."

Though his words seemed genuine, Sam knew there was a darker intention behind them. It was unspoken to the crowd but clear to those who knew that he was co-opting the sacred words of Scripture, distorting them for his own ends. He wasn't merely offering peace—he was manipulating the very principles that once guided faith, twisting them into tools to elevate himself.

The crowd, mesmerized by the cadence of his speech, reacted with growing adoration. He extended his arms, his gestures smooth and deliberate, as if to envelop them in his vision. "Under my leadership, there will be no more strife, no more division. We will forge a single will, a unified purpose, with all of us bound together in one destiny—my destiny. Together, we will build a future of strength, peace, and prosperity."

Sam realized the words Kesar spoke were not his own; they were taken from a place of divine truth and reshaped for his personal ambition. And while the people before him heard only promises of salvation, he knew exactly what he was doing: using faith to bind them to his will.

After Kesar finished his speech, the crowd's reverence was evident. With a practiced flourish, he turned toward the stage, and two figures emerged from the shadows.

"And now, to solidify our unity and vision for the future, I present to you two figures of immense power and wisdom—figures who stand beside us in this great mission."

The crowd erupted into applause, their faces a blur of eager excitement. But the roar seemed hollow to Sam, distant, like it was coming from miles away. The two men moved with a quiet grace, their steps deliberate, as if they were playing their part in a terrible, twisted show. To everyone else, they were nothing more than figures Kesar had presented to strengthen his narrative—nothing more than pawns in his grand performance.

Kesar stood tall, smiling with smug satisfaction, his eyes gleaming with arrogance. He raised his hand in an almost theatrical gesture, his voice a smooth, hypnotic baritone. "And now, to seal our vision for a new world, I give you these two great men—Moses and Elijah!"

The crowd applauded louder, their cheers echoing off the walls. Sam could feel his breath catch in his chest. *Moses* and *Elijah*. He knew them—trusted them, fought beside them. They were not supposed to be here. They were his leaders, his mentors. But now, they stood before him, placed under Kesar's control like actors in a grotesque play.

The two men stood there, their faces still, unreadable. He tried to make sense of it, but the crowd's adoration drowned out every other thought. Kesar's voice cut through the rising applause and cheers, smooth and confident. "Together, we will usher in a new era—a world united, free from division. These men stand with me, and together, we will rebuild the world in our image."

Sam's stomach turned. Why were they standing with him? Moses and Elijah—he was sure it was them. But this didn't make sense. Confusion swirled in his mind. What was happening? None of it made sense.

But then, the air shifted—like a storm cloud snapping the peace of a warm afternoon. The sound of gunfire rang out, sharp and brutal, slicing through the air like the crack of thunder. The crowd froze, their gasps hanging in the air.

Sam turned, his eyes instinctively following the source of the noise. And then he saw it—the two men who had walked onto the stage moments ago were now crumpling to the ground, their bodies collapsing like ragdolls. The gunshots had torn through them with brutal precision. The crowd screamed, scrambling in every direction, but Sam couldn't tear his eyes away. *Moses* and *Elijah*, the men he had followed, the men who had once spoken the truth, now lay lifeless, blood pooling on the stage beneath them.

The crowd around him was a blur; Sam couldn't move. His legs felt frozen, his mind numb. There, in front of him, the final, horrible truth was unfolding. *They were dead.*

Kesar remained still, a cold smile playing on his lips, watching the scene unfold as if it were nothing more than an inconvenience. The officials—his officials—didn't flinch, their faces cold and detached. The man the crowd thought of as a savior now stood in the center of it all, unshaken, as if he had orchestrated it from the beginning.

"Ladies and gentlemen," Kesar's voice rang out, unnervingly calm, "Let us not be distracted by this … momentary setback. We are here for a greater purpose. We will stand united against the forces that seek to destroy our way of life!"

He leaned into the microphone, his expression a mix of resolve and fervor. "I will not tolerate those who turn against Israel and her people. Together, we must root out those who seek to undermine our future!"

As Kesar's words grew louder, Sam became enraged. The rhetoric grew more aggressive, the implications darker.

"I call upon each of you to join me in this mission. I will issue new orders to seek out anyone meeting in secret. Those who are found will face execution on the spot! These traitors"—he gestured disdainfully toward the fallen bodies—"were part of a clandestine group that has betrayed us."

Sam's heart raced as he absorbed Kesar's words, the power of their ramifications sinking in. This was no mere rally; it was a call to arms. As Kesar continued to stoke the flames of anger and division, Sam realized that the stakes were higher than he had ever anticipated. The atmosphere crackled with tension, and he understood that he stood at a dangerous crossroads—one that could forever change the course of his life and the lives of those he loved.

He glanced at Damion. The camera was still rolling, but instead of filming the stage, Damion had turned it toward Sam. He was waiting for him to speak, to report—but Sam couldn't find the words. He felt the disbelief in his own eyes, the shock rooting him in place, his mouth slightly open, frozen. He didn't speak. For a moment, neither of them did. Then, silently, Damion stopped the recording and slowly lowered the camera. The bewilderment on Sam's face was mirrored in Damion's, but there was something deeper—a flicker of betrayal in Damion's eyes that sent a chill through Sam.

Damion, visibly shaken, held the camera down, his gaze fixed on the ground. Sam could feel the tension in the air, the gravity of the moment settling heavily between them. Damion's face instantly showed remorse as he looked up, and he mouthed, *I'm so sorry.*

"What did you do?" Sam demanded, confusion and anger rising within him.

"I'm so sorry, Sam. I had no choice," Damion replied, his voice barely above a whisper, but it struck Sam like a thunderbolt.

Before he could process the implications of Damion's words, instinct kicked in. Sam took off running, adrenaline surging as he sprinted toward his parents' house. Each step was fueled by a desperate need to protect them, a primal urge to shield his family from whatever storm was brewing on the horizon.

His mind raced with questions, but all he could focus on was reaching home. The streets blurred around him as he pushed through the thrumming fear in his chest, the urgency of the moment propelling him forward.

CHAPTER TWELVE

INTO THE WILDERNESS

As Samuel tore through the narrow streets, his heart pounded in his chest, each beat echoing the panic surging through him. The world around him blurred, but the image of betrayal and bloodshed clung to his mind, making every shadow seem dangerous. He pushed himself to run faster, desperate to escape the scene that had just unfolded, but the deeper he ran into his thoughts, the heavier his legs felt.

With every step, an uneasiness grew within him—a strong sense that something was wrong at home. He thought about the times spent with his family, the laughter and warmth that now felt so distant. Were they safe, or was he heading toward a devastating truth? The questions drove him forward, his mind racing with possibilities. He pressed on, feeling the weight of the situation and the isolation of the moment, knowing he had no choice but to face whatever was waiting for him.

Finally, as he crested a small hill, the familiar outline of his family's house came into view, nestled quietly among the trees. Relief swept over him momentarily, easing the fear that had gripped him. For a brief moment, he let himself believe that everything might be OK—that his family was inside, safe and unaware of the chaos he had just escaped.

As he drew closer, a sliver of hope took hold. The surroundings were calm, untouched by the upheaval of the city, and there was no sign of officials. It felt like a haven, a place where the outside world couldn't intrude.

But as the front of the guest house came into view, Sam's steps slowed. He focused on the door, which hung slightly open, swaying faintly in the breeze. He glanced around, scanning the yard and windows, but nothing moved. The house stood unnervingly still.

He stopped just short of the porch, his eyes fixed on the dark interior beyond the doorway.

"Mom? Dad?" he called out, his voice steady but low. No response.

The open door seemed to both invite and warn him. Swallowing hard, he stepped inside, listening intently for any sound. The silence was suffocating, thick with an unnatural stillness. There was no Shay, no little girl rushing toward him with her usual excitement. Where was everyone? An ominous feeling crept over him as he cautiously moved farther inside.

He made his way through the kitchen, which appeared untouched and eerily clean, as if time had frozen. The contrast of the pristine space against his growing unease unsettled him further. Moving into the living room, he was struck by the flickering light of the television, where clips of Kesar were being broadcast, interspersed with footage of Moses and Elijah —now shown lying lifeless in the street, their bodies having been moved there after the attack—taking him back to the horrors he had witnessed minutes before.

Pushing through, he ventured down the hallway, peering into each bedroom, calling out for his family with increasing desperation. Each empty room deepened his anxiety. Where were they?

Sam stepped back into the living room. The silence was staggering. A dark shape outside caught his eye. He turned quickly, a cold sense of urgency rising within him, and hurried through the doorway to the back porch.

As he stepped outside, the hair on his neck stood on end. There, face down on the ground in the yard, lay his father, their friend Asher, and his uncle in a pool of blood. The stillness around them was unnatural. Their bodies were frozen in place, limbs twisted at odd angles, their faces pressed into the dirt. The blood pooled beneath them, dark and thick. Sam's pulse spiked, and without thinking, he sprinted toward them, each footfall pounding in his ears as his mind raced to make sense of the nightmare.

When he reached his father, his stomach lurched. The stillness was too much. He doubled over, bile rising fast, and vomited onto the dirt, the acid burning his throat. Gasping for air, he wiped his mouth with a shaky hand, but his eyes stayed locked on the lifeless figure. His father was gone—irrevocably, horribly gone.

Sam's eyes landed on a crumpled note nailed to the back of his dead father, blood seeping around it. The paper bore the unmistakable stamp of Nero Kesar, stark and imposing. As he unfolded it, nausea rolled in his stomach again. The words hit him hard, each one echoing in the silence. It was a warning—a decree signed by Kesar and Chief Rabbi Weissman—detailing the grim fate awaiting anyone who practiced Christianity. Sam's breath hitched.

Then Sam's gaze fell to the ground beside his father's hand, where a Bible lay open, pages fluttering slightly in the breeze. Its presence felt like a cruel reminder of everything he had just lost.

Sam's mind raced as he scanned the yard. If the older men were gone, he couldn't help but fear the worst for the others. He called out for them, his voice breaking the quiet, but only the stillness answered back. Moving through the guest house again, he felt a growing unease with every empty room he checked.

Stepping outside the house, Sam paused, the evening air unsettlingly quiet. His eyes drifted toward the main house. Surely that's where his mom, Aunt Miriam, and Shay were hiding. He started toward it but froze mid-step, his gaze drawn to the nearby stairs. There, slumped against the porch of her home, was Adina's body. His stomach turned as he recognized her face, the awful certainty made clear—she was dead.

He forced his eyes away, fighting the nausea that threatened to rise again. As he scanned the chaotic scene around him, his mind raced. Where were the others—his mom, Shay, Aunt Miriam? And Moshe and Aharon—had they even heard that their leaders had been killed? Were they still somewhere on the property, unaware that everything had already changed? His eyes searched the landscape, flickering over the open fields, hoping for any sign of them. Then, a faint whimper reached his ears. He stopped, listening intently. The sound came again, sharper this time. Startled, he stepped back, his body tense as he prepared for the worst.

Gritting his teeth, Sam leaned down and pushed the bushes aside. His breath caught as he saw them—his mother and Aunt Miriam, crouched together, trembling, their faces pale and streaked with tears. Aunt Miriam was holding Shay tightly, the little girl whimpering softly as she clutched at Miriam, her tiny hands gripping the woman's dress as if afraid to let go. They were terrified, but they were alive.

"Mom? Miriam?" Sam's voice trembled as he pushed the branches aside, heart racing.

His mother looked up, tears streaming down her face. "Sam! Oh, thank God you're safe!"

He knelt beside them, relief sweeping over him as his eyes darted around, scanning for any sign of danger. "Are you OK?"

Aunt Miriam clutched Shay tighter. "We saw the men coming. Your father and uncle knew the danger. They ran outside, hiding us in the bushes for safety. But there wasn't enough room for all of us."

"Did they hurt you?" Sam scanned their faces, desperate for any signs of injury.

"No, we're OK," his mother whispered. "But what about your father?"

Sam's gaze flickered over the land again, his thoughts racing. He grabbed his mother's shoulders, his voice strained. "Where's Moshe and Aharon?"

Miriam's face tightened with concern. "They're still in town. They didn't come home yet."

Sam didn't respond immediately, still looking around. His mother's eyes locked on him, searching his face for answers. "Sam," she said more forcefully, "where is your father? Have you seen the men?"

When Sam hesitated, she asked again, her voice rising, "Where's your father, Sam?"

Sam's heart sank again, the weight of reality crashing back down. "He … he's gone. They killed them."

At his words, both women erupted into tears, their sobs echoing the grief that had shattered their world. Aunt Miriam, trembling, managed to choke out, "Where's Adina? Is she OK?"

Sam glanced at Shay, who was clinging to Miriam, then back at her. "She's gone, too," he said quietly, the words tasting like ash on his tongue.

Sam helped his mother and aunt out of the bushes, guiding them back inside their home. He urged them to keep their heads down, avoiding the bodies as they moved. The loss of their husbands was clear in their faces, the shock and sorrow impossible to ignore. Each step seemed more difficult for them. Sam's heart ached seeing their pain, but he knew what needed to be done now. It was time.

"Get the suitcases!" he shouted with urgency. He rummaged through the bedrooms, pulling out whatever he could find—clothes, essentials, anything that might help them survive. "Mom, grab the food and the seeds you've been storing! We need to go!"

Aunt Miriam's eyes were wide, shimmering with shock and disbelief. "No, Sam. I can't just leave my husband like this." Her voice trembled. "He deserves a proper burial." The anguish on her face was heart-wrenching, her hands shaking as she clutched at the fabric of her dress. Sam could see the disbelief holding her captive, the burden of her loss anchoring her in place.

"There's no time!" he insisted, desperation creeping into his voice. "We have to leave NOW!" He felt the gravity of the situation pressing in on them, knowing that staying any longer could mean the end for all of them.

Shay began to cry, her small body trembling as she clutched onto Miriam. Her face was tear-stained, eyes roving as if searching for her mother, but she held tightly to Miriam.

Sam's mother's eyes were wide, her breath coming in shallow gasps. "Where will we go?" she asked, her voice trembling as if she couldn't quite grasp the plans they had laid out so long ago.

Sam gently placed his hands on her shoulders, grounding her in the moment.

"Mom, remember our plans? We're going to the mountains," he said softly but firmly. "That's our only option now. We can't wait. Think about what Moses told us. After his death, the Antichrist will soon take full power and set himself up in the new temple. The mark of the beast has already spread to other nations, and it's coming for us next. They know who we are and will be back! If we stay, it will be too late."

His words cut through the air, sparking a flicker of resolve in his mother's expression. She nodded slowly.

Sam was relieved to see a newfound urgency surge through the women as they began to pack. Sam quickly grabbed a backpack and stuffed it with clothes, shoving them in with swift, determined motions. "Miriam, we can't take everything," he reminded her as she struggled to fit too many items into her own bag. "We have to travel several miles on foot to the mountains. We can only bring what we can carry."

Miriam hesitated for a moment but then nodded. Together, they moved to their secret hiding spot, a cleverly concealed cutout in the wall behind a shelf in the kitchen. The shelf was stocked with ordinary items, camouflaging the hidden compartment that had been storing their supplies for years. Inside, they found packets of dehydrated fruits, packets of seeds, and salt-dried meats—all meticulously prepared and stored away for this particular moment.

Each woman hurriedly packed her bag, gathering what essentials they could, making sure to include enough for Shay. They filled their canteens with water. As they prepared to leave, Sam saw them exchange a quick look, their faces set with determination.

Shay, clutching tightly to Miriam, cried out in a trembling voice, "Mami." With their bags packed and his resolve firm, Sam took one last look at the house before stepping out into the unknown, ready to face whatever came next.

✳ ✳ ✳

As dusk settled over the hills, Sam led his family through the rolling landscape dotted with farms and olive groves. The sun dipped low, casting a warm golden hue over the fields, and the sweet scent of ripening olives filled the air. They walked quietly, each step crunching softly on the gravel path, the day's fatigue and sorrow beginning to weigh on them after several hours of travel.

Soon, Sam spotted a sheltered nook nestled between two large boulders, surrounded by low shrubs and wildflowers, which offered a natural barrier from the wind and prying eyes. Carrying Shay in his arms, he approached the spot, his eyes scanning the area for any signs of danger.

"This will do," he said quietly, gently shifting Shay to a more comfortable position.

The ground was soft with a thin layer of grass, and the boulders provided a sturdy backrest. Sam quickly cleared away any twigs and stones, ensuring the area was as comfortable as possible.

Miriam looked around, her eyes wide with exhaustion. "It's perfect," she murmured.

As night descended, Sam watched the sky transform into a canvas of deep blues and purples, the stars beginning to twinkle overhead. He had set down their backpacks and helped the women settle against the cool stone, wrapping his arms around them to share warmth. The sound of rustling leaves and distant animal calls filled the night, creating a serene atmosphere that momentarily soothed his troubled mind.

Shay, nestled against Miriam, whimpered softly, her little stomach growling. Sam glanced down at her, realizing the hunger was becoming impossible to ignore. He could see it in the way Shay clung to Miriam, her small hands fidgeting with her dress, looking for comfort. They hadn't eaten in hours, and it was starting to take its toll on them all.

Just a short distance away, he noticed a small olive tree, its branches swaying gently in the evening breeze. "Stay here, I'll go get some olives," Sam said, standing up.

His mother, her face weary, quickly nodded. "I'll help," she replied, getting to her feet as well.

They approached the tree cautiously, mindful of their surroundings. Sam climbed up to reach the higher branches while his mother carefully picked the ripe olives within arm's reach. The fruit felt cool and firm in their hands, and with each olive they collected, a sense of normalcy returned, however fleeting.

With their newfound bounty, they returned to their resting spot. The simple meal of olives was a welcome relief. Sam took small bites, pairing them with some of the matzah they had tucked away in their bag. He savored the fresh, briny flavors against the dry, unleavened bread, reminding himself that, even in this dire situation, God still provided sustenance in the world around them.

❋ ❋ ❋

By midmorning the following day, they had already traveled several miles, the sun rising steadily and casting a warm glow over the landscape. The weather in September was mild, with a cool breeze offering some relief from the heat of the day. Despite the pleasant conditions, Sam and the women felt the strain of their long trek; his feet ached with each step, and the women's fatigue was evident.

They found a small patch of shade beneath a cluster of trees and decided to take a break. Sam sat down, his muscles sore, and wiped the sweat from his brow. The others settled around him. They ate what little food they had left from the night before, too tired to talk much, the quiet of the moment broken only by the sounds of wind rustling the leaves. Sam leaned back, closing his eyes for a brief moment of rest. When he opened them again, he noticed that Shay was no longer beside him. His gaze darted around the clearing, his pulse rising.

"Shay?" he called out, his voice tense.

In the distance, the faint sound of Shay's crying caught Sam's attention. He immediately jumped up, desperate to find her.

"Shay!" he shouted in a panic.

The women stood up at once, both looking around frantically. His mom's voice joined his, calling out her name, but Miriam was the one who followed him. He rushed toward the sound of the cry, which was growing louder and more urgent with each step. As Sam pushed through the thick undergrowth to finally spot the child, the unmistakable growl of a jackal suddenly pierced the air. The animal appeared just as it lunged toward Shay.

Without thinking, Sam grabbed a sturdy branch and swung it at the jackal, knocking it off balance. The creature yelped, retreating, but Sam didn't hesitate. He ran after the jackal and swung again, landing a harder blow that sent the jackal scurrying into the underbrush, whimpering as it disappeared.

The moment he turned, Sam saw Shay trembling in Miriam's arms, her face streaked with tears. As soon as she saw him, she reached out with both arms, her scream breaking into a desperate sob. Sam rushed to her, and Miriam gently passed the child into his arms.

She clung to him, her tiny fingers digging into his shirt. He held her close, murmuring softly as he checked her over, spotting a shallow scratch on her arm. Sam gently cleaned the wound, then pressed a kiss to it.

"Little Bird," he whispered, "you're OK… you're OK."

The moment his lips touched her skin, Shay's cries softened. Her sobs quieted into hiccups as her small body relaxed in his embrace. Sam turned to his mom, who was still standing a few feet away, visibly shaken, but relieved.

"We can't stay in one place too long," Sam said.

Gathering their things quickly, they set off again, the dangers of the world around them all too clear.

✳ ✳ ✳

After Sam and the others had walked nearly fifteen miles, the landscape slowly turned from hills adorned with lush trees and vibrant life to harsh desert sand and scattered rocks. The sun hung high in the sky, relentless in its heat, casting a shimmering haze over the horizon. Dust kicked up with every step, clinging to Sam's skin and filling his lungs, while a dry wind swept across the barren expanse, offering little relief.

Sparse vegetation dotted the landscape—scraggly bushes and the occasional resilient cactus stood as lonely sentinels against the vastness. The horizon shimmered, creating the illusion of water that was nowhere to be found. As they walked, the heat intensified, pressing down on Sam, and the sun beat down mercilessly, exacerbating his exhaustion.

Sam kept a close eye on the women, noticing the way they stumbled slightly, their feet sore from the unyielding terrain. He encouraged them to take breaks whenever they could, seeking out any patches of shade that offered a momentary respite from the sweltering sun. Despite the harsh environment, they pressed on with determination, driven by the hope of reaching safety.

As darkness settled over the desert, Sam found a quiet place to stop for the night. The air had turned sharp and cold, the wind cutting through the silence like a blade. He glanced over and saw Miriam wrapped tightly in her blanket, holding Shay close. She rocked the little girl gently, as if she were her own, brushing a hand through Shay's tangled brown hair as she slept.

Sam knelt beside them, noticing the way Miriam's eyes glistened in the moonlight. "You okay?" he asked softly.

Miriam didn't answer at first. She kept her gaze on Shay, her hand still moving in slow, comforting strokes. Then, quietly, she said, "I was just thinking about my daughter."

Sam's brows drew together. He waited.

"She was taken during the Rapture," Miriam whispered, her voice tight with emotion. "I wasn't saved then. I didn't understand any of this. One minute she was with me, and the next…" Her voice trailed off. "It took me a long time to accept what had happened. I used to talk with your mom late into the night, trying to make sense of the loss. My daughter… she's with Jesus. I know that now. I just—" her voice broke slightly, "I miss her."

Miriam fell silent for a moment, her eyes still on Shay. Sam didn't press her. The wind tugged at the edges of their blankets, but she didn't seem to notice. Her face had softened—not with grief now, but something quieter. Peaceful.

She gently brushed a strand of hair from Shay's cheek, her expression tender.

"I know now that God has a plan," she said. "And part of that is for me to care for Shay… to protect her as if she were my own daughter."

Sam watched her, the way she held the child close, rocking slightly in rhythm with Shay's breathing. He didn't say anything, but something about the way Miriam spoke settled in him. It wasn't just comfort she was giving the little girl. It was purpose. Redemption.

"Seeing all the stars is a good reminder that God is in control," Sam's mother said, glancing up at the twinkling lights above them. "I almost forgot how calming the night can be."

Sam nodded, appreciating the serenity in the moment. "Yeah, it is. It's such a contrast to everything we've been through." He looked around at the shadows cast by the flickering firelight. "I never thought I'd be camping in the desert like this."

She chuckled softly, though it was tinged with sadness. "I used to love our family camping trips. Remember how we would set up by the lake, just talking and laughing?"

"Of course," Sam replied, a smile creeping onto his face. "Those were good times. We never worried about anything back then."

He noticed that Miriam had fallen asleep as his mom's expression grew somber. "I miss those days," she said quietly, her voice barely above a whisper. "And I miss Andrew. It's hard not knowing if he's OK."

Sam could hear the worry in her tone. "I know, Mom."

She sighed, glancing down at the ground. "I just keep thinking about him out there, so far away. What if he's struggling? It's like I can't help but feel this … emptiness."

Sam reached out, wrapping his mother in a warm embrace. "We'll find a way to get through this. You and I are together, and that's what matters right now."

"And I miss my husband," she wept. "I can't shake the feeling of losing him so suddenly. How are we going to survive this without him? What if we don't have enough food to last us in the mountains?"

Sam felt the heaviness of her grief. "I know it's hard, Mom. But we have to hold onto hope. Like we just said, God has a plan for us, even when it feels impossible."

His mother paused for a moment, her gaze distant. She wiped a tear from her cheek and looked at Sam with a mixture of sadness and vulnerability.

"Sam," she began softly, her voice catching just slightly, "there's something I haven't told you. When you and your brother went off to college, things started to change with your dad. He started drinking, and we started drifting apart. I tried to hold things together, but he wasn't the same man anymore. He … he pulled away from me, and I didn't know how to fix it. Our marriage … it was falling apart. I loved him so much, but it felt like I was losing him." She looked down, her voice thin, almost lost in the air. "I honestly wasn't sure if we'd make it through."

Sam was quiet for a long moment, taking in what his mother had just said. He hadn't known any of this, and her words hit him harder than he expected. He'd seen some changes in his father over the years but hearing it from his mother's own lips—how bad things had gotten, what his father had become—it was a lot to absorb.

She fiddled with the edge of her blanket, her voice soft but steady. "It wasn't just the drinking, though. He wasn't the man I married anymore. He started drifting, not coming home. I found his clothes with strange perfumes on them. I knew. I thought, maybe, we were done." She shook her head, her eyes filling with emotion. "I loved him so much, but I didn't know what to do. And I wasn't sure if our marriage could survive."

Sam was stunned. He'd always known his father had his struggles, but this? This was something else. He didn't know what to say, so he just continued listening, his gaze steady on her face.

His mom sighed deeply, looking out into the night. "I thought maybe this trip to Israel would help. I was holding onto that hope, thinking it could bring us back together. But then—then when you started talking to us about God, about Jesus, about salvation … I began to see something in your dad. He stopped drinking. At first, it was little things—like he'd start praying in the mornings. And then we started praying together. We even started reading the Bible. Over time, he repented. For everything. I saw him change, Sam. He loves me. He loves us. And God … God gave us mercy. Our marriage was better. Better than it had ever been."

"Why didn't you tell me, Mom?" Sam felt confused and angry. "I don't understand how you could forgive him. It feels like the dad I knew is … someone else now. A stranger." He couldn't shake the sadness that grew for his mother, knowing the pain she'd endured in silence.

She took a slow breath, her gaze distant for a moment. "Because God gave me strength, Sam. It wasn't just your father who started praying. I prayed, too. And through that prayer, God gave me the ability to forgive him. If God could forgive me for all I've done, then I knew I had to forgive him, no matter how hard it was." She looked at Sam, her eyes full of quiet conviction. "I chose to forgive him, and I'm so thankful I did. It brought us closer, not just to each other but to Him. And that … that's what saved us, saved our marriage."

Sam tried processing his mother's words. The idea of forgiveness lingered in his thoughts. He had always thought forgiveness came after things were fixed, after the wrongs were corrected. But his mother's words challenged that idea. She had forgiven his father not because everything was set right, but because she trusted in God's grace to carry her through the pain.

She looked at Sam and took his hand. "I miss him so much. Without him, I just don't know how we're going to make it. Everything feels so uncertain."

He sat in silence for a moment, his mind replaying the conversation he'd just had with his mother. How would they survive this? The uncertainty, the fear, the loss—it was overwhelming. He thought about his dad, about how everything had changed for them, and about what his mother had said. She had chosen to forgive, to trust in God's strength, even when it felt impossible.

He looked up at the vast sky, searching for the right words, then back at his mother. The deep sorrow in her eyes made something in him shift.

After a long pause, he spoke softly, squeezing her hand in his as his thoughts began to take shape. "You know what, Mom? This is when we need to trust Him the most." He glanced down at the Bible in his hands, the one his father had used, before meeting her gaze again. "I'm really proud of you. God tells us to forgive one another, just as Christ forgave us, and you've done that. He's going to take care of us. I think we just need to remember Matthew 6:34—'Therefore do not be anxious about tomorrow, for tomorrow will be anxious for itself. Sufficient for the day is its own trouble.' We don't know what tomorrow will bring, but we can trust that God will provide for us today, and every day."

The next day dawned gray and weary, the sun barely peeking over the horizon. Fatigue clung to them, every step a reminder of their hunger and the distance still to cover. They took turns carrying Shay, as she soon grew too heavy for one person to carry for very far. "Just a few more miles," Sam encouraged, glancing back at the women. "We can do this."

As they trudged forward, the outline of the Judaean Mountains grew more prominent, their rocky peaks silhouetted against the pale sky. The sight stirred a flicker of hope within Sam. "Look! We're getting closer," he said, trying to infuse energy into their weary legs.

His mother squinted against the sunlight. "It feels like we've been walking forever," she replied, though a hint of determination crept into her voice.

Miriam nodded, her eyes fixed on the mountains. "We have to keep moving. It's not far now."

They pressed on, the terrain shifting beneath them. The dry, rocky ground was unforgiving, each stone reminding Sam of the struggle ahead. But as the mountains loomed closer, he felt a surge of resolve. They had come too far to turn back now.

"Just think of what awaits us in the mountains," he urged. "Safety, shelter, and a chance to start over. Come on, we can do this!"

As they approached the mountains, a narrow path wound through the boulders, hinting at a way into the caves that Sam hoped would offer them shelter. The landscape shifted from the rugged hills they had traversed to the jagged, sun-bleached rocks of the mountains, each step a test of endurance. The warmth in the air was intense, contrasting to the gentle breeze they had once enjoyed.

The heat shimmered off the ground, distorting the horizon, while the relentless sun beat down mercilessly, painting their skin in harsh reds and browns. With each labored breath, Sam could see the weariness etched on his mother's face, her lips cracked and parched. As he held Shay in his arms, he noticed his mom's hand trembled slightly, a sign of the toll this journey was taking. Miriam, her feet dragging, squinted against the glaring sun.

Then she stumbled and slipped on a loose rock. She hit her head against another stone, and Sam's heart dropped at the sight. Panic surged through him as he rushed to her side, handing Shay to his mom. He saw the way her eyes fluttered, a clear sign of how badly she was hurt. He would have to carry her, but the thought filled him with apprehension; he was already exhausted.

Just then, a ripple of voices echoed through the rocky terrain. Sam tensed, now on full alert. Was it danger? The urge to protect his family kicked in, and he stood rigid, waiting for whatever came next. As the voices grew louder, his mother's body stiffened beside him, her breath catching. Sam's thoughts quickly shifted, weighing the possibilities—friend or foe? Every second felt like it dragged on, the voices now carrying a sharpness he hadn't anticipated. He steadied himself, prepared for whatever might emerge from behind the rocks above.

Suddenly, a bearded man appeared. Sam instinctively moved to shield the women, ready to defend them, but the man held up his hands, speaking in rapid Hebrew. Sam listened intently, and a flicker of understanding dawned on him. The man wasn't here to hurt them.

"I saw you walking," the man said in Hebrew. "You need help." His voice was calm and reassuring.

Sam recognized the words, a flicker of hope igniting within him. He nodded, grateful for any assistance. The man stepped forward, offering his strength to help carry Miriam. Together, with two other men, they lifted her, and as they made their way into the caves, the shadows enveloped them, providing shade from the harsh sun outside. Inside, the cool air was a welcome relief, and Sam was immensely thankful for this stranger who had come to help.

As they entered the caves, Sam, Shay, and his mom were met with a flurry of activity. Men and women rushed to assist, their faces filled with concern and purpose. A group of women took Shay, cooing over her and smoothing her hair. A group of men gently took Miriam and laid her down on a makeshift cot. Women hurried to her side, carefully tending to her head wound, applying natural herbs with practiced hands, their movements calm and reassuring.

Sam glanced at his mother wide-eyed, then turned to take in the vastness of the caves and the enormity of the group within them. The dim light revealed a labyrinth of spaces filled with people, supplies, and the comforting scent of earth and herbs. A quiet relief settled over him as the tension that had gripped him for so long began to ease.

Men approached with water in hand, their smiles warm and genuine, offering a kindness Sam hadn't encountered in days. "Come, let us show you around," one of them said, gesturing for Sam, Lilah, and Shay to follow.

But before they turned to leave, Miriam slowly regained consciousness, her eyes fluttering open. Sam's mom rushed to her side in relief. "Miriam! You're OK! We're safe," she said, brushing a damp strand of hair from Miriam's forehead.

But Miriam's expression darkened, a shadow crossing her features. "No," she whispered, her voice shaky. "Remember what's coming next …"

The bearded man, standing nearby, furrowed his brow in confusion. He looked to Sam. "What does she mean?" he asked.

Sam took a deep breath. "We'll need to move everyone deeper into the caves soon," he explained, his voice steady. "The world is on the brink of war—nuclear war is coming."

The man's eyes widened, confused and concerned. "How do you know this?"

In response, Sam pulled out his Bible, flipping to the book of Revelation. "This," he said, pointing to the passages that spoke of tribulation and destruction, his voice firm with conviction. "We need to prepare."

CHAPTER THIRTEEN

GOODBYE FOR NOW

Jayne stood on the porch of a neighbor's house, handing over Finnley and Charlie, the two dogs she'd grown to love.

"I know you'll take good care of them," she said, forcing a smile as she passed the woman their beds and a bag of food. "We'll only be gone a few days," she added, the lie tasting bitter on her tongue.

The neighbor, a kind but sharp-eyed woman, frowned slightly. "Just be careful with everything going on right now," she cautioned, glancing nervously down the street.

Jayne nodded, swallowing hard. "We have to see Lawson's parents," she added, knowing full well that Lawson's parents had been gone for more than a decade. She could see the concern in her neighbor's eyes, but Jayne brushed it aside. "We'll be back before you know it."

As she turned to walk back to the house, her thoughts drifted to Sophie. Earlier that day, her daughter had been seething with frustration, arms crossed defiantly.

"Why can't we take the dogs with us, Mom? It's not fair!" Sophie's disappointment had cut deep, and Jayne had struggled to explain that they simply couldn't bring them and didn't have room.

Now, with her neighbor's anxious gaze still lingering, Jayne felt the burden of that earlier conversation. She wished she could take the hurt away from Sophie, but the reality of their situation seemed larger than the comfort of their pets.

Their car stood ready, bags packed and loaded. Sorting through everything they owned had been overwhelming—choosing what to leave behind and what might save their lives wasn't easy. She'd packed all the safety gear Lawson had insisted on—first aid kits, flashlights, anything he bought from Dante earlier that might help them survive the uncertain road ahead. Alongside that were clothes for different seasons, all neatly organized, a testament to her meticulous planning.

But it was the personal items that weighed most heavily on her heart. A piece of jewelry her mother had left her before passing, her mother's wedding ring, and old photographs of their parents, long gone yet ever-present in her memories. Each item carried a story, a piece of their history, and she felt those memories pressing down as she prepared to leave almost everything behind.

Jayne had decided to bring Ruth's Bible, along with the outline and notes her sweet friend had compiled. She wasn't bringing the other books—there simply wasn't room, and besides, she'd already read them all. Carefully, she hid Ruth's belongings in a compartment in the back of the car, covered by a weather mat that concealed the spare tire. She wanted to keep them safe, knowing that if they encountered any roadblocks or searches, they could be in danger simply for being Christians in a world turned hostile.

As Jayne turned the corner to head home, a jolt of fear shot through her. Military officials were gathered at the doorstep of Trevin and Sarah's house, their uniforms dimmed in the porch light. What were they doing there? "This was the last thing they needed right now. They were all supposed to meet at the designated spot soon—one final chance to say goodbye before going off-grid. A sickening realization hit her—Trevin and Sarah weren't coming with them after all.

She instinctively ducked behind a bush, her breath catching in her throat as she watched the scene unfold. The officials spoke in low, urgent tones, and Jayne strained to catch snippets of their conversation. Panic rushed over her—what if they came for her family next? As the officials began to cuff Trevin and Sarah, her stomach twisted. The finality of the moment hit her hard—they were being taken away. With trembling hands, she pulled out her phone and sent a quick message to the group:

"Trevin and Sarah just got arrested. We need to leave now."

Jayne began to cry when the doors of the military vehicle slammed shut. She had to get home. With a mixture of fear and determination, she sprinted back down the street, her mind racing. What did this mean for their plans? Every step felt heavier as the harsh reality of their situation took hold.

Jayne rushed into the house, her heart racing as she quickly scanned the street before shutting the door behind her. It was only when she caught sight of Tiffany standing on her nearby porch, casually smoking a cigarette, that a wave of unease washed over her. Jayne's stomach dropped. Tiffany had always had a knack for sniffing out secrets, and that smirk on her face confirmed Jayne's fear: She was the snitch. The realization hit hard—Tiffany had likely tipped off the authorities about Trevin and Sarah. They couldn't stay a moment longer. Jayne's instincts screamed that they needed to leave now, before the net closed in on them.

Jayne burst into the living room, breathless and frantic. "Lawson! We have to leave—now! Trevin and Sarah were just arrested!"

Lawson's face went pale, shock etched across his face. "What?" He shot up from the couch, anger flashing in his eyes.

"Didn't you see my text? There's no time to explain! Tiffany knows something and she might have tipped off the cops. We can't stick around!"

Lawson cursed, running a hand through his hair. He turned to the kids, who were now wide-eyed and alert. "Grab your things! We're leaving!"

Without hesitation, they jumped into action, gathering their essentials while Jayne hurried to the kitchen. Leaving her phone on the counter, she snatched up her purse and a few snacks, the urgency propelling her forward.

"Let's go! We can't waste another second!" she called out as she headed for the door.

They dashed outside, not even stopping to turn off the lights or lock the door behind them. Lawson jumped into the driver's seat, his hands gripping the wheel as Jayne hopped in the passenger seat and the kids loaded in the back of the Suburban.

The familiar streets blurred by, Jayne's anxiety spiking with each turn. As they reached the clearing just outside the neighborhood, she let out a shaky breath. Their friends—Camille, David, John, Maria, and Jake—were already there, looking worried.

"What happened?" Jake asked as Jayne and Lawson stepped out of the car.

Jayne took a shaky breath, scanning their faces. "I was dropping the dogs off at the neighbor's, and when I turned the corner… they were at Trevin and Sarah's house—arresting them. I don't know what happened, but I think Tiffany was the one that ratted them out.

David's face twisted in anger. "That snake! I wondered if it was her all along." The realization hit them all like a punch to the gut: This was it. They were leaving the neighborhood and the lives they knew behind, possibly for good.

Maria's eyes filled with tears as she turned to the others. "I can't believe we don't even get to say goodbye to them. What if we don't see each other again?"

Jayne hugged her tightly, and soon the women were all embracing, their sobs mixing with the somberness of the moment.

"Lawson, do you remember the route to Rockdale?" David asked, bringing Jayne's thoughts back to their escape.

"Yeah, I've got a map," Lawson replied, his expression serious.

Just then, David squinted at one of the vehicles. "Wait, is that a phone?" he said, pointing at a light in their Suburban.

Lawson rushed over and opened the door, his anger rising when he saw it was Sophie. "What are you doing with your phone?" he scolded. "I told you we can't bring them!"

Sophie looked up, her eyes wide with defiance. "I just wanted to text my friends!"

Lawson sighed, shaking his head. "No! We can't take any chances." He grabbed the phone and tossed it into the bushes.

Jayne felt a pang as Sophie's face twisted in anger. "That was my phone!"

"Do you want to get caught?" Lawson shot back, his voice stern. "This isn't a game!"

As Sophie pouted, the seriousness of their predicament became clear to Jayne. She looked around the group, a blend of fear and resolve taking root in her. This was it—there was no turning back now.

As they gathered for their goodbyes, Jayne's voice trembled. "Please, be careful out there. Remember everything we've talked about over the years. We all know what's coming. Nuclear war is looming, and we have no idea where it might start or what will be hit."

An ominous silence settled over them, and they drew closer, their shared fears apparent. "We need to try to stay in one place when it happens," she continued. "We can't risk moving around too much during the fallout. It's going to be dangerous."

Everyone nodded. They had prepared for this moment, but it didn't make it any easier.

Maria stepped forward, her eyes glistening with tears. "I'd like to say a prayer for us before we leave," she said softly. The group formed a circle, joining hands tightly.

"Dear God," Maria began, her voice steady despite the fear around them. "We come together in this moment, asking for your protection over us. Please watch over our families, send your angels before us, and place a shield of protection over each of us while keeping us safe from harm. Guide us as we navigate this uncertain future. Help us find strength in each other and in you. Help us to remember our plans, and help us to find shelter when the time comes. Please provide all we will need in the days ahead. May we be wise in our choices and strong in our resolve. In Jesus's name, amen."

"Amen," Jayne echoed with everyone else, their voices merging into a collective strength.

With a final squeeze of hands, they released each other, the reality of their separation sinking in. They exchanged tearful hugs and solemn nods, a silent promise to watch over one another from afar.

As Jayne turned toward the car, her heart felt burdened with the stress of what lay ahead. They were all stepping into the unknown, but she trusted the strength of their bond would carry them through whatever came next.

"Until we see each other again," she whispered, her voice barely audible as they drove away, each car pulling off in different directions toward unpredictable futures.

But as she glanced in the rearview mirror, doubt crept in. Would they really be reunited? Would she ever see her friends again? The lingering sense of dread clung to her, but beneath it was a flicker of determination— an unspoken assurance that they would fight to find each other again, no matter the obstacles that lay ahead in this vast and volatile world.

※ ※ ※

As Lawson drove through the desolate landscape, he gazed out the windows. Buildings that had once stood proudly were now crumbling, draped in graffiti. The schools, once filled with laughter, now looked abandoned, their windows shattered and dark.

"Look at that," Sophie said from the back seat, her voice small. "It's like a ghost town."

Lawson glanced at her in the rearview mirror, his heart aching at the sight of his daughter's wide, bewildered eyes.

"I had no idea all of what you were protecting me from," she said softly.

The remainder of the first hour of the drive passed in tense silence, the hum of the engine providing a dull backdrop to Lawson's unease. But just as a fragile sense of calm began to settle in him, everything shifted abruptly.

Ahead, he spotted flashing lights and a roadblock, a line of vehicles halted by armed guards. Lawson's heart raced. "Damn it!" he muttered under his breath, tension rippling through the car.

"Dad, what do we do?" Sophie asked, her voice unsteady.

"I'm going to find another way around," he replied, scanning the area for an escape route.

But before he found one, Lawson saw the officer waving him forward, and his stomach dropped. He knew he had no choice but to head toward the officer. As he approached, anxiety coiled inside him. Jayne turned to the kids, her eyes wide with concern.

"Everyone, be quiet. Don't say a word," she instructed, her voice low but urgent.

They crept closer to the guard, the tension in the car thickening with each passing second. Lawson rolled down the window, forcing a calm he didn't feel.

"Good evening," the guard said, his tone flat and authoritative. "What are you doing out here on the road? Where are you headed?"

Lawson took a deep breath, steadying himself as he faced the guard. "We're heading home after visiting my sick parents," he lied, forcing a calm tone despite the unease churning in his stomach.

The guard narrowed his eyes, glancing at Lawson's hand on the steering wheel. "Where's your QR code?" he asked sharply.

The guard shone his flashlight directly onto Lawson's forehead, scanning for the mark. "Uh, it's—" Lawson stammered, but the words failed him.

The guard's flashlight swept over Jayne and the kids, illuminating their anxious faces. "And why don't they have theirs?" he pressed, his tone skeptical.

Lawson's mind raced, searching for a quick excuse. "We just got our notice that it's our appointment day tomorrow to get them. That's why we're heading home." he lied.

The guard frowned, clearly not convinced. "Do you have any ID? Proof of your appointment?"

Lawson felt a wave of panic wash over him. They didn't have a phone, and he knew he had to come up with something fast. Just then, a call crackled over the guard's radio, drawing his attention.

"We've got a situation involving another vehicle," the dispatcher said.

The guard sighed, momentarily distracted. "Hold on," he said, glancing back at Lawson. "Just … make sure you get that code tomorrow," he said, waving Lawson through.

As they pulled away, Lawson finally exhaled, feeling like he'd been holding his breath this whole time. He glanced at Jayne, who sat silently next to him, her hands clasped tightly in her lap. Her lips were moving slightly, whispering prayers, and Lawson was grateful for her unwavering strength.

"Are we really going to be OK?" Sophie whispered from the back seat.

Lawson met Jayne's gaze, her eyes reflecting both fear and determination. "We will," he said, trying to sound more confident than he felt. "We just have to keep moving and stay smart."

As they drove further away from the roadblock, a deep sense of gratitude filled him for the protective hand of God watching over them. Every moment was crucial, and he understood the need to keep moving to reach their destination safely.

* * *

As they arrived in the small town of Rockdale, a vast expanse of land surrounded them, filled with fields and scattered patches of trees stretching into the darkness. It felt surreal to be in the country, the night air thick with the earthy scent of farmland. Lawson turned onto a gravel road, the crunch of stones beneath the tires echoing in the quiet night.

He pulled the car to the side of an iron gate that stood locked. He hadn't received any specific directions about what to do upon arrival, leaving him feeling a bit lost.

"I'll be right back," he said, glancing at Jayne and the kids before heading to the trunk for a flashlight. The darkness enveloped him, and the quiet was almost unsettling.

When he returned to the gate, the beam of his flashlight cut through the blackness, illuminating the area around him. Suddenly, he noticed something unusual: a walkie-talkie sitting on a stump next to the gate. Curiosity piqued, he picked it up and pressed the button.

"Hello?" he said, uncertain of who might be on the other end.

A crackle of static responded before an old man's voice came through, stern yet carrying a distinct country drawl. "Who's there? State your business."

"Uh, it's Lawson. I-I'm looking for the way in. I was told to come here."

"Lawson, huh? You got a code or something to get in?" the voice asked, skeptical.

"No, I wasn't given any code. I just arrived. I need to know what to do," Lawson replied, trying to sound calm.

Silence lingered in the air for a moment, and Lawson hesitated. "Hello? Are you there?" he called again, but there was no response.

Then he heard a strange noise coming from the trees beside him. Turning his flashlight in that direction, he caught sight of something moving—a camera, almost hidden from view, scanning its surroundings. Confused, he said, "Hello?" once more, but still, no one answered. Frustration bubbled within him. Maybe he had come to the wrong place. He set the walkie-talkie back down on the stump and returned to the car.

Jayne looked up as he approached, her expression filled with concern. "What happened?"

"They didn't have a code or any instructions for me," Lawson replied, exasperated. "And there's a camera over there. I don't know what to think."

He turned in his seat to see the kids exchange worried glances, confusion evident on their faces. Just then, Landon's eyes widened, and he said, "I see a light just past the gate."

Lawson spotted it swaying back and forth. As the light drew closer, a figure emerged from the glow of their headlights. The man's silhouette grew clearer as he approached the driver's window, cane in hand and a shotgun slung over his shoulder. His weathered face hardened into a cautious glare, and in a thick Southern drawl, he asked, "What's your name, son?"

"Lawson," he replied, trying to maintain composure. "This is my wife, Jayne, and our kids. We're from out of town. I was told to come here."

The man studied Lawson for a moment, his expression unreadable. Without saying another word, he swiftly unlocked the gate and pushed it open, urgency in his voice. "Drive through, quickly now."

Lawson exchanged a glance with Jayne, then pressed the gas pedal, steering the car through the gate. As they crossed the threshold, the old man locked the gate behind them, taking the walkie-talkie with him as he stepped away into the shadows.

Lawson drove up the long, winding gravel driveway that snaked through the tall trees, leading them to a rustic log home that stood proudly against the night sky. The house had an inviting charm, with its big wraparound deck made of sturdy cedar logs, each piece thoughtfully crafted to blend seamlessly with the natural surroundings.

The logs had weathered gracefully, their surfaces rich with texture and character, and the soft glow of light emanated from the windows, with a trail of smoke coming from the chimney, hinting at warmth inside. Lawson parked the car, and they sat in silence for a moment, absorbing the peaceful ambiance.

Finally, the old man reappeared, making his way back to the house with deliberate steps, his cane tapping softly against the wooden boards of the porch. He waved them in, urging them forward with a friendly gesture as he climbed the steps and opened the door, revealing a cozy interior filled with the flickering glow of a fire and the promise of refuge.

They all climbed out of the car, grabbing only the bags they would need for the night. Lawson led the way up the worn wooden steps to the front door, the creaks beneath their feet sounding both familiar and comforting. As they stepped inside, the man shut the door behind them, sealing out the cool night air.

"Welcome," he said with a warm smile, his Southern drawl wrapping around each word. "I'm Archie." He gestured toward the kitchen, where the faint aroma of something simmering filled the air. "This is my wife, Zella."

At the mention of her name, a small-framed woman clearly older in age appeared from a cozy nook, her apron dusted with flour. Zella's face radiated warmth and was framed by wisps of silver hair. She wiped her hands on her apron, her smile genuine and inviting.

"Oh, I'm so happy to have you all in my home," she said, her voice gentle and melodic, as if each word were a sweet note in a song. She stepped closer, her eyes sparkling as she took in the family.

She turned her attention to Sophie, Landon, and Andrew. "You'll be staying in the loft upstairs. There are plenty of beds to choose from, so pick whichever one suits your fancy!" Her enthusiasm was infectious, and Lawson watched the kids exchange excited glances before bounding up the stairs.

With them gone, Zella's gaze fell on Jayne, whose eyes showed her exhaustion. "Oh, dear, you look worn out," she said softly, stepping forward with genuine concern. "Why don't you and your husband take the spare bedroom downstairs? It's nice and cozy, just waiting for you."

Lawson could feel Jayne's gratitude and relief as Zella led them to the room. The space was charming, with a wooden-framed queen bed adorned with a handmade quilt, its intricate patterns a testament to Zella's love for her home. Zella reached into an antique wardrobe, pulling out another quilt.

"It gets a bit nippy at night," she explained, her hands moving with the familiarity of someone who had done this countless times before. She draped the extra quilt over the bed with care.

"Here's the bathroom," she said, opening the door to reveal a simple yet inviting space. "Feel free to freshen up. Dinner will be ready soon, and I'd love for you to join us."

As Lawson took in the warmth of the room and the kindness radiating from Zella, he felt a sense of safety envelop him. He embraced his wife as tears began to spill down her cheeks, and he knew they were in the right place, guided into the gentle hands of Archie and Zella.

CHAPTER FOURTEEN

SIMPLE PLEASURES

The morning light softly filtered through the window, casting a warm glow in the room as Jayne and Lawson stirred awake. It was the first night she had slept so well in what felt like ages, the comforting atmosphere of the house wrapping around her like a cozy blanket.

Jayne took a deep breath, catching the savory scent of bacon and fresh coffee drifting in from the kitchen. She couldn't help but appreciate how kind and generous their new hosts had been. She quickly dressed, a faint smile tugging at her lips as she headed to the kitchen. As she entered, she found Zella bustling about, her apron tied snugly around her waist. The kitchen was alive with the sounds of sizzling and the soft clatter of pots and pans.

"Good morning, dear!" Zella called out, her face brightening with a smile. "Come on in! I could use an extra set of hands."

The invitation brought a welcome sense of ease, and Jayne looked forward to sharing the start of a new morning together.

Zella set Jayne to work making homemade biscuits from scratch, guiding her through each step with patience and enthusiasm. As Jayne measured flour and mixed ingredients, she felt a bit strange in this kitchen, acutely aware of Zella's years of practice and expertise. The motions were familiar yet foreign, like a long-lost art she hadn't touched in years.

Memories flooded back of her childhood, helping her grandmother in the kitchen, laughter and flour flying as they created delicious meals together. But those moments felt distant, overshadowed by her busy life as a lawyer. Long hours had kept her away from home, often leading her to pick up food or order takeout for the kids, leaving little time for the joys of cooking and family.

As she worked alongside Zella, Jayne felt comforted. It was the normalcy of life as it used to be—the simple, familiar routines that had once filled her days. Zella's kind soul and nurturing presence reminded her of her grandmother, and for the first time in a long while, Jayne felt a sense of peace enveloping her. There was something soothing about this shared moment, a quiet connection that grounded her.

The others filed into the kitchen, their eyes bright with morning energy, practically drawn to the rustic wooden table by the rich smells of breakfast. Everyone settled in, eager to dig in, and Jayne felt a quiet gratitude for this simple moment of togetherness.

Archie leaned back in his chair, surveying the scene. His weathered face bore lines that told of a hard-lived life. His hair, mostly white and neatly cropped, carried the quiet dignity of someone who had endured many seasons. He wore a red plaid flannel shirt, soft from years of wear, the cuffs slightly faded, like it had seen a hundred quiet mornings. A cane rested against the table. Jayne didn't know the story behind it, but the way he moved made it clear the injury was old—something he'd long since learned to live with.

"Alright, y'all," he said, his voice firm yet inviting. "This leg slows me down more than it used to, and I've got a lot to get done today. I could use your help."

Archie pointed toward the mud room. "Boys, go grab some old boots and some coveralls hanging up in there."

Landon hesitated, glancing down at his shoes. "Can't I just wear these?"

Archie shot him a stern look, the kind that brooked no argument. "You won't want to wear those for what you'll be doing soon."

Landon exchanged a look with Andrew, and after a moment, they both nodded and headed toward the utility room to find the clothes.

Archie carried a certain hardness in his demeanor; he was a no-nonsense kind of man, someone you didn't want to cross or talk back to. But as Jayne watched the way the boys moved quickly to obey, without fear, she sensed there was more to him. Beneath that tough exterior, she suspected, was a heart that cared more than he let on.

"I'll be canning more veggies and fruits today to store," Zelle said to Jayne and Sophie, her voice warm. "Could use some help if you're up for it."

Sophie's face scrunched up in reluctance, and when she opened her mouth to protest, Jayne quickly interjected. "We'd be glad to help, Zella," she said, offering a smile that conveyed her sincerity. "Right, Sophie?"

Zella seemed to notice the exchange, her kind eyes softening as she stepped in. "That would be wonderful, dear."

Jayne was glad Sophie had gone upstairs to change instead of arguing, leaving just Zella, Archie, Lawson, and herself at the table. She glanced around, taking in the details. The home was clean and lived-in, full of charm, but one thing stood out: there were no family photos. No pictures of grandchildren on the mantel or framed memories lining the walls.

It struck her as odd. For a couple their age, she would've expected smiling faces, birthdays, holidays—some glimpse into the generations that came after. She wondered if they'd ever had kids. Maybe not. And maybe that was why Archie had looked at the boys the way he did earlier—not soft, but thoughtful, like he was watching something unfamiliar settle into his space.

Archie leaned back in his chair, looking at them curiously. "So, where are y'all from? What's been happening out there?"

Lawson took another sip of coffee and cleared his throat. "We're from a little town just south of Houston. We've been there until now." He hesitated, weighing his words. "Things have been bad, and we had to leave when the officials brought in the mark …"

Archie raised an eyebrow. "The what?"

Jayne realized instantly that they didn't know about the biblical mention of the mark of the beast. Lawson must have too because he quickly corrected himself. "The government service plan with the mark on the hands," he explained.

Archie gave him a funny look but didn't press the matter further. Instead, he nodded slowly, his expression grave.

"Yeah, it's coming here too soon, I reckon. I've been hearing it's worse in the cities. We don't have a lot of folks around these parts, so we've been pretty sheltered so far. We've been helping families for a while, on their way to safety. But when the time comes, we may have to leave as well." He paused, shaking his head. "I don't so much like the idea of gettin' a mark on me—sounds pretty intrusive. You can't even go to the store without it? More government control, if you ask me." He glanced at Zella, and they exchanged a knowing look, both clearly reluctant to consider leaving their home.

"How long do you plan on staying?" Archie asked, his gaze steady.

Lawson looked at Jayne, uncertainty flickering in his eyes. "Only a few days," he said carefully, though they both knew the unspoken truth: If war broke out soon, they might need to stay longer. Jayne felt their shared decision to keep the deeper realities from Archie and Zella for now.

In the kitchen a while later, Jayne and Sophie joined Zella, who moved about with a sense of purpose. The countertops were lined with jars, their surfaces gleaming in the morning light, each waiting to be filled with the bounty from Zella's garden. The rich, earthy scent of ripe tomatoes and fresh green beans mingled with the sweetness of apricots and figs, creating an atmosphere that felt both comforting and nostalgic.

Zella stood at the stove, where a large pot simmered with chopped tomatoes, their vibrant red promising a burst of flavor. Next to it, another pot bubbled with green beans, their bright green hue a testament to their freshness. "All right, ladies," Zella said, her voice warm and inviting, "let's get started on these preserves while the veggies cook."

Jayne watched as Zella expertly chopped apricots and figs, her hands moving with the grace of years spent perfecting the art. "Do you grow all of this yourself?" Jayne asked in genuine admiration.

"Every last bit," Zella replied, her eyes twinkling with pride. "This year's been especially good for the tomatoes and figs. I always make enough to last us through the winter."

Sophie, lingering a bit apart, crossed her arms and watched with a mixture of curiosity and apprehension. "I've never done any canning before," she admitted hesitantly. "It seems … complicated."

Zella chuckled softly, her demeanor reassuring. "It might seem that way at first, but it's really just about following the steps. Here, let me show you." She handed Sophie a knife and gestured to a cutting board. "Start by chopping these apricots into small pieces."

Jayne watched Sophie take a deep breath and step closer, accepting the knife with a hint of uncertainty. "Like this?" she asked, her focus sharpening as she concentrated on the task at hand.

Jayne turned to Zella, noticing the gentle way she guided Sophie. "You're so patient with her," she remarked, warmth in her voice. "It's nice to see."

Zella smiled, a soft light in her eyes. "Well, I remember when I was learning. My mother had the same patience with me. It's about passing down the knowledge, isn't it?"

"Absolutely," Jayne agreed, feeling a sense of connection deepen between them. "It's a bridge to our past, to our families."

As they worked together, the kitchen filled with laughter and conversation, a rhythm that echoed the simplicity of life itself. Zella shared stories of her early days canning with Archie, their youthful escapades in the garden, and the little joys that came from living close to the land. Jayne listened intently, feeling a soothing calm surround her as she sealed each jar, one by one, capturing the essence of their labor in a way that felt both sacred and lasting.

Zella's hands deftly moving from pot to jar as they talked. Jayne could see the tomatoes had thickened beautifully, their rich aroma filling the kitchen, while the green beans had softened just right.

"Okay, now we're ready to fill these jars," Zella said. "Sophie, you can help me with this part. Make sure to leave a little space at the top."

Sophie approached, her earlier hesitation gone. She watched as Zella ladled the steaming tomatoes into the jars, the red liquid splashing softly against the glass. "It smells amazing," she remarked.

"It tastes even better," Zella replied, smiling. "There's nothing like homemade canned goods. They'll keep us warm during the colder months."

Jayne joined in, filling jars with green beans, her movements becoming more fluid as she settled into the rhythm of the task. "How long do these usually last?" she asked, genuinely curious.

"Depending on how well you seal them, they can last years," Zella said. "The key is making sure everything is clean and hot when you pack them. Bacteria doesn't stand a chance against good canning practices."

Once they filled the jars, Zella showed Sophie how to wipe the rims to ensure a good seal. "Always remember, a little care goes a long way in canning," she said.

With the jars filled, they moved to the next stage: sealing. Zella showed them how to run a spatula along the inside of each jar to remove air bubbles before wiping the rims clean. "Air pockets can lead to spoilage," she explained. Then she placed the lids carefully on each jar and tightened them down with a metal ring. "Once they're sealed, they'll create a vacuum," she said. "That's what keeps the food fresh."

Finally, they placed the jars in a boiling water bath, watching as the bubbles danced around them. Zella turned to Sophie and Jayne, her face glowing with satisfaction. "And that's it! In a few hours, we'll have fresh preserves to enjoy."

As they cleaned up the kitchen, the atmosphere felt lighter, filled with the warmth of shared labor and newfound camaraderie. Jayne couldn't help but feel grateful for these moments, a brief escape from the world outside, as they created something lasting together.

As the jars settled into their water bath, Zella clapped her hands together, a gleam of excitement in her eyes. "While those finish processing, how about we make a homemade dewberry cobbler for dessert tonight?"

Sophie raised an eyebrow in curiosity. "What's a *dewberry* cobbler?" she asked.

Zella smiled warmly, clearly delighted to share. "Dewberries are similar to blackberries but a little sweeter. They grow wild around here, and they're perfect for pies and cobblers. It's one of my favorites, especially when I serve it warm with a scoop of vanilla ice cream."

"Sounds delicious!" Sophie replied, her enthusiasm growing. "But I've never even heard of dewberries. Where do you find them?"

Zella chuckled, moving a few steps away to gather ingredients from the pantry. "Oh, they grow all over this area in the spring, and we just freeze 'em till we need 'em. You just have to know where to look. My favorite spots are along the old dirt roads, where the sun hits just right. I've taught Archie a few tricks for picking them without getting scratched up!"

"So, what do we do first?" Jayne asked.

"Could you grab me some butter from the fridge, dear?"

Jayne opened the refrigerator door and was met with a sight that made her pause. There were about seven or eight containers of margarine, each one stacked and lined up, their labels faded from use. "Which one do you need?" she asked. "And why do you have so much butter?"

Zella let out a hearty laugh. "Oh, those aren't butter! Those are just empty margarine containers. I clean them out and use them for leftovers. Never understood the need for all that fancy Tupperware."

Jayne couldn't help but chuckle at the thought, imagining Zella's practical approach to life. "I guess that makes sense. You really do make the most of what you have," she said.

"That's the way to do it," Zella replied, her eyes twinkling. "Waste not, want not, as they say. Now, if you could find me the real butter tucked in the back, we'll get started on that cobbler."

Jayne rummaged through the fridge, appreciating the simplicity of Zella's method and the way she embraced the little things in life.

As they began mixing the ingredients for the cobbler, Zella turned to Sophie, her hands steady and sure. "You know, dear, I'd love to hear more about your life before all this. What was it like?"

Sophie hesitated for a moment. "Well, I was a freshman in college, just starting out. I joined a sorority and had a lot of friends. We had fun—dressing up, going to parties, and talking about fashion. I was a fashion major." She glanced down. "I really miss that life."

"I can only imagine. It sounds like you had a bright future ahead of you. Do you have a beau you're fond of?"

Sophie nodded slowly, her expression turning somber. "Yeah, it felt that way. But everything changed so quickly." She paused, taking a breath. "I had a boyfriend, Matt. We were really close."

Sophie's voice faltered, a sadness creeping in. "He's one of the missing. It's been hard knowing he's gone." Her eyes glistened with unshed tears. "But I'm starting to come to terms with it. I keep telling myself he's in a better place."

Zella regarded her with a mix of sympathy and concern. "How do you know that?"

"Because he was taken in the rapture," Sophie replied, her voice soft but resolute. "At least he's with God now, or at least that's what I've been told."

Zella's brow furrowed, confusion clear on her face. But Jayne was proud of the way Sophie shared the truth, even if she wasn't fully convinced.

✵ ✵ ✵

Once the cobbler was finished, Jayne felt a sense of accomplishment. Zella wiped her hands on her apron and turned to Jayne and Sophie with a purposeful smile. "Now that we've done some good work, let's take those cooled cans down to the root cellar for storage."

As they stepped outside, Jayne appreciated the crisp and fresh air, a gentle breeze rustling the leaves. Zella led them to a large wooden door set into the side of the house. With a firm pull, she swung it open, revealing a set of stairs that descended into darkness. "Watch your step," she said, guiding them down.

At the bottom, they encountered another door—this one made of heavy metal, with a handle that resembled something from an old war film. Jayne's curiosity grew as she wondered what lay beyond. Zella turned the handle and pushed the door open, and as it swung wide, Jayne's eyes widened in disbelief.

The space before them was immense. The walls were lined from floor to ceiling with meticulously arranged shelves brimming with canned goods—rows and rows of gleaming glass jars in every color imaginable, each labeled with its contents: tomatoes, green beans, squash, and more. It was a pantry that spoke of years of preparation, of survival in a world that had grown increasingly uncertain.

In one corner, jars filled with meats preserved in lard stood out prominently. Each jar was meticulously labeled with the type of meat and the date it was prepared, showcasing Zella's dedication to both quality and organization.

Nearby, packets of seeds were carefully organized, each one labeled with its variety and planting instructions, ready for the next growing season. A water filtration system and stacks of bottles filled with clear water were a testament to their foresight.

There was also an inviting living space, with a well-worn couch that had clearly been loved, its fabric soft and faded from years of use. Two comfy recliners flanked the couch, their cushions slightly misshapen. An afghan was draped over the back of one chair, a token of Zella's craft and care. The walls were adorned with skin pelts and hand-stitched frameworks with phrases like Bless This Home. A cast-iron wood heater stood in one corner, ready to provide warmth during the colder months. Jayne took it all in quietly, the decor striking her as both unfamiliar and strangely comforting—like stepping into a life she'd never known but somehow needed right now.

As Jayne took in the surroundings, her gaze fell upon a carefully sealed bucket labeled Lye. Curiosity sparked within her, and she turned to Zella. "What's that for?"

Zella paused, her expression shifting slightly. "Ah, that's for making soap and cleaning supplies. It's a bit dangerous if not handled properly, so we keep it sealed tight. We like to be prepared for everything, you see," she added with a nod, her eyes reflecting a wisdom borne from years of experience.

Jayne nodded, absorbing the information. This was more than a simple shelter; it was a carefully curated refuge, showing resilience and the spirit of survival.

As they moved deeper into the bunker, they entered a small kitchen area. It was equipped with a sturdy stove, pipes leading out of the bunker to vent smoke, cast iron pots and pans, and a work table cluttered with tools and utensils. Jayne noted how practical yet inviting it felt, with the rustic charm of home blended with the seriousness of preparation.

Beyond the kitchen lay two sleeping quarters. One room housed two twin beds, each made up with quilts that looked homemade. The other room was larger, filled with several twin beds, all neatly lined up and adorned with their own colorful quilts, each telling their own story.

Finally, they found a bathroom, surprisingly well-equipped for such a remote setting. A makeshift shower stood in one corner, and a compost toilet occupied the other, showcasing Zella and Archie's commitment to sustainability and self-sufficiency.

Jayne's thoughts raced with the implications of this space. Zella and Archie weren't just preppers; they were ready for something far greater than anyone else expected. This wasn't just a shelter—it was a home, a fortress forged from love and resilience. In that moment, Jayne silently thanked God for bringing them here, feeling that His hand had guided them to this place at the perfect time. This bunker— what Zella had affectionately called a root cellar—could become their sanctuary if war were to break out soon. Now Jayne knew she had to find a way to explain to Zella what she knew was on the horizon.

Landon positioned himself next to the large cow, his confidence high as he prepared to help with the milking. But just as he reached for the udder, he felt a sudden, sharp kick to his leg. "Oww!" he yelped, hopping back on one foot, his eyes wide with surprise.

Archie, nearby, rolled his eyes and chuckled under his breath. "You've got to be quicker than that, boy," he said, shaking his head. "Cows can be temperamental, especially if they don't know you."

Landon rubbed his leg, still wincing. "I thought I was being gentle!"

Archie stepped closer, his demeanor calm and confident. "Here, let me show you how it's done. First, you've got to be calm and assertive. They can sense your energy." He reached out to the cow, placing his hands gently on her side. "Just be firm but gentle. Start from the top and work your way down, like this."

As he demonstrated, the cow relaxed under his touch, and Landon watched closely, determined to get it right. Andrew stood by, chuckling at his friend's misfortune. Lawson leaned against one of the stall beams, observing with a half-smile, arms crossed. Archie glanced over at him. "You ever milked a cow before, Lawson?"

Lawson shook his head. "No, sir. But I'm learning just like they are."

Archie nodded with approval. "Good. We'll make country folks outta y'all yet."

The barn was filled with the soft sounds of the animals and the scent of hay and farm life, creating an atmosphere that felt foreign to Landon.

"Wow, the smells in here are burning my eyes," Andrew commented.

Archie glanced over at him with a twinkle in his eye. "Son, that's the smell of money," he replied. "This barn may not win any beauty contests, but it sure provides for us. You get used to it, trust me."

Half an hour later, Landon took a step back after milking, feeling proud of himself—until his foot landed squarely in a pile of fresh cow manure. "Ugh!" he exclaimed, lifting his foot in disgust. "I stepped in it!"

Archie laughed, shaking his head. "Aren't you glad you wore my old boots instead of those fancy sneakers you had on earlier?" Archie added with a teasing grin, "Just remember, boys, every time you take care of these animals, you're doing your part. It's all part of the cycle." He motioned for them to get back to work, and Landon felt the bond between the men growing stronger as they shared in the rhythm of farm life.

Just then, Archie let out a hearty call, and a chorus of bleats and whinnies filled the air as the goats, horses, and donkeys came bounding toward the barn. They skidded to a halt at the gate, blocking the entrance and eager for attention.

"Looks like they're ready for their breakfast," Archie said cheerfully. He turned to Andrew and said, "Go grab some feed from those large bins we've got stored in the corner. They're not going to wait all day."

Andrew nodded, moving toward the bins with purpose. The animals shifted impatiently, their eyes bright with anticipation. Landon and Archie shared a knowing look, their earlier laughter replaced by the simple satisfaction of tending to the animals.

Once Andrew returned with the feed, Archie pointed to the wooden fencing. "Now just sprinkle it in those troughs hanging on the inside," he instructed. Landon helped, and the boys poured the feed into the troughs as the animals began to nuzzle in, their excitement evident.

As the animals started grazing, Landon and Andrew couldn't resist getting closer to them. They began petting the animals, while curiosity surfaced. "Do they have names?" Landon asked, his fingers running through the coarse fur of a goat.

Archie rolled his eyes good-naturedly. "Well, this here is Woodrow," he said, pointing to a sturdy donkey. "That's Jake, Newt, Deets, Dee, Peach, and over yonder is Gus, our goat. And this is Lorrie Darlin'," he added, nodding toward the horse.

Lawson raised an eyebrow, intrigued by the names. "Lorrie Darlin'? Really?"

Archie huffed a chuckle. "Zella loves that old show *Lonesome Dove* and just had to name all the animals after those characters. Keeps things interesting around here." He shook his head, a fond smile creeping onto his face.

✳ ✳ ✳

After feeding the animals, Archie led Lawson, Andrew, and Landon out of the barn and onto a winding path that cut through the lush landscape of his property. The sun beat down from above, illuminating the greenery around them.

In the distance, a pond shimmered under the sunlight. Willows draped over the water, their branches swaying in the breeze.

"Wow, look at that!" Andrew said, pointing toward the wooden pier that stretched out over the pond.

"That pier looks like it's been there a while," Lawson said, shielding his eyes to take in the view.

Archie gave a nod. "It has. I built that not long after Zella and I got married. Bought this land from my daddy back in the seventies. We've been working it ever since."

Lawson glanced around, taking in the serenity of the place. "You can tell. Feels like the kind of land someone's poured their life into."

Archie gave a small, approving grunt. "That's exactly what it is."

As they walked along the path toward the pond, Lawson's eyes lit up at the sight of the water glistening in the sunlight. "So, Archie, are there any fish in here?"

Archie chuckled, nodding. "Oh, definitely! We've got some good-sized catfish lurking beneath the surface."

As they got closer, Archie leaned over, reaching into an old coffee can that sat at the edge of the pier. He pulled out a handful of something and tossed it into the water. Instantly, the surface erupted with splashes as the catfish darted to the food.

"What was that?" Lawson asked curiously as he watched the frenzy unfold.

"Just some dry dog food," Archie replied, a grin spreading across his face. "They love it! You'd be surprised what they'll go after."

Landon leaned over. "Really? Dog food? That's kind of funny."

"You make do with what you have, son. Besides, they don't seem to mind!" Archie laughed as he watched the catfish swirl around. "You ever fished for catfish, Lawson?"

Before Lawson could reply, Archie went and rummaged through a nearby shed, emerging with some old cane poles, their paint chipped and faded but still sturdy. He reached for a different can and pulled out a handful of wriggling worms. "All right, boys," he said. "We're going to catch our dinner!"

Lawson couldn't help but smile at the prospect. It felt so right, so normal, even amidst the chaos that lay beyond their little haven. As Archie handed him a pole, Lawson glanced around at the sprawling landscape. In that moment, he felt a wave of relief wash over him. Here, in this quiet slice of country life, the troubles of the outside world seemed to fade into the background. It almost felt surreal, as if they had stepped into a dream where everything was uncomplicated and peaceful.

And for now, he thought, *I will take it.* Even if it was just a fleeting moment of normalcy, it was a gift he wouldn't take for granted.

✳ ✳ ✳

Later that evening, Zella entered Jayne's room, intending to check if she needed anything before Zella went to bed. The space was surprisingly empty; a soft silence filled the air. Her gaze fell on Jayne's Bible and a scatter of papers strewn across the bed.

Zella felt a twinge of curiosity, reluctant to invade Jayne's privacy yet unable to resist the pull of the map that caught her eye. She stepped closer, drawn in by the meticulous details and the unsettling images etched upon the paper. As she began to read the outline titled "The

Last Plumb Line," she took a deep breath. Each item on the list seemed to echo with a dark resonance—missing people, the war in Israel, the emergence of a new world leader, and the rising specters of famine, disease, and death.

Archie had shared harrowing tales of those persecuted for their faith, and the chilling introduction of a new mark mandated by the government loomed large in her mind. Zella's breath caught in her throat as the weight of it all pressed down on her.

Just then, the bathroom door clicked, jolting Zella back to reality. With a quick glance back at the disarray, she slipped out of the room before Jayne came in, a growing sense of worry taking hold as an unsettling thought flickered through her—what else were Jayne and Lawson keeping from them, and what did those papers mean?

CHAPTER FIFTEEN

SECRETS BENEATH THE SURFACE

The next day, Jayne found Zella in the root cellar, surrounded by jars and crates as she organized more supplies. The rows of glass containers filled with fruits and vegetables gleamed in the light.

"Hey there," Jayne said, stepping inside. "Need a hand?"

Zella looked up, her face brightening. "Always! I'm just trying to get everything in order."

Jayne glanced around, taking in the neat rows of canned goods and the carefully labeled jars. "I have to say, I'm really impressed by all of this. You've created quite a setup down here."

Zella smiled, a hint of pride in her eyes. "Thank you! It's taken years to get it like this. Every jar holds a story."

Jayne leaned against a shelf, admiring the fruits of Zella's labor. "It must feel good to know you're prepared for anything. I can't imagine the work that goes into all of this."

Zella chuckled softly. "It can be a bit overwhelming at times, but it's worth it. It gives me peace of mind."

As they settled into conversation, Jayne's unease grew. She hesitated longer before each response.

"How are you holding up with everything?" Zella asked gently.

Jayne's gaze dropped to the floor, her voice trembling. "It's been hard. So much has changed in such a short time. The world feels upside down, and everything I thought I knew about life has completely changed my views." Jayne took a deep breath, wrestling with her thoughts. "Sophie's really struggling too. She acts out sometimes, almost like she's pushing everyone away. It's as if she can't see past her own pain."

Zella's expression was sympathetic. "That's understandable. It's a lot to process. Do you think she's starting to accept what's happened?"

"A little, maybe," Jayne said with a frown. "But it's like she can't let go of the anger and the grief from everything that's changed. I see her wrestling with it, and it breaks my heart."

Zella nodded thoughtfully. "Grief manifests in different ways. It's tough for young people, especially when they feel alone in their struggles."

She paused, then added quietly, "I may not know what it's like to be a mother, Jayne, but I do understand loss. Archie and I had to accept a long time ago that children just weren't going to be part of our story. That kind of grief... it stays with you, just in a quieter way."

Jayne looked up at her, a flicker of connection passing between them.

Just then, a loud boom echoed outside, rattling the shelves. Jayne jumped, instinctively ducking for cover.

Zella blinked, a puzzled look crossing her face. "Jayne, it's just thunder. It can be startling, but you're safe," she said, moving closer to help her up.

Jayne took a moment to compose herself. "Right … just thunder," she murmured, trying to shake off the fear.

Zella studied her closely. "You OK? That seemed to rattle you."

Jayne sighed, rubbing her arms. "I guess it caught me off guard."

"You're not alone in this," Zella said. "We're all navigating a lot right now. If there's something on your mind, you can talk to me."

Jayne hesitated, feeling the importance of Zella's kindness. She could sense the warmth in Zella's offer, but the thunder rolled again outside, and she found it hard to voice the fears lurking just beneath the surface. Instead, she simply nodded, grateful for the support.

As the rain began to fall, Lawson and Archie walked into the house, shaking off droplets like dogs after a swim. The rhythmic patter on the roof created a cozy atmosphere, but Zella's voice cut through the sound as they stepped inside.

"Boots at the door, gentlemen!" she called out, her tone light yet firm.

Lawson chuckled and nodded, kicking off his muddy boots. "You've got it, Zella. I wouldn't want to ruin this lovely floor."

Archie followed suit, his well-worn boots making a soft thud as they landed on the porch. "Can't blame a woman for wanting to keep a clean house," he added, a twinkle in his eye. He stepped inside, revealing a smudge of dirt on his heel.

Zella raised an eyebrow playfully. "Archie! How many times have I told you?" she said, shaking her head but unable to suppress a smile.

Lawson watched them with quiet amusement. He didn't know much about their history, but it was obvious they'd weathered a lot together. Their bond was easy to spot, even for someone like him who barely knew them. The way Zella raised an eyebrow when Archie tracked in dirt, and the way Archie grinned like he'd done it on purpose—it was the kind of teasing that spoke of a well-worn rhythm. Zella had a sharp eye for tidiness, Archie an easy-going charm, and together they moved through the moment like they'd done it a hundred times before—and probably would a hundred times more. Lawson laughed as he looked back at the rain-soaked landscape through the door. "Looks like we timed that just right. Perfect weather for a warm meal, huh? Zella, it smells amazing in here. Oh, here's some fish we caught." He handed her the cut filets in a sealed bag to be stored in the freezer.

Archie nodded, his expression shifting to a more serious one. "We need to make sure we keep an eye on the animals during this storm. I don't want anything getting spooked."

"Of course," Zella replied, her hands busy arranging some freshly baked bread. "We'll check on them after supper. For now, let's enjoy dinner."

As the storm intensified outside, Lawson felt the sense of community within the home deepen. As they settled around the table, the warmth of the bread and a hearty meal fueled their senses. The meal looked delicious, and in true Southern form, the fried venison and cream gravy sat beside a warm bowl of whipped mashed potatoes. Fresh green peas sat nestled in a container with a slab of butter on top.

As they began to serve themselves, Andrew looked up and said, "Would you all mind if we said a prayer before we start?"

Archie and Zella exchanged surprised glances, but they nodded in agreement. "Of course, son," Archie replied.

Andrew bowed his head, and the others followed suit. "Thank you for this meal and for bringing us together during these hard times," he began. "Please watch over our families, friends, and all those in need. Amen."

Lawson appreciated Andrew's simple prayer. He noticed Zella look up, a smile on her face as well. "That was a lovely prayer, dear. Were you brought up in the church?"

Andrew hesitated for a moment, a flicker of emotion crossing his face. "Actually, I'm Jewish, but I became a Christian when all this started," he admitted.

Lawson thought he saw curiosity pique in Zella's expression, but she only smiled gently and encouraged the others to dig into their meal.

After dinner, Jayne followed Zella into the kitchen, the sound of their chatter blending with the clinking of dishes. The kids had retreated upstairs.

In the adjoining room, Lawson and Archie remained at the table, their conversation shifting to the portable ham radio that Archie had set up years ago. With a practiced hand, he flipped on the switch and adjusted the dial, a series of crackles and voices filling the air.

"Listen to this," Archie said, his voice low and focused. He fine-tuned the frequency, and the static cleared, revealing urgent reports. Lawson leaned in closer, listening intently.

"… escalating tensions in Eastern Europe … reports of military movements … imminent threat of conflict …"

As the details unfolded, Lawson's expression grew grave. He exchanged a worried glance through the doorway with Jayne, who had paused in her dishwashing. Then she and Zella joined Archie and Lawson at the table.

"This is how I've been getting my information," Archie said. "I don't own a TV, and I've never trusted the mainstream media to give the real story. This"—he gestured to the radio—"is where I find the truth."

Lawson nodded, his eyes narrowing as he absorbed the details. "What have they been saying about the situation?" he asked, eager for clarity amidst the static.

Archie adjusted the dials again, homing in on a clearer transmission. "Tensions have been escalating everywhere—military movements, protests. They say World War III could be just around the corner."

Lawson turned to Jayne, noting the concern in her eyes. They were both acutely aware of the impending turmoil but uncertain of when it would strike.

Zella, sensing the tension between them, turned the volume down slightly. Her voice was gentle yet probing. She looked Jayne straight in the eyes. "Is there something more you two know? Something you aren't saying?"

Lawson shifted uncomfortably in his seat, and he saw the uncertainty reflected in Jayne's eyes.

"It's complicated," Jayne finally said, her voice barely above a whisper. "We've seen things … and heard things. It's hard to explain." She glanced at Lawson, seeming to search for reassurance, but he didn't know what to do.

Archie leaned back in his chair, his expression serious. "If you know something, now's the time to share."

Zella nodded in agreement, her gaze fixed on Jayne. "We need to know what's going on," she said, her voice steady. "I'm so sorry for snooping, but I went in your room last night to say good night and saw some disturbing things laid on the bed. Whatever it is, you can tell us. We're all in this together."

Lawson immediately felt a pang of guilt for not speaking up sooner. But before he could say anything, Jayne began to share everything they had discovered since the world turned upside down.

CHAPTER SIXTEEN

CINDERS IN THE WIND

When Jayne had finished, Archie replied, "Let me get this straight. You're telling me all these events—disappearances, wars, diseases, deaths, and even a new world leader—are part of some prophetic plan laid out in the Bible?"

Jayne nodded, hoping her expression showed her earnestness. "Yes, I know it sounds odd, but we've been connecting the dots. The signs align with what many believe are prophecies unfolding in real time."

Zella looked confused. "But how can we be certain? This is a lot to take in."

"You're right," Lawson chimed in. "When Jayne discovered these notes at our neighbors' house the day of the rapture—" Noticing Archie's puzzled look, he quickly added, "I mean, the day everything started—the day of the disappearances," he clarified.

"At first, it was just a simple gathering to check on each other. But then we started reading these notes that Ruth left behind. The war with Israel was already underway, and like you, we were skeptical at first. It all seemed far-fetched."

Jayne nodded as he glanced at her before continuing. "But as events unfolded exactly as described in those notes, we began to realize there might be some truth to them. Then came the earthquake, and soon after, a new world leader emerged. He allied himself with the chief rabbi of Israel."

Lawson took a breath, pulling the notes from the table to show them. "So, the notes suggest that these two could be the Antichrist and the false prophet."

Archie shook his head. "You mean to tell me that what we're experiencing isn't just random? There's a greater purpose behind it?"

As Archie examined the document, Jayne pointed to the first section and began to explain. "This part talks about the rapture—the moment when God's church, the believers, will be taken away. And after that, the rise of the Antichrist and the false prophet will follow. They'll form an alliance and sign a peace deal with Israel. That marks the beginning of the seven-year tribulation period—a time when God's wrath will be poured out on the earth."

Jayne traced her finger over the words, her voice tight with the weight of what she was saying. "This is where the four horsemen come in— the wars, the famine, the diseases. And it all builds to the mark of the beast, when people will have to choose between their faith and their lives. It will be a time of persecution, and martyrs will be killed for their belief in God."

"But why seven years?" Archie asked, his brow furrowed.

Jayne opened her Bible, flipping to the Old Testament passage in Daniel. "Let me show you," she said, her fingers tracing the worn pages. "In Daniel 9:25–26, it lays out a prophecy that speaks to these very events. It's pivotal for understanding the timeline.

"*Know therefore and understand that from the going out of the word to restore and build Jerusalem to the coming of an anointed one, a prince, there shall be seven weeks. Then for sixty-two weeks it shall be built again with squares and moat, but in a troubled time. And after the sixty-two weeks, an anointed one shall be cut off and shall have nothing.*"

Jayne paused to let the words sink in. "This part is talking about the time before the Messiah came to earth. It mentions 'seven weeks' and 'sixty-two weeks,' which adds up to sixty-nine weeks. In this prophecy, those weeks are actually years. And we know that Jesus, the Messiah, came to earth in the flesh about two thousand years ago. So, this prophecy was about the time leading up to His first coming, but it also leaves out the last week, which is about when He returns during the tribulation.

"After those sixty-nine weeks, there's a pause before the final week—the seventieth week. This week is often understood to be the seven-year period known as the tribulation. The Scripture says the Messiah will be 'cut off,' which means He won't be here. Instead, Satan will be allowed to show himself on earth and give his power to a man who is the opposite of Christ—he's called the Antichrist. This man will appear like a savior, promising peace and unity in a time of great need. But his power comes from Satan, and the peace he offers is fake. This is when God's final plan for the world will begin, and it will be a time of great trouble and judgment."

Archie listened intently, his head tilted slightly, the skepticism in his expression slowly shifting toward curiosity. "So, the tribulation is tied directly to this prophecy? How do we know it's not just going to keep going on indefinitely?"

Jayne nodded, encouraged by his engagement. "The Scripture makes it clear that this seven-year period is distinct. It's part of God's redemptive plan. Throughout the Bible, the number seven is associated with completion and fulfillment. This is the time when God will bring His judgment upon the earth but also offer a final opportunity for repentance. It's a critical chapter in the grand narrative of faith."

Archie leaned back. "So, all of this—the wars, the diseases, everything—is part of a larger picture? Something that's been laid out for a long time?"

"Yes, it's like a puzzle coming together," Jayne said. "These notes highlight how everything we're seeing aligns with what has been foretold."

Archie rubbed the back of his neck in thought. "I don't know … this is just a lot to take in. So why is this outline called 'The Last Plumb Line'? What's a plumb line got to do with any of this?"

Jayne glanced at Lawson before answering. "Well, we were confused on this for a while too until we did a little more research. Do you know what a plumb line is, Archie?"

"Of course I do." Archie nodded. "It's an older style tool for measuring straight lines. I've used one many times when building things around the farm. Even used one to help build the foundation of the barn. Without it, everything would've been crooked. It was the only way to make sure the walls didn't lean. If the walls weren't straight, the whole barn could've fallen apart."

"That's exactly it," Jayne said. "A plumb line is just a string with a weight at the end that hangs down, helping to make sure everything is straight and aligned."

Archie leaned back in his chair. "Okay, so the plumb line is a way of measuring, of testing if things are straight. But how does it fit with all this talk of prophecy?"

"It's the standard for what's straight … and for what's right," Jayne said. "In the Bible, God uses the plumb line as a symbol, a way of measuring His people—whether they're living in alignment with His truth.

"In the Bible, the plumb line is more than just a tool. It's a symbol of God's truth. In the book of Amos, God tells the prophet that He's set a plumb line among His people."

As Zella listened, Jayne could sense the wheels turning in her mind. Zella's eyes softened, and after a pause, she murmured, "So, He's measuring their faithfulness. He's seeing if they're living according to His righteousness."

"Right," Lawson added. "And in Isaiah, the plumb line is linked to justice and righteousness. God's justice is the line, and righteousness is the weight that keeps it steady, testing everything. The plumb line represents God's standard for us."

"Okay, but when you use a plumb line, you need a base to measure against," Archie said. "The base helps you see if the line is straight."

"Yes, Archie, that's right," Jayne said. "What do you use as a base?"

Archie thought for a moment before answering. "Well, usually, it's something solid—like a wall, a post, or even the ground if you're checking something vertical. You need something that's already steady and dependable to see if the line is true. We call it the cornerstone."

Jayne exhaled deeply, relieved to see the pieces falling into place. "Yes! And in the Bible, it says that Jesus is the cornerstone! He's the standard. He's the perfect measure of righteousness. When we say we need to align with God, we're saying we need to align with Jesus. He's the cornerstone, the foundation of everything."

Jayne was encouraged by Archie's reaction and began to elaborate. "A cornerstone is the first stone laid in a building. It's the most important stone because it determines the angle and direction for everything else. If the cornerstone is wrong, the whole structure will be out of line. Without the cornerstone, everything is crooked."

Lawson leaned forward and wrapped his hands around the Bible that lay before them. "Jesus is that cornerstone. He's the foundation of our faith. Without Him, there's no true alignment with God. Everything else, no matter how good it looks, will eventually fall apart."

"That's why we weren't raptured," Jayne added. "We weren't in alignment with God then. We didn't believe in Jesus. He's the one who holds everything together. Without Him, we're lost."

Zella's voice was soft, almost a whisper. "So, because we didn't believe in Jesus, we're still here?"

"Yes," Jayne replied gently. "But the good news is, it's not too late. We can still choose to make Jesus the cornerstone of our lives. That's the only way to be aligned with God's truth, to build on the right foundation."

Archie leaned back, his expression thoughtful. "So Jesus is the measure and we missed the boat."

Jayne smiled, relieved that he understood. "Exactly. He's the only solid foundation. And He's the one who can save us."

"But if the rapture has already happened, doesn't that mean it's too late?" Archie asked.

Lawson sat back in his chair, his expression serious. "No, not necessarily. This period is known as God's wrath on the earth, meant to punish those who have turned against His people, Israel, but it's also a time for the unbelievers. God is making a final effort to open their eyes to the truth—that there is only one true God."

He paused. "For so long, people have worshiped idols—whether they're made of gold, brass, or even wooden statues. Others idolize fellow humans or bow to nature itself, treating it as if Mother Nature can provide grounding or solace. But in this time of tribulation, God is trying to make it clear that these distractions can't save them."

"It's as if people have been lost in their own desires and misconceptions," Zella said with a nod. "They need to see the futility of those idols. I've watched as the world drifts further from its morals. Everyone's become so consumed with themselves, so in love with their own image, that they've lost sight of what truly matters."

"Even though these times will be the worst in all of history," Lawson said, "God is still reaching out to humanity. He's trying to get their attention, to show them the truth."

Archie looked skeptical but intrigued. "How is He doing that?"

"Even for those who missed the rapture," Lawson explained, "God's grace remains. It's not too late. Scripture tells us that even if they face death during this time, they can still go to heaven if they put their faith in Him now. It's a chance for redemption, a final invitation to believe."

Jayne felt optimistic they were reaching their kind hosts. "It's a powerful testament to God's love, even in the darkest of times," she said softly. "He desires everyone to come to Him, to seek refuge in faith, no matter the circumstances they find themselves in."

Archie's expression shifted, a flicker of hope glimmering through his uncertainty.

"Yes, there's hope," Lawson said firmly, "but right now, we can't put our hope in the idea of living in peace in this world anymore. Our hope has to be in the promise that Jesus will come back for us when all this is over. It doesn't matter what brand you are, what denomination you belong to, whether you were raised Catholic or Protestant, or whether you ever went to church at all. What matters is believing in Him now, turning away from sin and worshiping false gods, and focusing on having a relationship with Him."

In his pause, Jayne reached out, holding Zella's hands tightly, a gesture of unity and support.

Lawson continued. "You need to have a personal faith that Jesus Christ died for every sin you'll ever commit. He purchased and pardoned it for you and offers it to you as a gift of grace. You can't pay for it. You can't earn it; you definitely don't deserve it. All you can do is receive it. It's a gift. Ephesians 2:8–9 reminds us, *For by grace you have been saved through faith, and that not of yourselves; it is the gift of God, not of works, lest anyone should boast.'"* *

He glanced around the room, his voice growing more passionate. "Look at the world around us. You and Zella are the salt of the earth—amazing people with kind souls. Why are you here instead of among the missing? Why were those who committed heinous acts at one point taken, while you remain to endure this dark time? It's because, at some point in their lives, they chose to trust in Christ. Their sins were forgiven."

Lawson leaned in closer, his intensity growing. "Good people, who wouldn't harm a soul, are still here because they chose not to believe.

*Hal Lindsey

No amount of church services, no number of Hail Marys or good deeds can save you. Those actions won't work. It's only through the blood of Christ, who lived a perfect life free of sin, that you can be saved. His grace is a divine gift from God. You see, Jesus is the only way to enter heaven. The Bible tells us in John 14:6 that He is the way, the truth, and the life and no one can get to the Father, except through His Son, Jesus. Until we ask Him to be our savior, repent from our own sinful ways, and put our faith in Him, we won't be saved."

He looked into their eyes. "It's time to stop relying on our own efforts and to start relying on Him."

Jayne silently prayed for Zella and Archie as the room fell into silence. Archie sat motionless, his gaze distant.

Zella squeezed Jayne's hands tightly and bowed her head. When she finally looked up at Jayne, tears streamed down her cheeks, glistening in the dim light.

"I didn't realize …" Zella's voice trembled, barely above a whisper. "I didn't know. I just didn't know." Her eyes were wide with a blend of sorrow and newfound clarity. Jayne met her gaze and saw the hope and peace come into her expression.

"It's overwhelming," Jayne replied softly, her own heart aching for Zella's realization. "But we're not alone in this. We're in this together."

Archie continued to stare ahead, his expression unreadable. It seemed like a contemplative tension lingered between them. Jayne prayed in the silence.

Finally, Archie cleared his throat. He turned to Lawson, his voice steady but tinged with uncertainty. "So, it's been about three and a half years since this began. You say we have three and a half years left. What comes next?"

Jayne shot Lawson a meaningful glance, an unspoken understanding passing between them. She reached for Ruth's notes, her fingers tracing the outline of the next set of judgments. "The next phase is known as the trumpet judgments," she explained. "During this time, the mark of the beast will be implemented across all nations. People will face a critical choice: whether to receive it or not. Accepting the mark means pledging allegiance to the Antichrist and, ultimately, to Satan. Once it's taken, there's no turning back—no forgiveness from God and no hope of salvation.

"It's vital to resist, even if it means facing death," she continued. "The Antichrist will take over the new temple in Israel, and each trumpet judgment that follows will be even more devastating than the last."

Zella asked, "What's the first judgment?"

Jayne took a deep breath, her fingers resting on Ruth's worn notes. "According to Ruth, the first trumpet judgment points to a global nuclear war. Revelation describes hail and fire mixed with blood being hurled to the earth—one-third of the trees burned up, all the green grass scorched. She believed that wasn't just symbolic—it sounded like the direct aftermath of nuclear fallout."

She scanned the next section, her voice firming as she continued. "Ruth also connected it to Revelation 6, where it says the sky receded like a scroll being rolled back. John—trying to describe what he saw in ancient terms—may have witnessed something like a mushroom cloud. When it rises, the sky literally rolls back on itself. Then it says the sun turns black like sackcloth, and the moon becomes like blood. That's exactly what happens in the wake of nuclear detonation—the ash, the radiation, the choking sky."

Jayne looked up, her expression steady. "When you piece it all together the way Ruth did—the fire, the blood, the vanishing sky, the scorched earth—it stops sounding symbolic. It sounds like the beginning of something real. And devastating. And the judgments that follow only reinforce it: a blazing star falls and poisons a third of the rivers, making the waters bitter—exactly what you'd expect after widespread fallout.

If Ruth's right, nuclear war isn't just possible—it's the trigger that sets everything else in motion."

Archie slowly stood and cleared his throat. He turned to face them, his expression solidifying the severity of their situation. "Well, I guess it's time to get ready," he said, his words hanging in the air.

❋ ❋ ❋

Later that night, Archie lay in bed, the room as still and dark as the night outside. The faint patter of rain lingered on the roof, its rhythm soothing yet unable to quiet his restless thoughts. Beside him, Zella slept soundly, her steady, calm breathing contrasting the conflict churning in his mind. Staring at the ceiling, he replayed everything Lawson and Jayne had shared—their warnings, the prophecies—and the undeniable stirring in his heart, a pull toward something far greater than himself.

Archie felt restless and uneasy. It felt foreign to him, but in a moment of quiet determination, he closed his eyes and clasped his hands together, a gesture he had never before practiced. Taking a deep breath, he gathered his thoughts and spoke into the silence.

"God, it's me, Archie," he began softly. There was a rawness to his words, desperation in them, like someone reaching for a lifeline they never knew was there. He paused, unsure of how to continue, but something in him pushed him forward. "I don't know what to say. I've spent my life questioning you, not really knowing if you were real—at least not in the way they say you are. But … things have changed. Everything around me is changing, and I can't ignore it anymore." His voice quiet, as if speaking these words was cracking open something inside him. "I don't understand it all, God. But I know now that Jesus—He's real. He's … the Savior, my savior. And I guess … I guess now it's time to understand what that really means." It was a small step, but it felt monumental—a connection made, a conversation begun. In the stillness of the night, he continued to share his thoughts, feeling a flicker of peace begin to settle in his heart.

✳ ✳ ✳

A few weeks had passed since that pivotal conversation, and Archie and the others had done everything within their power to prepare for the looming war. Tensions hung as they worked diligently, uncertain of where the conflict would strike or how severe the consequences would be. Together, they had harvested everything from the garden, canning fruits and vegetables and storing them in the root cellar.

They had carefully relocated extra blankets, pillows, and essential supplies from the house to their makeshift sanctuary, creating a semblance of refuge. Lawson added his own provisions to what Archie and Zella had, bringing in gas masks and air filters, which had taken on a newfound significance given the escalating threats. With each passing day, they filled more containers with water from the well, ensuring they had enough stored in the root cellar. This preparation had offered Archie a fleeting sense of control, regardless of the uncertain future.

Now Archie crept quietly up the stairs to the loft just above the kitchen, the wooden floorboards creaking softly beneath his weight. He paused for a moment, listening for any signs of life. Just before the first light of dawn broke, he gently knocked on the door. "Rise and shine, boys! It's time to get up for the hunt."

Landon groaned, turning over to pull the covers closer to his chin, while Andrew blinked sleepily, still trying to shake off the remnants of sleep.

"Are you serious? What time is it?" Landon mumbled, his voice muffled by the blankets.

Archie chuckled but quickly cleared his throat to sound more stern than he really felt. "You'll thank me later. There's nothing like a morning hunt to start the day. Plus, we're not going to get anything if you sleep in."

Reluctantly, the boys climbed out of bed, rubbing the sleep from their eyes. They dressed quickly, the chill of the early morning air prompting them to bundle up. Archie led them to the kitchen, where Zella had already prepared a hearty breakfast of biscuits and gravy, the smell wafting through the air.

"Eat up, boys," Zella encouraged. "You'll need your strength out there."

After breakfast, they gathered their gear and met in the yard, Archie showing the boys how to check their hunting rifles, emphasizing the importance of safety with a firm but patient tone. He made sure they understood the mechanics of their weapons, how to load and unload them properly, and always to double-check before they fired.

Then, with a knowing glance, he reached for the bottle of scent-eliminating spray he always carried. He sprayed a generous mist over their clothes, ensuring the pungent scent of the forest would mask their human odor, making them less detectable to any deer nearby.

"Keep quiet," Archie instructed as they moved through the dewy grass, the world around them waking slowly. The woods loomed ahead, filled with the promise of adventure.

As they approached a massive oak tree, its gnarled branches reaching high into the sky, Archie gestured for the boys to quiet down. "This is where we'll set up," he whispered, pointing to a well camouflaged deer blind nestled among the leaves.

Landon and Andrew exchanged excited glances before they climbed the sturdy wooden ladder. Inside, the blind greeted them with the rich scent of wood and earth. Cutouts for windows framed a perfect view of the surrounding forest, and three stools were arranged for their comfort.

"Now listen up," Archie said, lowering his voice to a hush. "We need to be as quiet as possible. The deer are smart and can hear us if we're not careful." He motioned for them to settle down, his demeanor serious yet infused with a fatherly warmth.

"Stay still and keep your eyes peeled. If you see a deer, raise your rifle but don't shoot until I say so. We're waiting for the right moment."

Archie pointed out a deer feeder about fifty yards ahead, nestled just beyond a thicket of underbrush. Its weathered, metal surface glinted softly in the early morning light.

"That's our target area," Archie said softly. "The deer know this spot well. They'll be drawn in by the feed, especially at dawn when they're looking for breakfast."

Landon leaned forward, peering through the cutout window. The feeder stood as a beacon in the quiet forest, a promise of the wildlife that might come. Andrew fidgeted beside him as he adjusted his grip on the rifle.

"Stay focused," Archie reminded them. "It might take a while for them to show up. Just keep your eyes peeled and don't make any noise or sudden movements."

The boys nodded, their eyes fixed on the feeder. The air was still, and the world outside seemed to hold its breath, waiting for the moment when the deer would emerge from the shadows.

At precisely 6 a.m., the feeder sprang to life, scattering corn across the ground in a golden shower. Minutes ticked by, the stillness of the morning amplifying every rustle in the underbrush.

Then, out of the shadows, a silhouette began to emerge. Landon raised his rifle, peering through the scope. But Archie leaned in, his voice a conspiratorial whisper, each word sliding out slow as honey off a spoon, his Southern drawl dragging out every syllable. "Well, don't shoot Gus."

Landon turned to him, confusion etched on his face. "Gus?"

Archie chuckled softly, shaking his head. "Yeah, that's one of the goats. Looks like he must've gotten loose from the pasture."

Landon lowered his rifle. The tension in the blind dissipated, replaced by laughter and the boys' realization that hunting often meant sharing the woods with unexpected visitors.

The boys continued to watch the goat as it grazed on the scattered corn. But Archie's attention was drawn away. He squinted into the distance and, without a word, raised his rifle.

"Archie, what is it?" Landon whispered.

Just then, Archie fired, his shot echoing through the stillness. The boys jumped, and Archie pointed out the mountain lion he'd taken out. The tension in the air thickened, a sharp reminder of the danger lurking in the wild.

"A mountain lion?" his wife exclaimed, her voice tinged with disbelief as she entered the kitchen, where Archie and the boys had gathered after their morning adventure.

Archie was busy putting his gun away, shaking his head as he spoke. "It's odd indeed. I haven't heard of a mountain lion in these parts for over fifty years. This land used to be full of 'em, but they all disappeared long ago."

The boys exchanged glances. "What does that mean, Archie? Are they coming back?" Landon asked.

Archie leaned against the counter, concern crowding his thoughts. "Could be, I reckon. I just can't have them eatin' all my livestock. If they're wandering back, it means something's changing out there." He glanced out the window as Zella busied herself making lunch.

That evening, the warmth of the campfire enveloped the kids as they gathered around, roasting marshmallows and sharing stories. The crackling blaze flickered against the gathering twilight, casting dancing shadows on their faces. Meanwhile, Archie and the other adults lounged on the back porch, engaged in quiet conversation, the air thick with the scent of woodsmoke and impending night.

Suddenly, a strange noise cut through the evening calm. It started as a distant murmur but quickly grew into a sharp, discordant series of quacks. Archie paused, and everyone's heads turned in unison toward the sound. Just above the ancient post oaks, a massive flock of ducks appeared, their wings beating together, creating a symphony of calls that echoed through the air.

Archie stood up, squinting against the fading light and feeling bewildered. "What in the world?" he muttered, astonished at the sheer number of birds—hundreds, maybe thousands—streaming overhead, flying south in a chaotic formation.

Lawson joined him at the porch railing, his eyes wide. "That's unusual, isn't it?"

"Sure is. I can't remember seeing so many at once. Something's driving them out." Archie and Lawson exchanged a look, the unease between them a silent acknowledgment of the uncertainty beyond their small sanctuary.

❈ ❈ ❈

Later that evening, Archie decided it was time to check in on the latest developments and switched on his ham radio while Jayne and Zella prepared stew for dinner.

He and Lawson leaned closer, their expressions shifting from casual interest to growing concern as they tuned into the chatter. The voices crackled through the speakers, reporting that the first strikes had begun, with parts of Israel and the surrounding regions facing devastating attacks.

Andrew, who had joined them, listened intently, worry etched on his face. "I can't believe this is happening," he murmured, gripping the edge of the table.

As they continued to listen, the reports detailed threats against the US and smaller—yet increasingly violent—attacks in major cities. The chaos seemed to spread like wildfire. Unsettling accounts of strange behavior among animals reached their ears: migratory patterns shifting, creatures acting erratically as if sensing an impending storm.

The following day, Archie, Lawson, and the boys were hard at work, securing the barn's windows and doors from the outside. They filled gaps and cracks with hay, determined to protect the animals from any potential fallout that might soon be upon them. Each thud of a hammer and rustle of materials created a sense of urgency.

Archie could see Jayne and Zella nearby, taking sheets off the clothesline. His wife loved the way her sheets smelled after being air-dried in the sun.

Suddenly, an unearthly light exploded on the horizon, a flash so bright it seemed to tear through the very fabric of reality. For a moment, the world held its breath, the air vibrating with an anticipation that felt almost sentient. Then came the roar—a sound so deep and primal it shook the barn's wooden beams and rattled the nerves of every living thing within earshot.

Archie saw the sky begin to unfurl, curling back like a scroll, revealing a grotesque ballet of orange and yellow that writhed and churned, casting an unnatural glow across the landscape.

He, Lawson, and the boys stood in stunned silence, their tools forgotten. Time stretched, and the ground beneath them felt alive, trembling as if the very earth was recoiling from what it had just witnessed. Then, from the haze of confusion, Archie spotted it: a monstrous mushroom cloud rising in the distance, unfurling like the gaping maw of some ancient beast, its dark tendrils reaching for the heavens.

He stood there in awe, caught in a moment of disbelief as the scene unfolded before him. The world around him faded into a backdrop, each heartbeat echoing in his ears. But instinct soon kicked in; he knew they had to return to the house.

With urgency, Archie locked the animals inside the barn, the boys and Lawson helping. They reached the women outside, and without hesitation, everyone sprinted toward the root cellar.

"Where's Sophie?" Jayne called out, her voice rising in panic as she scanned the area.

Lawson called, "I see her coming from the pond!"

"Sophie!" Jayne shouted.

She reached them just as they were opening the cellar door, breathless and wide-eyed. But then she stopped, her gaze fixed on the horizon. Light, powdery flakes drifted silently from the sky.

"Why is it snowing?" she asked.

Archie stepped beside her, staring upward. "No ..." he paused, his voice tightening. "That's not snow." He exhaled sharply. "It's the ashes from the fallout. Get in—now."

Lawson grabbed Jayne's hand, pulling her toward the steps. They hurried down into the shelter, locking the heavy door behind them.

CHAPTER SEVENTEEN

THE MESSENGER'S WARNING

The sudden commotion at the entrance of the cave's great room pulled Sam to his feet. Shouts echoed off the stone walls, sharp and urgent, breaking through the heavy silence that had settled over the group for weeks. He pushed through the hunched forms of the others, the whispered prayers, the startled gasps.

Then he saw them. Two figures stumbled into the dim light, their clothes streaked with dust, their steps frantic. Sam froze, his breath catching in his throat. Moshe. Aharon. Their faces were gaunt, streaked with sweat and ash, their eyes wide with something between relief and exhaustion. They looked like they hadn't slept in days, like the city had taken everything from them on the way out. The cave around them rumbled faintly. Distant explosions thudded like heartbeats beneath the earth, shaking loose dust from the high stone walls. Ahead of him, his mother Lilah and Aunt Miriam reached the men first. Miriam's cry broke through the murmurs, a sharp and unrestrained sound. She threw her arms around her sons. "God be praised," she choked out. "You're here. You're alive."

Moshe stood stiffly at first, as if the weight of her embrace might knock him over, but then his arms rose, folding around her. Aharon's chin dropped to her shoulder. The three of them clung together in silence.

Sam slowed as he neared them. His cousins, his brothers in every way that mattered, were alive. Their clothes were tattered, sweat traced muddy lines down their faces. He wanted to say something, but his throat tightened. "You made it," he said finally, the words barely audible. Three weeks. It had been three weeks since they'd last seen them—since Moshe and Aharon were trapped inside the city.

Moshe looked at him, his face gaunt. He nodded once. "We barely got out," he said, his voice low and raw. "The city … it's gone. It's burning."

Sam's jaw tightened. There was nothing to say. He stepped closer, unscrewing a canteen as he reached Aharon. Wordlessly, he placed a hand on his shoulder and handed him the water. Aharon glanced at him, his face grim and hollow, but he gave a small nod before taking a slow sip.

Together, the family moved deeper into the cave, leading Moshe and Aharon to a quieter place.

The cave shook with each blast from the surface, the ground trembling beneath the feet of those gathered inside. Sam sat with his mother and Aunt Miriam and encouraged his cousins to join them. The faint glow of lanterns cast shifting shadows on the walls. Across from him, Sam watched as Aunt Miriam handed Moshe her canteen, then reached up to brush some of the dust from his face. Her touch was soft, steady — one that spoke of a mother's care.

"Sam," Moshe said, his expression grave. "It's true. Everything we feared is happening. Just like the Bible said it would."

Sam nodded, already aware of the unfolding horrors. "Moses and Elijah?"

Aharon's words came slowly, each one heavy with the memory. "They brought their bodies to the street and left them there." He said, his voice rough. "Kesar made sure no one touched them. He wanted them there, for all to see."

Sam didn't speak, just let the silence stretch between them, listening. Aharon took a breath, like he could still taste the dust of the city. "Then, three and a half days later, just like that—without any warning—they stood up. Breathing. Moving. Like nothing had happened. They just looked around."

He stopped, shaking his head as if he couldn't get over it. "And then, in front of everyone, they ascended. Right there. In the middle of it all. People started shouting. Some of them dropped to their knees, the others just ran."

Sam sat in silence. He had known it would happen—he had read the words, studied the prophecy. But hearing it spoken by someone who had seen it unfold made it feel heavier. He pictured them—Moses and Elijah—men he had followed, learned from, left lifeless for the world to mock... then suddenly rising with the breath of God in their lungs. Standing. Looking. Ascending. Just like the Scriptures said they would.

Nearby, little Shay had been playing a simple game of rolling pebbles with a few other children her age, their quiet giggles offering a rare moment of innocence in the tense atmosphere. But when a particularly strong blast reverberated through the cave, sending a small shower of dust from the ceiling, Shay froze. Her wide eyes darted to Sam before she ran to him, clutching his arm tightly and burying her face against his side.

Sam pulled Shay closer, her dark curls brushing against his chin as she clung to him, trembling. Her wide, innocent eyes revealed both fear and the unspoken trust she placed in him. She wasn't family, but the bond they'd formed felt just as strong. He was her protector, her safe haven.

"Shh, it's OK, Shay," he murmured softly, his hand gently smoothing her hair. "You're OK. You're safe." Another tremor shook the cave, dust trickling from the ceiling, but Sam kept her close, determined to be her shelter in the storm.

Sam glanced back to his cousins. "It's been three weeks... where have you been staying?"

Moshe shifted. "At first, things were tense. The city felt... off. People were shaken after Moses and Elijah were killed, but it was like Kesar was just... waiting. Watching—almost like he was holding back, figuring out his next move." He paused, then added, "We tried to get out, but roadblocks were going up fast. The guards were checking every car, every bag. It wasn't safe. So we stayed with some friends on the outskirts of the city and waited... hoping it would at least give us a window."

Aharon picked up quietly, "But after Moses and Elijah stood up— and the people saw them alive again—that's when everything shifted.

Kesar didn't hold back after that. He set himself up in the Temple—just walked right in like it belonged to him. He hung his own picture inside, called himself the one true god. No more sacrifices, no more worship. You either follow Kesar or you die."

Murmurs rippled through those nearby, but Aharon kept going.

"The Chief Rabbi's backing him. Preaching that Kesar is the Messiah. They're calling it the new order. And now there's this emblem—his symbol. You have to hang it over your doorway. If you don't, they come for you. Imprisonment… or death."

Sam took a slow breath, the grim reality settling in. "What about the mark?" he asked, already bracing for the answer.

"He's forcing everyone to take it or face starvation," Aharon continued. "People are desperate to escape, but the officials are blocking all exits. The only reason we made it here is because—"

"Because we had a plan," Moshe said. "We knew about the hidden routes beneath the city from Moses and Elijah. They had told us about the ancient winding tunnels, tight burrows, and broad chambers hewn into the rock. A few months ago, we scouted them out, knowing they'd be our lifeline if things went south."

Sam listened, jaw tight.

"We couldn't find you," Moshe continued. We got word that the family had been killed, but only found the bodies of our father, uncle, Asher and Adina. We just prayed the rest of you got out in time. We knew we couldn't stay. The tunnels were guarded, day and night. So we decided to hide in an old bomb shelter near the tunnel entrance and lived off stored supplies as long as we could. We waited for a guard shift, slipped into a tunnel, and followed it until we got out."

Aharon's eyes darkened. "When we were in the tunnel, we knew nuclear war had started. We heard the bombs and felt the tremors through the ground. We stayed in the tunnels as long as we could. We knew we had to stay underground for at least a few days to make sure the fallout had settled."

He looked up, meeting Sam's gaze. "We hoped you'd made it here. It was the only place left."

Sam placed his hands on his cousins' shoulders, a silent gesture of respect for the strength he saw in them. "You were prepared." He said as Moshe glanced at the flickering lights overhead, taking in his new surroundings. "But we made it. And now we have to find a way to survive down here while this nightmare continues."

Aharon nodded, his eyes reflecting fear and determination.

As they settled deeper into deeper conversations, more men from their group began to gather around Moshe and Aharon. Their faces were relieved as they welcomed the men, grateful for their safety. Sam felt the atmosphere shift, a collective understanding passing among them as they began to share stories.

Sam paused, collecting his thoughts before he spoke. "I learned something new. Our group—these Jewish men from all over Israel— we're the 144,000 believers prophesied in the Bible."

A quiet spread through the group. Sam saw the words stirred something in the eyes of those who listened. There was hope in their gaze, but also a somber recognition. They were part of something much larger, a plan unfolding as the world outside crumbled away.

Sam felt a surge of gratitude for Moses and Elijah, who had started their group and taught them the truth. Without their guidance, they might have remained lost in the darkness, unaware of their purpose.

Moshe and Aharon exchanged a look, something unspoken passing between them.

Aharon spoke slowly, as if measuring each word. "We're more than survivors," he said, his voice low. "We're a remnant, chosen for something. We have to stay strong, hold on to our faith, no matter what."

✳ ✳ ✳

Weeks passed in the dim light of the caves, their temporary refuge now feeling to Sam both like a sanctuary and a prison. The echoes of war had faded into an unsettling silence, but the fear of the fallout kept them hidden deep within the twisting tunnels.

The underground aquifer provided fresh water, a lifeline that trickled steadily from the rock. Sam and the others from their group ventured cautiously to fill their containers, the cool liquid a welcome relief.

Food was another challenge. Their supplies were limited to the dried goods they had managed to bring with them—salted meats and dehydrated vegetables packed tightly in canvas bags. Meals consisted of rehydrated vegetable stew, the flavor muted but comforting in its familiarity. They boiled water from the aquifer, letting the dried ingredients soak until they softened.

Gathered in small groups, they shared what little they had. They savored the hearty bites, laughing about the tastes of their former lives while pushing aside the unease that lingered in the background. As the evening settled around them, Sam, Moshe, Aharon, and the other men sat together, their faces illuminated by the soft glow of lanterns. This nightly gathering had become a ritual, a moment for reflection and connection amid the uncertainty of their lives in the caves.

Sam looked around the circle, his eyes meeting the familiar faces of those who had walked with him through so much. They had been through momentous times together, and tonight felt especially significant. "Let's pray," he began, drawing the group in.

Moshe nodded and lowered his head, leading them in a prayer of gratitude for their continued safety and the sustenance they still had.

Sam added his own heartfelt words, asking for strength and wisdom as they navigated their new reality. "Lord, we don't take this for granted. Every step, every breath—it's all because of You. Give us wisdom to know what to do next, and courage to follow through. Help us to stand firm, even when everything around us falls apart. We trust You, even here." He lifted his head slowly, his eyes scanning the faces around him—tired, worn, but still holding on. Each man followed suit, sharing their thoughts and hopes, drawing from a well of faith that had deepened in the darkness of the caves. Many among them had transitioned from their Jewish roots to embrace the teachings of Jesus, finding a new sense of purpose in this collective journey. Their shared beliefs were signs of their resilience and unity.

As the prayers came to a close, they naturally flowed into quiet conversations. Sam was filled with a sense of belonging and support. They shared stories, laughter mingling with the remnants of solemnity, creating a bond that was both comforting and empowering. In that moment, they were not just isolated individuals; they were part of a community forged through faith and shared experiences, standing together against the darkness outside.

One of the men in the circle interrupted the flow of conversation, a puzzled look crossing his face. "Why did God choose Israel for such a pivotal role in these end times?" His question made the others pause, their gazes shifting to one another in silent contemplation.

As various explanations filled the space—echoes of historical narratives and theological beliefs—the tall, bearded man stepped forward. Sam recognized him as the one who had helped his Aunt Miriam when she stumbled on the rocks. He had since learned the man's name was **Eitan**, a name that suited his quiet strength. Known for his wisdom and thoughtful silence, the group instinctively quieted when he began to speak, eager to hear his words.

"My brothers," he said, his voice low but steady. "The land of Israel is bound by a promise that cannot be undone. It was given by God to His people, and though a man may sell his land, it is never truly lost. There's always a right to reclaim it, even when times are hard. This right, this promise, was recorded on a scroll sealed with seven seals. Each seal on this scroll represents a term of the sale, and when they're broken, the scroll opens."

He paused, letting the silence speak before continuing.

"This isn't just about land," he said slowly. "It's about the covenant God made with His people. He set Israel apart for a reason, and that purpose has remained through every trial and hardship. God's promise is eternal, and no man can change that."

The men listened quietly, their eyes fixed on him. He went on.

"In the book of Revelation, it's as if God is reclaiming His land, breaking each seal one at a time. This isn't just about judgment. It's God's declaration that He's taking back the earth from the grip of Satan."

A hush fell over the group as they absorbed the words. The idea of the scrolls, their seals, and the profound significance of reclaiming land resonated deeply in Sam. It wasn't just about Israel; it was about a divine promise, a restoration woven into the very fabric of their faith.

Weeks turned into months, the days bleeding together as Sam and the others settled into their new, harsh reality within the caves. Their routines centered around prayers, shared stories, and rationing what little supplies they had. One morning, Sam and Moshe were chosen to scout outside the caves. Their task was simple in name but heavy in its burden: to find out if the world they had hidden from for so long was still a place to walk or if it had turned into something unrecognizable.

They moved together through the winding corridors, their steps cautious but steady. The stones, cold and rough beneath their feet, murmured with the sound of their passing. It was the sound of time lost, of days spent in silence, their every step a reminder of the darkness they had come to know. This wasn't just a walk into daylight—it was a mission. They needed to see how much of the world was still standing. The nuclear strikes had come months ago, but the full weight of what was left couldn't be understood from the safety of a cave. They were looking for signs of life, of food, of survivable land.

As they stepped closer to the tunnel's mouth, a sliver of light appeared at the end of the tunnel. At first, it was a faint thing, barely noticeable, but it grew as they walked, slow and steady, until it filled the passage with a brightness that was almost painful. Sam felt his heart speed up. What waited for them outside, he did not know. They emerged into the light, and it hit them like a wave. Their eyes, unused to the brightness, struggled to adjust, blinking against the glare. It was the first light they had seen in months, and it burned with a sharpness they had not expected.

When their sight cleared, Sam took in the land before him. The earth, once familiar, was now foreign and broken. The sky above them was a muted gray, tinged with a strange stillness. Trees—what few remained—stood like skeletons, their branches bare and scorched. Fields had turned to ash. Blackened soil and deep craters marred the landscape where explosions had torn through, leaving only remnants of the world they had once known. The silence was all-encompassing, save for the distant, muted sounds of destruction echoing from the far-off horizon.

Sam stood motionless for a moment, trying to absorb the sight of it all. He couldn't make sense of it. The world had changed beyond recognition, and yet here they were—on the edge of it.

Suddenly, he heard small, hurried footsteps behind him. He turned, and there she was—Shay. Her dark curls bounced as she ran toward him, her little hands outstretched as if trying to reach across the distance between them.

Sam blinked in surprise, not sure how she had found them. He hadn't seen her leave the cave. But before he could say anything, she was there, clutching his leg with all the strength her small body could muster.

"I go, too?" she asked, a soft tug of confusion in her voice.

Sam's heart tightened. She was only three. What was she doing out here?

Without thinking, he bent down and scooped her into his arms, cradling her small form against him. Her tiny hands rested against his chest, and he could feel the warmth of her innocence.

"You stay with me, Shay," he whispered, holding her tightly.

She didn't answer, but her wide eyes met his, and for a moment, there was nothing but the simple trust of a child in her gaze.

Sam adjusted his grip on the girl, her small hands curled closely around his neck. He glanced out over the broken earth, unsure of what to make of it. The world was utterly unfamiliar, and the city of Jerusalem seemed so far away, its silhouette barely visible against the horizon.

"Come on, I've got you," Sam whispered, his words more for himself than for her. The little girl's wide eyes were still filled with wonder, unaware of the reality they now faced.

Sam squinted toward the horizon, where the silhouette of Jerusalem sat low against the haze. It looked small. Distant. "Can't tell much from here," he said quietly.

Moshe nodded, then tilted his head toward the ridge to their right. "If we climb a little higher, we might get a better view of the city."

Sam hesitated. Shay still clung to him, her small arms around his neck, her body light but ever present in his arms. He glanced down at her, then at the path ahead. "We should take her back first," he murmured.

Moshe looked around, scanning the terrain. "There's no one out here. It's dead quiet."

Sam tightened his grip on Shay. She wasn't fussing. Just watching. Wide-eyed and calm. He nodded reluctantly.

Together, Sam and Moshe started up the path. The climb was not difficult, but it was slow. Sam held Shay in his arms, her small body warm against him. She rested her head on his shoulder, her soft breaths whispering in his ear. The rocky ground shifted beneath their feet, a few small stones tumbling down the slope. Sam's gaze shifted occasionally to the landscape in the distance, searching for any sign of movement, any sign of the world he once knew.

At the top of the mountain, they stopped. The wind, dry and constant, brushed against their faces as they looked down. Sam could see the outline of Jerusalem more clearly; it was still there, though everything around it had changed. It seemed far away. The land between them and the city lay in ruin. Broken earth and scattered stones stretched across the valley, the remnants of something that had once been.

Shay stirred slightly in his arms, and he adjusted his hold on her. She was quiet, still, as children often are in the face of something too big to understand. He kept his gaze on the distant city, shocked at what the area around it had become.

They didn't speak. There was nothing to say. Sam looked to Moshe, who nodded once, then began moving down the slope, looking toward the horizon. As they descended, Sam noticed movement in the distance. Two figures. Slowly, they drew closer. One of them was stumbling, his movements slow and unsteady. His companion was holding him up, guiding him along. Sam's eyes narrowed. The man was badly burned, his skin raw, his face a grimace of pain. Sam's hand tightened around Shay.

When the two men saw them, the uninjured one raised his hand in greeting, his voice hoarse when he called out, "Over here!"

Sam paused, looking down at the injured man, unsure of what to do. He motioned to Moshe, and they walked down the slope toward the men, each step slow but deliberate. As they came closer, Sam could see the severity of the wounds, the way the burned man winced with every movement.

"An attack," the uninjured man said as they approached. "We were ambushed."

Sam's mind worked quickly, considering what to do. He glanced down at Shay. She was still quiet, resting in his arms, her small fingers curled gently around his shirt. There was no time to waste.

"We'll help," Moshe said, kneeling beside the injured man. Sam nodded, adjusting Shay in his arms as Moshe helped lift the burned man. Sam, too, moved to help, lifting one of the man's arms over his shoulder. The burned man groaned but didn't speak.

They didn't go far before Sam felt the change. The unscathed man urged his friend to keep moving, but the burned man hesitated, his body trembling and his eyes wide with fear. Moshe and Sam stepped forward, offering support, but he moaned in pain. Desperation flashed in his eyes as he tried to pull away, recoiling from their touch.

"Please, let us help you," Sam said, keeping his grip steady on the man's arm. Moshe mirrored his efforts, gently encouraging him to accept their aid. Yet the burned man continued to act erratically, eyes darting around as if searching for an escape, lost in a world of anguish that they couldn't fully understand.

"Hold on," Sam whispered, trying to steady him, but the man's face twisted in pain.

Sam saw that his mouth was badly burned, his tongue nothing more than charred flesh, rendering him unable to speak. The man struggled weakly against their hold, panic flickering in his eyes as they tried to support his weight. Moshe's breath quickened; it was clear the pain was consuming the man, and they could do little more than try to ease his suffering.

As Sam and Moshe focused on maneuvering the burned man, Moshe gave a sudden cry and collapsed, unconscious.

Sam's pulse quickened as he looked around to see what had happened. The burned man struggled to crawl away, his face tight with fear. His wide eyes seemed to speak, trying to warn Sam, but the message was lost. Sam's gaze flickered to the boulder behind him, where movement caught his eye. Another stranger emerged, his face hard, eyes cold, knife in hand.

"Lead us to the caves," the man growled, his voice a low rasp that seemed to press in around Sam.

The world shifted. Sam looked back at Moshe, lying unconscious on the ground, and the burned man, inching away in terror. The situation had changed, and Sam felt a cold knot tighten in his stomach. This wasn't a random encounter—it was an ambush. Sam quickly pieced it together—the uninjured man had used the burned man as a distraction, a way to draw their attention, while the other man had been lurking behind the boulder, waiting for the perfect moment to strike. Now, it was two against one— and Sam was the one holding Shay.

He felt the fear rising in him, but he held it back. Shay was with him now. He couldn't let anything happen to her. Her cry reached his ears, sharp and sudden, as she looked at Moshe's crumpled form on the ground.

Sam tightened his hold on her. "Get back," he said, his voice low but steady. He had to buy time, think through the next step, but his mind was scattered. The men were moving closer, their knives glinting in the light. Their intent was clear.

They took another step toward him, and the sunlight glinted off the blades. Sam's thoughts were erratic; his heart was hammering against his chest. His only focus now was Shay.

His grip tightened on the girl. He would protect her. No matter what it took, no matter what came next, he would make sure she was safe. There was nothing more important.

Sam looked down at Shay. Her little head was bowed, her eyes squinting shut as if she could block out the world that was closing in on them. Her small form trembled slightly in his arms, but she made no sound now, trusting him to shield her.

His heart twisted, but his resolve hardened. He knew what he had to do. Without thinking, he whispered a prayer under his breath. It wasn't much—just words formed from the depths of his heart. Words that he hoped would reach beyond the moment, beyond the danger.

"God, protect us," he murmured, his eyes never leaving the men who moved closer. There was no other choice but to pray. He couldn't fight this on his own.

"Lord, please!" Sam pleaded again, and as the words left his lips, a strange quiet settled around him. Time slowed, the moment stretching out before him like an endless sea. A warmth wrapped around him, like a blanket on a cold night. He felt it there, guarding him, steadying his hand as he held Shay close. The men before him stood still. Sam couldn't grasp what was happening, but something told him that everything had changed.

Then, as if the earth itself had shifted, the two men wielding knives and the burned man dropped to the ground in unison. Sam blinked, confused, but his heart still raced. His eyes moved between the fallen men and Shay. She was still in his arms, her small body trembling softly. The air felt thick now, charged with something beyond comprehension.

From the dust, a figure moved toward them. Slowly, deliberately, he walked, his presence commanding attention. There was a grace in his step, an easy rhythm, as though he was not bound by the same laws that governed Sam's world. His shape shimmered in the light, a blur of brightness, soft and strong, like something that belonged neither to earth nor sky. As the figure drew closer, Sam felt his confusion settle, the air cooling around him as calmness spread through his limbs.

The figure stepped forward, his form radiant, casting light across the desolate landscape. For a moment, time seemed to stand still, and Sam felt an overwhelming sense of forgetting everything around him. He realized then that he was in the presence of something beyond this world—eyes gleaming with an understanding deeper than anything Sam had ever known. The smile on its face was one of perfect calm, as if it carried a peace that transcended all the fear Sam had ever felt.

Despite the racing of his heart, there was a sense of reassurance, like he was being watched over in a way he couldn't fully grasp.

"Do not be afraid," the angel said, his voice clear and steady, filling the space between them. It was a voice that seemed to belong to the earth, the heavens, and everything in between. "You are not alone."

The men on the ground began to stir. Sam's breath caught in his throat, the panic crawling back, but the figure raised his hand, and the world seemed to grow still again. No sound, no motion, just peace.

"They will not harm you," the figure spoke once more. "Trust in the path before you."

Sam's mind spun. He didn't understand. "Who are you?" he asked, his voice a mere whisper, strained with awe.

"I am a messenger of hope, who stands in the presence of God." the angel said, his voice like the wind passing over a quiet sea. "I am here to protect those who seek the truth."

Sam stood, still holding Shay, her soft weight against him. The figure gestured toward the horizon. Dark clouds hung there, swirling like the edges of a storm, promising something more to come.

"You must stay in the caves," the angel continued. "It is where you will be safe. Do not drink from the streams. The waters are poisoned. The sea will bring you nothing. Instead, drink from the aquifer below. God will provide."

The messenger's face grew somber, and his words deepened in weight, like a shadow falling over the land. "The world outside will grow darker. The stars will fall. Fire will scorch the earth. The sun will be veiled in darkness, and the moon will turn red like blood. The prince of darkness will release his army. Two hundred million will sweep across Israel, unstoppable like a flood."

Sam's breath caught as the angel's words painted a scene of unspeakable destruction. The angel continued, his voice clear and deliberate. "These warriors will ride on cavalry with the heads of lions and tails of snakes. Their armor will gleam in red, blue, and yellow, and from their mouths, fire, smoke, and sulfur will pour. Then kings from the east will cross the dried Euphrates River, moving toward Jerusalem for battle."

He paused, locking eyes with Sam. "It is crucial that you stay within the caves. Your safety lies there, and it is there you will fulfill the purpose you've been called to." The angel's voice softened, almost reassuring. "Do not leave until your food runs out. Only then will God provide just outside the caves. Trust in God, in His perfect timing."

Sam awoke suddenly, the remnants of the angel's words echoing in his mind. He blinked, disoriented, as the sun began to set. Moshe stirred beside him, groggy but his eyes scanning the surroundings. Sam looked down and saw Shay still in his arms, her small face beaming up at him.

"Did you see that too, little bird?" he asked softly. She smiled and raised her arms, holding them out wide, as if trying to show him how big the angel was.

The two men and the angel had vanished, leaving behind a chilling silence. Sam glanced around, searching for any sign of what had transpired. The burnt man was gone too, leaving only an unsettling emptiness in his place.

"Sam? What happened?" Moshe asked, rubbing the sleep from his eyes.

"I-I think I saw an angel," Sam said, struggling to grasp the reality of it all. "He warned me about what's coming."

Moshe's expression was somber as he remained silent. Sam took a deep breath as the angel's warning echoed louder in his thoughts.

"Stay in the caves," he whispered to himself, feeling the urgency of the message.

As they climbed the rugged path back to the cave's entrance, a sudden shout broke through the stillness. "Shay!" Miriam's voice rang out, panic evident in the call. Lilah and a few others appeared from the shadows, their faces drawn with worry. Their eyes locked on Sam and the girl in his arms.

"She's here. She's safe." Sam called.

Miriam rushed toward him, her hands trembling as she reached for Shay. "Thank God," she breathed, pulling the little girl into her arms. "We thought we lost you."

Before Sam could respond, a sudden burst of light in the sky caught their attention. They turned just in time to witness what looked like stars plummeting toward the ground in the distance, fiery trails streaking across the twilight. Each brilliant flash lit up the darkening sky, casting an eerie glow over the sea.

Then, a series of massive explosions erupted on the water's surface, sending towering waves crashing against the shoreline. The force was so great that they could hear the thunderous roars of ships being obliterated, swallowed by the monstrous swells. It was a spectacle of destruction, each explosion a grim reminder of the angel's warnings.

With a final glance back at the horizon, where fire met water in a violent dance, they stepped into the shadows of the cave. The fight for survival was far from over. Sam felt as if the very walls of the cave were holding their breath, waiting for the storm to break.

CHAPTER EIGHTEEN

STRENGTH IN GOD'S DESIGN

5½ years since start of the tribulation

Jayne stood over the bubbling pot of goat's milk, her hands steady as she stirred, the warmth of the liquid providing a small comfort against the chill in the air. The sweet, tangy scent drifted up, momentarily distracting her from the world outside. Zella worked beside her, their movements in sync, their shared routine offering a sense of normalcy.

As the milk heated, Jayne monitored the temperature, recalling the steps she'd learned over the past two years. When it reached the right point, she added rennet and salt, watching as the mixture began to curdle, delicate white clumps forming before their eyes. The transformation felt almost magical, a reminder that life could still yield something worthwhile.

After several minutes, Jayne carefully cut the curds with a long knife, creating small squares that released whey. The yellowish liquid pooled at the bottom of the pot. She and Zella ladled the curds into a cheesecloth, pressing out the excess whey, the rhythm of their work bringing a brief sense of calm.

"Can you believe this is what we've come to?" Jayne said with a hint of irony, a faint smile crossing her lips.

"It's a skill worth having," Zella replied, her tone light.

It had been two years since they had arrived at Archie and Zella's farmhouse, which proved to be a sanctuary for the time being. Now, five and a half years into the tribulation, the shadows of nuclear war lingered in their lives. They were never directly in the blast zone, but its effects forced them into the root cellar for weeks, which had seemed spacious at first. But as the days wore on and seven people shared its confines, the cellar felt smaller, the walls closing in with every passing hour.

To keep the fallout at bay, they had to seal off the vents from the stove that led outside, eliminating any chance of cooking with limited heat. This made Zella's canned goods a crucial lifeline. Protein came from soaked beans and the preserved meat stored in lard, which had felt strange to Jayne at first but quickly became a staple her tastes learned to crave. Daily, they gathered around the dim light of a single candle, sharing meals that were less about nourishment and more about survival. Jayne was grateful the gas masks had been on hand— they had been a wise precaution. In the end, they were only needed during the first few weeks after the fallout, and even then, only Archie used one when stepping out to tend the livestock. Determined to keep the animals alive, he made quick trips to the barn alone, slipping in and out with as little exposure as possible. She often thought back to those tense days before the blast, watching Archie, Lawson, and the boys work tirelessly to pack hay into every gap and crack of the barn. Their effort and foresight had likely saved the animals that now sustained them. With wildlife still unsafe to consume, the barn and its growing offspring remained their only reliable food source. Jayne found a quiet sense of purpose in assisting with the birth of baby goats, working alongside Archie through each delivery. Every new life felt like a small triumph in the midst of hardship. Survival had become their way of life, and they leaned heavily on one another, bound together by trust and shared resilience.

Eventually, when the worst of the fallout had passed, they returned to living in the house above, though the world they came back to had changed. Now, with no electricity, every meal was a test of ingenuity, prepared over an open fire. The warmth offered Jayne little comfort against the biting cold of the world beyond. Zella's well-stocked pantry had once felt like a safety net, but now it was thinning, each empty shelf reminding Jayne of their dwindling resources.

Water from the deep well was their only supply, but after the fallout, it had to be filtered. They set up solar stills to purify it, using clear plastic sheets to trap moisture. As the sun heated the contaminated water, it evaporated and condensed, allowing them to collect clean water for cooking and drinking. Each drop felt precious in this new reality. The fallout had also contaminated the ground, rendering the soil unusable for their garden and with it went their hopes for fresh produce.

The ham radio usually hummed quietly in the background, its steady connection powered by the sun—a small yet vital link to the outside world. News trickled in about the devastation caused by nuclear war, a conflict that pitted every country against each other, ultimately destroying more than a third of the planet. The blasts had not only obliterated cities but ignited wildfires that swept through the land, leaving charred remains in their wake. Even their own farm bore scars from the destruction, though it had narrowly survived thanks to a rainstorm that had quelled the flames. Radiation from the fallout didn't just claim lives on land; it extended to the seas as it decimated ocean ecosystems and ruined fresh water supplies.

Zella's voice broke into Jayne's reflections. "Sophie, would you like to help with the—"

But Sophie brushed past her, her silence loud enough to fill the room, and headed straight up the stairs to the loft.

Jayne felt a rush of frustration, glancing at Zella. "I'm so sorry, Zella. I don't understand her. She's still acting like a child, and it's infuriating."

Zella frowned with concern. "She's been through so much, Jayne. We all have. She's still figuring things out."

"I know, but ignoring us won't help," Jayne said, crossing her arms and letting disappointment flow through her.

Just then, Landon and Andrew burst through the door, breathless and wide-eyed, urgency in their tone.

"Where's Archie? Where's Dad?" Landon gasped, looking around frantically.

Jayne exchanged a worried glance with Zella.

"What's wrong?" Zella asked.

"We saw a car by the front gate," Andrew panted, trying to catch his breath. "Through the trees."

Fear gripped the ladies as memories of past encounters flooded back—visitors who had looted their supplies, desperate men threatening their safety. Jayne's stomach churned at the thought.

They stopped what they were doing and hurried toward the barn with the young men.

"What's going on?" Archie demanded when they burst in.

"There's a car by the front gate," Landon explained, breathless. "We saw a man and a woman. They looked suspicious."

"Stay back," Lawson said, motioning for the women to keep their distance. He and Archie exchanged a quick glance, the situation clear.

✳ ✳ ✳

Lawson and Archie moved cautiously toward the gate, weapons ready. They approached the car warily.

A man leaned against it, his clothes torn and caked in dust, giving the impression he hadn't seen a clean change of clothes—or a bath—in weeks. Beside him, a woman stood with her back to them, her posture rigid, as if she were waiting for something.

Lawson raised his weapon, voice steady but firm. "What do you want?"

As the woman slowly turned around, Lawson's breath caught in his throat—she was visibly pregnant, her face pale and anxious.

The strange man quickly raised his hands, palms open. "We mean no harm," he called out. "My wife is pregnant. We're just looking for safety."

The men came closer to the strangers, guns still drawn. Archie kept his shotgun aimed squarely at the man, while Lawson moved to the vehicle, eyes scanning for any signs of danger.

"You can search the car if you want," the man said, his voice calm.

Lawson nodded, cautiously circling the vehicle. He opened the door, rifling through the sparse contents—a couple of worn blankets and some empty water bottles. Nothing concerning, but the unease between the couple was evident.

"Now, what do you want?" Lawson asked again.

The man's eyes widened, pleading. "Please, just let us in. We're starving. My wife needs food. We've been on the road for days, and I'm worried about her and the baby."

Lawson glanced at Archie, searching for his partner's thoughts. Archie nodded slowly, his grip on the shotgun relaxing just a fraction. "All right, one meal. Then you'll have to go."

As they neared the house, he spotted Jayne and Zella standing on the porch, watching. Their eyes were fixed on the approaching strangers. From where Lawson stood, he could see the unease etched into their expressions—the silent questions written in their eyes: *Who are they? What do they want? Can they be trusted?* Jayne didn't move at first. Her arms were crossed, and her eyes were sharp with suspicion. But when she saw the woman's swollen belly and unsteady steps, Lawson could see something in her softened. She glanced at Zella, then gave a small nod—almost to herself—and stepped down from the porch.

"Are you OK?" she asked.

The woman stood awkwardly, her clothes tattered and dirt-stained, a noticeable odor clinging to her. Exhaustion was evident in her face, she had dark bags under her eyes, and her hair was a tangled mess. She tried to straighten her blouse, but it did little to change her disheveled appearance. "I'm … I'm fine," she whispered, though everything about her said otherwise.

Zella stepped forward, her voice gentle. "Come inside. You look like you could use a rest."

While the women guided the pregnant woman inside, Lawson and Archie stayed out front with the man. Their weapons were lowered, but their guard remained up. The stranger kept his hands visible, his movements deliberate—fully aware he was still being evaluated. Lawson and Archie intended to ask a few questions, get his story, and determine exactly who they were dealing with and why they had come.

❋ ❋ ❋

Once Jayne and Zella were inside, they settled the woman onto a chair and offered her a glass of water. Jayne's heart ached as she took in the sight of her—so vulnerable and weary.

"What's your name?" Jayne asked softly.

"Jennie," the woman replied, her gaze downcast.

"How far along are you?" Zella continued, trying to keep the conversation flowing.

"Five months," Jennie murmured, a hint of fear creeping into her voice.

Zella stepped forward, her voice gentle. "You look like you could use some help. Are you hungry?"

The woman nodded, her eyes pleading. "Yes, very."

Once the woman took a few sips of water, Zella continued, "While I'm making your food, would you like to take a bath? It might help you feel better."

Jennie hesitated for a moment, then nodded gratefully. "That would be wonderful."

"Great. I'll get the water heated for you," Jayne said, moving to the wood stove. The comforting crackle of the fire filled the silence as she prepared to fill the tub. She found a set of clean clothes to offer their guest as well.

After Jennie finished her bath, she emerged looking refreshed, though her exhaustion still lingered. The pants Jayne had found were a bit snug around her growing belly, so she left the top buttons unfastened.

As Jennie sat down at the table to eat, the aroma of Zella's cooking filled the air. The men soon entered the kitchen, drawn by the smell, their expressions shifting from wary to curious as they took in the scene.

Jayne immediately offered the man a bowl of beans and rice. "Here you go," she said, her voice warm.

The man looked up at her, grateful. "Thank you," he said quietly. "I'm Kevin."

"Nice to meet you, Kevin," Jayne replied, offering him a small, reassuring smile. He accepted the bowl and took a seat next to Jennie, diving into the meal with eagerness.

"So, where are you two from?" Jayne asked, her tone casual but probing.

Between bites, the man wiped his mouth with the back of his hand. "Virginia," he replied, almost absentmindedly. "Been on the road for over a year now, just stopping wherever we can to sleep for the night." As he spoke, Jayne noticed the faint outline of a QR code on his right hand, inked into his skin. The woman, however, had no such mark.

Archie leaned forward, crossing his arms. "How are you managing to travel right now? Gas is scarce."

The man paused, chewing thoughtfully before responding. "We barter where we can. Most places are shut down, but I siphon gas from random vehicles when I need to. Keeps us moving."

Jayne exchanged a concerned glance with Zella, his words making her uneasy.

As the meal came to an end, Zella looked at the couple with a mix of empathy and caution. "You two look like you could use a place to rest. Why don't you stay the night?"

Jennie's eyes brightened at the offer, while the man nodded appreciatively.

Archie shot a glance at Zella, clearly irritated at the suggestion. But her steady gaze didn't change. After a moment's pause, he nodded, relenting. "There's a small room off to the side," he said, turning back to Jennie. "It's mainly used for storage, but we can set up a cot for you. The couch in the living room can be your husband's bed for the night."

"That would be great, thank you," Kevin said, his voice softer now.

Later that night, Jayne awoke to find that Lawson was sitting up in bed, his gun close. She could sense his anxiety, but she felt a sense of peace as she drifted back to sleep.

The next morning, Jayne and Lawson woke early to find Archie already in the kitchen. "Did you manage to sleep at all last night?" Lawson asked.

Archie shook his head. "The man's gone," he said, gesturing to the empty couch where the blankets were neatly folded. Lawson looked as confused as Jayne felt. "The car's gone, too," Archie continued, "but he left the woman. She's still here."

Jayne hurried to peek into the other room, where Jennie was still asleep, blissfully unaware on her cot.

As the week went on, Jayne and Zella worked to make Jennie as comfortable as possible. They provided her with clean clothes and warm meals, but the shadow of her husband's departure loomed.

Though Lawson and Archie had been hesitant at first, the women had convinced them that Jennie, especially with her pregnancy, would need all the help she could get in such uncertain times. She seemed to be in shock at first, but later she confided to Jayne that her husband hadn't wanted to raise a child in the world they were living in.

"And maybe he was right," she said. "How will I manage to have a baby in such uncertain times?"

Sophie leaned against the counter, feeling the weight of the world pressing down on her. Since everything had changed, she had been struggling to accept this new reality, retreating into herself as the world fell apart around her. Depression had settled in, clouding her thoughts and sapping her motivation. She watched her family adapt, finding ways to survive, while she felt increasingly inadequate. But today was different. Determined to step up and contribute, she resolved to try her hand at baking homemade bread, hoping to find a sense of purpose.

As she mixed the flour and water, she felt a flicker of hope. She shaped the dough, kneading it with a bit more force than necessary, wanting it to rise perfectly. After wrapping it in a cloth, she placed it near the warm embers, hoping the heat would help it rise.

But as she returned to check on it later, she was greeted with disappointment. The dough had flattened instead of rising, and when she placed it on the makeshift baking surface above the fire, she lost track of time. The bread soon blackened, the acrid smell filling the air. Sophie stood there, frustration bubbling inside her. She had wanted so badly to help, to make something for the family, but instead, she felt like she had failed once again, only wasting what little supplies they still had.

The next day, she ventured into the only fields that remained, navigating the charred remnants of what had once been lush greenery. Armed with a small basket, she hoped to bring back something useful. She spotted dandelion greens and wild garlic, both promising finds among the desolation. As she picked more, her eye caught a cluster of vibrant berries nestled among the spindly branches of a bush, their bright color contrasting sharply with the ashen landscape. She was convinced they would be a great addition to their meager meals.

When she returned home, her excitement was quickly spoiled. As she presented her haul, the looks on the others' faces told her everything.

"Sophie, those aren't safe," Zella said, her voice showing concern.

Sophie felt her cheeks burn as the realization hit her: They were poisonous. Once again, she had tried to help, only to fall short. Her frustration and despair boiled, and she wanted to scream. Why was it so hard to do something right? She stood there, feeling more lost than ever.

❋ ❋ ❋

Sophie sat by the pond, her back pressed against the rough bark of a willow tree. The shade cooled her face, but nothing settled the unease in her chest. She listened to the soft rustle of leaves above her, the gentle lapping of water against the bank. Still, her thoughts churned.

She heard the cane before she saw him—the familiar rhythm of Archie's steps moving slowly toward her. She didn't look up. She didn't need to. His presence alone brought a strange comfort. When he lowered himself to the grass beside her, she didn't speak, and neither did he.

Archie didn't ask. He just sat there, the quiet between them saying more than words could. The wind stirred the pond's surface, sending tiny ripples across the reflection of the sky. Sophie watched a single leaf drift along the water, carried without effort, and wished—for once—that something in her life could feel that easy.

Finally, he broke the quiet. "It's a hard world we're in, Sophie. We all have our battles." His voice was gentle, carrying the wisdom of someone who had seen much and learned from it.

Sophie nodded, staring into the water. "I just want to help."

Archie leaned back against the tree, taking a deep breath. "Sophie, have I ever told you how I injured my leg?"

Still looking at the water, she shook her head.

"It was during the Vietnam War, in a place I'd rather forget. We were in the middle of a mission, trying to secure a village that had been overrun. I was part of a team tasked with clearing the area, and we thought we had everything under control."

He paused. "I spotted some movement in a building and decided to check it out. I was so focused on being brave, thinking I could prove myself, that I didn't notice the trap they'd set. I stepped on a hidden mine. The blast knocked me back, and I was left with a shattered leg."

Sophie's gaze remained on the water as she processed his story.

"I remember lying there, feeling helpless," Archie continued. "My squad rushed in to help, but I felt like I'd let them down. I was just trying to be a hero, but all I did was put us in danger."

She nodded slowly. "So, it was an accident?"

Archie paused, his eyes distant as he looked down at the ground. "Yes, but it's what came after that was the real lesson," he said, his voice quieter now. "I became very depressed. I was in the hospital for months, and at one point, they told me I might lose my leg completely. They said I might never walk again. I was medically discharged from the military, and I had no idea what I was going to do with the rest of my life. I was angry—angry at everything, angry at the world. But then Zella helped me see things differently. She showed me that it was OK to not be perfect. She helped me see that life still had meaning, that there was a new path ahead of me. She made me keep trying. Every day, she helped me get back up, no matter how hard it seemed."

Sophie was thoughtful as she looked at him. "I guess I'm just struggling to find my place, too. I want to help, but I keep messing up."

"You're trying, and that's what counts. Everyone stumbles. What matters is that you keep getting back up."

Sophie sighed, trying to summon the strength she didn't quite feel. Archie sat in silence for a moment.

"Turn around and look at that," he said, pointing. "Do you know what that is?"

Sophie shifted her gaze to the trunk of the willow tree behind her, her curiosity piqued. "That's a caterpillar's cocoon," she replied in wonder.

"Yes, but do you know what it's doing in there?" Archie asked, his tone inviting her to think deeper.

She shook her head, prompting him to continue.

"Inside that cocoon, a remarkable transformation is happening. The caterpillar is changing, breaking down into something new. It creates this protective casing, using its own body to form it. And look," he said, pointing to a small hole at the top of the cocoon, "there's an opening. Soon, that caterpillar will break free."

Sophie watched closely, fascinated.

"I could help that caterpillar by gently tearing that opening a bit more, making it easier for it to escape," he continued. "But if I did, it wouldn't develop the strength it needs to survive outside. It needs to struggle to emerge, to grow into a butterfly."

He paused. "Just like that caterpillar, you're in a season of transformation. You're in the middle of something difficult. It's slow, it hurts, and it feels endless, but this is where change happens. And change, the kind that lasts, is never easy. The struggle shapes you, makes you stronger. God doesn't promise that life won't be tough. He promises He'll be with us in it. I didn't get it before, but I do now. Even when it seems like He's not answering, He's still there. He's working in ways we don't always see. You're not alone. Don't stop praying, even when you can't hear His voice."

"I'm really trying to change, Archie. I've started praying, asking God for help, but it feels like He's not listening. It's like He doesn't hear me—or maybe He just doesn't care."

Archie cleared his throat, looking off for a moment. Then, in a quiet, deliberate tone, he said, "Let me tell you a story. It's one I've been reading over and over lately. The parable of the shepherd—Jesus called Himself the Good Shepherd. Said there were a hundred sheep, but one wandered off. So, He left the ninety-nine to go find that one."

Sophie watched him, unsure where this was going, but something about his voice made her still.

"He didn't leave the ninety-nine because they weren't important. But because the one that was lost mattered just as much. He went after it—wouldn't stop until He brought it home."

Sophie shifted slightly, her arms wrapped around her knees. "I don't know if I've ever felt... found," she murmured. "I've always kind of assumed I'd figure it out eventually, but... sometimes it feels like I've just been walking in circles."

Archie glanced at her, and there was something in his expression, something gentle but sure. "You're not the only one. I was that lost sheep for over seventy years. I used to think I was doing all right," he said, "but I didn't know the truth. Then your parents came, and God used them to reach me. And He brought you here, too, Sophie. That's not an accident. You know what else hit me?" He went on. "I thought about those shepherds the night Jesus was born. They left their ninety-nine in the fields, too—but this time, they weren't looking for one lost sheep. They went to find the One. The One who wasn't lost at all. The One who came to save."

Sophie lowered her eyes, letting the silence stretch as the truth settled somewhere deep inside her.

"That's the difference," he said. "Jesus left heaven to find us. And those shepherds left everything to go find Him. That's what we're all meant to do. Leave the ninety-nine—the life we've known, the safety, the control—and go after the One. Go after Him."

Sophie's chest tightened. It felt like he was speaking directly into something she'd been trying to ignore. "But how can there only be one way?" she asked, her voice low.

Archie didn't answer right away. He watched her for a moment, calm and unshaken, like someone who had wrestled with the same question long before she ever voiced it.

"You're not the only one who's ever asked that," he said softly. "And being honest about it is a good place to start."

She looked down at her hands, her voice hesitant. "It's not that I don't believe in Jesus. I do. I believe He's real. I believe He died for us. But... I don't understand why it has to be Him or nothing. Why does salvation only come through Jesus? What if someone believes in God—really knows Him, follows Him with everything they have—but they were raised to call Him something else?"

Archie nodded slowly. "That's a hard question, Sophie. And it's one that hits deep, especially when you think about people you care about."

He leaned forward a little, elbows resting on his knees.

"But here's the thing—Jesus didn't come to start a religion. He didn't show up just to give us one more spiritual option. He came because no one else could do what He did. No prophet, no teacher, no amount of good intentions could carry the weight of sin and destroy it. And the truth is—no one else ever has. Only He did. Because Jesus isn't just a man, He's God in the flesh. The Son of God who came to us as one of us, so we could know the Father through Him. You can't have a relationship with God apart from Jesus—He's the only way to the Father."

She didn't say anything, but for the first time, she looked at him directly. Her mind was quiet for a moment, trying to absorb everything he'd said. It was like the pieces were starting to fall into place, but something still wasn't quite right.

"It's not that other people aren't sincere," he continued. "Some are more devout in their faith than most Christians I've ever met. But sincerity doesn't equal salvation. If I drink something thinking it's water, but it's poison... it doesn't matter that I believed it would help me. It still leads to death."

Sophie swallowed hard. "That feels... unfair."

"I know," Archie said. "But fairness isn't the measure. Truth is. And the truth is, Jesus didn't say He's *a* way—He said He's *the* Way. If there were another path, He wouldn't have had to die. But He did. Because it was the only way to bring us back to the Father."

Sophie's voice wavered slightly as she spoke, a thought that had been lingering on her mind for some time. "But... I feel like it's not our place to judge someone else's relationship with God. What if they're following God the best they know how, even if it's not exactly the way we understand it?"

Archie paused, meeting her gaze with a steady, compassionate look. "That's something our culture praises, isn't it? Tolerance. But biblically, that mindset sidesteps the truth. It sounds loving, but it leaves people blind to the seriousness of eternity. Yes, only God can judge hearts, but He's already given us His judgment in His Word. And what we do with Jesus—that's the judgment. If we accept Him, we find salvation. If we don't, we're lost."

Archie's expression didn't harden—Sophie could see it break with compassion. "I know you don't want to think of people getting left out. But do you think you love them more than God does?"

Her eyes darted to his.

"He made them, Sophie. Every heartbeat, every thought, every breath they've ever taken—He's known it. And He's been more patient with them than we ever could be. But He won't force them through the door. Jesus *is* the door. And God's not hiding Him from anyone."

She sat in that—still as the water beside them. The breeze had died down. Her defenses, too.

A tear traced her cheek. She didn't brush it away.

After a long pause, she whispered, "How did you know? That you were saved?"

Archie let out a slow breath, eyes on the rippling pond.

"When I stopped trying to earn it. When I stopped making excuses. I realized I was guilty—really guilty—and that there was nothing I could do to fix it. I believed Jesus already had. I asked Him to save me, and He did. I can't explain the peace that came with it. I just... knew."

She nodded once, barely.

Then, voice barely above the wind, "Would you help me?"

Archie nodded.

And there, beside the pond, they bowed their heads.

Later that evening, Sophie and the rest of their group settled into their seats on the porch outside, the day's fatigue easing. Jennie emerged from the house, her face tired but content. Sophie quickly got up, offering her seat and wrapping a quilt around Jennie's shoulders. Archie noticed and shared a knowing wink with Sophie, a moment of unspoken approval.

Her mom also noticed and smiled broadly at Sophie. But before she could respond, a low hum began to fill the air, cutting through the silence. Sophie paused, confused as the sound grew louder. She turned her head, squinting into the fading light, trying to make sense of the dark shape approaching.

The buzzing intensified—too loud, too close. She exchanged anxious glances with the others, unsure of what was coming. The bug landed on Sophie's shoulder with a soft, almost casual thud. She froze. At first, she thought it might just fly away. But it didn't. It sat there, its tiny legs gripping her shirt, its body a sickly greenish-brown.

She blinked hard, trying to push it out of her mind, but the buzz grew louder, more frantic.

Before Sophie could react, another one landed—this time on her mother's arm. She froze, and Sophie's heart skipped. Jayne's expression hardened as she slowly looked at the others, her voice quiet but steady.

"They're here," Jayne said, her voice low—carrying a weight that told Sophie she understood exactly what this meant.

CHAPTER NINETEEN

SILENT SACRIFICE

The moment the locust landed on Jayne's arm, a chill coursed through her. Its small, rigid body pressed into her skin. The buzzing sound grew louder, a hum that seemed to vibrate through her bones. She looked down, and there it was—an abomination. Not like any locust she had ever seen.

In a movement too slow to be natural, it turned its head toward her. The creature had the face of a man—sharp, pinched features. Its mouth was too wide, its teeth like the jagged, yellowed bones of a long-dead animal. Its body was sleek and armored, glinting with a strange, sickly golden sheen. Its wings, like fragile, shimmering filaments, stretched wide in a pattern that resembled an ancient, twisted battle flag. Its eyes—black and cold—stared right through her. It was sinister and evil. The thing wasn't just a locust—it was *something else entirely*.

Around her, the swarm was coming—rising from every corner of the earth. She couldn't see them all at first. The noise was deafening, like the rumble of a storm building on the horizon. Then, they were everywhere. Locusts. The outside walls, the porch railings, the floor—covered. Some fluttered in frantic, erratic movements, while others crawled, their wings scraping the air like dry paper. The sound of them, the sickening rhythm of their wings, filled the space around them.

Jayne's heart quickened. She opened her mouth to scream, but the noise swallowed it up, leaving only a hollow, trembling breath. Her eyes darted from one insect to the next, all were like the one on her shoulder. She reached up, shaking it off with a jerk, but it had already joined the swarm.

"Inside!" she yelled, her voice thin, panicked. "Get inside!"

They scrambled, pushing into the small, narrow doorway. The swarm pressed after them. The locusts were relentless, a living, shifting carpet of buzzing, clacking, darting bodies. The group burst inside just as the door slammed shut behind them. But hundreds had already made it through—swarming in wild, frenzied circles, ricocheting off the walls, their wings snapping like brittle paper in a deafening storm. Then, just as suddenly as it had begun, the frantic buzzing dimmed. The locusts that had swarmed wildly around the group began to peel away—first a few, then hundreds—drawing back from the others. Their movement changed. It was no longer erratic. Now it was focused. Jayne turned and gasped. Every locust was zeroing in on their prey.

Jennie.

Jennie was standing in the middle of the room, swatting frantically at her arms, her face twisted in pain. Jayne blinked, disbelief settling in. The locusts weren't just surrounding her—they were *biting* her. Their small bodies were clinging to her skin, digging in with their scorpion-like tails, and the sight made Jayne's stomach turn.

"Jennie!" Jayne shouted, rushing to her.

Jennie didn't respond, her mouth working soundlessly. She slapped at her arm, her face pale, her eyes wide with panic. The skin around the bites was already starting to darken, swollen and raw.

"What are these things?" Jennie finally screamed, her voice rising to a new octave. She ran to the kitchen, trying to pull away from the swarm, but the locusts seemed to follow her, biting again as if they had chosen her—singled her out.

"Why is it only her?" Sophie asked. Her eyes stayed fixed on Jennie, who had dropped to her knees, struggling to hold herself upright as if the air itself was pressing against her.

They pulled Jennie to her feet, frantically trying to brush the locusts from her skin, but nothing slowed the swarm. More locusts were crawling into her clothes, biting into the soft flesh of her neck, her arms, her hands. The rest of them could only watch in horror.

Jennie's screams filled the space, the only sound that mattered.

Jayne and Sophie hurried to Jennie's side, grabbing her under the arms and helping her toward the bathroom. Her movements were jerky, like someone in shock, still trying to process what was happening to her body. The locusts had bitten her mercilessly, and now the blood from the wounds had begun to drip, staining her skin. Her eyes were wide, frantic, darting around the room. Once inside the bathroom, Sophie slammed the door shut, the sound echoing in the small space, sealing them off from the madness outside.

Jennie ran toward the sink. "I don't understand," she muttered under her breath, her voice low, as if speaking to herself. She wiped at her eyes, her skin clammy. The confusion in her expression was unmistakable.

Jayne crouched down and started pulling the locusts off her skin, brushing them aside as quickly as she could. They were small but vicious, their bodies like sharp little hooks digging into her flesh. As each bug landed on the floor, Sophie smashed them with her shoe, her face grim as she stomped down hard on another locust that had crawled across the floor. With each crushing blow, the noise of their bodies cracking underfoot seemed to echo in the tight, suffocating room.

"Jennie," Jayne said trying to hold back panic. "Hold still, OK? Just— just hold still."

But Jennie wasn't listening. Her eyes were unfocused, her fingers clutching at her arms like she could keep the pain from spreading. Her voice came out in a raw, strained sob. "Make them stop. Please, make them stop."

"We're trying," Sophie said. She looked up, meeting her mother's gaze. Jayne could see the raw, trembling fear in Jennie's eyes and didn't know how to help.

Just outside, the living room was filled with urgency. Lawson, Landon, and Andrew worked quickly, stomping and smashing locusts as they swarmed. They moved fast, crushing the insects underfoot, using anything they could find to kill them. Andrew swung a pan down with a sharp crack, scattering a group of locusts. Out of the corner of his eye, he saw Landon grab a towel and slam it down on another cluster.

Archie and Zella were sweeping up the remains, working in tandem to clear the floor. The sounds of chitin cracking, the sharp scrape of brooms, and the occasional squelch of squashed bugs filled the air.

Lawson moved toward the door, stomping out the last of the locusts beneath his boots. The surge had passed; nothing else was getting in.

"It's safe," he said. "Jennie can come out."

Zella rushed to Jennie as she emerged from the bathroom and sat in a chair. "This will help with the swelling," she said gently, kneeling in front of Jennie with a small jar of ointment. She uncapped the ointment and began to spread it on the bites. But when Jennie flinched, Zella looked up, her face tight with concern. "It's not going to fix it, but it might help a little. I'm sorry."

Jennie barely reacted to the statement. She winced as Zella dabbed the ointment on the open wounds, her sobs rising again. "Why … why is this happening?"

Jayne hesitated, then took a breath. She wasn't sure if Jennie was ready to hear it, but it wasn't something they could ignore. "It's … the fifth trumpet," she said. "The locusts. They've been released."

Jennie blinked up at her, confusion twisting her face. "The fifth … what? Locusts?" Her voice cracked. She looked at each of them. "What do you mean? What does that even *mean*?"

❋   ❋   ❋

Three-and-a-half months had passed since the locusts descended.

The quiet that had followed their initial swarm was never truly silent. The buzzing, though less intense now, was always there in the background, a constant reminder to Jayne of what had come—and what was still to come. The house had become a sort of fortress as they'd kept the windows sealed tight, the doors locked, trying to protect Jennie from the worst of it.

Jennie, now nearly nine months pregnant, had spent those months inside, sheltered from the locusts that still roamed freely outside. They didn't eat the earth; the pests only seemed to attack Jennie. When it was absolutely necessary for her to leave the house, it was like walking through a minefield. They had watched as the locusts came and went in waves, thick clouds of them covering the sky for days at a time.

Every time she stepped outside, every time she ventured too close to an open window, they came for her—relentless, sinking into her skin, stinging her with their bites. Her body was marked with wounds and scars from the constant onslaught, a map of torment across her skin. At one point, the pain had driven her to her breaking point, and she had pleaded desperately for the suffering to end, wishing for death to take her away from it all. It had broken Jayne's heart.

One afternoon, as Jennie sat near the window, her eyes tracing the movement of the locusts outside, she asked again, "Why is it just me?" Her voice was frustrated, though weak from months of confusion and persecution. "Why aren't you all getting bitten? Why do they only go after me?"

Jayne sighed and glanced over at Lawson, who was busy in the corner, his back to them. They had tried, over the past couple of months, to explain what was happening—what they believed to be happening— based on Ruth's notes. They'd tried to explain the concept of God, the tribulation, but Jennie's eyes had always been clouded with skepticism. She couldn't believe it. Not yet.

Jayne stood slowly and walked to the table where Ruth's Bible lay open, a book they'd read from often. She turned the pages carefully, the quiet rustle of paper almost drowned by the ever-present hum of locust wings outside. She found the passage she needed—the one that kept coming back to her in her recent dreams.

"It's in Revelation," Jayne said softly. She sat down beside Jennie with the Bible. "Listen. This is what it says about the locusts."

Jennie looked at her, her face still full of confusion, but she nodded.

Jayne cleared her throat and began to read aloud:

"In Revelation 9:1–6 it says, *And the fifth angel blew his trumpet, and I saw a star fallen from heaven to earth, and he was given the key to the shaft of the bottomless pit. He opened the shaft of the bottomless pit, and from the shaft rose smoke like the smoke of a great furnace, and the sun and the air were darkened with the smoke from the shaft. Then from the smoke came locusts on the earth, and they were given power like the power of scorpions of the earth. They were told not to harm the grass of the earth or any green plant or any tree, but only those people who do not have the seal of God on their foreheads. They were allowed to torment them for five months, but not to kill them, and their torment was like the torment of a scorpion when it stings someone. And in those days people will seek death and will not find it. They will long to die, but death will flee from them.*"

Jayne paused, looking at Jennie, her eyes searching for any sign that the words were making sense.

Jennie sat frozen, her hands clutching the edge of her chair. She didn't speak for a long time. The buzzing outside now seemed to fill the room. Jennie's eyes flickered toward the window. "So, it's not just happening to me? They're attacking other people who don't believe, too?"

"Yes," Jayne said gently. "It says the locusts were released from Satan, the *'star fallen from heaven,'* as part of the judgment. The fifth trumpet.

They don't harm the land; they don't touch the trees or plants. Only those who don't have the seal of God. And—" She paused, glancing at Lawson before looking back at Jennie. "We believe … that's why you're the only one of us they come for."

Jennie stared at the Bible.

"Judgment?" she echoed, her voice tight. "What do you mean *judgment?* Why are they here? Why is this happening?"

Jayne didn't answer right away. She simply looked at Jennie, feeling the heaviness of Jennie's struggle.

"We're in the middle of the tribulation, Jennie," she said quietly. "The world has changed. It's all happening exactly as it is written in the Bible. These locusts … they're not just any insects. They've been given authority by Satan himself. They've been sent to torment those who refuse to believe in God and who haven't accepted Christ as their Savior. But those who have been marked by God, those who have His spiritual seal on their foreheads, will be spared from this agony. Only they will be protected from the locusts."

She paused, feeling the weight of the truth. "Unfortunately, with the next judgment, Satan will also release his worst demons into the world—ones that Christ Himself cast out long ago because of how vile and destructive they were. They've been waiting for this moment, for their release. Their mission is to kill a third of the remaining human population on earth, and they will not show mercy. Unfortunately, the Bible doesn't make it clear whether believers will be spared from death during this judgment."

Jennie sat back, her eyes scanning the floor as if trying to find something that could make it all make sense. "I'm just not sure what I believe. The Bible, the tribulation, the locusts and demons—it all sounds too impossible, too much like something out of a horror novel."

✳ ✳ ✳

A few days had passed since the last attack. The room was quiet except for the clink of spoons against bowls. The last of Zella's oatmeal sat cold on Jayne's plate. No one spoke. Every movement seemed measured, as if to avoid breaking the uneasy calm.

The radio crackled to life as Archie fiddled with the dials. First came the sharp, jarring static, then the unmistakable sound of voices—raised and muffled, filled with panic.

A scream tore through the noise. "Get inside! They're coming!" The sounds of a door slamming and frantic footsteps followed.

"Hide! *Hide!*"

Jayne froze, but Archie was already on his feet, knocking his chair back. He grabbed the radio, twisting the dial with quick, frantic movements. The voices became clearer, their terror unmistakable.

"They're coming!" a man's voice shouted, nearly drowned out by the static. "We can't hold them off—"

Gunshots. Multiple shots. Loud, sharp, echoing through the radio's speakers, causing Jayne to jump. Then silence.

Everyone was still, waiting. Jayne dared not say a word, and it seemed as if they could all feel the moment stretching out. Then, a deep malevolent voice came through, clear and cold.

"We've found you," the voice said, each word slow, deliberate, as if savoring the fear it was stirring. It was dark, almost guttural, a tone that made the hairs on the back of their necks stand up. There was a faint laugh in the voice, a kind of cold amusement, but it was the kind of laugh that made your skin crawl.

"We know who you are. We know where you're hiding. We have a list of those in the underground system. We're coming for you, and we *will* find you."

The radio crackled once more, then its static faded into a dead hum. Archie turned the dial, but the screen was blank now, and there was only a flat, empty tone. The connection had been severed, leaving only silence in its wake.

No one moved. Jayne felt the words hanging in the air, thick with malice, and for a moment, the room seemed darker. The voice felt like it was crawling out of the radio, like it was already in the house with them, just waiting to claim them.

"Who was that?" Jennie's voice broke the quiet.

"No idea," Archie muttered, his fingers still resting on the radio. "But they're coming."

Jayne exchanged a brief glance with Lawson—no words needed.

It was time.

"Kids, upstairs," Lawson said, his voice clipped. "Pack your stuff!"

Zella stood up, moving quickly toward the back door. Jayne followed her to the root cellar, and their eyes scanned the shelves before the two women grabbed crates and filled them with whatever food was left—bags of rice, canned beans, and the last of the dried goods. They worked quickly, but Jayne could see the strain behind Zella's eyes, like her thoughts were already somewhere darker than the cellar.

When the women brought their loads to the Suburban, Archie was bringing the rifles and ammunition from the gun safe. The tension in his jaw was visible.

"I've got the gas masks, tents, and water purification tablets," Lawson said as he stowed duffle bags in the vehicle.

Once the car was packed with the food and supplies, he turned to Jennie. She stood on the porch, her belly swollen, her face pale. The weight of her pregnancy seemed heavier now, more real than ever.

"You're coming with us," Lawson said, his voice soft but firm.

Jennie hesitated. "Where are we going?" she asked confused, looking around in fear.

Instead of answering, Jayne approached the young woman and gently guided her into the house to pack.

Landon, Sophie, and Andrew passed Jayne and Jennie as they came downstairs, their bags slung over their shoulders, their movements quick and purposeful as they moved quickly outside.

Jayne followed Jennie back into the room and helped her gather what they could. Jennie's hands trembled as she stuffed clothes and supplies into her bag, her breath uneven. Jayne didn't say much—there wasn't time, and there wasn't anything that would make this easier.

They zipped the bags, slung them over their shoulders, and stepped out into the hallway. The weight of what they were walking into hadn't fully hit yet. Jayne just kept moving.

Outside, the SUV waited.

"Lawson … where are we going?" Jennie asked, her voice tight and filled with worry as she climbed into the vehicle.

Lawson looked up from the Suburban, his face hard, but his eyes betraying a flicker of concern. He took a deep breath before answering. "We're heading for the caves," he said. "We can't stay here. The farm isn't safe anymore."

The words stung, laden with finality.

Jayne moved to help load the SUV, taking the items that Zella and Archie handed her, but she noticed Zella wasn't moving quickly anymore. Jayne stepped over to her, her own face wet with tears. She put a hand on Zella's shoulder, trying to offer comfort, but the words didn't seem to matter anymore.

Jayne's voice broke as she spoke. "We're going to be OK, Zella," she whispered, though she wasn't sure if she was trying to comfort her friend or herself.

Zella didn't answer; she only nodded weakly, wiping her eyes. Her shoulders were hunched, her entire body shaking with the burden of her grief. Jayne stayed close, holding her in a gentle embrace.

The ground was still damp from the morning dew, the wet earth giving off a faint, musty scent. Jayne watched Lawson check and recheck their supplies—every can of food, every jug of water, every rifle. There was no margin for error.

Zella was quiet, more subdued than usual. She worked as if in a trance, loading extra blankets, extra supplies, as if preparing for something she knew would come but didn't want to face. Archie was just as silent, his eyes distant as he checked his rifle one last time. He didn't need to say anything. No one did. They all knew what was coming.

Lawson handed Archie a map, showing him the route to the caves, his finger tracing the lines with precision. "Stay close," Lawson said, his voice a low murmur. But Archie simply nodded, his expression unreadable. He wasn't looking at the map, but beyond it, his mind already somewhere else.

Jennie sat inside the vehicle, her hands resting on her swollen belly, her eyes following the movement of the others, but it was clear to Jayne that she was lost in her thoughts. She hadn't fully grasped all that was happening. Zella stepped up to the open SUV door where Jennie sat. Without a word, Zella reached in and handed her a quilt—a simple thing, but lovingly made, each stitch a quiet offering of the love she held for the life soon to come. Her hands trembled slightly as she passed it over. Zella's eyes were filled with something unreadable, but she didn't speak. She just handed the quilt to Jennie and then, almost as an afterthought, gave her a hand-crocheted sling for carrying the baby when the time came. It was beautiful, delicate, and so full of tenderness that Jayne's throat tightened as she watched the interaction.

Jennie's eyes welled, and she whispered, "Thank you."

But before Zella could answer, a dark ripple moved across the sky. A locust swarm was coming.

Zella's expression hardened. She reached up and pulled the door shut.

A single gunshot echoed in the distance, sharp and jarring against the quiet of the morning.

"They're here," Archie said, his voice low but edged with urgency. His gaze shifted toward the horizon, where the sound had come from. There was no shock in his words—only a quiet recognition of the inevitable. "They've found us."

There was a faint sound of the gate being rattled. "I think they've broken the lock," he said.

Lawson didn't hesitate. "Get in the car," he said sharply, turning to face the others. There was no argument, no time to waste. Jayne and the young adults all moved quickly, scrambling to get inside their vehicle. The air was tense, but no one spoke. The sounds of the vehicle starting, doors slamming shut, was all that broke the silence.

From her spot in the back seat, Jayne's eyes darted toward the front gate, her mind racing. She couldn't see anything yet—no movement, no sign of who was out there—but there was an unspoken understanding that the enemy was here. Lawson's hand tightened on the wheel.

"Back gate," Archie said from next to the vehicle, his voice calm. He didn't need to explain. Lawson nodded without a word. He knew exactly where the back gate was, knew it well enough to get them out of here fast. No hesitation.

Just as Lawson shifted the car into gear, Jayne's eyes caught something out of the corner of her vision. Zella. She was standing on the porch, staring out into the distance, her posture rigid and still.

"Zella!" Jayne shouted, her voice cracking with alarm. "Get in your car! Now!"

But Zella didn't move. She just stood there, clutching her hands, her face unreadable. It didn't make sense. They didn't have time for this.

Lawson's hand froze on the gearshift. He opened his mouth to shout at her, but the words never came.

Archie had started walking toward the front gate, rifle in one hand, cane in the other. His steps were slow, deliberate. There was no fear in his movements—only a calm resolve, as if he had already accepted what was to come.

Jayne's stomach twisted. She knew what this meant. Archie and Zella weren't coming with them. Not now. Not ever.

But she didn't want to accept that. "Lawson!" Jayne's voice was frantic now, tearing through the disbelief. "We can't leave them! We have to wait!"

But Lawson didn't stop. He couldn't. The decision had been made. He slammed the car into drive, his foot heavy on the gas pedal. The engine roared to life, and they lurched forward. Jayne screamed his name, but the sound was drowned out by the rush of the wheels turning.

As they pulled away from the house, the finality of it hit Jayne hard. The image of Zella standing alone on the porch, Archie walking toward the front gate, was burned into her mind.

And then, in the distance, two gunshots shattered the quiet.

Jayne's breath caught in her throat. The sound hit her like a physical blow, like something inside her snapped. She didn't need to look back. Archie and Zella had made their choice—had *chosen* to stay behind. Their sacrifice was the price of their family's survival. The cost had been written in blood—and they would carry it with them forever.

CHAPTER TWENTY

DEMONS IN THE NIGHT

Under the dull ashen sky, Jayne's group made their way down a narrow, paved road, the Suburban kicking up clouds of dust behind them. Hours had passed since they left, but the landscape never changed. The world outside was a wasteland. The sky, a sickly shade of gray, stretched over the barren landscape, casting everything in a muted, oppressive haze. The sun barely broke through anymore—if it ever did—and the days seemed shorter, darker, as if the earth itself was exhaling its last breath. Every tree they passed was dead or dying, their skeletal branches reaching up like the hands of the lost. The roads had long since cracked, weeds overtaking the pavement, but they had no choice but to keep moving forward.

Lawson gripped the steering wheel, his eyes fixed ahead, scanning the horizon. They were taking the back roads now, avoiding the main highways where danger might lurk. Jayne kept watch out her window, and the ones in the back were silent, absorbed in their own thoughts. Even Sophie, who had always been the first to break the tension, was quiet. The earlier chaos, the panic, had quieted down, but something heavier now filled the space between them.

A tension lingered that Jayne couldn't shake, an awareness that they were no longer just running from what they'd lost but also from everything that was hunting them. The land outside seemed to stretch on forever, empty and unforgiving, as if the earth itself had grown tired of humanity.

Landon sat beside his father, his face drawn tight, eyes scanning the rearview mirror as if expecting someone—or something—to appear.

Andrew was in the far back with Sophie, just visible if Jayne glanced over her shoulder.

Jennie sat silently beside Jayne, her hands resting on her swollen belly, her face pale. The bites on her arms were healing slowly, but the marks left behind were still red and raw, a constant reminder of how the locusts had singled her out, even now. Jayne had tried to give her comfort, but she had stopped seeking it.

Jayne's eyes occasionally flicked back to Jennie, like a mother watching a child carry pain she can't take away. There wasn't much she could do for her. The locusts had made their choice, and it seemed there was no escaping it.

The loss of Zella and Archie was a blur of raw emotion for Jayne. At first, she had been consumed by grief, unable to make sense of it, the sharp pain of their sacrifice cutting deeper with each passing hour. She had been hysterical, frantic, her mind unable to grasp that they had actually done it—that they had chosen to stay behind so that the rest of them could escape.

Zella had not only been a friend to Jayne; she had been family in every way that mattered. The kind of person who never asked for anything in return but always gave, always took care. It felt as if a piece of Jayne's own heart had been ripped away. Zella had welcomed them into her home when they'd had nowhere else to go, provided safety when they thought it was no longer possible. She hadn't known then what kind of preparations Zella and Archie had been making for years, the quiet stockpiling of food, the hidden supplies, the underground system that had kept them alive. They hadn't known what they were preparing for, but it seemed Zella somehow had known deep down. She had prepared them all for this—a safe place in the midst of turmoil, this fight, this escape. All those years of what seemed like simple, prudent living, now making sense in the cruelest way.

Jayne had never asked, never questioned Zella's intentions. She had just trusted her. And now, leaving the farm and everything they had once considered home, she realized just how blessed she was to have known them. To have had the time they had, even if it felt like too little, too late.

With time, the tears slowed, and the hysterics ebbed away, replaced by a kind of solemn clarity. Zella and Archie had given them a chance to survive, a chance to live, but at the cost of their own lives. The pain still burned, but the gratitude—heavy, layered, suffocating—was there too. And as they drove, Jayne's heart ached, but she also felt something else. A new kind of resolve, a deeper understanding of what she had to do to honor their memory. There was no going back now. The road ahead was uncertain, dangerous, but she couldn't afford to lose sight of the fact that they had been given this gift: survival. It wasn't just for them. It was for Zella. For Archie. For everyone who had made the ultimate sacrifice.

Jayne glanced back at Jennie, her hand resting lightly on her belly, her face drawn in pain and exhaustion. She couldn't let them down, not now. Not after everything.

Jayne yawned as Lawson pulled the Suburban into a small, overgrown campground, the gravel crunching under the tires. The place was quiet, deserted. He parked the vehicle behind a thick cluster of trees, the shadows already stretching long in the fading light. The woods around them were silent except for the occasional rustle of the wind, the only sounds of the day slipping away.

Jayne noticed the stillness and felt quietly grateful for it. The locusts didn't seem to be around at the moment; they came and went without warning, and though she knew better than to trust the quiet completely, for now, it was a small mercy.

"We'll stay here for the night," Lawson said, his voice low. He looked around, scanning the tree line one more time before he shut off the engine. He pointed to a small trail leading through the trees. "This trail looks like it leads to the campsite. Get the tent up. We'll keep the fire small."

Jayne squinted through the trees, catching sight of a small fire pit tucked just ahead, the faint remains of old fires scattered around it. The spot seemed secluded, exactly what they needed right now.

The others moved quickly. Andrew and Landon pulled out the tent, pitching and staking it into the hard ground, while Sophie and Jayne gathered some of the sparse dry wood they'd found nearby and worked to start a small fire. Jennie, visibly uncomfortable, sat by the fire with her arms wrapped around her knees. The night was growing colder, the air biting at her skin.

The fire crackled to life, its orange glow flickering against the dark woods. They passed around a can of beans, eating in silence, the metallic taste of the food almost a comfort—one of the few familiar things left in a world that had long since unraveled.

They talked quietly among themselves, their words drifting in the cool night air. Jennie, her hands now resting on her rounded belly, felt a sudden kick. She paused mid-sentence, a smile crossing her face. "He's moving," she said softly, looking down at her stomach.

Sophie leaned in and placed her hand on Jenni's stomach. "I can feel it," she murmured, her voice full of wonder. "Do you think it's a—"

Before she could say more, the sound of leaves rustling sharply cut through the conversation. It was faint at first. Jayne's head snapped up. The others froze. No one spoke.

Through the trees, three figures emerged into the dim light of the fire.

Lawson stiffened, his hand drifting to the gun at his hip. Andrew and Landon shifted slightly, their rifles within reach.

The first man was tall, his broad frame casting a shadow in the firelight. His long, dark hair, streaked with gray, was pulled back into a messy ponytail that hung low against his neck. A rough, scruffy beard covered his weathered face, and dirt clung to his skin like it had been there for days. He wore a grimy tank top, the fabric stretched over his chest and shoulders, revealing veins that ran like cords along his sinewy, muscular arms. His bloodshot eyes were dull, unfocused, and the bottle of whiskey in his hand swung lazily at his side as he took a slow, uneven step forward.

Behind him, a shorter man shuffled into the light, his movements jittery and unsteady, like a marionette pulled by unseen strings. His shaggy, sandy blond hair hung unevenly to his shoulders, as though cut with no care or precision. Sparse patches of a beard clung to his jaw, rough and untamed, the kind of growth that could only come from weeks of neglect. His pale face was gaunt and damp with sweat, the hood of his stained, zip-up hoodie pulled tight over his head, casting shadows over hollowed eyes. Dirty jeans clung to his thin legs, stained and frayed at the cuffs. His hands shook constantly, a nervous energy rolling off him in almost visible waves.

A woman followed behind them, thin and wiry, with long auburn hair cascading over her shoulders. Big, round eyes scanned the space with a watchfulness that felt invasive, her freckled face betraying nothing of her thoughts. She moved quietly, her steps deliberate, as though she was used to bending the world around her to her will. Her clothes had a thrown-together, earthy feel—layers of flowing, mismatched fabrics in muted tones, with beaded necklaces hanging loosely around her neck. A makeshift wreath of dried leaves and brittle flowers sat atop her head, a fragile crown that swayed with her movements, lending her an odd, uneasy presence.

Jayne watched warily as the first man took another swig from the bottle, his eyes locking onto Lawson and the gun that was holstered securely on his hip.

"We don't mean no harm," he said, his voice slurred, but the edge in it was clear. "My name's Roman," he said, his voice carrying an air of confidence. "This here's Sawyer, and the woman goes by Jo." He looked them over, eyes flicking over their faces before resting on Jennie, her swollen belly catching his gaze. "But we could sure use some food. Got anything to spare?"

Lawson didn't flinch. He kept his hand on the gun at his side, but he didn't draw it. Not yet. "No," he said, his voice steady but firm. "We've got enough for our family and that's about all. You need to keep going."

Roman raised an eyebrow but didn't argue. He tilted the bottle to his lips and took another long drink. He didn't seem to care much about the answer—only the fact that it had been given.

The woman stepped forward then, her eyes fixed on Jennie. There was something unsettling in her stare, something predatory. She looked at Jennie for a beat too long, her lips curling slightly. "When's the baby due?" she asked, her voice soft, but too soft, like the whisper of a snake in the grass.

Jennie glanced nervously at Jayne. "Any day now," she said quietly.

The woman—Jo—gave a slow, chilling smile. It didn't reach her eyes. Her gaze flicked back to Roman for a moment, a silent exchange passing between them, before she turned away.

Roman, still swaying on his feet, seemed to enjoy the moment. He eyed Jennie again, his smile too wide, too pleased. "Time's up," he said, his voice like gravel, low and dangerous.

Jayne's blood ran cold. She didn't know why, but the words struck her like a slap. She straightened, her heart pounding. "What did you say?"

Roman's grin widened, and he looked over his shoulder at her. "I said, I guess time's up." The words were drawn out with a rhythm, like a song she couldn't place.

Jayne's breath caught in her chest. A jolt of cold horror shot through her, but she couldn't move. The air around her seemed to thicken. This wasn't a coincidence. There was something wrong—something she couldn't quite place, but it gnawed at her, a dark whisper at the edge of her mind.

And then it clicked. His face. That face. It wasn't just some stranger's look—it was the man from her dream years ago. The one who had stood in the courtroom, watching her. The man she prosecuted for the brutal murder of a child. The one who had spoken in a voice that felt like ice, who had made her skin crawl with terror.

Her stomach twisted; her pulse spiked. This wasn't just some drifter wandering into their camp. This wasn't random. This was something she had been warned about, something she couldn't escape. She tried to look away, but his gaze seemed to hold her, as if he knew everything.

Roman stared directly at Jayne. His face twisted for the briefest moment, his features molding and distorting like wax melting, as if it could no longer hold its shape. His eyes went black, his skin seemed to stretch and twist. In the span of a heartbeat, his face turned monstrous—fanged and cruel. It was the face of something that didn't belong here. It was the face of something from the dark places of hell.

Jayne couldn't breathe. She couldn't look away.

But then, just as quickly, it was gone. Roman's face was normal again, that same smirk on his lips. As if nothing had happened.

He turned, nodding to the others. "Let's go," he said, his voice no longer slurred but sharp, like a command. He didn't wait for a response, just walked back into the trees with Jo and Sawyer trailing behind. They disappeared into the woods without a sound, like smoke dissipating in the night.

For a long moment, no one moved. The crackle of the fire was the only sound.

Jayne's heart pounded in her chest, her breath shallow. "Did you see that?" she whispered, almost to herself.

Lawson didn't answer immediately. His eyes were still fixed on the spot where Roman had stood, searching the trees beyond the firelight.

He didn't need to say anything. She knew. Whatever they were—whatever that had been—it wasn't over.

Lawson hadn't seen it. He hadn't seen Roman's face twist. He hadn't heard the words in that low, guttural tone. When she asked the others, Sophie, Landon, and Andrew all shook their heads. They saw a drunk man—a man with sores and too much whiskey on his breath, a drifter with a grin that was unsettling but nothing more.

Jayne swallowed, trying to calm her fears. Had she imagined it? Maybe it was the stress, the fatigue, everything that had been building up over the last few days. Maybe it was the fear that had started to eat away at what little peace she had left. Was it just a trick of the mind?

"We need to leave," she muttered, more to herself than anyone else, but the words came out weak, unsure.

Lawson glanced at her, his voice steady, but there was a quiet edge to it. "It's OK. We're OK." He turned to the others. "We'll keep watch. We'll be fine."

He wasn't asking for reassurance; he was giving it. Jayne wasn't sure if she believed him, but there was comfort in his certainty. She nodded, swallowing the fear that had risen in her throat, trying to hold it together.

Later that night, after securing themselves in the tent, Jayne lay in the dark, trying to ignore the creeping anxiety at the back of her mind. The sound of the wind in the trees, the occasional snap of a twig— everything felt magnified in the stillness of the night. But mostly, it was that feeling. The one she couldn't shake. The thought that something was out there, watching. Waiting.

She closed her eyes, wishing for sleep, but every time she drifted close, Roman's twisted grin would flash in her mind. It was the face from her dream. The same man, the same *smile*.

The first light of dawn barely cut through the trees as Jayne moved quickly, almost frantically, packing their things. She couldn't stay there any longer. The night had been a blur of restless fear, each passing hour dragging her deeper into panic. She hadn't slept. Not really. Her mind kept replaying Roman's face—no, that *thing* in Roman's face—and the words he'd said: *Time's up*. Her heart wouldn't stop racing. Her skin felt like it was crawling, every muscle tight with the memory of his grin.

But it wasn't just that. It was the noises in the night. The sounds from the strangers, coming from somewhere close by.

It had started with chants. Low, rhythmic, almost hypnotic—like some kind of twisted incantation or prayer. It had made her skin prickle, her pulse race, but she tried to ignore it, tried to tell herself that it was just the madness of the world they now lived in. But it didn't stop. The chants shifted into something else. Something worse.

Later, she heard the muffled sounds of them—*all of them*—moving around the woods. Their voices had shifted, more animalistic now, as they started to … *worship* each other. She didn't know how to describe it, but the sounds they made were unmistakable. Groans, the wet sounds of bodies moving against each other, their frantic, desperate moans echoing through the trees. She had almost felt it—heard it—in her own bones. It had been repulsive.

Jayne's stomach turned at the memory. She didn't care how quiet they were now. She and her family were leaving, and they were leaving now.

Jayne and Jennie brought the last of their belongings to the vehicle where Lawson and the boys were already hastily shoving their supplies in the back. She turned to Lawson, her voice tight. "It's time to go. Now."

Lawson nodded, his face hardening. He didn't ask why. He understood. They all did.

They were done here. The strangers had claimed the woods as their territory, and it was a place Jayne and her family never wanted to be again.

Jayne's eyes flicked from Lawson to the camp, then back again. She could feel something starting to tighten in her chest. She took a slow breath, steadying herself as she looked around. *Where was Sophie?*

"Jayne," Lawson said, his voice strained, "I thought Sophie was with you."

Jayne froze. "She wasn't with me," she replied, trying to keep her voice even, but the words felt too sharp. "I thought she was with you! Sophie said she was going to wash her face and bring her things to the car," Jayne muttered, her voice tight with rising panic.

They both stood there for a moment, just looking at each other, as if neither of them could believe what was happening. Lawson turned away from her and scanned the campsite and the woods surrounding them. He moved to the car, checking the back seat. No Sophie.

Her breath caught. "Where is she, Lawson?"

He didn't answer right away. He glanced around, then looked at her again, his jaw tightening. "I don't know."

And that was the moment Jayne knew—something was wrong. A cold rush of fear swept over her, sharp and unrelenting. Sophie was gone.

Her breath caught as her eyes darted to Lawson, then to the rest of the group, her thoughts tumbling over one another. Without hesitating, she turned sharply, scanning the area. "Sophie?" Her voice cut through the air as she moved, calling out again, louder this time. Each step quickened, her focus narrowing as her instincts took over. Where could she have gone? Jayne refused to let herself stop. She had to find her daughter.

They all ran back to the campsite, urgency driving their steps. Lawson was ahead, running so fast Jayne could barely keep up, catching only glimpses of his red T-shirt flashing through the trees. Branches scratched at her arms as she pushed herself forward, her breath coming hard and fast. When they reached the clearing, they scattered, scanning the area, desperate for any sign of Sophie. But there was nothing—no tracks, no clue. Only the echo of their own footsteps crunching through the dry dirt.

"Landon," Lawson said quietly, his voice hard, the sharp line of his jaw set in that way she knew too well. He was going into protective mode, and she could see it in the way his eyes narrowed, his body becoming all business. "Come with me. Andrew, you stay with Jayne and Jennie."

Landon didn't hesitate. With his rifle slung over his shoulder, he fell in behind his father without a word.

Jayne watched them head down the path, terror creeping through her, jagged and relentless. Her breath caught slightly as the fear settled in, quiet but unshakable.

Jayne turned back to Andrew and Jennie, her mind shifting to the next step. "Come on, we're going to check the others' camp," she said, her voice steady with a clear plan. "Stay close." She didn't know what they'd find, but she knew she had to keep moving.

Without a word, the three of them set off through the woods, their feet crunching over the dry leaves and dead twigs that littered the ground. Jayne's mind raced as they moved through the trees. She couldn't shake the feeling that something had gone wrong—*terribly* wrong. The strangers weren't just random drifters. Roman, Sawyer, and Jo—she could still see them clearly in her mind, their unsettling smiles, their unsettling presence. They weren't the kind of people who simply passed through. They had a purpose. And Sophie was missing.

As they neared the strangers' camp, the unnatural quiet hit them first. No sounds of movement, no signs of life. The usual rustle of leaves or distant calls from animals were absent. All that remained was a deep, almost suffocating silence. The air felt wrong. Jayne's skin prickled.

They arrived at the edge of the camp—just a few rundown tents, half collapsed and sagging, their remnants scattered about. The fire pit was cold, the ashes gray. It was as if whoever had been here had simply vanished.

Jayne motioned for Andrew and Jennie to stay back. She moved forward, her heart pounding. The place reeked of something foul, something beyond the decay of an abandoned campsite. There were scraps of clothing, a few bottles of liquor half buried in the dirt, and old, twisted remnants of what looked like broken tools. It was a mess. A place that no one would want to call home.

"Sophie?" Jayne called out, her voice strained. "Sophie, where are you?"

No answer.

The wind blew lightly through the trees, carrying with it the faint smell of something burning. Jayne looked back over her shoulder at Andrew and Jennie. Both of them were tense, their eyes scanning the area nervously.

And then Jayne saw her.

Jo.

Sitting cross legged on the ground at the back edge of the camp, her back straight, her hands resting flat against the dirt. Her eyes were closed, her face expressionless, as though she was in some kind of trance. There was no movement except for the slow rise and fall of her chest. For a moment, Jayne thought she might be asleep, but the longer she watched, the more wrong it felt.

Jo's lips moved silently, her fingers twitching ever so slightly against the earth. It was as if she were drawing something from it, something ancient, something dark. Her head tilted just a bit, and a soft hum—a chant—escaped from her mouth. The sound was low, almost like a prayer, but it felt too much like a ritual, a twisted invocation. Her palms pressed deeper into the dirt, her body still as stone, absorbing the land's vibrations like a starving animal.

She wasn't just connecting with the earth, Jayne realized. She was *taking* from it. The way her fingers dug into the ground was not reverence but a desperate need to bind herself to something beyond the natural world—something older, something wrong. This wasn't peace she was seeking, Jayne thought, but power. She wasn't offering herself to the earth; she was bowing before it, treating the dirt as a god, submitting to the forces it promised in return. The earth beneath her seemed to answer, humming with low, guttural energy, as if feeding her. The land was no longer a refuge. It was her idol.

Jayne's stomach turned. She had no idea what kind of ritual this was, but it wasn't something she wanted to witness. Her first instinct was to pull Jennie back, to get as far away as possible, but her legs wouldn't move. She was frozen, caught in the eerie stillness of the moment.

Jo's humming stopped. Her head snapped up, and her eyes—those wide, dark eyes—opened slowly. They were unnaturally still, unblinking. There was no humanity in them, no warmth. Just an empty, endless stare. It felt like being watched by something ancient and dark, something that shouldn't be alive.

Jo's lips curled into a smile. A slow, sinister smile that made the hairs on the back of Jayne's neck stand up.

Jayne's breath hitched. She couldn't look away.

And then Jo spoke, her voice a whisper, but it cut through the silence like a blade.

"You shouldn't have come here."

Jayne's body went cold. The realization hit her like a wave. *The strangers had been waiting for them.*

Before she could react, Jo's smile widened even further, and without another word, her movements became unnatural, jerky—as though her body was not entirely in her control.

Jayne's instincts kicked in. *Get out of here. Now.*

She could see Sophie was not there. She turned to Jennie. "We need to go. Now!"

Andrew's rifle was raised, his eyes scanning the trees. His grip tightened on the weapon, and he gave a sharp nod.

A sudden crackle sliced through the silence, sharp and jarring. A noise—faint, distorted, caught in the static—punctuated the stillness of the woods. Jayne froze, her eyes snapping toward the sound. Then it came again, clearer this time, piercing the quiet.

Was that—? She took a step back, eyes locked on the trees, pulse thudding hard against her ribs.

Then came the burst—rapid fire, a string of shots in quick succession. Too many. Too fast.

Jayne's hand flew to her mouth.

Silence again. Just for a moment.

Another string of gunfire.

And then—

A voice. Shattered. Unmistakable.

"DAD!"

Lawson and Landon had stuck close together, each step deliberate, the path narrowing as the dense woods had begun to open up into a clearing. The lake ahead lay dull and still, its surface a flat mirror reflecting the muted sky above. Relief had washed over Lawson when he saw Sophie standing at the water's edge, a towel pressed to her face as she wiped off the dampness from her skin. She was safe.

Out of the corner of his eye, something stopped him dead in his tracks. A flicker of movement, just beyond the tree line, half hidden behind thick brush.

Roman and Sawyer.

They were crouched low, barely visible, eyes fixed on Sophie, staring at her with a cold, deliberate intensity. They hadn't noticed Lawson yet, but the air between them felt wrong, charged with something dangerous.

Lawson's jaw clenched. He was frozen for a moment before his hand instinctively went to the pistol at his hip. The grip was familiar, reassuring in its simplicity, and within a breath, he had it free, the cold metal cool against his palm.

"Stay back, Landon," Lawson hissed, his voice low and clipped.

Landon quickly stepped back, his fingers brushing the rifle strapped to his chest.

Lawson's breath came quicker now, his mind racing with the implications. Roman and Sawyer were still oblivious to his presence, and for a moment, Lawson's eyes locked onto the two men, the simmering fury in his chest quickly morphing into something darker. The intensity of their gaze toward his daughter made his blood boil. This wasn't curiosity. This wasn't some chance encounter. It was something else entirely. She was their prey, and the realization sank in like a blade through his chest.

Lawson took a step forward, every nerve on edge, his finger hovering near the trigger. He didn't care about the consequences.

"Hey!" Lawson's voice cut through the silence, hard and sharp. "What the hell do you think you're doing?"

Roman didn't flinch. He simply turned his head slowly, his eyes locking with Lawson's, a smirk spreading across his face—a smirk that crawled down Lawson's spine like a rotting hand. Sawyer didn't budge. He stayed rigid, eyes narrowed, his whole body taut like a spring waiting to snap.

Sophie, unaware of the danger, lifted her towel from her face and stilled when she saw her father, eyes flicking past him. Her gaze fell on the two strangers standing just out of the trees.

"Dad? What—"

Lawson gripped his gun tightly, the barrel steady and aimed directly at Roman. The man was still smiling, his posture relaxed, as if this was some sick joke. But the look in his eyes—cold, calculating—told a different story.

"Don't you dare touch her," Lawson growled, flicking off the safety lock on his gun, his finger hovering over the trigger. His eyes did not leave the bushes, where the two men lay in wait.

Everything in him screamed to protect his daughter, but the silence between them stretched, the seconds weighing heavier with every passing breath.

Roman's smile stretched across his face, slow and deliberate, like a predator savoring its next meal. His eyes, dark and unreadable, held Lawson's gaze as if he could see through him, down to the very marrow of his bones. There was no fear in Roman's eyes, just a quiet, unsettling certainty.

"Sophie! Now, move!" Lawson's voice cut through the air urgently as he called for his daughter to come to him.

Then Roman slowly stepped forward and spoke. His voice was low, rough, like gravel scraping over stone, but it carried power—like the words were a summons, like they were pulling something out of the air, something ancient, something dangerous.

"She belongs to us now."

The words hit Lawson like a blow, sharp and venomous, but they only fueled the fire of a father's protective rage. His grip tightened on the pistol as a deep, primal urge to protect his daughter surged through him. Every fiber of his being screamed to shield her, to keep her safe—no matter the cost.

Roman's statement wasn't just a threat—it was a promise. And Lawson could feel it. His fingers twitched on the trigger.

At her father's command, Sophie had begun to run toward him, her feet pounding the earth beneath her, but in the next second, it happened. Sawyer was already out of bushes, his reach closing in on her. Sawyer lunged, his body moving with predatory speed, his eyes locked on Sophie, the prey.

Lawson's hand was on his pistol, his aim steady, as he squeezed the trigger. The shot cracked through the air, sharp and loud. It slammed into Sawyer's shoulder with a sickening thud just as he was grabbing Sophie, causing him to howl in pain, blood pouring from the wound as he stumbled back. His grip loosened, and she dashed toward Lawson, fear and relief flashing across her pale face as she escaped.

Lawson's focus didn't waver from Sawyer, the pistol still raised, ready for the next shot. Sawyer, his glare venomous, retreated into the shadows, slinking back to Roman. The threat was far from over, but for now, Sophie was out of harm's way.

Lawson's gaze locked onto Roman, who stood at the edge of the clearing, his face unreadable, but the way he watched—half amused, half calculating, only fueled the fire in Lawson. Every muscle in his body ached to protect his daughter, to end this now. There was no fear, only a cold determination.

Lawson's finger itched against the trigger. His grip tightened on the gun, knuckles white, as Roman's lips curled into a grin—a smile that stretched too wide, too cold, like it didn't belong on a human face.

"You think you can stop this?" Roman's voice slithered through the air, low and guttural, like the growl of something that had taken human form. He began to move toward Lawson, his steps deliberate, like a predator closing in on its victim.

Out of the corner of his eye, Lawson could see Sophie freeze beside Landon. The tension was unmistakable as though the very ground was holding its breath.

Roman's eyes glinted, a flash of something ancient and terrible passing through them, his gaze carrying the presence of something pure evil, as if the darkness within him had taken form.

And then, it happened.

In the blink of an eye, Roman's body *shifted*. His posture straightened, his shoulders widening, the skin on his face rippling like liquid beneath a mask. It was unnatural, grotesque. For a moment, Lawson couldn't breathe. His vision blurred as Roman seemed to grow taller, the muscles in his body bulging in ways that defied reason, stretching his clothes until the seams threatened to split.

Roman's eyes, now black as midnight, were no longer his own. They were hollow, an empty vessel for the demon that had claimed his body. The soul that once inhabited him was gone, leaving only a terrifying void. Those eyes didn't just look at Lawson—they pierced through him, as if they could strip away everything, leaving only fear in their wake.

Lawson's gun wavered in his hands, the weight of it suddenly too heavy. His muscles screamed in protest, his body betraying him, refusing to move.

Roman stepped closer.

Each step sent a tremor through the ground, like the earth itself was buckling beneath his feet. Lawson aimed the gun again, but his arms were like lead. Roman's gaze never left him, his mouth pulling back into that grin, revealing teeth too sharp, too jagged to belong to a man.

Lawson's finger twitched on the trigger. He had no choice now. *Protect Sophie*, he thought. *Protect my family.*

With a final, desperate yank, he squeezed the trigger.

The shot rang out with a deafening blow.

But Roman didn't move. He didn't flinch, didn't even *acknowledge* the bullet that ripped through his chest, leaving nothing but a hole that seemed to swallow the very light around it. The bullet passed clean through his body—through him—as if Roman wasn't even there.

Lawson's finger squeezed the trigger again and again, the gunshots ringing out in rapid succession, each one striking Roman with unyielding precision. But Roman didn't fall. His face didn't flinch. His body jerked with each impact, but the demon inside him seemed untouched by the bullets. Lawson's mind raced, trying to process what was happening—how was this possible?

"Get back!" Lawson growled at Sophie, his voice raw, desperate. He fumbled for a new magazine, his hand shaking as he tried to reload. But before he could, Roman was on him—his grip like steel, seizing Lawson's wrist with an unnatural strength. It was as if the demon had no human limitations, no weakness.

Lawson gritted his teeth, tried to break free, but Roman's grip tightened, crushing his bones, forcing him to his knees. It was like fighting against a storm—powerful, inevitable. His body screamed, but he couldn't make it move. The gun slipped from his hands, crashing to the ground in a spray of dirt and dust.

Roman leaned in close, his breath foul and hot against Lawson's ear. His voice was a low rasp, a cruel whisper. "You should've just let me have her."

Lawson's breath caught in his chest. Before he could react, Roman's hand shot out, fingers like steel claws, gripping him by the throat. With one flick of his wrist, Roman lifted Lawson off the ground like he was a ragdoll, his feet dangling uselessly.

Lawson gasped for air, his throat tightening, the pressure unbearable. Roman's face leaned in, that wide, manic grin never leaving. But his eyes—those black, hollow eyes—bored into Lawson like they were reaching inside him, tearing apart his very soul.

"You're weak," Roman hissed, his voice a rasping growl, as though it were coming from a place far deeper than a man's throat. His words seemed to vibrate in the air around them, a distortion of reality.

Out of the chaos, Lawson caught a blur of movement—Landon. His son's rifle was already up, his face set with grim focus. Lawson heard the first shot crack through the air, then the sharp click of the chamber. Another shot. Then another. Roman didn't react. No flinch, no stumble—just that same twisted grin. A fourth shot followed, and still, the demon stood untouched. Lawson's heart sank as he realized what Landon must be thinking—what he must be feeling. Then came the hollow click of an empty chamber.

Lawson's hands instinctively clawed at Roman's wrist as two of the shots slammed into the demon's side. His nails scraped uselessly against skin that felt more like stone than flesh. It was no use. Roman didn't even flinch. Lawson couldn't move. His body refused to respond. His strength was gone. Betrayed by his own muscles, all he could do was fight to breathe as the darkness pressed in.

And then, in a sudden burst of brutal strength, Roman hurled Lawson across the clearing. He flew through the air, crashing hard against the ground, the impact jolting his entire body. His vision blurred, and his lungs screamed for air, but the world seemed to close in, everything slipping away.

Through the fog in his mind, Lawson heard footsteps—fast, thundering. Before he could process it, Roman's strong hands grabbed him, lifting him off the ground and pulling him swiftly into the woods. The world around him blurred as they moved, Roman's grip relentless, dragging him further into the trees.

✳ ✳ ✳

Landon had stood frozen, his empty rifle still aimed. His eyes had been wide, staring in disbelief at the two men—no, *monsters*—who had just torn his world apart.

His father, the man who had fought for him, who had protected him for as long as he could remember, was gone.

Landon's chest had tightened. He had opened his mouth, but no sound came out. The words, the scream, the *rage* inside him—it all had turned to ice.

A wave of cold realization had hit him like a slap. His father—*his father*—was gone, taken by something that didn't belong to this world.

"DAD!" he had screamed, his voice breaking, desperate and raw.

But there was no answer. Just the wind, rustling through the trees, and the echoes of the forest, carrying his cry farther than he could reach. The shadows swallowed his father, swallowed the man who had been his protector, his everything.

The woods swallowed the sound of his anger, as if the earth itself had absorbed his pain, leaving him alone in the hollow quiet. The weight of the rifle was now unbearable, like a hundred pounds of guilt pressing down on him, and still, he couldn't stop himself from staring into the dense shadows where his father had disappeared.

He lowered the rifle slowly, his chest heaving, and the world around him seemed to narrow. There was no more fight. There was nothing left but the haunting image of his father, taken. Gone.

Landon and Sophie crashed through the trees, breathless, terror written across their faces. The gunshots still echoed in Landon's ears as they stumbled back toward the clearing. Sophie's face was ghostly pale, her eyes blank, her feet barely keeping up with her brother's hurried pace.

When they broke through the brush, Landon saw the others. His mom was already moving toward them, alarm in her every step. Jennie was right behind her, her hand outstretched, ready to catch his mother if she stumbled. But it was the sight of Sophie that froze his mother.

Her body jerked back, her eyes wild. "Where's Lawson?" she demanded, her voice tight with fear. "Where's your father?"

Landon couldn't answer right away. He just stood there, staring at his mother, the words lodged in his throat. He looked at Sophie, her trembling form like a shell, unable to speak.

"Andrew!" Landon finally barked. "Get Sophie in the car. We're leaving, now!"

Andrew grabbed Sophie, pulling her toward the car, but she didn't respond, her body limp and uncoordinated. Jennie scrambled to follow. Landon shoved his mother toward the vehicle, his hands shaking.

"No, we can't—" Her voice broke, her eyes flicking toward the woods. She was looking for him.

Landon didn't waste a second. He grabbed his mother, pushed her toward the car without a word. She tried to resist, eyes wild with terror, but his grip was firm.

"Landon, where's your father?" his mom shrieked, her voice raw, as she stumbled toward the car. "Where is Lawson? Tell me! Please!"

She reached for him, her hands shaking. "Landon! Please, you have to tell me—what's happening?"

Her breath came in frantic gasps. The fear in her voice cracked through the air, but Landon didn't stop. Without a word, he shoved her into the car, the door slamming shut behind her.

The engine roared to life as Landon threw the car into drive, tires screeching on the gravel. She screamed, trying to open the door.

"Landon, please!" She shouted again, eyes wide with terror, looking back, willing him to stop, to tell her what had happened. But there was no explanation, no answers, only the sound of the car tearing through the woods, the weight of silence pressing in.

"They have him," he said. "He's … he's gone."

His mom's breath caught, her face crumpling in disbelief. The world seemed to collapse around them as the words hit her. Landon didn't say anything else. He didn't need to. The truth hung between them, undeniable and final.

CHAPTER TWENTY-ONE

A PURE GIFT

Hours passed in an oppressive silence, broken only by the occasional sound of the car's tires on the road. Jayne sat in the passenger seat, staring blankly out of the window, her eyes swollen and face streaked with tears. Her mind was a blur—flooded with images of Lawson, of Landon's words. She could still hear him, his voice shaking as he recounted everything. How they had come for him. How her husband had been taken. And now, here she was, running with her children in the middle of nowhere.

Her chest felt hollow, as if every breath she took was too shallow to fill it. She couldn't cry anymore; the tears had run dry, but the ache remained. Her heart was shattered, but the pieces kept slipping away, too far gone to grasp. She wanted to go back. To find him. To make it all stop. But she knew the danger. She couldn't risk their lives. She couldn't put her kids in harm's way, not again.

She saw Landon glance at her from the driver's seat. But she turned to stare out the window, absorbed in the passing scenery.

"Mom?" he said softly, but she didn't respond.

She heard Jennie shift in the backseat, but Sophie and Andrew were quiet and still in the back. The only sound was the steady rhythm of the tires on the road, as if no one dared to break the silence left in the wake of what they'd been through.

Without saying a word, Landon eased the car off the main road, steering it into a deserted neighborhood. The houses were dark, lifeless, with windows boarded up and weeds overtaking the yards. He pulled the car into an alley that led to the back of one house.

"We're running on fumes," he muttered as he climbed out. Jayne was vaguely aware of him grabbing a siphon hose and a gas can from the trunk and moving toward an abandoned car. Andrew followed. His hand rested near the pistol strapped to his hip.

Landon crouched next to the car, jamming the hose into the gas tank and starting to siphon. Andrew stood a few steps away, his back to the vehicle, keeping watch with tense focus.

Behind her, Jayne heard Jennie crack her door open and step out cautiously. She turned to look, but she couldn't rouse herself to ask if the young woman was all right.

"You OK?" Landon asked.

"I'm fine," Jennie said quickly, though her voice betrayed her. She took a shaky breath and leaned against the car for support.

"Jennie," Landon said, standing up from the gas tank. "What's wrong?"

"I said I'm fine," she insisted, but as she spoke, another wave of pain hit, and a small gasp escaped her. She bent slightly at the waist, gripping the car.

In the car, Jayne finally stirred to action. She opened her door and stepped out, her eyes darting toward Jennie. "What's happening?" she asked with alarm.

Landon looked back at his mother. "Something's wrong with Jennie," he said, his own worry evident.

Jayne's gaze locked on Jennie, taking in the way she clutched her belly and leaned against the car. "Jennie," she said softly but urgently, stepping closer. "How long have you been feeling like this? How far apart are the pains?"

Jennie hesitated, guilt flickering across her face. "A while," she admitted, her voice cracking. "Maybe since we left. They were coming about every five minutes or so, but now they're—"

Another contraction hit, and Jennie gasped, her knees buckling slightly. Jayne caught her arm as the realization hit her.

"You're in labor," she said calmly but insistently. She steadied Jennie as Andrew glanced over, tense but keeping his focus on the surroundings.

"Jennie," Jayne continued, "this baby is coming."

The house smelled of dust and decay, its walls were scrawled with graffiti, and broken furniture was scattered across the floor. Jayne was still grateful that Landon had found an unlocked window so they could get indoors. Now, they huddled in the dim light, scanning the space for any sign of movement.

The back bedroom was vacant, the floorboards creaking underfoot as they helped Jennie inside. The room was bare except for a sagging bed with an old comforter thrown over it. A faint smell of mildew lingered in the air.

"Lay her down, slow and easy," Jayne said calmly but urgently as she guided Jennie onto the mattress. Sophie hovered nearby, adjusting the blanket beneath Jennie's head.

Jennie winced, her breath catching. "It's … it's starting again," she whispered, clenching her fists against the pain.

Jayne knelt by the bed, placing a hand on Jennie's shoulder. "You're doing great," she said. "Just breathe through it." She turned to Landon, shifting into business mode. "Get the first aid kit from the car. And a towel—something clean."

Landon nodded and hurried out, his footsteps echoing down the hallway.

Andrew stood in the doorway, his hand resting on the grip of his pistol, his gaze scanning the street outside through the front windows.

Jayne adjusted Jennie's position on the bed. Sophie was by her mother's side, dabbing a damp rag across Jennie's forehead, trying to ease her discomfort.

Landon returned, arms full of supplies—water, the first aid kit, and a few blankets. He set them down in a haphazard pile beside the bed.

"Good," Jayne said, quickly sorting through the items. "Help me get her more comfortable."

Landon nodded, stepping in closer, but Jennie groaned with discomfort, curling into herself.

"Stay with me, Jennie," Jayne said firmly but gently. "You're OK. We're here. Just focus on breathing. One contraction at a time."

Jennie's face twisted with pain again, but she nodded weakly.

Hours passed. Jayne had sent Landon and Andrew out of the room. But Sophie stayed by her mother's side, her hand gripping Jennie's as she tried to offer comfort. Jennie's body convulsed with pain, each contraction bringing her closer to the breaking point. She was sweating, breathing raggedly, her face pale and drawn. But through it all, she held on, determined to see this through. She had no choice.

Jayne was a steady presence beside her, guiding Jennie through each contraction, each wave of pain. Her voice was low and firm, giving Jennie the reassurance she needed to hear. "Breathe, Jennie. Focus on the breathing. You can do this."

Jayne wasn't new to this. She remembered birthing her own children, the pain and the work, the uncertainty and the beauty of bringing life into the world. She could still feel her own mother's hands guiding her through it, and now, she was the one doing the guiding. The knowledge and experience were in her bones, a natural rhythm that seemed to take over as soon as Jennie's labor began to intensify.

Sophie, too, was no stranger to the process. She had assisted with the birth of calves and goats on the farm alongside her mom and Archie.

Her hands were steady, her movements precise as she helped Jennie, gently positioning her legs and holding them back as Jennie pushed.

Jennie's cries echoed through the walls as her body struggled against the pressure of labor. Sophie's voice cut through, calm and focused, telling Jennie to breathe, to push. Jayne's hands guided Jennie's body through the final stages of delivery.

"Come on, Jennie," Jayne encouraged, her voice steady despite the tension. "PUSH!"

Sophie moved closer as another contraction hit. Jennie cried out.

And then, the moment came.

With one final push, the baby's head emerged. The room fell silent for a heartbeat. Jennie gasped in pain, but she was almost there.

Jayne moved quickly, guiding the baby the rest of the way, her hands steady. Sophie continued to help Jennie, holding her leg, her voice urging her to keep going. And then, the baby was out—small, fragile, but crying with a strong, loud wail.

Jennie collapsed softly against the bed, gasping for air, her body trembling with exhaustion and relief. The baby's cry filled the room, and for a moment, the world outside seemed to pause.

Jayne cut the umbilical cord with practiced precision. She wrapped the baby in a towel, moving quickly to keep the infant warm. Jennie, still breathing heavily, reached out for her baby, her hands trembling.

Jayne carefully placed the baby into Jennie's arms, her voice soft with emotion. "I'd like you to meet your daughter."

Sophie stood by, her eyes brimming with tears as she watched Jennie hold her newborn. Jennie's expression was a blend of awe and disbelief, her eyes glistening as she gently cradled the tiny girl. The room was quiet except for the soft sounds of breathing, each of the women overwhelmed by the tenderness of the moment. They stood together, taking in the beauty of new life.

Jayne watched as Jennie held her newborn daughter against her chest, the world outside forgotten for a moment. She had made it. They had made it.

And for the first time in hours, a small flicker of hope stirred in the air.

Later that night, the house was still. The only sound was the soft, rhythmic suckling of the baby at Jennie's breast as she nursed her. Landon's tired eyes scanned the darkness outside while Andrew took his turn to doze. Sophie slept in a chair beside Jennie. Her head lolled slightly, the pull of sleep too strong to resist.

Jayne, sitting on the bed next to Jennie, watched the scene before her. The baby, so small and fragile, was held in the comfort of her mother's arms. She felt a quiet relief wash over her—everything had gone as it should, and the baby was healthy, safe. She gave a silent prayer of thanks, grateful for God's protection and guidance through it all.

But as she looked at the tiny new life, something inside her broke open. Just hours ago, she lost her husband—gone without warning, without a goodbye. And now here was this precious child, beautiful and breathing, full of everything he had lost. The sharpness of it cut through her. Sorrow came fast and full, almost too much to carry. But even in that storm, a quiet gratitude stirred—small, but steady enough to remind her that life still held beauty. Her tears, silent, held both truths. "She's beautiful, Jennie," Jayne whispered, not wanting to break the moment. She gently stroked the baby's hand, watching her tiny fingers curl around Jennie's thumb.

Jennie's gaze was fixed on her daughter, her face soft with love and a quiet disbelief. "She is," Jennie said softly. "Thank you … for everything. I couldn't have done this without you."

Jayne smiled, her heart swelling. "You're not alone in this, Jennie."

There was a brief moment of silence as Jennie's eyes softened, captivated by the delicate new life in her arms, unable to tear herself away from the miracle before her. Her lips trembled with pride, then, almost shyly, she met Jayne's gaze. "I've decided on a name," she whispered.

Jayne raised her eyebrows, curious.

"Reyna," Jennie said softly, cradling the baby closer. "It means 'pure'. I just feel like, in all this darkness, she has to be something pure. Something untouched by all the evil around us, something from God—something good and pure to hold on to."

Jayne's heart lightened, the weight of Jennie's words resonating. "Reyna," she repeated softly. "In a world like this, pure feels like the most precious thing. God's reminder that even here, in the worst of it, He still gives us something to believe in." She looked at the tiny, fragile life in Jennie's arms. "She's a gift. A sign of hope, of light in the midst of it all."

CHAPTER TWENTY-TWO

PROVISIONS OF MERCY

6½ years since start of tribulation

Sam shifted fitfully in his sleep. His body twitched on the cold stone floor, beads of sweat clinging to his brow despite the cave's chill. In his dreams, something was with him—no, *on* him. Icy fingers trailed his face, the touch searing in its coldness. He tried to scream, but his voice lodged somewhere deep in his throat. The thing whispered, its voice slithering into his ears like poison, a language he didn't understand but instinctively recoiled from.

Sam bolted upright, gasping, the dream dissolving into the suffocating reality of the cave. He slapped at his face, the phantom touch lingering like an itch he couldn't scratch. Drip. Drip. Something warm hit his forehead. His breath stilled. Slowly, he looked up, expecting … what? A face in the dark? Glowing eyes in the shadows?

But it was just the ceiling, rough stone glistening faintly in the dim light of his lantern. Water trickled from a crack above. He exhaled, shaky but relieved. Then he wiped his face with his hand, and his stomach dropped.

Blood.

The realization hit hard. His trembling hands glistened in the flickering lantern light, wet and crimson. Not water. Blood. His pulse quickened, his thoughts racing. The judgment. The bowl judgment. The waters were turning to blood, just as Scripture foretold.

He scrambled to his feet, reaching for the rag he kept tucked in his belt. He scrubbed at his face, harder than he needed to, as if he could erase the growing horror around him. The drip became a steady patter now, the blood running down the cave walls, pooling in shallow crevices on the floor. The cracks above wept red, as though the earth itself were bleeding.

Sam grabbed his lantern and stumbled toward the aquifer. It was deep in the cave, their last source of clean water, hidden from the outside world and its decay. He reached it, knees hitting the stone as he crouched. He dipped trembling hands into the water. It was still clear, still fresh—for now. He splashed his face, the coolness grounding him as he stared into the small pool. But he couldn't shake the image of blood creeping toward them, tainting everything.

The caves had once been a refuge, a shield from the horrors outside. But they weren't safe from the evil spirits released into the world. For months, they'd endured torments no stone walls could keep out. The demons had found ways in—slipping through cracks, materializing in dreams, crawling into the fragile minds of those sheltering within. People woke with scratches carved into their skin, their blood leaking onto the rugged ground. Some wandered in their sleep, blank- eyed and murmuring words in languages that felt ancient. Others screamed awake, clutching at shadows, their voices hoarse from terror.

Sam and his group had fought back with everything they had. The Scriptures had become their lifeline, a road map through the unrest. Each judgment was marked, expected, prepared for—if preparation was even possible. They had weathered the early waves of the tribulation, the first judgments that seemed almost distant compared to the horrors that followed. But now, as they neared the end of the seven years, the weight of prophecy was pressing closer.

They heard the screams from the world outside, carried into the caves like echoes from hell—the dying, the wars, the earth splitting apart. Nuclear devastation had paved the way for the judgments that followed. First, the locusts from the abyss, tormenting those without God's seal for five months, their stings driving people to madness but sparing no lives of the unbelievers. Then came four angels released at the Euphrates, unleashing a demonic cavalry that slaughtered a third of mankind. The first bowl judgment brought festering sores, tormenting those left behind. And now, the final bowls poured out God's wrath—the waters turned to blood, the sun burned hotter than ever, scorching the land, and dehydration claimed those who'd survived. The air was thick with decay, suffocating, and still, the Scriptures warned of more to come.

The end was near. Sam knew it, felt it in every tremor of the ground beneath them. They were not merely living through prophecy; they were teetering on the edge of the last pages foretold in Scripture. The time of decisions was past, and only God's mercy could sustain them now. The final battle was coming.

But for now, they held fast. When the demons came, they spoke Christ's name with authority, and the spirits fled. For a while, at least.

Sam wiped his face again, the rag now streaked red, and rose unsteadily. He stared at the cracks in the ceiling, blood dripping in uneven rivulets, tracing jagged paths down the stone walls. The bowl judgment wasn't a warning. It was here. And their fragile sanctuary was crumbling under its influence.

He tightened his grip on the lantern and turned back toward the main chamber. They had no choice but to stay. The blood was a stark reminder that their refuge was not impenetrable, yet it was where God had placed them, and here they would remain. Not because it felt safe. Not because they understood His plan, but because they chose to obey.

Sam stepped into the main chamber of the cave, the faint lantern light hovering over his mother. Lilah crouched near the fire pit, her frail frame illuminated by the dim glow. She had once been a sturdy woman, her laugh warm and inviting, her presence a comfort. Now, her frame was rail-thin, her cheeks sunken and gaunt. The dark, glossy hair she used to pin neatly behind her ears hung limp and dull, streaked with gray and tied back in a loose, fraying braid. Her hands trembled slightly as she stirred the pot over the dying embers, her knuckles prominent and skin pale.

Shay sat cross-legged on the cold stone floor nearby, surrounded by a few of the other small children, her slender fingers clutching the worn photograph of her parents. Her dark curls spilled over her shoulders, now long enough to rest in soft, unruly waves past the middle of her back. Her big brown eyes, wide with wonder and innocence, studied the faces in the picture as if memorizing every detail. Despite the somber air of the cave, Shay carried a sweetness that softened even the hardest hearts. Her gentle smile and quiet giggles often lit up the gloomy corners of their refuge

Miriam knelt beside her, her voice soft and steady as she recounted another story about Shay's parents—how kind they were, how much they loved her, and how they were waiting for her in heaven. Shay listened intently, her little face glowing with curiosity and comfort. She nodded as Miriam reminded her of the promise that one day, they'd all be reunited with Jesus.

Sam watched from a short distance, a faint smile tugging at his lips. Shay had a way of weaving herself into everyone's heart, but the bond he shared with her felt special. She often sought him out, her tiny hand slipping into his when she needed reassurance or her laughter bubbling up when he tried to make her smile. Shay had become a bright spot in their dark days, a little flame of innocence and joy that reminded them all why they kept enduring.

"This is it," Lilah said, stirring the pot of broth. Her eyes flicked toward Sam, weary but determined. "The last of the food." Around her, others huddled close, muttering their frustrations. It was a familiar scene—grumbling over the food and the lack of it, the gnawing hunger that pressed on them all.

Sam stood nearby, his arms crossed. He stayed quiet, his thoughts churning as he looked at his mother. The dim light of the cave barely touched her weary face as she stirred the pot, her focus steady despite the hopelessness around them.

Before Sam could sink further into his worries, a small figure approached him. Shay. Her dark curls bounced lightly as she crossed the room, the picture of her parents still clutched in one hand. Without a word, she climbed into his lap, her presence a welcome distraction. She handed him a small wooden brush and looked up at him expectantly. It was their routine, one of the few things that brought them both comfort. Sam managed a faint smile and began to run the brush through her curls, the gentle motion steadying him.

He sighed as he worked through a knot. "What are we going to do, little bird?" he murmured, the nickname slipping from his lips as easily as breathing.

Shay didn't answer right away. Instead, she stopped his hand and held up the photograph, her big brown eyes intent. Sam hesitated, puzzled. He'd seen the picture countless times, but something in her expression made him take it carefully. Turning it over, his eyes landed on the faint, handwritten note on the back— "To my Little Bird, God will always take care of you, even in the smallest of ways." Beneath that, in his familiar handwriting, was the verse: Matthew 6:26, which he had written there for Shay as a reminder, though he hadn't thought about it in a long time. "*Look at the birds of the air: they neither sow nor reap nor gather into barns, and yet your heavenly Father feeds them. Are you not of more value than they?*" Sam read aloud, his voice soft. He blinked, and then, almost involuntarily, a laugh escaped him.

"Bird," he chuckled, shaking his head as he looked at Shay. "Of course." The word stuck out, echoing in his mind. Little bird. It was as if God Himself were smiling down, sharing a quiet joke. A God-giggle moment, as Sam had come to call them—those unexpected, unmistakable instances when he knew God was nudging him, showing His hand in a way only He could.

Sam grinned at Shay and leaned closer, the laughter fading into quiet reverence. "But how is He going to provide?" he whispered, more to himself than to her.

Shay reached up, her small hands cupping his cheeks, forcing him to look directly into her steady gaze. Her voice was gentle, but her words carried a wisdom far beyond her years. "Remember what the angel told us," she said, her tone unwavering. "When the food runs out."

Sam stilled, her words breaking through his restless thoughts. He nodded slowly, brushing a curl from her face as a sense of peace settled over him. If God could care for the birds of the sky, He would care for them too. Somehow, someway. He looked into Shay's big brown eyes and smiled softly. "Yes, little bird. Yes."

The others sat in silence. Moshe and Aharon, listening nearby, shared a glance that spoke volumes. Sam could tell they were thinking the same thing: *The angel. When the food is gone, God will provide. But how?*

As dusk painted the cave's entrance in fading gold, Sam, Moshe, and Aharon ventured toward the opening. The air carried a faint tang of decay, mingling with the silence that stretched over the wasteland beyond.

The sight brought them to a halt, their steps slowing as the extent of the devastation became clear. The land, already scarred, was in an even worse state than they had seen before. Jerusalem, once the heart of Israel, lay in ruins. The temple, once a towering symbol of faith, was gone, reduced to rubble. The spires, the walls—everything that had defined the city—was destroyed. The landscape was a mixture of shattered stone and charred remnants, the debris of a once-proud city now buried under layers of devastation.

The Dead Sea shimmered in the distance, reflecting the last slivers of daylight, but its surface was no longer water. It was blood—deep, red, and thick, sluggishly churning as though alive. The sight was grotesque, otherworldly, a visceral reminder of the judgments that were upon them.

The three men stood at the edge of the destruction, their gazes fixed on the wreckage before them. There was no need for words—the scene before them spoke for itself. The land lay in ruin, the city of Israel reduced to nothing but ash and stones.

"We'll sleep here," Sam said finally, his voice low, almost reluctant to disturb the quiet. He gestured to the darkened space just inside the entrance of the cave. "Tomorrow ... tomorrow we'll look again."

The night passed uneasily. Sam lay awake for hours, staring at the jagged cave ceiling, his mind racing with prayers and questions. He didn't remember falling asleep, but when he woke, it was to Moshe's urgent whisper.

"Sam. Wake up."

Sam sat up, rubbing his eyes, disoriented. Moshe crouched nearby, his face illuminated by the faint predawn light.

"Something's out there," Moshe whispered.

Together, they crawled to the cave's mouth, Aharon joining them silently. Shapes moved on the horizon, faint at first, blending into the landscape. But as they approached, the shapes became clearer.

Sheep. A small herd, their wool glistening faintly in the soft light of dawn, moved steadily across the broken landscape. But it wasn't the sheep that made Sam's breath hitch. Scattered across the ground behind the sheep was something strange.

"What is it?" he murmured, the words slipping out almost involuntarily. Tiny, pale flakes covered the earth, catching the light like frost on winter's edge. He stepped closer and whispered again, "What is it?" The question lingered in the air, a name as much as an expression of awe—*manna*.

"Manna," Moshe whispered, his voice reverent. He clutched Sam's arm tightly. "It's manna!"

Sam paused for a moment, a sense of relief settling in. Despite the devastation around them, God had not abandoned them. He had provided.

Aharon knelt, hands raised to the sky, his voice trembling as he recited Deuteronomy 8:3 aloud: "*He humbled you and let you hunger and fed you with manna, which you did not know, nor did your fathers know, that he might make you know that man does not live by bread alone, but man lives by every word that comes from the mouth of the LORD.*"

The sheep and manna were proof. God's hand had reached into their desperation and delivered exactly what they needed.

Though Sam knew he should not be shocked by God's mercy, he was. A stunned silence hung over them, the magnitude of the moment leaving them speechless. Each of them whispered fervent prayers of thanks, words barely audible against the desolate backdrop. Sam thanked God for His mercy, even in the face of such ruin. His protection, His provision—undeserved yet undeniable—was a gift he could only grasp in awe, as the world he once knew lay in pieces before him.

❋ ❋ ❋

As Sam rose and stretched his back, his eyes drifted to the horizon, where the manna still sparkled faintly across the earth. The sheep, a small herd, grazed nearby, their wool contrasting against the gray, desolate landscape. "That's the last of it," Moshe said, eyeing the last few handfuls of manna. The food was welcome, but they all knew it wouldn't last.

"We can take these back to the cave," Sam said. "We'll ration it out, but we can't waste any."

Aharon nodded and moved toward the sheep, gathering them together and securing them as best as he could. They had no choice but to bring them in, to protect whatever they could in this desolate wasteland. The last of their resources—meager as they were—had to be preserved. Sam wiped his brow as he looked around at the lifeless land. It was a hollow shell of what it had once been.

The last of the manna was gathered, and the sheep were herded into the cave, their hooves clicking against the stone floor as they skittered uneasily in the confined space. Aharon and Moshe had done their best to keep them together, looping strips of torn fabric and twisted vine around their necks to fashion makeshift leads. Still, the animals were skittish—too much time in the barren wilderness had made them nervous and unpredictable.

Morning light spilled through the cave's entrance, stretching a pale glow across the stone floor and illuminating the first few feet of the tunnel ahead. Sam carefully led the way as the tunnel began to twist and narrow, the stone walls closing in tighter with every turn. The further they walked, the more the outside light faded behind them, swallowed by the winding passage. Soon, only the flickering glow of their lanterns remained, dancing across the uneven rock.

The cave walls were rough, worn by time and streaked with mineral deposits that shimmered faintly in the lamplight. The ground beneath their feet was hard and uneven, scattered with loose stones and patches of grit. The sheep balked and pushed against one another, their hooves slipping now and then as they squeezed through the narrowing gaps.

Up ahead, a warm flicker of light broke the darkness, distant but steady. Lanterns. Torches. People were waking. Sam felt a surge of relief as he realized they were nearing the main chamber. Others were stirring. And soon, they'd see the food God had provided.

The cool air inside was a welcome contrast to the stillness of the tunnels behind them. In the winding corridors, the air could grow stale and tight, but here, the space opened up. Sam stepped through the arching stone entrance, the warm glow of torches lighting the faces of those already awake.

Murmurs rose quickly as heads turned—eyes widening at the sound of hooves and the sight of baskets brimming with manna. Lilah looked up from where she sat near the wall, a blanket still wrapped around her shoulders. Her face lit with surprise.

"Look what you've found!" she said, a half-laugh in her voice.

Aharon and Moshe stepped forward, each carrying baskets filled to the top. They began to show the group, holding the provision up for others to see—offering it as both sustenance and proof that God had not forgotten them.

But Sam's eyes were already searching for her.

Shay stood partly hidden behind Miriam, her small hands clutching the edge of the woman's worn skirt. Her brows lifted in curiosity as she peeked around the folds of cloth, eyes locking on the animals that fidgeted near the chamber entrance. She didn't move at first, just stared—wide-eyed and silent.

Sam realized she'd never seen one, she'd been just a toddler when they entered the caves.

The sheep, restless and noisy, sniffed at the ground and one another, their bleating loud in the stone-walled space. Sam crouched slightly, gesturing to her.

"Come see, little bird," he said gently. "Look at what God's given us."

Shay's eyes darted to Miriam, then back to Sam. Her steps were hesitant, but curiosity slowly pushed past the shyness. She crept forward.

Sam could see the wonder in her eyes, her inquisitiveness battling with a hint of fear. She lingered at the edge of the group, her gaze fixed on the sheep nearest her, its wool matted but full.

Sam crouched beside the sheep. "Go on," he said softly, reaching for her hand. "You can touch it."

She glanced up at him, uncertain. Slowly, he took her small hand in his and guided it forward until her fingers rested on the sheep's head.

Her breath caught for a moment, then her hand moved gently, stroking the wool. A small smile spread across her face.

"It's soft," she whispered.

Shay's hand moved over the sheep's head, her fingers brushing through the soft wool. She smiled, her eyes lighting up with wonder.

"Can we keep them?" she asked softly, her voice filled with awe.

Sam nodded, his gaze lingering on her face. "Look what God has given us," he said gently, his voice steady. He watched her a moment, then added, "Just like He promised."

As Shay continued to stroke the soft wool of the sheep, a sudden noise from behind made Sam flinch. One of the sheep, startled by the tight space, jumped with a high-pitched bleat, sending a ripple of nervous energy through the rest of the flock. Its wild movement knocked into the others, and soon the chamber was filled with the frantic sound of hooves scraping against the stone floor.

Sam turned just in time to see one of the sheep rear back, startled by the commotion around it. It leapt, its hooves slamming into the jagged rocks along the cave wall. A sharp crack echoed through the chamber, and a large piece of stone broke loose, tumbling to the ground with a thunderous noise. Dust billowed into the air, and the smell of earth filled the space as the sheep bleated in alarm.

Frightened, their bodies pressed together in a tight, frenzied mass. One bolted toward the wall in confusion, its hooves striking against the rock. Then came a deep rumble, stone shifting, splintering. Another slab fell, tearing loose as the rock overhead began to collapse.

Sam's eyes shot upward. The ceiling was giving way. "Run!" he shouted, but when he saw the rock breaking loose above her, he instinctively yanked her back just as it crashed down where she'd been standing. Dust flooded the air. The echo of falling stone drowned out everything else.

With a deep groan that seemed to echo from the bones of the cave, the rock face above them shuddered. Cracks webbed across the ceiling. Then, with an earth-shaking roar, another section gave way, collapsing in a thunderous cascade. The ground trembled beneath their feet.

Sam grabbed Shay and pulled her closer, his body instinctively shielding her as stone rained down. Dust and debris swallowed the light. The sound of rock hitting rock was deafening.

There was no time.

The ceiling gave way in one last thunderous collapse, rocks falling like a torrent of destruction. Sam's body hit the ground hard as he pulled Shay close, shielding her with everything he had.

Chunks of rock struck the ground beside them, some grazing Sam's back and legs as he curled around Shay, bracing for impact. The roar of the cave's collapse drowned out everything except the frantic, shallow rasp of Shay's breath in his ear.

The world around Sam was a void of crushing darkness. The air was thick with dust, choking his lungs, and every breath felt like it took a lifetime to pull in. His leg was pinned beneath the weight of the rocks, a sharp, burning pain shooting through it with every twitch of muscle. The pressure was suffocating, each movement feeling like a battle to break free. His hands, slick with sweat, skimmed through the debris, reaching for anything, for her.

"Shay?" he gasped, his voice rough from the dust in his throat. He found her hand, cool against his, and gripped it tightly. "Are you okay?"

She didn't answer. There was only silence, thick and suffocating, broken only by the faintest sound of her whimpering. His heart pounded in his chest, panic rising.

"Shay, please. Hold on," he urged, his voice trembling. His chest heaved with each strained breath as he tried to calm himself, tried to find a way to move, to do something.

Her hand shifted slightly in his, a weak squeeze, like a fragile thread of hope. He clung to it, but the darkness felt endless, oppressive, and suffocating.

"Talk to me, little bird," Sam whispered hoarsely, his fingers tightening around her hand. "Hang on for me. They're going to get us out. You hear me? They're going to get us out."

But the seconds stretched into an eternity, and the warmth of her hand slowly started to fade. The weak grip she'd given him lessened, then stopped entirely.

"Shay?" Sam rasped, his throat tight, the words barely escaping. His lungs burned as he tried to fill them, but the air was too thin, too heavy. The dust and debris were choking him, and his mind was swimming in and out of consciousness. He couldn't see anything, couldn't hear anything but the distant crash of rocks settling, the pounding of his own pulse in his ears.

Her hand, still in his, didn't move. He forced out another breath, his chest feeling like it was collapsing in on itself, the darkness pressing down on him from all sides. "Please, Shay," he whispered again, tears blurring his vision as he blinked against the dust.

But there was no squeeze, no flutter. Her hand, still in his, felt impossibly still, growing colder as if the very life within it was fading away.

CHAPTER TWENTY-THREE

THE WEIGHT OF WAITING

Sam sat in the main chamber of the cave, his leg stretched out in front of him, the makeshift splint clumsy and worn. They'd hoped it wasn't broken, just badly bruised or sprained, but without proper care, there was no way to know. The cold stone pressed into his back, but the discomfort barely registered anymore. Everything had faded into the background. Only the pain in his leg remained sharp. Every time he shifted, it flared up, a bitter reminder that he wasn't whole.

It had been three days. Walking had become a slow, uneven shuffle, more dragging than stepping. The cane Moshe carved from a twisted branch served its purpose, but it felt like a mark of defeat. Every time he leaned on it, he was reminded of what he'd lost—not just the strength in his leg, but the part of himself that used to feel capable.

They said he was barely conscious when they found him, trapped beneath the wreckage, Shay pinned beside him. The others had dug through the rubble with their bare hands, calling their names until finally, someone heard Sam groan. It took hours to pull them free.

What none of them could explain—what no one dared call anything but a miracle—was how they'd survived.

When the cave collapsed, the first slab that crashed down had split clean from the ceiling and landed just beyond where they stood. That single, massive sheet of stone had formed a barrier of sorts, catching much of the falling debris and sparing them from being completely buried. Everything beyond it was lost under the rubble. But where they lay, cocooned in dust and rocks, there was just enough space to breathe.

Sam didn't remember much—just the roar of the collapse, the choking dust, and the feel of Shay's hand in his. He'd reached for her in the dark, held on, and prayed she was still alive. A rock must have struck his leg during the fall, and by the time they pulled him out, it was twisted and swollen.

Shay had been worse.

She had been pulled from the wreckage with only the faintest heartbeat, her small body battered, her head wound deep. She had yet to regain consciousness, and the doctors, if you could even call them that, didn't think she would. They told Sam the odds were against her, that they didn't expect her to survive.

Now, she lay just off the main chamber in a small, makeshift room the women had prepared. They tended to her around the clock, doing what they could with what little they had, but despite their care, there was no change.

Sam had stepped out just long enough to give the women privacy as they washed her, but his gaze kept drifting back to where she lay. He couldn't shake the image, couldn't stop seeing her like that. His little bird.

The flickering fire in front of him cast long, tired shadows across the chamber, offering the only warmth they had left. But it was the people around him who caught his eye. They were huddled together, scraping the bottom of their bowls for the meager portion of manna God had provided that day. Their faces were gaunt, hollowed by hunger and exhaustion. As Sam looked at them, he saw the same weariness in their eyes that had crept into his own soul.

Hope had withered, and in its place was a bitter emptiness. The faith he had once clung to felt paper-thin, fragile against the slow, relentless torture of the days that kept coming.

His attention shifted to the children playing quietly nearby. Shay should be with them, laughing, running, full of life. But she wasn't. And he didn't know if she ever would be again.

He was angry—angry at God, angry at the world, and most of all, angry at himself. There were moments when he'd stare at his mother, now frail and diminished from the woman she used to be, and wonder what the point of all this suffering was. Once the heart of their little family, she now sat by the fire barely able to stir the pot without help. His father was gone. His brother, distant. And Sam—crippled and hollow—could do nothing to fix any of it.

Many had died in the caves. Their bodies, too frail and weak from the hardships, succumbed to infections, fever, and the relentless strain of survival. The caves were thick with death, the stench of sickness clinging to the walls, and the burden of carrying the dead out of the cave had become a grim daily task. They had to dispose of the bodies far from the caves, for fear of spreading disease. The sight of men carrying the lifeless forms of their friends and family had become so common that it hardly caused a stir anymore.

Sam remembered when they had feared for his aunt Miriam's life, when the fever had come for her, and it seemed like there was no way she would survive. But somehow, she had pulled through against all odds, defying the sickness that claimed so many others. As for the men—the Jewish men in their group—none had died. Not one. They clung to life, as if protected for some greater purpose, a reason they couldn't see. It was a blessing, yes, but it also felt like a curse. Sam didn't know if he could keep carrying the weight of survival any longer. What was the point of living, when each day felt like a punishment, when the future was nothing more than an endless struggle for bare existence? He almost wished for the end. It was as though being part of this small, protected group had become a heavy burden—a reminder that they were being kept alive for something bigger, something he could no longer comprehend or care about.

Voices suddenly broke through the quiet and his thoughts, drawing Sam's attention to Shay's room. The voices, once distant, were growing louder—urgent, laced with panic. His heart skipped a beat as the cries pierced the stillness, and his stomach twisted. He grabbed his cane and shuffled down the dimly lit corridor, each step heavier than the last. His mind raced with possibilities, none of them good.

Lilah and Moshe reached him quickly, both drawn by the commotion. Moshe glanced at Sam, his gaze heavy with unspoken questions—the same ones that churned in Sam's own mind. But Sam didn't need to ask. Moshe's silent, worried expression said everything he feared.

They reached the entrance to the small room where Shay lay. Moshe pushed it open, and Sam's eyes immediately fell on the familiar forms gathered around the bed. The others were there, some kneeling, some standing, all of them with their heads lowered. Sam's breath caught in his chest. His legs felt weak beneath him, the cane trembling in his grip. He thought he might collapse right there.

He stumbled forward, fighting to stay upright, each step harder than the last. It felt as though every ounce of strength was slipping from him, leaving him raw and exposed. The thought struck him with brutal clarity: Shay was gone. His little bird.

The room grew louder with cries and murmurs as he made his way through the crowd, maneuvering past the people gathered around her bed. He neared the small circle of figures blocking his view, then he made his way around the last person standing between him and Shay. A faint sound stopped him—a soft, unmistakable whimper—and it froze him in his tracks.

He froze, eyes wide, searching. Was it real? He barely breathed, waiting for another sign, any sign that his heart wasn't playing tricks on him.

And then—there it was again. A soft, innocent cry, the sound of his little bird alive and breathing.

Tears welled in his eyes, this time not from grief, but from relief so overwhelming it felt as though he might shatter. The weight of understanding settled in Sam. The weeping in the room wasn't born of sorrow, but joy. Sam knelt beside her, pressing his lips to her forehead.

"Shay?" Sam whispered, his voice hoarse with disbelief.

Her eyes fluttered open slowly, and when she saw him, her small face broke into the faintest of smiles. The room exhaled collectively, but Sam stood there, overcome by the miracle unfolding before him.

Shay was still alive.

CHAPTER TWENTY-FOUR

THE HIDDEN MESSAGE

7 years since start of the tribulation

The sun hung high in the sky, its heat relentless as Jayne and her small group trudged across the barren desert plains. The land stretched out before them, endless and unforgiving. Jennie, weary and frail from the hardships they had endured, walked with a slumped posture, clutching her daughter close to her chest in the tattered sling Zella had made.

Reyna, just over a year old, lay still in her arms, her innocence a sharp contrast to the brutal landscape that surrounded them. Her skin had taken on a pale hue from the lack of nourishment, and Jayne thought her wide, searching eyes seemed to grasp more of the world's cruelty than any child should. Together, Jayne and her family were nothing more than a scattered group of survivors, broken by time and suffering.

Landon walked beside Jayne, his hand resting on the hilt of his pistol, eyes scanning the horizon. Andrew was a few paces ahead, his back hunched under the bulk of their supplies—what little they had left. Sophie walked behind her mother, but Jayne could picture her drawn face, her hollow and tired eyes.

Their appearances reflected the toll the world had taken on them. The once-familiar clothes they wore were now little more than threadbare rags, the holes in their shirts and pants large enough to expose their skin to the unforgiving sun. Their shoes had long since lost their soles, barely held together by frayed laces. Blisters covered their feet, arms, and faces from the constant burn of the intense heat.

They hadn't bathed in what felt like a lifetime—Jayne couldn't even remember the last time they'd washed, their bodies caked in dust and grime, their hair tangled, their skin raw. The air felt stifling, the sun a merciless hand pressing down on them, but still, they pushed forward, driven by the hope of reaching the caves.

The earth around them was burned and barren. The world Jayne had once known was gone, scorched by the final bowl judgments, and most of humanity was lost. Yet she kept moving, kept putting one foot in front of the other. There was nowhere else to go, no refuge left to seek—only the distant, uncertain hope that the caves might offer even a bit of shelter, even a sliver of safety. If she stopped, if she gave up, the only other option was to lie down and die.

Jayne had tried to stay strong for them all, but the days blurred together. She could feel the changes in her body—thin, weaker, her bones aching from exhaustion. The hunger that gnawed at her every day had eaten away at her strength. And her mind … her mind had started to betray her too. Once, she had been the rock, the one who held them all together. But now, with each passing day, her resolve was slipping. Her feet dragged. Her body was so tired, so beaten. The weight of the past year had hollowed her out, and she couldn't remember the last time she'd felt anything other than pain, fear, and a constant hunger.

She glanced at Andrew's back, and she could see the tension in his shoulders. He, too, was on edge, always waiting for something to happen, for the next attack, the next loss. There was no more talk of safety, no more belief they would be OK. It was just survival now.

And survival was running thin.

They had no water, only the small trickle of moisture they managed to extract from cactus plants. The prickly pear was a blessing—a rare gift in the unforgiving desert—but it never lasted long. Jennie would kneel over a small, hastily built fire, the flames licking at the dry wood they had scavenged. Her hands, raw and bleeding, would work with grim determination as she peeled away the sharp needles using a battered knife. It wasn't much, but it was all they had. Every drop felt like borrowed time, a desperate offering in the face of the desert's cruelty.

Jayne could feel the weakness in her legs, the sharpness of dehydration beginning to take hold. She swallowed, but her mouth was dry. They had been walking for hours, and the sun had been merciless. Jennie's face was pale beside her, and the baby—still cradled in her arms—was silent, her tiny face pressed against her mother's chest.

"Almost there." Landon's voice cut through her thoughts, rough and strained.

Jayne looked up, her eyes squinting against the harsh light, but the distant shapes on the horizon blurred and swayed like an illusion. She knew what it was, the same as always—the heat was playing tricks on him, distorting the landscape. It wasn't a settlement, a shelter, or anything that could offer hope. It was just the mirage of a weary mind, the last desperate flicker of hope in a world that had long since taken it all away.

They had tried to leave earlier. The day after Jennie had given birth, they had packed their things, desperate to flee to the caves, but the Suburban had failed them. The engine coughed and groaned but refused to turn over, choked by the bad gas Landon had siphoned from an abandoned car the day before. They had searched the neighborhood for another vehicle, but all the cars had either been looted or left to rot. Nothing worked. Nothing was left to salvage.

The days bled into weeks, and the weeks into months. They remained in the town, Brownwood, clinging to a faint optimism that the world would offer them something—anything—that would allow them to move forward. But with each passing day, the strain of survival began to wear down even the strongest among them. Food became a distant memory, a fleeting luxury from another time. They scavenged through homes, searching for whatever cans of food had been left behind. There were a few cans of beans, some rice, a handful of dried pasta, but it was always the same—so little, never enough.

Snow had been their only salvation, the frost covering the ground like a temporary reprieve. But it had soon melted away, giving way to the oppressive heat of the next judgment. They would collect what they could, melting it drop by drop just to drink, but it never felt like enough. The nearby streams, once lifeblood for the land, had turned to blood themselves—mocking them with the certainty of their own demise, a constant reminder that even nature had turned against them.

"Just a little longer," Landon muttered under his breath, though there was no belief in his voice.

Jayne closed her eyes, pressing her hand to her forehead as the world spun. It was getting harder to focus, to think. She wanted to lie down, close her eyes, and never open them again.

An hour passed, and still, they trudged through the desert, their steps slow and exhausting, the sunbaked earth stretching endlessly beneath their feet. The ground seemed to rise up and meet them like an unyielding wall. Each footfall felt pointless, like they were walking in circles, not getting anywhere, and with each passing moment, the question gnawed at Jayne: *Do we even know where we're going anymore?*

How much longer would God let them suffer like this? The thought deepened her despair. The weariness in her limbs, the relentless sun burning their skin, the hunger, the thirst—they were all too much to carry. It would be easier to just lie down, give up, and let the desert have them.

"Almost there," Landon repeated suddenly, his voice rough. Jayne barely registered it. She couldn't understand him, couldn't focus on anything but the grating ache of her body, the crushing heft of exhaustion pulling her down with every step. She kept her eyes low, her feet moving on instinct, hoping she wouldn't fall.

A shadow fell over her. It was large and dark, sweeping across the barren ground. She blinked through the dust that stung her eyes, squinting at the shape before her. At first, she thought it was another mirage—another cruel trick played by the heat—but no. Her eyes slowly tracked upward, and as they did, she saw it: a shadowed cross in the desert sand.

She looked further up. It was a church. The silhouette of a steeple rose against the sky, tall and stark against the fading light. Real, solid. For a moment, she didn't know whether to laugh or cry, her breath catching in her throat.

"Is it real?" Sophie's voice was quiet beside her, as if she, too, feared it would vanish.

Landon and Andrew didn't wait for an answer. They took off, picking up the pace, their tired bodies moving with renewed energy. The church hadn't been a mirage. It was there, standing at the edge of a ghost town, untouched, forgotten by time, but still standing.

Andrew and Landon approached the front doors, which had been battered by years of neglect. Landon kicked them open, the old wood groaning in protest. The door splintered, and with a final shove, it gave way.

The air inside was thick with dust and the smell of old wood, but it was shelter. It was real. It was a break from the blistering sun. Jayne's legs buckled, and she crumpled to the ground, her body finally giving in. She barely registered the worn pews, the crumbling stone walls around her, as her limbs refused to move any longer. All she could focus on was the dull throb in her head.

Jennie sat near the altar, her toddler cradled gently in her arms. She, too, was silent, staring at the child in her arms as if she was the only thing in the world that mattered. There was a calm there, even in the face of everything they had endured. No one spoke. No one moved. The stillness of the church seemed to press in on them, the silence broken only by the occasional creak of the building settling. The others collapsed where they stood, too tired to do anything but fall into whatever space they could find.

❋ ❋ ❋

Jayne slowly came to, her body resisting the command to move, every muscle protesting as though the weight of the world had pressed her into that cold wooden floor. Exhaustion clung to her like a relentless ache buried deep in her bones that no rest could cure. The air in the dim church was stale, thick with dust and silence, broken only by the faint sounds of sleeping breaths around her.

Trembling, she wiped at her face, but the gesture only smeared dirt across her skin, a reminder of how long it had been since she'd felt clean—weeks, maybe months. She wasn't sure anymore. Summoning her strength, she pushed herself up, her hands shaking under the effort, every movement a battle against the weariness that threatened to consume her.

Moonlight streamed through the fractured windows, pale beams illuminating the crumbling room. Landon and Andrew lay near the door, their positions awkward, their bodies contorted on the unforgiving floor. Landon's broad shoulders and the set of his jaw stood out in contrast to the boy she had raised. He was the protector now, taking on the mantle of a man who now had to keep their family together, safe. Andrew was sleeping nearby, his posture stiff and vigilant. She saw the lines of manhood in him now, the soft, carefree youth long gone. Seven years without his family. Three years without a single word from them.

But it was her daughter—her grown-up daughter—who pulled Jayne's gaze. Sophie was sleeping on a nearby pew, curled into the shadows, her face slack with fatigue, her breath slow and steady. She should be finished with college by now, maybe even planning a wedding or holding her own child in her arms. But instead, here she was—caught in a world that had torn away everything. Jayne's chest ached as she looked at her. There was a time she would've brushed the hair from her daughter's face, whispered promises about the future. Now, all she could do was watch and wonder how much more this life would take from her. The girl she'd raised was gone—not lost, not broken—but changed in ways Jayne could barely comprehend. The change had quietly woven itself into Sophie, a transformation Jayne had only now fully seen. It wasn't a single moment, but a slow shift, shaped by survival and struggle. Before her was no longer the girl with the innocence she once had, but a woman—strong, hardened by the world. In that quiet moment, Jayne recognized the adult Sophie had become, with all the strength and resilience that came with it.

Near the altar, Jennie slept with her small daughter, holding the child against her chest as though she could shield her from the broken world around them. Her tiny breaths were peaceful, oblivious to the heaviness in the room. Above them, the wooden cross loomed on the wall, stark and splintered against the cracked plaster. Jayne's chest tightened at the sight. What kind of world would that baby grow up in now? What would become of her in this shattered, destroyed place? How could God let this happen to them? It felt cruel. The pain of it was too much to contain, and her body trembled with heartache and rage as she thought of her own husband who was now gone.

It was too much. The baby shouldn't grow up like this. None of them should.

Her throat constricted, anger and grief threatening to choke her. The questions she'd kept buried clawed their way to the surface. *Why?* she wanted to scream. *Where are you now, God?* The silence from heaven had stretched on too long, and the pain of it was unbearable.

She forced herself to her feet, her legs unsteady beneath her. The effort left her lightheaded, and she leaned against the wall for support. She needed space. The walls of the church felt like they were closing in, suffocating her. Her breath came in shallow gasps as she stumbled toward the back of the building.

The bathroom door creaked as she pushed it open. Inside, the air was damp, the faint stench of mildew clinging to the peeling walls. A cracked mirror hung above the sink, and for a moment, she avoided her reflection. She wasn't ready to face the stranger she'd become.

But the pull was too strong. Slowly, she lifted her gaze.

She hardly recognized the woman staring back. Her face was hollow and pale, with dark circles etched beneath her eyes and skin that was dry, cracked, and scorched by the relentless sun. Her lips were chapped and raw, and her hair hung in limp, tangled strands that framed her gaunt features like a shadow. When her trembling fingers brushed against her blistered skin, a sharp sting made her flinch, a souvenir of how deeply the world had worn her down.

Jayne let out a ragged breath, turning away from the mirror. Her fingers fumbled for the towel in her bag, and she pressed it against her face, scrubbing harder than she should have. The dirt wouldn't come off. It clung to her as if it had become part of her.

She closed her eyes, sinking onto the edge of the sink. Her tongue throbbed, swollen and raw from the thorns she'd pulled from her mouth. The bitter flesh of the cactus they'd found yesterday had barely been enough to hold off hunger, and the moisture it contained had done little to ease her thirst. It was a cruel mockery of survival—just enough to keep going but never enough to truly feel alive.

She wasn't sure why she was still trying, why she was attempting to make herself look anything other than what she had become—broken, beaten down by a world that had no mercy left. She reached for her bag, hands shaking, lifting it as a thud sounded from the ground. Her eyes flicked down, and there it was—the Bible. Ruth's Bible. It lay open-faced on the ground, its pages worn, its cover cracked and faded from years of use. She stared at it for a moment, the sight of it stirring a swell of frustration deep inside her. It felt like a cruel reminder of everything she had lost.

Her hands tightened into fists. She didn't want to keep going.

Her breath came in ragged gasps, and the room seemed to close in around her as she fell to her knees, fists clenched so tightly her nails dug into her palms.

She couldn't breathe. The burden of it all was crushing her chest, suffocating her, drowning her in a sea of hopelessness.

"Where are you, God?" The words came out barely above a whisper.

Tears swelled in her eyes as her voice rose, shaking with fury. "Where are you? Why have you left us here? Why don't you take me?" she choked. "Why don't you just end this? I can't—I can't do this anymore!"

The words burned in her chest, as though she had been carrying them for lifetimes.

Her face yielded in desperation, tears blurring her vision. "I can't do this anymore!" she shouted, her voice cracking. "I've tried—I've fought with everything I have, and it's never enough. I can't keep going. I can't keep pretending. I just … I just want to see you. I want to be done with all of this—done with the pain, done with the emptiness. Just … take me home, Lord." Her body wracked with sobs, her words lingering in the air long after they had fallen silent.

She needed more—needed Him. "Where are you?" she wept, the words torn from her like a scream from the deepest part of her soul. "I need you *now!*" Her voice cracked and broke, raw with every unanswered prayer, every moment of silence that stretched longer than she could stand. She shook, her body trembling with a rage and desperation she could no longer contain.

The silence that followed felt like a final blow.

Her stomach turned. She didn't want to touch the fallen object. She didn't want to be reminded of the faith she had once clung to. It had failed her—had failed all of them. The promise of salvation felt distant, a lie whispered into the wind.

Still, her fingers found the Bible, and with a sharp breath, she threw it against the wall. The force of the impact sent it sliding to the floor, the pages fanning out like a prayer she no longer wanted to hear.

She collapsed in the dust on that cold bathroom floor, her breath coming in short, jagged gasps. Tears mixed with the dirt on her cheeks as she cried, the sobs wracking her body, making her feel weaker than she ever thought possible.

And then, as if the world was offering her a final cruelty, her eyes caught something—a note— poking out from the edge of the broken Bible's casing, almost taunting her with its presence.

For a moment, she stopped crying, the tears still running down her face, but her curiosity won out. She reached for the note, the paper crinkling beneath her fingertips. She unfolded it carefully, unsure of what she would find, and began to read.

My Dearest Jayne,

If you are reading this, it means my deepest fears have come to pass, and my heartfelt prayers have been answered in ways I never wished for. I'm so sorry that you find yourself among those left behind. My heart aches for you in this difficult time, but I have faith in your strength and resilience. I always knew you would use the key I kept in your safekeeping to come check on Isaac, the dogs, and me. Your gentle spirit and nurturing heart have always drawn me to you. I've cherished our sweet moments together, and your family has left beautiful memories etched in my soul that I will carry with me always.

The timeline I've provided has been carefully laid out from my many years of research into prophecy and the Bible, guided by the Holy Spirit. I wrote these notes specifically for you, knowing you would find them, if you were not taken in the rapture. God placed it on my heart to leave it for you, trusting that your compassionate nature would lead you to share this wisdom with others. The outline labeled "The Last Plumb Line" will be your guide, helping you understand the sequence of events that will arise during this difficult judgment period God has laid upon the earth.

You will learn that a plumb line signifies the coming judgment on Israel and the world. In Amos 7:8, God asks Amos what he sees and

Amos replies, "A plumb line." God then says, *"I am setting a plumb line / in the midst of my people Israel."* This plumb line represents God's standard of righteousness, a tool to measure how straight and true His people are in their faithfulness to Him.

Just as a plumb line helps builders ensure their walls are straight, God uses this symbol to guide His people back to His path. It reminds us that He desires order and integrity in our lives. If we find ourselves off course, the plumb line invites us to realign with His truth.

The reason I titled this outline "The **Last** Plumb Line" is simple, yet so important. These final seven years on earth are humanity's last chance to align with God's righteousness. The plumb line is more than a symbol of realignment—it's God's final call. A call to bring the world back into right standing with Him before it's too late. This is God's last attempt to draw His people back. It's the last opportunity for salvation, the last chance to be saved, before judgment falls. After this, there will be no more time to change. "The Last Plumb Line" is exactly what it represents—our **last** chance to realign ourselves with God's truth and accept Jesus as our Savior.

I pray that you take my Bible and read the Scriptures I've highlighted. I hope they bring you peace and strength during these trying times. It's vital to know that you can still be saved if you believe in Jesus and accept Him as your Savior. Your faith can be a beacon of hope, not just for you, but for those around you.

I feel for you, dear friend, and my heart aches knowing the challenges you and your family will face during the tribulation. It's crucial to prepare yourself by studying God's Word, remaining strong in your faith, and seeking salvation. You have a light within you that can shine through the darkest of times.

As it says in Romans 15:13, *"May the God of hope fill you with all joy and peace in believing, so that by the power of the Holy Spirit you may abound in hope."* Remember that hope is a gift, and you are never alone.

Even when you feel as though everything is lost and your strength is fading, do not give up. God is always there, even in the darkest moments. When you think there's no hope left, trust that He is with you, guiding you through the storm. Keep your faith, Jayne. He will see you through.

As it says in Proverbs 17:17, *"A friend loves at all times."* Remember the love we've shared and the bond that remains, even in difficult times.

Until I see you again, I'll be waiting, holding onto the hope that our friendship endures beyond this life.

With all my love,

Ruth

✳   ✳   ✳

Jayne sat on the cold, cracked tiles of the bathroom floor, Ruth's letter crumpled in her shaking hands. Her eyes were wide, still trying to process the words that had just unraveled everything she thought she understood. The letter—the years of painstaking research, the prophetic timeline, the Bible Ruth had left—it all made sense now. Ruth had poured her heart and soul into preparing this, all of it, for *her*. It was as if the ground had shifted beneath her, her mind reeling as the full weight of Ruth's actions hit her all at once. The enormity of it—Ruth's years of meticulous work, the tireless hours of study, all of it meant for *her*, for this moment— flooded Jayne with a wave of disbelief and profound gratitude. God had known exactly what Jayne would need and when she would need it most, and it felt like a lifeline in her darkest hour.

Jayne's eyes blurred with tears as she let the letter slip from her hands, the paper falling softly to the floor. Sobs wracked her body as her tears dripped down her face, falling onto the paper and smearing the ink. But she didn't care. The words no longer mattered. The power of God's love, along with Ruth's foresight, was more than she could bear. It made her ache in a way she couldn't explain, but it also reignited something deep within her.

Tears streamed down her face as she pressed her hand to her chest, silently thanking God for this moment of grace. She had so little left inside her, but this—this gift of hope—had reignited something. She *couldn't* give up.

Just then, the bathroom door creaked open. Sophie stepped in, her footsteps slow, hesitant. When she saw her mother on the floor, weeping, she dropped to her knees beside her without a word. Sophie's arms circled Jayne's shoulders, her face pressed against her mother's cheek. And without hesitation, Jayne wrapped her arms tightly around her daughter, holding her as though she might never let go.

The rawness of it—the depth of the pain and love and fear they both shared—was almost too much. They sat there, in the dim light of the small room, silently holding onto each other. Jayne buried her face in Sophie's hair, still sobbing uncontrollably, a broken prayer slipping from her lips.

"Lord, please forgive me. Thank you for this strength when I thought I had none. Please help us endure, give us hope in this darkness. Guide us through, Father, and carry us when we can't go on. We need you."

Andrew and Landon peeked in the room, probably drawn by the noise. Landon opened his mouth to ask if she was all right, but the words caught in his throat when he saw the raw, unguarded emotion etched across her face.

Jayne looked up at him, her tears still flowing, but she managed a small smile.

Landon cleared his throat, swallowing the lump that had formed there. "We're gonna be OK," he said, his voice barely above a whisper. "We found a car. In the shed behind the church. It runs. We have a way to get to the caves now."

Jayne closed her eyes, clutching her daughter tightly. Tears continued to fall, and she let them. She looked up toward heaven, her heart full of gratitude, and whispered, "Thank you."

CHAPTER TWENTY-FIVE

THE FINAL BATTLE

BOOM!

Sam flinched as the thunder cracked, ripping through the night like the strike of a war drum. Lightning tore across the sky, its jagged blaze illuminating the cave through the openings—a flash that felt like the hand of judgment carving the heavens. The rumble that followed was deep, rolling through the earth, shaking the cave walls until they groaned under the strain. The storm surged with a fury that seemed alive. The mountains trembled as violent reverberations shook loose bits of rock and dust from the cave's ceiling. The grit stung Sam's eyes and clung to the moisture in his breath. Wind, sharp and unforgiving, whipped through the cave like a living thing, tugging at his clothes and driving an unnatural chill deep into his bones. The lanterns shuddered against the gale, their flames flickering with the strain. One by one, they surrendered, plunging the group into a suffocating blackness.

The storm passed as quickly as it had come, leaving a stillness in its wake. The cave felt heavy, as though the earth itself was holding its breath. Silence settled over them, thick and suffocating. The only sound Sam heard was the rapid, uneven beat of his heart.

He spoke, his voice low but sharp, cutting through the quiet.

"It's begun."

The chill lingered as they relit their torches. The flames flickered weakly at first, reluctant to hold against the lingering draft, but soon they burned steady again, casting a pale glow against the stone walls. No one spoke. Words felt irrelevant in the face of what they all knew was coming.

Sam was drawn by an unseen hand to the cave's mouth, the others moving with him as one. They carried their lanterns, the dim light bobbing with each step. Sam paused only long enough to slip the binoculars over his head, letting them rest against his chest. He knew they would be needed—for whatever they were about to witness.

Outside, the path ahead seemed sharper, more unforgiving. The Judaean Mountains stretched before them, jagged peaks rising like sentinels against the darkened sky. Around them, more emerged from various nearby caves—survivors from different directions, all drawn by the same pull.

Sam began climbing. At the peak, he paused, breathless from the climb. The last light of day lingered as the sun hovered just above the horizon, its light now softened, dipping low into the land. Sam's gaze shifted from the ground beneath them to the sprawling valley below. Megiddo. The valley stretched out like a great stage, waiting for its final act. The sun's dying light still lit the land, painting it with hues of amber and crimson, though the shadows were deepening. The ground was cracked and worn, scarred by the years of conflict, yet for now, it held a strange calm, as if it, too, was waiting.

The valley itself was dry from years of desolation. It was a barren scar in the land, as if the earth had borne witness to so many conflicts that it no longer had the strength to heal. But it had remained untouched by the worst of the destruction until now. Sam felt a strange stillness hold the valley in its grip, almost as if it had been waiting for this moment, for the storm to arrive. In the distance, the hum of military engines grew louder—tanks and artillery gleaming. The machines of war were assembled, their massive forms casting long shadows across the plains. The wind kicked up, swirling dust across the valley floor, creating a haunting image of what was to come.

Sam surveyed the armies that had gathered throughout the valley. Nations from every corner of the earth were assembled, their flags unfurling in the wind. Bright banners, dark emblems—each a declaration of allegiance. Dragon symbols, lion motifs, and ancient seals marked the presence of kings and generals long prophesied.

They had all come for one purpose. To destroy Israel.

The valley of Megiddo had become a funnel, pulling the world's hatred into one place. Israel stood at the center—not just geographically, but spiritually. This was the final war, and Israel was the target of it all.

The armies were arrayed across the expanse, preparing for the confrontation foretold since the beginning. Soldiers shifted in formation, the clang of metal and the scrape of boots the only sounds breaking the charged stillness. No orders were shouted, no commands given. Only the low growl of engines in the distance and the relentless rumble of far-off thunder disturbed the quiet.

And still, the earth held its breath.

The last rays of sunlight faded, but still, the light clung to the land, enough for Sam and the others to see it all. He lifted the binoculars around his neck, pressing them to his eyes. Through the lenses, the vastness of the battlefield unfolded before him—more than just a valley. It was the stage of history. The cradle of fate. Every step they took, every glance across the horizon, confirmed the magnitude of the moment. This wasn't just a battle. This was Armageddon.

The armies of the East stretched from horizon to horizon, a coordinated wave of power moving with precision and might. Their allegiance was not to a cause, but to the beast—Nero Kesar—whose influence had deceived the nations. They had marched not to liberate, but to conquer, to crush Israel and defy the God they did not know. Sam watched through his binoculars, heart sinking. These men had no idea what they were truly walking into. This wasn't a war for territory or power. It was a war against heaven itself.

From the western edge of the valley, the first movements began. Armored vehicles rolled forward, their steel exteriors catching the fading light as they advanced. Tanks followed, their turrets swiveling, casting long shadows over the cracked earth. Troop carriers rumbled behind, their weight pressing deep into the brittle ground. Soldiers emerged, moving in disciplined lines, their combat gear shining with the precision of modern warfare. Their uniforms were dark and sleek, blending with the land as the last light played tricks on Sam's eyes. Helmets with angular visors reflected the dim glow, giving them a faceless, robotic presence as they marched forward, shields raised and weapons ready.

The steady thud of boots was lost beneath the mechanical growl of vehicles. Low-flying helicopters hovered at the valley's edge, their rotors slicing through the tense air, sending gusts of dust spiraling upward. Overhead, drones swarmed like scavengers, their glowing sensors flickering against the darkening sky. The faint crackle of radio transmissions drifted across the field. It all created a dissonant symphony of war that heralded the world's breaking point.

The battlefield stretched before them like an open wound, waiting to be torn apart. But with the first movements, something had shifted. Sam noticed the banners ripple harder in the wind, and the dust that had settled over the plain began to stir again, carried on sudden gusts that seemed almost alive. From the far horizon, a shadow emerged. It grew larger with every step forward, swallowing the distance with a relentless, deliberate pace.

Thunder rolled across the valley, deep and menacing, as the first figure broke through the haze. Nero Kesar rode at the forefront of his army. His black steed moved like a predator, muscles coiling with each step, its eyes glowing with an unnatural, hellish light. His armor gleamed like liquid obsidian, sharp and cruel in its design, etched with twisted symbols that crawled across its surface as if alive. His face was a mask of unnatural perfection, the sharp planes of his features marred only by the hollow void of his eyes. When he grinned, it was a predator's smile, his expression mocking and triumphant. In one gloved hand, he held a jagged black sword, its blade pulsating with an unholy energy that seemed to vibrate in the air.

Behind him, his army advanced—an abomination of steel and shadow. Strange, otherworldly machines looked like a sickening blend of advanced technology and demonic design. Sam was sure they were not of this world. Their metallic bodies pulsed with dark energy, sharp edges gleaming, mechanical tentacles writhing like serpents. The air seemed to tremble in their wake, as though even the earth itself bowed before them.

The armies of the East, unaware of the true force they faced, advanced with confidence, ready for battle. But they had no idea that this fight was not theirs to win. Not against what followed. They were here for a reckoning, but Sam knew they would soon find that their struggle was nothing compared to the true power of what was coming.

As Nero Kesar raised his sword high, the ground trembled beneath him. The wind screamed, tearing through the valley, whipping the banners into violent flurries. The sky darkened in an instant, clouds boiling above as lightning cut jagged streaks through the heavens. Each flash illuminated the battlefield in stark, merciless light, highlighting the masses of soldiers and machines, the cracked earth beneath their feet, and the horrifying figures advancing at the Antichrist's command.

Thunder split the silence. The armies of the world surged forward, marching under the banner of the beast. Their weapons were drawn, their formations tight, moving like a tide across the valley. But across the field, Israel stood ready too—outnumbered, surrounded, but not unprepared. This was their soil, their stand. Nero Kesar's grin widened as he lowered his sword, the signal given.

The valley erupted. The final battle had begun.

A roar shook the earth with the fury of mankind's final war. The sky burned, streaked with fire as missiles and bombs rained down from the east, each detonation ripping across the horizon in blinding flashes. The ground convulsed beneath the onslaught, breaking apart as explosions carved deep wounds into the battlefield. Israel's forces, though resolute, were dwarfed in both numbers and firepower. Their defenses buckled—soldiers falling to the relentless barrage, tanks reduced to flaming husks, and vehicles twisted into unrecognizable wreckage. The air reeked of burning flesh and fuel, acrid smoke swirled in choking clouds, and the screams of the dying were swallowed by the endless percussion of war.

Above, drones swarmed in dense swarms, striking with ruthless precision. Israel's interceptors retaliated, their missiles streaking upward in fiery arcs, but the enemy's advance was unstoppable. Soldiers in sleek, high-tech combat suits pressed forward, their movements synchronized, their weapons cutting down anything in their path. Pulse cannons flared, their energy beams raking the ground, and railguns fired with earsplitting cracks, tearing through defenses as the battlefield descended into a nightmare of blood and fire.

Shay flinched at the thunder of a nearby explosion, her body trembling uncontrollably. Sam reached her in an instant, pulling her close before panic could fully take hold. His arms wrapped around her protectively, his voice calm but firm.

"Cover your ears," he commanded, his tone leaving no room for argument. He pressed her head against his chest, his hand shielding her eyes from the carnage unfolding around them. She obeyed, her small hands pressing tightly over her ears, her breaths quick and shallow. Sam held her, his grip unyielding, his focus entirely on keeping her safe amid the chaos.

The minutes stretched into eternity, the battle a relentless tide of violence and destruction. What had started as an earth-shattering conflict between nations was unraveling into something far more sinister. The ground beneath the armies cracked and groaned, the scars of war deepening into jagged chasms. The proud armies of the world, gathered for their final reckoning, faltered. Their weapons, so fearsome moments ago, now seemed impotent. The silence between detonations and gunfire grew, as if the battlefield itself hesitated, waiting for what would come next.

Then the earth gave way with a deafening roar. The crevices widened, splitting open to reveal yawning voids of blackness. From these fissures, a new nightmare emerged—grotesque forms that defied all logic and reason. The first creature clawed its way free, its massive body a grotesque fusion of sinew and scales, blacker than the abyss it had come from. Its limbs were unnaturally long and wiry, ending in claws that glinted like blades. Its head was a twisted, nightmarish mesh of eyes and teeth, its maw opening to reveal rows of jagged fangs dripping with viscous, dark fluid. Sam tightened his hold on Shay.

The creature moved with horrifying speed, leaping into the nearest group of soldiers. Screams rang out, sharp and fleeting, as it tore through them with mechanical efficiency—razor-sharp claws slicing through flesh, its monstrous jaws crushing bone. Blood sprayed across the battlefield as more fissures erupted, each one birthing new horrors. Hulking forms with shifting, amorphous features dragged themselves into the light, their guttural roars drowning out even the sound of gunfire.

The armies of men, their strategies, and their weapons were now meaningless. This was no longer their war. The battlefield was now a stage for something ancient and unstoppable; it had been claimed by forces far beyond their comprehension.

From another rift came a creature of much larger stature—a hulking form, so massive it seemed to block out Sam's view of the sky as it rose. Its flesh was a mottled, sickly green, slick with a viscous, black slime that oozed down its grotesque body. The demon towered above the battlefield, a twisted mockery of life itself, with four massive arms, each ending in claws as long and sharp as swords. With every swing, it carved through men and machines alike, sending bodies and debris hurtling through the air. Its fiery red eyes glowed with a malevolent light, scanning the battlefield as though selecting its next victim. When it roared, the sound reverberated across the valley, a bone-chilling wave of unholy fury that shook the earth.

From the same fissure, smaller demons poured out, swarming across the battlefield like a tide of pestilence. They scuttled around on twisted limbs, their distorted forms blending traits of insect and beast into nightmarish hybrids. Rows of jagged fangs glistened with blood as they attacked with terrifying speed, their claws piercing armor and flesh with ease. Their eyes were bloodshot, gleaming with a hatred that was both feral and calculating.

The valley was no longer a battlefield—it was a hellscape, overrun by the legions of darkness. The armies of man, once so confident in their strength, were now insignificant against the onslaught of demonic power. Soldiers fell in droves as the demons fed on their destruction, growing stronger with every life taken. The ground was littered with the remnants of human defiance—shattered weapons, burning vehicles, and broken bodies—but the demons pressed on, relentless and unstoppable.

This is no mere war between nations, Sam thought. It had transcended into a spiritual battle, a physical manifestation of the ancient war between light and darkness. The soldiers fought with desperate bravery, but their efforts only delayed the inevitable. The forces arrayed against them were not of this world; they were demonic hordes, unleashed to bring devastation to humanity's final hour.

Sam held Shay tightly, shielding her from the horrors before them, yet his own eyes were fixed on the carnage below. The cries of the dying mingled with the guttural roars of the demons, creating a cacophony that seemed to shake the mountains themselves. Fire and smoke consumed the valley, and the air was thick with the stench of blood and sulfur. Sam could see it all—men and machines swallowed whole by the sea of darkness.

The blood-soaked valley became an unholy abyss, the prophecy fulfilled in horrifying detail. Rivers of crimson spread across the battlefield, pooling into a vast lake of blood that swallowed the land. From his vantage point in the mountains, Sam and the other survivors could see it clearly—the blood had risen to the height of a horse's bridle, just as foretold. It was a staggering, almost incomprehensible vision, the sheer magnitude of death overwhelming.

Yet, amidst the devastation, there was an undeniable sense that this was not the end. As the demons advanced, as the armies crumbled, the ground itself seemed to tremble with anticipation. The air shimmered faintly, charged with an energy that defied understanding. Sam felt as though something far greater, far more powerful, was stirring beneath the surface of this broken world.

He and the others stood in silence, their hearts heavy, their spirits worn. They knew this battle was not theirs to fight. It was beyond them, beyond any human force. They waited—not in fear, but in hope. Somewhere in the chaos, they knew the promise still held. This was the final battle but not the final word. Darkness had come, but the light had yet to speak. And Sam clung to that truth, waiting for the One who would bring it all to an end.

Sam stared, mesmerized, his heart pounding, yet no one moved. It was as though the very air held its breath, thick with anticipation. The dust from the shattered mountains hung like a veil, a ghostly shroud over the valley, muting the chaos for one brief, agonizing moment.

And then, Sam saw it.

At first, it was no more than a glimmer, a faint shimmer on the horizon, as if the very fabric of reality had begun to fray. But it grew, slowly at first, until it illuminated the entire sky, expanding with a brilliance that defied explanation. Sam felt every eye in the valley turn toward it, captivated and unable to look away. Hearts thundered in unison, breaths were held as though the act of inhaling might disturb whatever divine force was making itself known.

The light intensified, impossibly pure and radiant, and tears streamed unbidden down Sam's face. No one spoke. No one could. The impossible was happening, and it felt as if time itself had paused to bear witness.

Above the battlefield, the sky began to churn violently, clouds boiling and writhing as if caught in an unseen storm. The wind howled, shrieking with an unnatural force, and through it came the sound— trumpets, building to a piercing crescendo that cut through the air like a blade. Then came a flash so blinding that it seemed to split the heavens apart.

From the brilliance, they descended.

The angels.

They poured from the heavens on steeds of blazing fire, their wings unfurled in radiant majesty. Light cascaded from them in waves, consuming the darkness below. Each angel wore armor that shone like molten gold, their faces fierce and resolute, eyes burning with the fire of heaven. In their hands were swords of unearthly brilliance, blades that shimmered as though forged from the very essence of the divine.

A trumpet blast shattered the air, a sound so commanding that it seemed to resonate through every soul on the battlefield. Every being stilled as all creation seemed to bow beneath its reverberation. The sky, alive with swirling clouds and golden fire, suddenly parted with a force that felt like the culmination of eternity.

And there, amidst the parting clouds, He appeared.

The figure that emerged made even the mightiest of demons recoil in terror. His robe, drenched in blood, rippled as He rode forward on a white horse that blazed with heavenly fire. On His head were many crowns, their gleam a declaration of His sovereignty. His eyes burned like flames, piercing all they beheld, and from His mouth came a sword—sharper than any earthly blade, its power more piercing than the deepest wound. It was the Word of God, alive and active, its edge cutting through the hearts of men and demons alike, a judgment none could withstand.

His face was a storm of wrath; He was a king come to execute a final judgment. Written on His robe and His thigh was the title: KING OF KINGS AND LORD OF LORDS. As He rode forward, His voice roared across the valley, a sound that split the heavens and shook the earth. It was a voice of unrelenting judgment, a decree that none could escape.

As He descended from the heavens, His voice thundered across the valley, resonating like the roar of many waters. It was a voice that commanded creation itself, a proclamation of judgment and victory that left no room for resistance. The demons shrieked, their grotesque forms writhing as they tried to flee the unstoppable light. But there was no escape.

This was not a battle, Sam realized—it was the glorious execution of justice, the fulfillment of all that had been foretold. Heaven had opened, and the King had come, not to plead but to conquer. With Him descended His saints, a multitude of souls dressed in robes of pure, radiant white linen, their presence like a river of light flowing with divine purity. They were a vision of unmatched beauty, a display of holiness that outshone the darkness below. Their faces, bathed in the brilliance of His glory, reflected the joy of victory and the peace that only His presence could bring. It was a scene of perfect majesty, a breathtaking testimony to His power and the unwavering certainty of His reign.

And then, He touched the earth. The ground trembled as He descended, His feet landing upon the Mount of Olives. Instantly, the mountain split in two—east to west—forming a massive valley that stretched as far as the eye could see. The earth groaned under the weight of divine judgment, and with each crack in the earth, creation itself seemed to acknowledge the King's return. The rift was a physical manifestation of the breaking of the old order, an undeniable sign that what had been was gone and what was to come would never be the same.

The ground continued to shift as if the earth itself could no longer bear the weight of sin and rebellion. The heavens seemed to echo this monumental change, reverberating with a sound like thunder, a sound of finality. The very foundation of the world seemed to be crumbling beneath the weight of the King's glory.

All of creation seemed to pause, holding its breath.

And then, from the shadows, two figures emerged. Nero Kesar, the self-proclaimed ruler, stood atop a hill, his black armor stained with blood—silent tributes to the countless lives he had crushed beneath his boot. Though he was still a man, Sam knew the powers he wielded were not his own. They had been granted to him by Satan, the prince of darkness, who sought to extinguish all light and holiness. Beside him stood his false prophet, a shadowy figure whose every word was a lie, a whisper that had misled many into destruction.

Kesar's gaze swept over the battlefield, scanning the devastation with a hardened focus. His posture remained confident, as if victory was still within reach. But Sam could sense a shift, something in the air that hinted at growing unease. The false prophet's earlier certainty seemed to waver, and the weight of what was coming pressed on him, despite the façade of control.

And then, Kesar saw Him. The one who stood as the greatest threat to his reign.

Jesus.

Kesar was filled with fury and desperation. He felt his eyes glowing with an unnatural light as he burned with the unrelenting desire to dominate. His dark hair clung to his sweat-drenched forehead, and his lips twisted into a snarl as his teeth clenched in rage.

In one hand, he gripped a jagged blade, its surface blackened and uneven, as though forged in the pits of hell. The weapon seemed to vibrate, humming with energy. His other hand flexed and twitched, fingers curling like talons, a physical manifestation of his barely contained wrath.

Nero Kesar's gaze locked onto Jesus.

He could feel the darkness within him stirring, urging him forward. His every step was a march of inevitability, a journey toward the one who stood as the embodiment of everything he despised. The ground beneath him seemed to tremble as he moved, the very earth groaning in protest of his presence. He was the deceiver, the destroyer, and now he would finish what he had started. Jesus would fall, just as he had planned.

He advanced with monstrous resolve, the jagged blade in his hand cutting through the air with a low, sinister buzz. The winds began to howl once more, as if the heavens themselves were warning him.

But as Kesar closed the distance, something stopped him. A force so pure, so overpowering, that it made him falter. Jesus, still upon His horse, remained unmoving. His stare, fierce and unshaken, was fixed on Kesar, radiating divine power. There was no hesitation in His eyes, no weakness.

Kesar reached for the sky, summoning the full force of his dark power, attempting to smother the light that burned from Jesus. Lightning crackled around him, but it was as if the very heavens refused to listen. The ground shook beneath their feet, but still, Jesus stood unyielding.

But Jesus was not here to be defeated—He was here to put an end to all of it, to end the reign of darkness once and for all. From the depths of the abyss, the Deceiver himself rose. Satan, the ancient enemy, the father of lies, was a swirling mass of darkness and flame. His eyes blazed with unholy fire, and his voice seemed to shake the very foundations of creation itself.

Satan's growl rumbled through the air, deep and venomous, as his form loomed larger, vast and terrible. His wings stretched wide in twisted glory. His gaze locked onto Jesus, hatred burning in his eyes, a sneer curling on his lips.

"I have ruled this world since the dawn of time," Satan said. "The nations have bowed to me. The hearts of men have fallen under my sway. I have led them astray with lies, consumed countless souls in my darkness. You, pitiful light, will never undo what I've wrought.

Satan's laugh was cruel, tearing through the silence. "You will not break me. I will tear your kingdom down. Your light will fade, your reign will crumble, and I will watch as you are cast into the pit with all who dared defy me. You think you've won, but you've only set the stage for your own destruction."

Jesus stood unmoved, His eyes brimming with righteous fury. This moment had been ordained since the dawn of creation. It had been building since the first whisper of rebellion, when Satan—once the most glorious of angels—chose pride over worship and cast mankind into darkness. All of it had led to this. And now, the time had come to rid the earth of the Deceiver, to end his reign forever.

Every sin, every death, every tear shed at the hands of Satan—every moment of suffering caused by his hand—had echoed through time, and now the reckoning had come. The atrocities, the pain, and the suffering had been laid squarely at the feet of Satan, the one who had introduced sin into the world and had tempted mankind into rebellion. He had deceived billions, torn countless souls from the truth, and been the driving force behind the murder of Jesus Christ—the innocent Lamb of God, tortured and crucified for the sins of the world.

But Jesus had risen.

Now He stood before the Deceiver, His body bathed in the full power of God—the fullness of the Father, Son, and Holy Spirit in perfect unity. Jesus, God in the flesh, stood as the eternal Word made flesh, the second person of the Trinity, who had come to earth not only to redeem but to execute final judgment. The weight of all history, the agony of every lost soul, and the staggering cost of His sacrifice burned within Him.

His hands, raised in defiance of the darkness, poured forth radiant light from the deep, jagged holes in His palms—the marks from the nails, of the ultimate sacrifice, the price of redemption, carved by the blood of the Son of God. That blood, shed for the sins of the world, had soaked into the earth, tearing through the very veil of hell itself. Each wound spoke of a sacrifice so profound that it had shattered death's grip and crushed the forces of darkness. The victory of His blood, now written in His hands, was a decree that would never be undone.

In this moment, the Triune God—Father, Son, and Holy Spirit—was revealed in His fullness. The Father's will was made flesh in Jesus, and the Spirit was present, empowering the Son for His purpose. In Him, the Godhead stood in absolute authority, bringing final judgment upon Satan. Jesus was not only the Savior but also the Judge, the Creator who had now come to end the reign of sin and death. This was no mere man standing before the enemy—this was God Himself, fully present, fully triumphant.

The time for mercy had passed. The time for vengeance had come.

Without a word, Jesus raised His hand. The sky above darkened instantly, the clouds swirling as if stirred by an ancient storm. And then, with a single, earth-shattering cry, Nero Kesar and his false prophet were no more. Before their crumbling bodies could even touch the ground, they were seized by a divine force and cast into the abyss of hell. The very darkness they had once wielded was consumed by the blinding light of Christ's judgment. Their forms, once so full of defiance, disintegrated, turning to ash, scattering like dust as their souls were bound for their eternal torment.

The ground trembled as Jesus's actions fell like fire upon the earth. Satan, the once-proud fallen angel, stood before Him, trembling. There was no longer any defiance in his eyes—only fear. The fear of the inevitable. The fear of the light that consumed him.

The final battle had been fought. The Deceiver's reign was over.

Jesus stepped forward as fury filled Him. His hand rose once more, and with a single command, the prince of darkness was undone. The earth shook as Satan's figure began to collapse under the weight of Christ's authority. No power remained in him, no strength to resist. He fell to his knees, his kingdom of lies shattered.

And then, with one final, resolute action, it was done.

The very air seemed to fracture as the heavens themselves trembled. With a single command, Satan was cast down into the pit of hell, a place of eternal torment from which there would be no escape.

The war was over. Sin was undone. The Deceiver, once the prince of darkness, was no more—his reign shattered beyond all hope of restoration. The light had triumphed, and Jesus, the Lamb who was slain and the Lion who reigns, stood victorious.

The curse of sin had been broken, death defeated, and the eternal victory secured. The world, though still shuddering, would never again be the same. It was finished.

The sight of Jesus, standing tall in His unshakable power, was enough to make the very earth quiver. Those who had gathered on the surrounding mountains—survivors, witnesses, those who had endured the horrors of the tribulation—could do nothing but watch in awe. The force of His presence was overwhelming, and the heavens seemed to vibrate with the weight of it all.

✳ ✳ ✳

Sam set Shay down, his heart racing. He gently reached over and uncovered her eyes. She blinked, taking in the sight. The world before them had shifted; the ground quaked beneath their feet, but in that moment, it felt like nothing could touch them. Shay gasped, her face lighting up as she saw the Lord.

The others around them—those who had lived through this nightmare, survivors of the tribulation—fell to their knees in awe. Some wept; others cried out in praise, "To God be the glory," their voices trembling with reverence.

The truth of it all settled in. The world they once knew was gone. The age of darkness had ended, and in its place, the first light of a new era began to break through. As that light poured into the world, there was something miraculous unfolding before them.

Then Sam's gaze moved. Through the crowd of angels, he saw them—the saints of the past, the mighty figures of the Bible, his family, his friends, and his dad, all standing among the resurrected and redeemed. For a moment, his breath caught in his chest. They were here, alive and glorified, bathed in the same light that enveloped the King, their faces radiant with the glory of the Lord. In that sacred assembly, surrounded by the victorious, they stood as living proof of the promise fulfilled, and Sam felt a rush of emotion so profound it brought him to his knees. These people were no longer lost, no longer separated by death. They were here, in the presence of Jesus, with bodies made new, their lives now forever part of His eternal victory.

Sam slowly lifted his hands, pointing toward the group. Shay's eyes widened as she looked, and a sweet, radiant smile spread across her face. With a sudden burst of joy, she raised her arms toward them, calling to them in a voice that carried the weight of years of longing.

"Look, little bird," he said softly, his voice filled with awe. "There's your mom and dad."

CHAPTER TWENTY-SIX

THE PROMISE FULFILLED

Earlier the same day, 11,700 miles away

In the distance, the soft coo of a small child echoed, reaching across the barren expanse of dry plains to find Jayne perched on a boulder—a gentle reminder of life within the caves' sheltering walls. The land stretched wide and open before her, the sandy earth shimmering in the early light, while the occasional rustle of wind through desert brush created a rhythmic backdrop to her quiet surroundings. As she gazed over the rolling terrain, beyond weathered ridges and sparse tufts of sage, she saw the sun rising over the horizon, casting its glow on the endless landscape.

The rugged cliffs of New Mexico stood watch over the wide-open area, their rigid yet serene beauty carving a lasting impression that Jayne now cherished deeply. It was a remote, isolated sanctuary, far from the chaos she had left behind. The occasional shadow of a hawk drifted over the land as it glided on the warm currents of air, its presence blending into the stillness. The region, scarred but resilient, carried whispers of battles fought and survived, telling stories of endurance and faith.

Seated on the massive rock, Jayne held a small canteen of water, its cool touch grounding her in the present. Her boots gently tapped against the rock beneath her, the faint sound blending with her thoughts. The morning sun climbed higher, its warmth stretching over the jagged hills and casting long shadows across the dry earth. The faint scent of smoke from the previous night's fire mingled with the crisp desert air, reflecting the stark beauty of her surroundings and offering a moment of peace. It was fleeting, though, for as she drank in the quiet, the echoes of the journey that had brought her here began to settle over her.

With a sigh, she glanced toward the mouth of the cave behind her, feeling the weight of everything they had endured pulling her out of her brief reprieve. The serenity she'd briefly found in the morning light was slipping through her fingers, replaced by the reality of what lay ahead. Yet, as she turned back to face the horizon, the soft sound of the child came again, carried by the wind, and she allowed herself to hold onto the fragile promise of hope for just a moment longer.

Jayne's gaze softened as her thoughts began to drift. The warmth of the morning light on her face mirrored the faint warmth of a memory— her back porch, the steady whistle of the morning train, the world she had known so well. The rhythmic creaks of the old wooden swing, the scent of coffee mingling with the dew-kissed grass. It felt like a lifetime ago, a fragile, fleeting dream compared to the heft of all that had come after. Now, the sounds of life around her were different. The soft cries of a baby, murmured prayers, and the shuffle of those waking within the cave behind her. The echoes of survival, fragile but real.

Her thoughts drifted back to the day everything changed. The rapture had come like a thief in the night, and with it, the world had fractured. It wasn't the chaos or the devastation that had scarred her most, though—it was the loss of certainty. In those early days, Jayne had clung to the familiar, to what she thought she knew. But as the world slipped further into darkness, she had come to understand that survival wasn't about what you held onto, but about what you could let go. The foundation she'd built her life on had crumbled, and in its place, faith became something she had to lean on in ways she'd never imagined.

The years since had been shaped by loss, but they had also shown her what it meant to live with resilience. Every trial had been a lesson, though some had been more brutal than others. Archie and Zella— two souls who had given her hope—had paid the ultimate price, but in their loss, she had found a deeper strength. She had learned that love and faith didn't die with them. They lived in her, in the memories they left behind.

But the loss that cut deepest was her husband. His absence had hollowed her out in a way nothing else had. It wasn't just grief—it was the unraveling of everything she had leaned on. She remembered the dark days, the desert, when the weight of everything almost broke her. There had been a moment in an abandoned church, standing alone in the silence, when despair had almost swallowed her whole. But it was there, in that broken place, that she had found Ruth's note—a note that reminded her of God's presence even in the deepest of darkness. That moment, that simple message, had been a lifeline.

Jayne had learned that survival wasn't just about enduring the storms that raged around her, but about trusting in the promise of His return, finding grace in the quiet, and drawing strength from her faith in the midst of the weakest moments. The world had broken, but through it all, her faith had been the anchor that kept her grounded, remaking her in ways she never could have imagined.

Her heart lifted slightly as her thoughts shifted to the present. Just a few months ago, they had finally reached the caves—the sanctuary they had prayed for. And there, waiting for them, were their friends, faces glowing with relief, eager to share the stories of their own survival. She could still see Camille's face, tear-streaked and radiant with relief, as she rushed out to meet them. Jayne had barely stepped off the rocky path before Camille's arms were around her, squeezing her tightly. They had both wept, a tangle of laughter and sobs, as the stress of years fell away in that warm embrace.

The sound of soft footsteps pulled her from her thoughts. She turned to see Jennie approaching, little Reyna cradled in her arms. Jennie's eyes were tired but bright, the quiet strength in her face unmistakable. Without a word, she settled beside Jayne on the boulder, the child cooing as Jennie gently rocked her. Jayne smiled, reaching out to brush a finger against Reyna's tiny hand.

They sat in silence, the open plains sprawling out before them, until Jennie's voice quietly broke the stillness "Jayne," she began softly, her eyes still fixed on the horizon, "I need to thank you. For everything you've done … for helping me and Reyna. I don't think I could ever express how much it's meant to me."

Jayne turned slightly to face her, the warmth of the sun reflecting in her eyes. She could see that Jennie's gratitude was sincere, but there was something deeper, something unspoken, waiting to be said.

"Jennie," Jayne said gently, "what's really on your mind? I can tell there's more you want to say."

Jennie hesitated, the words seemingly stuck in her throat. Finally, she spoke again, her voice barely above a whisper. "Do you think …" She paused, exhaling deeply. "Do you think God can ever truly forgive someone? Someone like me?" She swallowed hard, her eyes brimming with uncertainty. "I've been so lost … I've done so many things … things I'm not proud of. I just … I don't see how someone like God could ever truly love and forgive someone like me."

Jayne felt a deep compassion rise within her as she looked at Jennie, her heart aching with the heaviness of her words. She gently placed a hand on Jennie's, her voice quiet but full of conviction. "Jennie, you're not alone in that feeling. Every one of us has fallen short in some way, and no one is perfect: not me, not you, no one. But that's exactly why God sent His Son—to offer us grace and forgiveness, not because we deserve it, but because He loves us."

Jennie looked at her, still unsure, but there was a glimmer of hope in her eyes. "But how can God forgive someone like me? After everything I've done?"

Jayne smiled, and she spoke with a tenderness that only love could convey. "God doesn't look at our sin and compare it to others. He doesn't see you through the lens of what you've done in the past. He only wants you to accept Him as your Savior. You don't have to be perfect. None of us are. Repentance—it's about turning away from that life, acknowledging the wrong we've done, and asking for His forgiveness.

"And repentance doesn't mean you'll never sin again. It means that you no longer desire that life, and instead, you choose to walk with God, to build a relationship with Him. The Holy Spirit comes to live inside of you, guiding you, not out of obligation, but because you want Him to. It's a process, a journey, but God's grace is what makes it possible. He's not interested in how many times you've fallen, what you've done in the past, how bad you've been or how 'good' you think you are. He's only interested in that personal relationship you're choosing to have with Him, understanding Jesus is the only way to be saved.

"Romans 3:23 says, *For all have sinned and fall short of the glory of God.'* That means every one of us, Jennie. We're all in the same boat. But that's why God's grace is so amazing. It's not about being good enough on our own—it's about receiving the love and forgiveness He offers, no matter what we've done. He wants to restore you, to heal you, and to give you peace. You don't have to earn it. It's a gift."

Jennie's expression softened, her eyes glistening with tears as Jayne's words seemed to take root in her heart. A quiet sob broke free, and she quickly wiped her cheek.

Jayne squeezed her hand gently, offering a quiet comfort that didn't need words. But then Jennie looked at her, eyes filled with vulnerability, and asked, "Will you pray with me, Jayne? I don't know how to do this, but …"

Jayne nodded, her heart swelling with love and compassion for the woman beside her. She leaned in a little closer, her hand still holding Jennie's, and smiled softly. "Of course, Jennie. Let's pray together."

Jennie hesitated before finally speaking. "God, I don't know how to do this … how to believe … but I want to try. I've made so many mistakes. I've hurt people. I've hurt myself. And I'm so tired of carrying it all. Please … forgive me."

Her voice broke as the words flowed from her heart, and Jayne squeezed her hand tighter, offering silent support. Jennie continued, her words coming slower now, each one heavier than the last. "Jesus,

I don't know what it means to follow you, but I want to. I want to know you. I believe you gave your life for me, and I don't want to walk away from that anymore. Please, come into my heart. Be my Savior. I need you more than I've ever needed anything."

Jayne watched as Jennie took a shaky breath, feeling the quiet stir of the Holy Spirit around them, and she whispered, "He hears you, Jennie. He's here."

Jennie's tear-filled eyes opened. Uncertainty still lingered, but hope had begun to break through. "I didn't realize how much I'd been holding inside," she cried. "It's like a burden I didn't even know I was carrying is finally starting to lift."

As they said "Amen" and embraced, the quiet was filled with a profound sense of peace. Jennie's prayer lingered in Jayne's heart, an echo of hope and humility. Sophie, Landon, and Andrew emerged from the cave, their faces tired but joyful. Sophie gently took Reyna into her arms, and the child nestled against her, safe and warm.

Together, they sat on the boulder, the breeze gently rustling the grass. For a moment, no one spoke. They sat in comfortable silence, as if the world around them had slowed, giving them time to breathe.

Jayne's thoughts turned inward, the memory of Jennie's words still fresh in her mind. She glanced out at the horizon, her eyes unfocused, her thoughts drifting. It was then that something began to take shape on the plains.

At first, she thought it was a mirage, a trick of the light playing with her vision. But the figure slowly became more distinct, and as her gaze sharpened, Jayne's heart began to race. The shape, still distant, was moving toward them.

Then she saw it.

That red T-shirt.

Her pulse quickened. *No … it couldn't be …*

But as the figure grew closer, the shape of the person became undeniable.

It was Lawson.

Her heart stopped, then surged back to life, pounding in her chest. She couldn't think, couldn't process. She didn't need to know how or why—she just knew, and that was enough.

"Lawson!" Jayne cried out, her voice breaking the stillness. She was already moving, rushing down the path toward him, her arms reaching out, her feet pounding the earth.

As Jayne's voice rang out, she vaguely heard others began to stir from the cave, drawn by the energy of her cry.

"It's him! It's really him!" Sophie shouted, disbelief mingling with joy.

Footsteps, laughter, shouts, and joy all blended together behind her as Jayne drew closer to him.

But just as the noise reached a fever pitch, a new sound cut through the air. It was sharp, commanding, and ancient—a trumpet blast that echoed across the plains. The earth seemed to tremble with it. The sky began to shift. The clouds parted, and a glow—brilliant, radiant— pierced through the gap, pouring down in a cascade of divine brightness. The sight was almost too much to bear, the brilliance of it overwhelming, and yet they couldn't look away.

And in the midst of this overwhelming light, a figure took shape.

As Jayne's heart filled with praise, she knew, without a shadow of doubt, that this was the moment they had all been waiting for. The moment they had fought for, prayed for, hoped for.

It was happening.

With the sky opening above them and the final trumpet's call echoing through the heavens, Jayne's heart swelled with peace. She was no longer waiting, no longer questioning, no longer wandering. She only saw Him, felt Him. And in that instant, she knew the King was coming, and all that remained was to fall to her knees in awe, for the world was about to be made new.